ZEN AND THE ART OF ANAL BLEACHING

A BACKDOOR JOURNEY FROM DARKNESS TO LIGHT

OLD HAIRY JESUS

APOCRYPHILE
PRESS

Apocryphile Press
PO Box 255
Hannacroix, NY 12087
www.apocryphilepress.com

Copyright © 2024 by Dave Holmes (aka OHJ)
Printed in the United States of America
ISBN 978-1-958061-82-4 | paper
ISBN 978-1-958061-83-1 | ePub

Please join our mailing list at www.apocryphilepress.com/free. We'll keep you up-to-date on all our new releases, and we'll also send you a FREE BOOK. Visit us today!

CONTENTS

To the real Eddie and Cowboy.

While I thought we were just sharing a couple of beers during our sidewalk chats, you were prying open my mind and my heart, setting me on a journey that transformed all of who I thought I was. I never got a chance to thank you; hopefully, this book will at least honor your memory.

Very rarely, in this day and age,
does anyone stop at their teeth.
—*Dan Drohan*

CHAPTER
ONE

"Yep... Yep... Yep...Hang in there. Looks good so far," he said with a calm indifference bordering on arrogance.

"Looks good?" I asked between deep breaths, trying to appear calm and relaxed.

"I mean, everything appears to be just fine," he said.

"Seems like you're getting a little rough there, Doc."

"Hey, to do this right, I've got to get an angle on the sides," he explained condescendingly. "And for the record, this is hardly rough. Now there! We're all done," he concluded, extracting what was indeed an uncommonly large finger from my rectum and snapping off his glove with bravado.

"So things look OK down there?"

"Things felt normal. Looks like hell, though," he kindly informed me. You're how old again, Toby?"

"Thirty-seven."

"Yeah, you got the asshole of a seventy-five-year-old," he stated, handing me a paper towel to clean myself up and starting to jot down a few notes.

"We'll, that's great news, Doc. What the hell does that mean?"

"You've been dealt kind of a bad hand. No fault of your own. Genetics are the most likely cause of your advanced discoloration."

"Oh. Of course. Yeah...this is the first I've heard about this discoloration thing. How does something like this happen? Do I need to be worried about it?"

"No. You can't really help it. The skin is darker than usual due to genetics, like I mentioned, friction, and sometimes both. Usually it's gradual, whereas yours seems aggressive for a man your age."

At this point, my ego was more violated than my sting ring. Not that I fancied myself as a butt-bead model or anything, but a guy likes to think he's reasonably attractive and not hiding a hideous deformity that he can't even keep an eye on.

"I suppose I should avoid the nude beaches from here on out. Changing disorders, what are the next steps on the VD tests?"

"I'll call you with the results. If they are positive, I'll call in a prescription to your pharmacy. Should be about 48 hours before the results are back," he said, looking at his notes.

"OK. Call my cell, would you? I don't want to set off any alarm bells around the house. It's probably a bit paranoid even coming in here, but I am a bit paranoid."

"Understood. Anyway, we'll be in touch and try not to worry too much until we know if there is anything to worry about," he said, as if it were only that easy, opening the door of the sterile white office. "We'll be in touch," and he walked out, closing the door behind him, leaving me to finish getting dressed and emotionally gather myself. I wondered if, technically, I had just been raped. He was being kind of rough, and I'm pretty sure he knew it.

Within a couple of minutes, I had slinked out of the office, carefully avoiding eye contact with all the employees and patients in the lobby, positive they were solely there to catch a glimpse of a guy packed full of venereal disease with a beat-to-hell sting ring.

I stepped out the door of the building, pausing a moment as my eyes adjusted to the sunlight, then navigated the stairs down to the sidewalk. The fog had been reduced to a thin veil, retreating towards the ocean as blue skies took command of what was fast becoming a beautiful San Francisco day.

"Hey man, hoping you can help a brother out. I'm down on my luck and trying to get back to Sacramento, but I lost my wallet. All I need is ten dollars more to get a bus ticket, and I can get back home and get my life—"

"Shut the fuck up," I said, interrupting the unshaven rumpled kid, who looked either hungover or severely sleep-deprived, likely both. "You and about thirty other guys, all playing the same angle of the poor victim trying to get bus money. Can't you think of anything novel or unique? Or better yet, give enough of a shit to...I don't know...actually work? They have things called jobs, you know?"

What the hell was the city coming to? Upper-middle-class white kids heading to San Francisco for the summer, trying to relive the glorious hippie stories from the sixties, or drug addicts looking for their next fix littered the streets like discarded food wrappers. They were multiplying exponentially, doing a fantastic job of ruining the city for everyone else. Pride and self-discipline were no longer in vogue, and human feces on sidewalks was as common as planter boxes on doorsteps.

"Sorry, man, just trying to get by. Damn!" the kid (probably in his early twenties) responded as I continued to the corner to catch a bus to, of all things, a job.

Approaching the bus stop, I shifted my thinking to the important stuff. Today was the big interview day. The interview was almost a formality, but I wasn't taking any chances. This promotion was my ticket out of the reactionary chaos of high-tech middle management and into a fulfilling director role. I needed a change and an opportunity to demonstrate that I could also contribute at a strategic level. Plus, some additional stock options and a raise never sucked.

Someone was hosing the filth off the sidewalk in front of the bank, spurring a couple more irritated homeless residents to relocate further down the block. I took my place in the bus stop line with the others, all lost in our phones, as we waited for the #7 Haight to arrive and take us downtown. I logged into my email to see what unplanned emergencies might require immediate attention. Being a Sales Operations Manager is a fool's game if you're after any day-to-day predictability. Unless you become a Director or VP, long days and working weekends are always part of the game. I was excited to get to a level where I could delegate this shit to those lower on the totem pole.

Luckily, my inbox was blissfully uneventful, except for an email from Jim with the subject 'Open with Discretion.' Jim was our Director of Facilities and the closest thing to a "friend" I had at work. I was a "get shit done" type of guy, which meant holding people accountable and driving projects, which I suppose also made me kind of a dick. My Dad always said that nobody makes it up the chain by sitting around and waiting to be told what to do. Jim was cut from the same cloth, so we got along well and shared a similar disdain for mediocrity despite our jobs having nothing in common.

On the last page of a giant flip board on the easel in the corner of Jim's office, we kept a list of all the coworkers we wanted to jack in the face. This was cathartic for both of us; the list had become impressively long over the past three years. Jim's office was our "safe space" where we could talk about anything and anyone and blow off steam. My cubicle was not. Jim was a Director, and Directors got offices.

More importantly, Jim had a great sarcastic sense of humor. However, we had a fierce rivalry going. We entertained ourselves by trying to elicit shock and awe from one another by finding clips of progressively more extreme sexual encounters that one couldn't help but stare at in paralyzed horror, as though at a dead body. Jim too was no stranger to perusing the finer cinematic arts. He was, in fact, a connoisseur.

I turned the volume down on my phone and opened Jim's email, which contained only a link called "Tub Girl." I took a moment to prepare myself, then clicked the link.

"Holy fucking shit!" I exclaimed. Where does he find this stuff?

"Are you OK?" asked a middle-aged woman next to me, who was wearing entirely too much eyeliner. I was a bit surprised there were people out there who still cared about others. These days, a person could be getting knifed in broad daylight, and people wouldn't consider pausing or, God forbid, helping.

"Sorry. I'm fine. Thanks for asking," I immediately flipped over my phone to protect my dignity in case she was tempted to steal a gander.

The bus pulled up; we filed on, and miraculously, I found a vacant seat, allowing me to focus on finding an appropriate response to Jim's latest challenge. Shifting my mindset to interview mode would need to wait. First things first, and humor always tops the list.

Jim was more skilled at this game than I was, but after about fifteen minutes of scouring the darker corners of the web, I finally found the coup de grace and was anxious to plant my flag on top of pervert peak. I quickly fired off an email with no subject line—just a link to a clip called "The Flying Fister Family."

Although I hated riding the bus downtown to work, there were two distinct advantages. First, it was a hell of a lot cheaper than parking downtown, and second, looking around at the other passengers couldn't help but make me feel pretty good about my own life. Of course, everyone looks sad and melancholy while riding the bus to work unless you are about to interview for a big promotion. It occurred to me that maybe I just had more to be hopeful for that day than my riding companions. They would have another day just like yesterday and indistinguishable from tomorrow. The slightly rumpled-looking woman across from me, the one with egregious amounts of eyeliner from the bus stop, was most likely an accounts receivable processor. She had realized too late that the world's a grind, and maybe she should have bitten the bullet and gone to college before she married the dock worker and had three kids. While some of us build avenues for hope, others look back and wonder where things went wrong.

But because I was the forward-thinking type, I wrestled my

laptop out of my "satchel" and reviewed my talking points regarding my most significant accomplishments over the last three years and my future vision for the department.

Twenty minutes of jostled interview prep later, we arrived at First and Market Street. I disembarked and began walking to my office building one block over on First and Mission.

I didn't think about the fact that I couldn't stand high-tech and that there was little to no meaning in supporting a sales team that basically sells IT plumbing to Fortune 500 companies. I didn't think about the ten pounds I'd gained and what a non-engaged father I was. No, I thought about what a responsible, successful professional I was and a family man to boot.

More than anything, I didn't think about how much I hated my wife.

"Good morning, Jeff," I said, flashing my employee badge at the lobby security guard.

"Morning, Toby. Have a good day, buddy."

"That's the game plan. And thanks for securing the lobby before my arrival. Feels very safe in here," I joked, making my way to the elevators.

"Can't have my main man attacked before he even gets to his desk," Jeff replied with a chuckle.

My company's offices were on the seventh and eighth floors of a shared office building. I stepped off the elevator and took the long way to my cubicle. This way, I would pass Jim's office and acknowledge the impressive photographic art he had forwarded earlier. His office door was closed, and he was meeting with someone at his desk when I peeked in the narrow floor-to-ceiling window to the left of the door. He was sitting at his desk, facing my direction, talking to a frail woman I didn't recognize from the back. Eventually, he looked up and caught my eye, and I silently mouthed in an exaggerated fashion, "TUB GIRL? What the Fuck?" Jim gave a slight shrug, fought back an emerging smirk, and quickly returned his attention to his guest.

Within moments, I arrived at my little gray-felt cubicle. It was furnished with a computer docking station, a monitor, one file cabinet, and a chair. It was exactly like everyone else's, except for a few personal effects. Mine consisted of a bamboo back scratcher, a few workplace achievement awards, a framed picture of my wife, and another of our two kids. I wasn't big on turning a cubicle into a personal statement. After all, I was a man of action and only had a half hour before my interviews kicked off.

First, I would interview with the SVP of Global Sales, then the Senior Director of IT Applications, followed by the Director of Marketing Operations, and finally, the VP of Global Sales Operations, my new boss. Four forty-five-minute interviews, starting at the top of each hour with a fifteen-minute break between them. Luckily, over the last eight years, I'd had the opportunity to work with each of these characters directly or indirectly. They were all intelligent people with a track record of success, each with their character flaws —most notably, the Senior Director of IT Applications had a penchant for anal, or so it was rumored.

Initially, three outside candidates and three internal candidates had been considered for the role, but now it was down to me and another internal candidate named Ted. Ted was our Order Management team's polished and effective young Manager but had only been with the company for eleven months. It would be easy to position the value of experience within the organization against him and flaunt my understanding of the history of our company's processes and systems.

"Hey, just stopped by to wish you good luck today." I looked up to find Ted himself extending his manicured hand over the front of my cubicle. He looked ridiculous in his coat and tie. We have a casual work environment where even a polo shirt and jeans are considered almost heretically formal. Ted was a douche.

"Thanks, Ted. You look dapper today. A bit over the top, but I suppose it shows you care," I said, forcing a smile and shaking his hand.

"Well, I think that no matter which of us gets the job, they'll be in good hands," he replied with a manufactured smile.

"And if it doesn't work out for you this time, I'm sure you'll get the next one. Thanks for stopping by, Ted," I responded, refocusing on my computer screen, signaling this tête-à-tête had concluded. Ted moved on, and I made my way to the restroom for what looked to be a close call.

Luckily, I only got a little bit of poop juice on my boxers. Nothing that couldn't be handled with a good toilet paper dabbing. I chalked this up as my first victory of the day. The rest of the morning followed suit. The VP of Global Sales Ops, Richard Flannigan, even spent the last ten minutes of the interview discussing the transition and ideas to backfill my current role. Our discussion culminated with, "Excellent job, Toby. I'm excited about this."

I was ascending to the next level, and work would be palatable again. Same company, same problems, same douchebags, but a new angle and something to prove: it would be the welcome change that I needed.

I was back at my desk, mired in email hell, when I got a Slack message from Jim: "Sorry. I've been in back-to-backs since 8 a.m. I'm finally free and in my office. Stop by whenever."

I was having a problem transitioning from the high of crushing my interviews to the depths of the mayhem now flooding my inbox, so I headed straight over to Jim's office, shut the door behind me, and sat in the chair in front of his desk.

Jim had decided the theme of his office would be the Golden State Warriors basketball team. On the left front corner of his desk, there was a basketball signed by Harrison Barns, an assortment of player bobbleheads on the right front corner, and a corkboard on the wall near the door with about forty ticket stubs from the games he had attended.

The *pièce de résistance*, directly behind his chair, was a framed signed Steph Curry jersey, illuminated by a picture light from above. Anyone talking with Jim at his desk had no choice but to take in the glory.

"The word in the senior management underground is that you're a unanimous lock for your Director role, big feeler," Jim said as he leaned back in his chair, hands behind his head.

"Dude, things went great this morning. I asked each person on the panel what concerns they might have with my ability to be successful in the role. Nobody raised anything more significant than, 'Remember that you catch more flies with honey than vinegar.' Richard even started talking about transition plans."

"Well done, sir. Now that you're in upper management, you're as fucked as I am. But...getting fucked isn't all bad if it's a novel fucking you haven't experienced before. Sometimes success is found in the most unexpected places. For example, thanks to you, I just researched a critical topic related to impressive performance in the least likely of places."

"What the hell are you talking about?"

"Oh, you know what I'm talking about," he said with a sly nod. "The 'Flying Fisters' are indeed a real family of trapeze artists with a brilliantly unique way of connecting in midair. This clip was much more than just awe-inspiring cinematography. It was biblical talent on many levels."

"Ha! How about that one? I was snickering on the bus when I stumbled across that baby!"

"You are such an ass. I was running late for a meeting with Frank (our General Council) and saw your email with no subject, and I thought I better check it in case it somehow involved your interviews. I clicked the link and was bitch-slapped by your genius find. Then, in my meeting, I failed to keep the occasional giggle at bay, causing Frank to ask, 'What the hell is so funny?'"

"Shit, Jim, I hope you didn't tell him. Did you?"

"Jesus, no! I told him some bullshit about my two-year-old

daughter's unsupervised attempt to repaint her bedroom with her own feces, starting with the floor and her stuffed animals. He seemed to buy it."

"Brilliant!"

"I thought so," he said. "And, by the way, the feces painting is a true story."

"Someone should give out parental merit badges or something for enduring that type of adversity. On another topic, I just learned from a recent college grad that it's no longer OK to say the word 'retarded' at work. What do you think about that?"

"Sounds retarded," he answered. "Hey, any chance you can bust out around 4 p.m. today? We should have a celebratory drink to consummate your meteoric rise up the management rungs."

"I'd say there's about a 100% chance. Meet downstairs in the lobby and head over to the 21st Amendment?" I asked.

"Sounds good. Now get out of here. I need to put out a few fires, you Flying Fister wannabe."

"Fine, ass clown. Don't let me forget to tell you about my trip to the doctor this morning. Not to be believed," I said, walking out, reminded that I was most assuredly incubating a fatal venereal disease.

IT WAS NOW SHORTLY past seven in the evening. Jim and I had been comparing and contrasting northern California IPAs for the last few hours, concluding that Simcoe and Mosaic hopped varieties were superior.

I had filled Jim in on the rectal assault at the clinic earlier in the day. Even though it was still too soon and at my expense, the humor was not to be debated.

"Congratulations again on the promotion...or the soon-to-be-announced promotion," Jim said as we stood outside the bar, punching our destinations into our Uber apps. "Looks like I need to head down to the corner of Second and Brannen for my pickup," he said. "But I got eight minutes."

"Thanks for the beers," I said. Seeing that my ride was going to pick me up right out front, I remained right there on the sidewalk.

The sun had just set, and the daytime white-collar tech workers were being swapped out by the seedier elements of the South of Market population. The fog had not yet reclaimed the city; a slight offshore breeze exhaled the remnants of the daily commerce buzz into the cool evening air.

A homeless woman, dressed in a black hoodie over a hunter green rag of a dress, scurried around me, chasing a dollar bill that the wind propelled off the curb. It became apparent she was utterly oblivious to the garbage truck barreling down on the intersection in an attempt to beat the yellow light. Instinctively, I lurched into the street, grabbed her outstretched arm, and yanked her back towards the sidewalk as the truck suddenly turned, barely brushing against her left shoulder. Of course, I tripped over the curb as I pulled her out of the street, landing on my butt and her in my lap. "Are you alright?" I asked. She buried her head in my chest and started shaking. I was a bit in shock myself. However, the putrid smell of her greasy, matted black hair immediately brought me back to my senses. "Are you hurt?"

"No...no. I think I'm alright," she stammered, scampering off my lap and pulling herself to her feet.

"Fuck! That was close," Jim said, eyes wide. "Here," he said to the shaken woman, still dazed, who looked to be at least in her early forties. Jim pulled a five-dollar bill out of his wallet and handed it to the woman, who stared expressionless at him. "Go ahead, take it," he said, still holding it out.

She snapped to and snatched the bill out of his hands before he changed his mind. "Thank you. Thank you very much," she said. I had just gotten to my feet, and she gave me a quick and awkward hug. "Thank you too," she said and rushed off down the street, disappearing around the corner and down an alley.

"These goddamned homeless people," I muttered, brushing myself off. "You're a better man than me, Jim. I never give them money. They just spend it on drugs."

"No. You save their lives instead," he said with a chuckle.

It appeared nobody even noticed the near vehicular homicide. Everyone was still moving with purpose on their way to their various destinations. Another crazy was now standing on a piece of luggage up against the outside wall of the bar and began preaching.

"My ride is almost here," Jim said as he walked across the street. "See you tomorrow, hero."

"Whether you like it or not," I replied.

I glanced down at my phone; for some reason, my driver was still seven minutes out. Great.

"The King! The King! He has a story just for you." The homeless woman had reemerged from the alley and appeared to be addressing me. I looked to where she was pointing and realized she was referring to the crazy guy standing on the suitcase behind me against the wall.

He was dressed in black from head to toe: black jeans, black tennis shoes, a black t-shirt, and a black raincoat in complete disrepair that hung almost to his feet. He even had a black fedora with a scarlet red feather tucked in the side of its black band.

"He walked without a care in the world, save himself," the man roared, looking me straight in the eye. "He was on a mission to save himself from himself but didn't even know it. That was all, but yet not an easy task. For he was haunted by darkness he couldn't escape. A darkness that had enveloped him for so long it was all he knew. Darkness with an appetite that had to be constantly fed but couldn't be satiated. It had consumed him, like cancer, without him even being aware of it." He paused, took a drink from his water bottle, and smiled a sincere yet unnerving grin. "Want to know what happens next?" he asked.

Realizing it was just the two of us on the sidewalk, three with the homeless lady down the block, clearly he was talking to me. Where had everyone else gone? I glanced at my phone. The driver was now eight minutes away. How does that happen? Figuring I was stuck for a while, I replied, "Why not?"

He spun in a circle, somehow maintaining his balance, and continued, "He wandered through the crumbled ruins of his life that once was, determined to recreate what had been lost, even build a more glorious version; however, he soon learned that reality doesn't always respond to our desires. Something had changed. What had come easily now didn't come at all. Fascinating, huh?" he asked me.

"Yes, fascinating," I played along, already losing interest. However, traffic seemed to have died down, and the wind started up again, blowing a McDonald's wrapper up against my ankle, where it stuck for a second, and then continued down the sidewalk after depositing a mustard stain on my pant leg to prove it had paid a visit. I looked back up at the lunatic, who had somehow gotten his hands on what appeared to be a black scepter or a very long cane with no handle. He slammed it on the sidewalk with a crack, which seemed to temporarily stop the wind, leaving us staring at each other in complete silence. "Indeed fascinating," I said, a bit nervous now, as this character seemed utterly unpredictable. I glanced toward the alley's opening, and the homeless woman, still there, started clapping wildly. I checked and validated my wallet—it was still in my pocket; she hadn't lifted it when I saved her.

"He tried in vain to find himself because a self-lost cannot always be found where one left it." He then produced a cigarette from his jacket pocket and steadied his scepter against himself as he reached into his other jacket pocket, produced a lighter, and lit it. He took a long, deliberate puff, holding it in and slowly exhaling. "Hmm....smoke, dissolving into the air like a fading dream. Who was this man now? He clamored to the past for solace, but ghosts seldom bring peace. The future, more tentative than he had ever realized, offered only hollow hope but no answers. He soldiered on, looking for clues as to how he might proceed, but the world had forgotten him and refused to play along anymore. And thus began his lonely journey home."

He hopped off the cloth-covered suitcase that had strangely supported him, took another drag on his cigarette, and quietly sat down as he rolled the cigarette between his thumb and forefinger, contemplating it.

"Is that the end?" I asked. I couldn't believe I was having this conversation, but it seemed a valid question.

"Oh no, my friend. That's where the story begins," he said with a comforting smile. "A frightful but fascinating story it is."

"What the hell? He starts a journey home, but his home is gone. So where does he go in his search?"

"That's always the question, isn't it?" He asked, leaping to his feet and spinning around again. "Where is the only place we can ever go that always remains unchanged?"

"You're the storyteller. You tell me." I was starting to get frustrated with him and myself for even engaging in the first place.

"Much like him, you are lazy and looking to someone else to provide all the answers, I see," he said with a condescending shake of his head.

"It's your damn story!" I exclaimed. "Maybe you should stop being lazy and answer the question?"

"Despite your rudeness, tonight is your lucky night, fellow traveler. You saved a woman's life, and maybe, just maybe, the answer may save your own. What was the question again?" he asked as smoke slowly emerged from his eerie grin.

"You said, 'Where is the only place we can ever go that always remains unchanged?' That's the question."

"Of course it is," he nodded.

Just then, my phone vibrated, notifying me my Uber was arriving. I started to walk towards the corner, trying to locate the black Nissan Leaf that had come for me, when someone grabbed my arm and pulled me around. I found myself face to face with the bizarre storyteller, his eyes wide with crazy. I could smell the clove cigarette on his breath. "The only place we can go that always remains unchanged is, of course, right now!" he said. "May luck be on your side."

As I turned around to get the hell out of there, he gave me a quick slap on the ass and exclaimed, "Enjoy the ride," and he skipped off down the street— that was again filling with people— pumping his scepter above his head, his guttural cackle resonating in my ears. A robust tingling sensation started where he had smacked me and migrated down my ass crack, settling in my sphincter. Or maybe it was still just sensitive from my doctor's visit that morning.

"Those panhandlers are relentless these days," the driver said as we pulled away from the curb.

"This city has become a damn zoo," I responded, focusing my attention on my phone to avoid any more unwelcome conversations with strangers. I hoped the kids would still be awake when I got home.

CHAPTER

TWO

The following morning, I was in our closet, picking out an outfit for work that would exude a management vibe. It was the day my new role would be announced. Although anyone could wear whatever they wanted, the upper echelon maintained a slightly more professional look. I settled on a nice pair of jeans, loafers, and a button-down shirt designed to be worn untucked. The brand was remarkably called Untuck-it or something of that sort. Equally important, it was an excellent cloaking device for my emerging gut. This new development, combined with the recent discovery of the accelerated aging of my rectal region, was making me feel old and slightly insecure.

I could now hear my wife ambling around the bedroom, which meant she was awake early, and I would soon have to engage in exchanging pleasantries with the unpleasant.

If the perfect marriage could be described as a divinely orchestrated sonata, ours was a fraudulent riff on a broken banjo.

"Good morning, Toby," Gina said as she passed the walk-in closet and entered the bathroom.

"Good morning. Looks like I fell asleep before you got home last night. What time did you end up getting in?" I asked.

"Around eleven-thirty. Another late work dinner with colleagues in town from the East Coast. We didn't even sit down to eat until almost nine," she answered from the bathroom. Gina's work required more dinners and travel, which was fine, as we could afford the extra nanny time. However, I now suspected it may be more than work dinners keeping her out.

Gina was moody. You never knew which version of her you were dealing with until she opened her mouth. You'd also never guess she was a mother of two in her mid-30s. She was attractive, intelligent, and at one time, I think I recall, charming.

"Aren't you going to ask how the big interview went yesterday?" I asked, trying to decide if it mattered what kind of belt you wore with an untucked shirt. "Actually, it was four interviews." I concluded that the comfortable blue canvas belt would be a better way to go, although it didn't match the brown loafers. It flexed to accommodate my love handles better than the brown leather one, which cut into my muffin top like a knife, regardless of what hole I used.

"Oh yes, how did your big interview go?" she asked in a tone devoid of sincerity.

"I'm glad you asked. It went....what're the right words? Fucking awesome! The new boss discussed my transition into the role before the interview even ended. Jim heard from others in management that I did impress." I was now fixating on sock options but continued, "About time we get some payoff for the ridiculous hours I've been working for the last however many years. We're talking an extra fifty thousand a year, and the quarterly bonus goes up from fifteen to twenty percent of my base. That's almost another ten thousand a year plus twenty-five thousand more stock options."

"Well, that's good news! Do you think you'll have to work more? The kids hardly know you as it is. I don't want to be a single parent, you know?" she asked. How silly of me! I forgot that advancing my career and putting more money in the bank for the family would be such an inconvenience for her.

"Probably be less work after the transition, but I'll be traveling a bit more—hopefully not too much."

"Well, that's nice. When will they announce it?" she asked almost indecipherably. She'd begun brushing her teeth, and I could hear the water running, which she knew drove me crazy. For God's sake, we're in a drought, and she's letting water run down the drain because it's easier than twisting a faucet handle.

"Pretty sure today is the day," I answered. "Hey, got some disturbing news from the doc yesterday during my prostate check."

"Tell me you don't have prostate cancer. Jesus, you're only thirty-seven years old, Toby."

"Fortunately, no, but he kindly informed me that I have the discolored beat-up asshole of a seventy-five-year-old man! That was a bit of a shocker."

"Oh yeah...that," she threw out nonchalantly.

"Yes, that! So you've noticed this and kept this dirty, dark secret from me?" It seemed like I was the only one, literally and figuratively, in the dark on this travesty.

"Well, I always assumed you had to have known about it. And you can be pretty sensitive about such things. Is this really news to you?"

"My God, Gina! I had no idea. I'm not always poking around down there. How would I know?"

"Figured someone must have said something to you before now."

"Before now? How long have you known about this?" I asked.

"Well, I remember talking to my sister about it when we had just started dating. So that must have been seven years ago or so. What does it matter?"

"Well, it matters a lot! What do you mean you were talking to your sister about it? Was she like, "Hey Gina, he seems like a nice guy, but how does his asshole look? How does a conversation like that even come up?"

"It wasn't the first thing out of my mouth, for Christ's sake, Toby. I'm sure I was telling her how I met this great guy, and she probably asked if I had any reservations or something like that."

"Reservations! So it was reservation-worthy? So were you like, "Yeah, Nancy, we've got a code brown here?"

"Well, obviously, it wasn't a deal breaker, but it did take some getting used to."

"Holy hell, Gina. So, everyone's been talking about this behind my back for years. The ogre-esque handicap that haunts the neighborhood kids in their dreams. A horrendous urban myth that happens actually to be true!"

"Toby, I seriously doubt the neighborhood kids are spreading the word of your condition around town like a prairie fire unless, unbeknownst to me, you've been in the front yard sunbathing in the nude. You need to chill out. We all have things about our bodies we don't like that we can't change."

"My condition? I suppose this does count as a 'condition.'"

At this exact moment, I found myself at eye level with a closet shelf, holding a stack of folded jeans. This, in and of itself, isn't relevant, but it's essential in context. However, the shockingly giant crazy-eyed spider standing on top of my jean stack, just three inches from my head, was a crisis of biblical proportions. He was obviously gearing up to pounce on my face and would take a shot at getting into my mouth or at least try to get away with a good little bite out of my eye. Right before he sprang, my catlike reflexes kicked in, launching me backward through the air while my hands commenced erratic sweeping motions in front of my face so I could bat it away mid-air. I landed in the hall outside the closet with no idea of where my assailant had come to rest. I needed to escape, as the chase was on, and those things could move lightning fast. Executing a flip to my stomach and an explosive crawl, I retreated into the bathroom on my hands and knees, slamming the door behind me.

"Towel!" I yelled to Gina, who stood motionless with her toothbrush paused in the corner of her mouth, eyes wide.

"Jesus," I added, snatching a towel from the rack myself and stuffing it under the door. I immediately executed a whole body brush-off with my hands in case the sneaky bastard had hitched a ride. "I think we're safe for now, but we have a situation."

"I'd say we do," Gina confirmed, toothpaste running down her chin. "Wouldn't happen to be another spider sighting, would it?"

"Those fuckers are always somewhere watching us, aren't they? I can't imagine how many we don't see for each one we do. We need to get an exterminator out here."

"I've seen only a handful of spiders in the six years we've lived here. Seems like a pretty normal amount to me."

"This one is different. Some tarantula/garden hybrid. The aggressive jumping kind." I was now getting frustrated fighting on two fronts. Apparently, I was the only sane person in the chaotically insane world. "Worse, the fucker has us trapped. Do you happen to have your cell phone?"

"NO! Who are you going to call? The police? 'Yes, officer, send everyone you got! We have a situation.' Toby, you need to get it together, and I don't want those kids to wake up."

I had totally forgotten about the kids, lying there, defenselessly sleeping, as the pissed-off killer, determined not to be defeated, executed the logical next move—killing the ones the target loves most. "Holy shit, the kids!"

Finally, understanding the magnitude of the situation, Gina was as pissed as I was and, God bless her, was taking action. She blew by me, ripping the towel out from under the door with her right hand and simultaneously opening the door with her left. Speed was critical here, and she was leveraging the element of surprise in her attack. "Where the hell is it?" she yelled.

"Last seen in closet jumping! Could be anywhere. Careful." When Gina was mad, nobody was safe. I realized she might have a shot at taking the thing down.

I peeked out the door, and she had already secured a land bridge from the bathroom to the closet entry, clearly forcing the arachnid into retreat, unless, of course, the unthinkable had already happened and it was now beelining down the hall to the kids' room.

"I can't find it!"

"He's after the kids!" I yelled.

"He's not after the kids. He can't move that fast!" She had clearly underestimated her enemy. "Where in the closet was it?"

"When it attacked me, I ran for safety. Couldn't risk slowing down to look back!" My frustration was starting to peak.

"Where was it before the attack?" She asked in a tone I didn't appreciate. I was now outside the closet, watching her scour the floor.

"It jumped at me from the top of my stack of jeans on the shelf. It could be anywhere now. We're so screwed!"

"It's still there."

"Where? It's back in the closet? Kill it!"

"No, you idiot! It's still there on top of your jeans," she said.

"I can't imagine how it got back up there that fast. Maybe it has babies up there somewhere that it fell back to protect. It's obviously grooming them to attack pack style."

"Or maybe it never attacked at all?" she suggested, grabbing a t-shirt and swishing up the spider inside it. "Nice. What a brave man you are. Jesus, I can't believe this."

"Is that my Kid Rock shirt you just used?" Her callousness knew no bounds.

Like most matters, we had different opinions about reality. She then deposited the spider outside and my favorite concert t-shirt into the laundry bin and waltzed past me, shaking her head in what could only be construed as disdain. She had no idea how lucky she was that the spider was too tired to leap a second time. Anyone can kill a winded spider, I suppose.

Deep down in the dark basement of my mind, a part of me wondered if it would have been awful if the spider had gotten her.

WE FINISHED GETTING DRESSED in silence. I headed down to the kitchen and started preparing a pot of coffee. Moments later, Gina announced her arrival with a "statement question." She had perfected the art of judgment and wielded the skill like a Jedi warrior does a lightsaber.

"Are you making just enough for yourself?" she asked.

"Of course not," I said, putting in another scoop of grounds, knowing full well the thought never occurred to me to make more. Most likely, being primarily a tea drinker, she didn't even want coffee, but she recognized an excellent opportunity for conflict when she saw it.

"What time are you planning on being home tonight?" she asked.

"Not sure yet. Big promo will be announced today, and not sure if anyone will initiate any celebratory after-work plans. Why?"

"Well, you know Tuesdays are my book club night, right?"

"If you say so," I responded.

"Well, I hope that after three years, it may have breached your awareness by now."

"Can't Jessica stay late? She always seems to be pretty flexible."

"Only if we check with her in advance. She has a life too, you know? I realize you may not recognize it, but your life intertwines with others' every now and then." Here we go. Gina failed to recognize that her routinely unanticipated work dinners, last-minute business travel, and spontaneous girls' weekends caused Jessica to adapt on the fly constantly.

"Well then, it seems like, when she arrives, you may want to talk to her about tonight being a later one," I said as I grabbed my Yeti coffee mug from the cabinet, made my way to the fridge, and started rooting around for the half-and-half. "Hey, are we out of half-and-half?"

"Possibly. You're the only one that uses it. If you used it up, I assume you'd have put it on the list for Jessica to pick up."

"Gina, I have a lot going on right now. I work my ass off and am trying to get us in a position where we can move out of this two-bedroom condo into a proper house and maybe eventually afford a good private school for the kids. I'm sorry if I'm not focused hour to hour on what food and drink we are about to run out of."

"Toby, it appears that you have been too busy to notice that I also work full time, work long hours, and am also responsible for managing the entire house, the nanny situation, all the kids' activities, their doctors' appointments, as well as our social calendar. Of course, since these things, much like emptying the dishwasher and doing the laundry, seem to 'magically' happen, I can see why they might not catch your attention. But God forbid, we're out of half-and-half, and you're offended that your needs aren't being accommodated. Jesus Christ." She had a point, but her bitchy tone made it impossible for me to acknowledge its validity.

"Yeah. I just sit around on my ass reading sports articles and watching the grass grow. Of course, it gets magically mowed, as do the bills get magically paid, and the cars get magically washed." I don't know where I was going with that, but it was vitally important that she understood it worked both ways.

"Toby, let's be clear. We work because we have college educations and don't want to be financially dependent on the eventual inheritance from my folks. But we both know that neither of them is in good health, and we will inherit a few million dollars in the not-too-distant future. Maybe my job isn't glamorous, but it helps pay the bills and cover childcare. I'm content with our small condominium and older cars and feel a public-school education has a lot of advantages. Don't forget that we both went to public schools."

"Well, it doesn't ever seem like you're that content to me."

"How would you know? I can't remember the last time you even asked how my day was, what I was reading, or what sounded fun to do this weekend. If it's about you, we can talk all night. Your career, your running workouts, your golf game. You have all these big aspirations to be a VP one day, have a nice single-family home in San Francisco, a BMW, run another marathon, blah blah blah. The rest of us are just a support system for you to stand on while you try to 'become somebody.' It's always about you trying to prove yourself to yourself or somehow validate yourself against some ideal you have. However, no matter what you achieve, you're never happy for long and only focused on the next goal. Do you know what sucks, though? They aren't team goals. They are Toby goals; you assume everyone else is on board for whatever sacrifice is required. But you know what I've realized?"

"It seems you've realized a lot of things. But I'll play along. What have you realized, Gina?"

"Well, thank you for asking, Toby," she said in a tone far beyond patronizing. "I have realized—and it's taken me painfully too long to see this—that you do not know how to be happy. And unfortunately, when you aren't happy, you make it damn difficult for anyone else to be happy around you."

"Well, I'm sorry I don't settle for mediocrity and a pathetically normal life. I'm going to get coffee on the way to work. Coffee with half-and-half in it, and you won't have to talk to my unhappy discolored ass anymore this morning. That ought to make YOU happy."

And with that dramatic declaration, I snatched up my briefcase and marched out the door. As it was closing, I couldn't be sure, and maybe it was just the wind outside, but I am pretty sure I heard, "I'm happy that I'm not scared to death of spiders!"

THREE

I entered the office with a fresh cup of creamed coffee and just the right amount of swagger. Sure enough, in my email was a meeting invite from my new boss, Richard Flannigan, titled "Next Steps." Clearly, Richard was anxious to get things kicked off, and the meeting was scheduled at 9 a.m., in just a half hour.

This provided me a nice little window to go online and research advanced symptoms of chlamydia. It seemed the initial burning during urination may have subsided, which I was sure clearly meant this disease had elevated its attack, targeting more critical life support systems. Swollen or tender testicles didn't seem to be an issue yet, nor did pain and discharge or bleeding around the anus, thank God. My anus was already on its last legs. What was taking the lab results so damn long? I also learned I could have a urinary tract infection and prostate cancer. It's incredible how time flies while researching one's ailments. Luckily, I only had a half hour to peer into the details of my untimely death before grabbing my notebook and making my way to the conference room to receive my promotion, all the while paying particular attention to whether my testicles were the least bit tender.

"Have a seat," Richard said, motioning towards the other side of the small round table. "I asked Julie to join us as well." Julie was head of Human Resources. Of course she'd be there, as there would be an offer letter to sign, maybe something for stock options, what my title would be, etc.

"Good morning, fun seekers," I said, sitting down directly across from Julie with Richard on my left. "So we're here to discuss next steps, huh?"

"Indeed we are. Might as well get right to it," said Richard.

"Toby, we have a situation that's...um...wellunfortunate," Julie stated matter-of-factly.

This wasn't good. I knew before another word was uttered what it was. We weren't forecasting the best quarter from a Sales revenue perspective. I'm sure the CFO must have proactively shut down all open hiring requisitions to get ahead of the problem by reducing expenses and protecting margins until the Sales engine ramped back up. I'd seen it a dozen times at least, which would mean a delay in my promotion. I also noticed my left testicle might be sensitive.

"Yeah, Toby...uhm...we saw the email you sent Jim yesterday," Richard informed me. After a moment of awkward expressionless silence, he continued, "As you're aware, we have a zero-tolerance policy towards pornography in the workplace."

"This is outrageous! I have no idea what you're talking about. I must have left my computer without the screensaver activated, and someone either sent it from my computer or maybe I was hacked." I felt that emphatic denial—much like when your Mom asks if you ate the entire rest of the carton of ice cream—offered the most potential.

"We were hoping that could be the case, but when examining your email history, which is company property, there seems to be a pattern with many back-and-forth emails of this nature. I'm sorry, Toby. We all lose in situations like this," Richard kindly informed me. "The company has decided to terminate your employment, effective immediately."

I wanted to share what I was thinking, but no such thing was happening. I was in complete mind-numbing shock, not unconvinced that this all might be a dream.

Julie then took over. "Because this is considered gross misconduct, unfortunately, we won't be able to extend you COBRA benefits. I have your final paycheck here. You own all vested stock options; however, the company fully retains all unvested options." She proceeded with other scripted declarations, which I was no longer paying attention to.

Richard escorted me to my cubicle, where I stuffed my two framed pictures, bamboo back scratcher, and Yeti coffee thermos into my satchel and grabbed my jacket. I left my stupid achievement awards as they now seemed hollow. The walk of shame to the elevator was punctuated by cheers coming from the far corner of the floor.

"Here's to Ted, our new fearless leader!" someone shouted.

"Way to go, Ted!" someone else chimed in as their group raised what appeared to be shots of some alcohol and downed them in unison. At that point, I would have preferred a colony of fire ants in my loins than witness Ted celebrating what should have been my promotion.

A guy never really daydreams about standing out in front of his office building, holding his personal effects, and wishing his company would have at least given him a demotion. It seemed I had just gotten swept into life's undertow, unsure of how far out to sea I would end up.

"You too, huh?" a voice asked from directly behind me.

I wheeled around to see Jim walking out the door carrying a box of his shit with a scowl anchored across his brow. The box under his arm had a basketball poking out the top, and he had his framed Steph Curry jersey in his other hand. We looked at each other standing there, trying to make sense of what had just happened, like two Survivor contestants that had just been voted off the island.

"How the hell did they get into our emails? I don't recall any memos saying anything about their right to troll through our private stuff?" I asked Jim.

"Well, I found out I didn't activate my screensaver before I rushed off to my meeting with Frank. I didn't anticipate that Katie from Marketing would be dropping off her team's new seating chart for my team to execute. It appears that Katie isn't a Flying Fister fan," Jim informed me.

"She was always colder than a whore's heart," I pointed out.

"Well, I'm fucked, dude," Jim said. "I can't tell my wife the truth. Maybe I can, but there's no rationalizing this. I mean, the thing is, there was never any intention to make anyone, other than maybe you, uncomfortable. What a shit show."

I deduced that the company's sensitivity to these infractions was most likely increased after last month's incident involving Kurt, the Director of Marketing Communications. He was caught in a last-minute attempt to find a receptacle, tossing his load into a plant in his office. It seemed like a high-risk move to me, but Kurt was in a pickle, which I completely understood. Kurt remained employed, so his moral infraction was more of a corporate misdemeanor than the felony we had inadvertently committed.

"How about you blame me one hundred percent for sending the email and whatever else? Then I'll blame you when I tell Gina. They've never met and likely never will. We'll each play the victim card, and the beauty of being a victim is that it's never the victim's fault. I heard a TED Talk on that once. It's an amazing psychological defense mechanism."

"I imagine we'll need to be pissed at each other for getting each other fired. Probably worth a hiatus from calls or texts. It's more believable if I tell her I won't even talk to your pathetic ass," he said with a remorseful chuckle.

"Yeah, I don't want to see your irresponsible, reckless ass again either," I said, shaking my head, still in disbelief. "Alright, man, I got to straighten my head and figure out a plan before confronting Gina."

"Let me know if you need a reference in your job search. Just tell me what you want me to say, and I'll lie my ass off for you," he offered, setting his picture frame on the ground against his leg.

"Likewise," I said, shaking his free hand, and we departed on our new respective life journeys just like that.

And that was the lynchpin that unleashed the fuckering of my life. One day you're on a trajectory straight to the top, and then, out of nowhere, life's flyswatter slams your ass back down to the pavement with one well-placed stroke.

As the bus I was riding approached my stop, I remained in my seat, unable to push the button signaling I wanted to get off. So I continued west. There was only one other person on the bus. A young, angry-looking boy, around fourteen or maybe sixteen, dressed in a black Megadeth t-shirt and black jeans. He was working hard to maintain an exaggerated scowl, staring out the window directly across from him. He probably got kicked out of school for smoking a J on the playground or something and would, much like me, have some explaining to do when he got home. We had a lot in common. He wasn't pushing any buttons either. Eventually, we were approaching the ocean, and I decided to get off at Thirty Eighth Avenue and make my way over to Spreckles Lake in Golden Gate Park. It seemed like a good place to ponder life. Plenty of benches around a beautiful manmade lake with seagulls, pigeons, and remote-controlled boats, all teaming up to create a bizarrely tranquil space safely nested in the densely populated city.

I hung out there the rest of the afternoon.

The logical next step was to find another job. I definitely didn't seek out a career in Sales Operations. However, the reality was that it was the only thing anyone was willing to pay me to do. When you are making decent money, have expensive rent, two kids, and a keep-up-with-the-Joneses wife, you don't have the luxury of taking a step back to ground zero to test out a different career. You're in the trap. And when you're in the trap, you first convince yourself you want to be there, and then, technically, you're not trapped. But now I wasn't in the trap. I wasn't anywhere. Deep down, it was clear that I needed to get back into the trap and find a way to like it. While coming to grips with this, my phone rang.

"Hi, this is Toby," I said.

"Hi, Toby, Dr. Beck. Got your lab results back. Everything looks normal."

"Wait, you're saying I'm not stuffed full of chlamydia?"

"Nope. Nor do you have gonorrhea or human papillomavirus. Blood and urine tests were clean as well. Also, no urinary tract infection."

Well, maybe Gina wasn't fucking around on me after all. Still, the late nights out, phone calls taken outside, and growing disdain lent itself to suspicion.

"Well then, why the burning when I pee? Do I have dick cancer?" I asked.

"Has it started to subside?" he asked in response.

"What, the burning? Yeah, it's almost stopped. What does that mean?"

"Can I ask you a personal question?" Which struck me as amusing since things couldn't get much more personal.

"Of course."

"Do you masturbate in the shower?" This definitely qualified as more personal and a little creepy.

"Yeah. So?"

"With soap?"

"So?"

"Pretty common, actually," he informed me.

"Well, I'm glad a bunch of us guys toss off in the shower with soap. Where are we going with this, Doc?"

"If you get soap or shampoo inside the opening of the urethra, it irritates the sensitive inner lining and, while it's inflamed, it burns when you pee."

"Really?" I asked. How would I not know something like this by now?

"Really. I'm surprised you wouldn't know something like this by now. The good news is now you do, and you don't have to worry about having a venereal disease anymore.

"Well, this is a breath of fresh air. It's been a hell of a day, Doc. Thanks for the good news," I said, feeling optimistic that maybe there was still a God out there somewhere, potentially on my side.

"One more piece of advice, Toby."

"Yeah, what's that?"

"Use conditioner instead of soap. Doesn't seem to have the same adverse side effects."

"Right. Appreciate the tip. Thanks, doc," I said, hanging up. I was excited about this conditioner revelation until I remembered I had just been fired for pornography. Now I just felt dirty talking to a medical professional about a masturbatory accident and tips and tricks for more pleasurable shower spanking. Maybe this was the life of a porn addict, and until now, I never realized I was that guy. Hell, I had never been aware of my geriatric anus until a couple of days ago. I wondered what other nasty little details were hiding in plain sight, waiting for just the right time to maul my self-esteem.

FOR THE FOLLOWING WEEK, I pretended to go to work while I crafted a suitable lie to spare my wife from digesting the bitter pill that her husband was a fan of hardcore porn and was ruining both their lives. For the record, that effort counted as staying in touch with my compassionate side.

I split my time between working on my spiel about how Jim had irresponsibly torpedoed our jobs and frantically reaching out to everyone in my network who might be aware of potential job openings.

Another interesting tidbit of information— Jim had broken our new "no contact protocol" to share with me that Gina's college freshman dorm mate Hadley, as luck would have it, worked in the HR department at the company that had shit-canned me. I was not aware of this, having never met her, although, as luck would have it, she knew exactly who I was. I also learned that women's loyalty to each other doesn't fade even through twelve years of not keeping in touch when an evil man rears his ugly and increasingly flabbier head.

DAY 9 PF *(Post Firing)*

I returned home from "work" to find Gina in the kitchen sitting at the kitchen island with red eyes and a large glass of matching red wine without a smile. As any husband knows, this can mean many things, and one doesn't benefit by hastily jumping to conclusions. These symptoms could have resulted from a fight with her sister, which wasn't unusual. Maybe the kids pushed her off the end of her rope. Possibly, but unlikely, she was super high.

"Uh oh, rough day, hon?" I said with compassion.

"You could say that. Is there something you want to tell me?" she asked. Checkmate.

Nope.

Get me a beer.

You don't look as hot with puffy eyes.

I don't think I like your tone.

All these options would have made for a better story later but wouldn't have ultimately affected the outcome.

In a Hail Mary attempt to mitigate the situation with a cocktail of admirable transparency and a splash of lie, I blurted out, "Fired for porn. Fucking Jim's fault."

My heart rate had impressively escalated from normal to cardiac arrest in under three seconds.

I didn't know exactly what she knew, but according to plan, I decided it would be best to position it as Jim had sent me some inappropriate email, and I was the misunderstood victim in the saga.

"The fucking Flying Fisters, Toby?" Gina asked. I guess she knew more than I had hoped.

"Actually, it's The Flying Fister Family, but a common mistake," I answered, weaving sarcasm into the noose that would soon hang me —another bad decision.

I wanted to think this is something couples work through every day with a good therapist and maybe come out of it closer in the end, but it wasn't just The Flying Fister Family email that got under her craw. The other seventy-six video files and two hundred eighty images found on my hard drive made the "Jim's Fault" into an indisputable lie and me into a much worse person than when I walked in.

"Toby, not only can I not trust you, I don't even know who you are anymore, and I'm not sure you do either. Your actions have consequences for everyone else in your life. You need to figure out what you're all about and make some changes in your life, or at least consider being more than just a shitty person. Life is who you are, Toby, not what you achieve."

That's a lot to unpack, but it's just new-age bullshit, most likely from the latest selection from her book club. Who does she think she is now? Some fucking shrink. She isn't Mrs. Happiness herself; she is always complaining about the neighbors who blow their leaves, what seems like every day, or going on about her friends who never initiate and wait for her to organize everything or the lists of all the household projects that seem to fall into her lap. I had built a career, started a family, stayed in good shape (until recently), and had a plan for the future.

Gina's emotional charge on the situation ensured that this conversation would yield no productive outcome. Like oil in water, the truth eventually worked its way to the surface, and Gina had a point. Maybe I wasn't very good at being happy. At that moment, I was so unhappy, not to mention irritated, that she showed not the slightest empathy that I elected to neutralize the situation by removing myself from it.

I walked out, got in my car, and rode into the sunset. While it helped me to clear my head, it did nothing of the sort for Gina.

———————

THE NEXT FEW weeks of failed attempts on my part to beg, plead, promise, and grovel did nothing to prepare me for the pain, shame, and self-hatred I felt when reading the words "irreconcilable differences" in the divorce papers I was served in Room 206 of the not so *Super 8 Motel* on Lombard and Divisidero. Although it wasn't explicitly listed, I was pretty sure my beat-up, discolored anus must have played a role in her decision-making process.

I learned the domino effect is real; I was fucked, hated myself, and cried a lot for the next couple of months. Often it felt like I was living an out-of-body experience, watching this poor fuck wallow and ruminate in a new world that was so absurdly different from his previous life that it must just be a movie or a shitty dream. I was transitioning from denial to dread, or whatever grieving stage typically follows denial. Acceptance was too far off to seem like a realistic possibility.

So that was the end of my life as I knew it and a beginning—the beginning of the end of much more than I could have imagined.

CHAPTER
FOUR

Six Months Later

S
I opened my eyes and tried to register what day it was. I began working up the courage to face the crippling current of woe I knew I'd swim against for five to seven hours while my hangover raped my day.

This pattern had steadily increased in frequency over the last five or six months. In addition to alcohol, I was also developing an impressive tolerance to shame.

A quick body scan revealed that I was at least dressed and in my own apartment. From experience, I knew it could be worse.

I began a fishing expedition for the events that had transpired throughout the previous evening, complete with counting each drink consumed before the amnesia set in. Seven, while not my lucky number, appears to be the foundation upon which today's headache was built. My life was off the rails.

We've all been there to different degrees, not always with the good fortune of staggering evidence of a substance abuse problem. Sometimes, the first blow hits us when we are blindsided by a big promotion being hijacked by an unexpected career execution. Other times, it's when your wife announces, "You've destroyed my trust in you and my false reality of who you are. That's a deal breaker, but more importantly, the kids need a better role model, and frankly, I deserve better." For other folks, it could happen when getting out of the shower and accidentally noticing an extremely white, fat, and haggard-looking man in your bathroom staring at you from the mirror with a surprised look on his face.

A few of us are blessedly fortunate to experience all of these epiphanies simultaneously. The life I had proudly built up from nothing and consciously scripted through meticulous planning, self-sacrifice, and positive affirmations had somehow miraculously returned me to the starting line of "nothing." The only thing worse than starting with nothing was achieving what you thought was everything and watching it blow up in an apocalyptic detonation, revealing only the ashen ruins of who you thought you were and what your life once was, complete with all the rubble, dust and smoke to choke on. I was stuck in a holding pattern, waiting for a comeback that appeared to have taken an extended leave of absence.

I sat on the edge of the bed and paused while the dizziness settled, the taste in my mouth confirming I hadn't wasted time brushing my teeth before retiring the night before.

That is how the morning of June 1st, 2018, settled into existence. Cocktail hour was at five o'clock and couldn't come soon enough, as a shot of Patron with a Corona backer always released me from my rumination shackles. Plus, waiting until five—regardless of the torture involved— did create the illusion of self-discipline, control, and almost earning that first drink. Additionally, it was proof I was not a day drinker.

What it didn't make me was skinny, lean, or fit. I had exceeded the capacity for all my sneaky techniques for sucking in my gut to have any noticeable effect. I was fat. I had been at least ten pounds overweight before the "big life change," but now I was at least thirty or forty.

I won't be the first person, and certainly not the last, to claim the

McDonald's McRib Sandwich helped ruin my waistline. If you haven't tried one, don't. It's like playing with dynamite—fascinating, exciting, and most definitely dangerous if you get too close. I got too close every day for the last six months. The thing about the McRib isn't just the perfect shape imitation of a small rack of ribs, dripping with a BBQ sauce that's in a league of its own, nor is it the brilliance of the pickle and onion to sauce ratio or the breaded delivery vehicle, most likely baked fresh daily. The thing about the McRib is that it pairs perfectly with most beers, providing incredible variety and flexibility. My choice is Coors because it's a banquet beer. Coors Light, however, won't work because the ferocity of the tang of the delectable McRib sauce immediately overpowers it. I am very disciplined about only going with classic Coors on such occasions. Seems harmless enough, right?

As it turns out, this well-thought-out menu choice and pairing does have its sneaky drawbacks. The first major one is that it's cheap, fast, and yummy. The second major drawback is that you are always only blocks away from one in the United States. The third is that it's almost impossible not to drink beer with it. The fourth major drawback is that the McRib is not always on the menu, nor do you know when it may return. As all psychologists asked to weigh in on this will tell you, this is a perfect storm for creating a scarcity mentality that forces one to eat as many as possible, as often as possible, until this window from heaven slams shut on your sauce-stained fingers for God only knows how long, possibly forever.

In this case, the window exceeded everyone's expectations and stayed open for over five months, precisely how long it takes a guy to pack on thirty pounds if they strictly follow this diet. Four out of five doctors who chew gum agree that for men, rapid weight gain like this will be the result 96% of the time, especially if a pre-existing porn addiction is involved. That was undoubtedly not footnoted on the McDonald's menu, which is why I no longer patronize that establishment.

It's strange, but online dating sites don't mention that attractive single women will generally try to avoid getting banged by a fatty. Hot women who crave sloppy fat guys, as we all learned in elementary school, are like unicorns and are super hard to find. For now, I had little choice but to remain monogamous in my relationship with lotion and Kleenex.

I shifted my focus out the window to see what the loud rain, which made a wooden spoon hitting a copper pot sound like gentle white noise, looked like. Not surprisingly, it looked like lots of rain. Watching extreme weather of any type is still fascinating, even after 37 years of life.

My attention was captured by some activity in the backyard two doors down. In San Francisco, two doors down means fifty feet, as the houses are packed tight like a stuffed bookshelf. I had been aware of some building project going on over the last month but had been too busy being lazy to make the twenty-second trek to investigate things. The only part of this gloomy picture that wasn't rendered in black and white was a tiny bit of yellow moving around the misty gray yard. Upon closer examination, it turned out to be an old rain jacket like we all wore in elementary school. Of course, this particular one was being modeled by a grown man with a shovel in his hand, relocating a massive pile of dirt to the right five feet from the starting pile, one scoop at a time. Christ! What does someone have to do to earn that kind of karma? I could only assume he must have ax-murdered a nun or two in a past life, or maybe it was some construction worker's initiation.

Then a voice inside my head suggested maybe he got shit-canned from his previous job, packed on the pounds eating McRib sandwiches and swigging cheap beer, and likely had his wife walk out on him, leaving his fat, lonely, broke ass with little choice but to take employment where he could find it. In his case, it was the rainy backyard two doors down. That solidified my dislike of this mean little voice in my head. Until then, I had never had much empathy for people in these jobs. However, it appeared I was on the fast track to becoming one of them.

I needed to recapture my life, or at least most of it. Most importantly, I needed to be happy again with a respectable job and good cash flow, have purpose again, and find a woman willing to take a chance on a complete train wreck. That last one, however, would be challenging without the job and income. Not a lot of women want to rescue a charity case.

It was time to get disciplined. That day, I decided I wouldn't have a drop of booze until after 6 p.m., and I needed something healthy for breakfast. As luck would have it, I had woken up dressed, so I grabbed my rain jacket off the orange, slightly cracked bean bag chair marking the beginning of my living room and angled towards what at one time may have been a proper couch, a mere six feet away, marking the end of my living room.

I opened the front door of the apartment building and began to navigate the crumbling cement stairs that led down to the sidewalk. The heavy rain had faded to a drizzle, adding a nice texture to the puddles on the sidewalk.

"Top of the morning to ya!" The local homeless guy— who had chosen to reside next to our building— raised a 24-oz Tecate can towards me from his reclined position under a tarp extended from his shopping cart, which had created a small "front porch." He then took an impressive swig to punctuate his greeting. There's nothing like having a homeless guy be the first thing you see when you walk out your door and the last thing you see before you walk in to ensure you know you are just one step away from his world. So far, this guy had always been pleasant and hadn't once asked for money, shouted crazy shit, or left any noticeable defecation or needles in the area. However, the next one might not be as amiable. Just in case, I had filed a complaint a week before to the property management company as a proactive measure.

"Top of the morning," I replied in an obligatory manner as I passed by, reveling in how fortunate I was to live within walking distance of Chick-fil-A.

Ten minutes later, head pounding and eyes burning, I struggled back to my apartment, wielding a bag of Chick-n-Minis, a bacon, egg, and cheese muffin, hash browns, and a fruit cup. I was feeling good about also ordering the fruit cup.

I had planned on ramping up the job search, but now it felt like just getting through the morning without puking would be a more realistic goal. It had become evident that not doing something can be as much of a habit as doing something. In my case, not searching for a job had become a habit I wasn't yet equipped to break. I had started aggressively networking only to realize I didn't have quite the network that I thought. Sure, I had been in high-tech for eight-plus years, but in all honesty, it was more like a couple of years of experience repeated over and over again. Being that all eight years were with the same company, I interacted with pretty much the same people every day. I also discovered that most of those same people either still worked there, where I wasn't going to get a job ever again, or had moved on and didn't even like me enough to return a call, email, or LinkedIn message. One can interpret that in many ways, but luckily, Jed, who was willing to pick up the phone and take my call, translated the true meaning for me. "Dude, I'm not going to beat around the bush. You were a fucking asshole," is how he positioned it.

I occasionally responded to a posting here or there, hoping my resume would cut through the competition and that whoever was screening applications didn't know me. This resulted in about twenty or thirty applications being submitted and two interviews in six months, neither of which progressed to the second round.

Ultimately, I had to accept that I may be unable to pick up where I left off professionally. The thought of taking a lower-level Sales Ops job and the grinding, soul-sucking, thankless hours involved only reminded me I'd be back in a prison I wasn't convinced I could ever escape. Sadly, I had no other skills to fall back on. Outside of tech, I'd be pretty much on par with any recent college grad with no experience.

Then my Dad's words would cruelly dance through my head:

"You only get one shot to play this game called life, son, and the culmination of what you go out and take from it defines your legacy." My legacy was starting to look like a collection of empty Chick-fil-A and Taco Bell bags. If life rewarded effort, this must be what happened when you couldn't muster any up.

I spent the rest of the day contemplating the enormity of my gut and trying to make sense of who I was becoming. And like sand through the hourglass, these were the days of my life.

IN STARK CONTRAST, I woke up feeling uncommonly great the following day. While tangled in the web of my thoughts the night before, I had forgotten about drinking. For that matter, I forgot about eating dinner as well.

I had lain on the couch for what seemed like hours, fabricating stories to explain raincoat man's lot in life and the path that led to shoveling mud piles in the pouring rain. Had he, too, lost what he believed to be a happy life? Maybe he couldn't read, write, talk, or think, reducing his career choices. Possibly an ex-con out on work relief? Were we leading parallel lives, or was his burden such that his misery was his alone and I had more upside? It's amazing how, when your life story falls to shit, your mind desperately clamors for a new story to make sense of everything. My mind hadn't been able to pull this off just yet, and although I was rooting for it, I somehow knew I could make good money betting against it.

I showered and dressed and realized I had no idea what to do next. I couldn't remember the last time I was awake this early without burning eyes and the constant need to take exaggerated deep breaths. I also noted that getting the toothpaste onto the tooth-brush is easier when both are not shaking around in your hands.

Yesterday's rain had finally stopped sometime during the night. The early morning sunlight brushed a tangerine stain across the city, beckoning me outside.

I donned my coat and strode out my front door and directly into Brian, the resident manager of our little apartment building. His presence there took me by surprise, as my spontaneous emergence must have him. This resulted in the only logical response on my part: accusation.

"How long have you been lurking outside my door, Brian?"

Brian was a suspiciously nice guy whose over-exuberant passion was that of someone who had just come out of a Tony Robbins weekend retreat. It was all but certain he would sign up for Tony's fire-walking workshop next to prove his invincibility.

I'd estimate him to be in his late 20s or early 30s, medium height, with well-coiffed hair and no signs of gray or evidence of a receding hairline. Brian was a guy eager to conquer his weaknesses and the world, which grated on me because he was my mirror opposite, reflecting a ghost of who I once was and the distance between that version of myself and the current husk of that version that I had tragically morphed into.

He was in his usual uniform: khaki trousers, a tucked-in and neatly pressed button-down shirt, and loafers. His wrist supported one of those oversized watches that pilots always wear, announcing that "time is of the essence," best communicated with ostentatious jewelry. This irritated me far more than it should have. One of my still intact superpowers was masterfully judging people I didn't know.

I just hoped I'd be fortunate enough to witness him suffer some sort of crushing defeat.

"Actually, just arrived, Toby, my friend," he proclaimed. It's funny what qualifies as being a friend these days. In Brian's case, two conversations within three months about whether the mail had come yet and when the electricity may come back on checked off all the boxes on his list. "Everything OK in there? I heard some banging around."

"I guess OK is relative," I replied, wondering if I had been banging around or if snoopy Brian was a bit of a liar.

"Oh, good. I'm just checking, buddy," he replied. He gave me one of those fist bump extensions. I obliged and met his fist with mine, making haste to the front door.

THE CRISP MORNING air embraced me as I descended the front stairs to the sidewalk, the morning dew infusing the air with fragrant subtleties. I could smell the pine trees as I strolled down the block, something sweet like lilac, and possibly even the morning sunlight itself. It was a glorious day. Within five minutes, my destination was upon me.

With a sudden shift in olfactory pleasure, I was now in 7-Eleven, making my way to the frozen food cooler. The best part of the 7-Eleven burrito (I go with sausage, egg, and cheese) is the perfection of the 7-Eleven microwave's heating ability. The piping hot outside and the still frozen center hitting your palate simultaneously with an explosion of flavor, seldom found outside of Mexico, makes a guy feel truly alive. Today, I was feeling action-oriented, so I elected not to eat in and took my neatly wrapped pocket of yum on the road, savoring the tangy spice lingering on my back palate between every bite.

The day was moving in the right direction, and I still had the scrumptious burrito butt to look forward to as I jaywalked across the street toward home. It was right about this point when I heard the beeping sound of heavy construction equipment reversing. If a giant excavator has ever backed over anyone, they were either totally deaf, a complete idiot, or likely both.

This seemed as good a time as any to check out the construction project. After a quick stroll up the driveway and scanning the scene, I realized I had no idea what was happening. Then, one of the workers approached me.

"You must be the inspector?" the construction guy said. He was a few inches shorter than me, maybe 5' 7", Hispanic, mid-forties, with weathered skin. His jeans and sweatshirt were remarkably clean, but the day was still young.

"Yes, sir. Thought I'd make sure things are up to snuff. You can call me Toby. So what's going on here?"

Looking slightly perplexed, he asked, "Are you from the city?"

"I'm originally from the East Bay, but I've lived here in San Francisco for over twenty years now. Does that count as being from The City, or is there a minimum tenure requirement that disqualifies me?"

"No, I mean from City Planning?" The construction dude clarified as he peered a little closer, trying to make sense of me with a curious frown.

"Nope. That sounds like a job, which I don't currently have, so I guess not. Sorry to disappoint."

He was less than jovial, so I wrapped up my little act. "Just curious what this project is all about?"

"Oh. Yeah...just leveling the yard, digging a new basement, and putting in a new foundation." He extended an arm towards multiple disorganized piles of cinder blocks, dirt, and gravel, bordered by trailers, white pick-up trucks with roof racks, and a couple of randomly deposited jackhammers. I took a quick liking to the red one.

This type of project would be easy enough if you were a real man. I knew this because, by any definition, I was not and was moving farther in the opposite direction every day. I would be ripe for a sex change in about another month at the current rate.

"Hey, by any chance, were you the guy moving that big pile of dirt over there with a shovel in the rain yesterday?" I figured as long as I was here, I might as well get to the bottom of the fascination that had consumed me.

"Full of questions today, huh, Curious George?"

"Well, I suppose I am. If you want to be stuck up, you don't have to answer," I responded with equivocal rudeness.

"Backhoe had a fuel line leak, and we had to get ready for the excavator today. I'm the newest hire, so I got to take the lead on that one."

"What a beautiful initiation ceremony. Where were you working before you started this gig?" I was bracing myself to hear my own story and confirm my fears of realistic future employment options. This guy didn't seem like the idiot I was hoping for. I was, however, still anticipating his story might leave me feeling better about the shit sandwich life generously deposited on my fate plate.

"Not around here. I lived in San Carlos, Mexico, making bricks. But, because of the drought, we didn't have enough water to make the clay, and most of us lost our jobs. Luckily, my cousin, who works for this company, told me they needed help that didn't require much experience except being willing to work hard. Why am I even telling you all this? I've got to get back to work, man."

I hoped, for his sake, he had at least been able to keep his porn collection. Then I realized he said '*Luckily.*' It seems like luck must be a relative concept these days. At this point, I was grilling a complete stranger about his employment history without an explanation. Kind of dickish of me. However, each answer he gave only raised more questions in my mind.

"I realize I didn't introduce myself," I said, extending my hand. "My name is Toby, and I live two doors down. Have only been in the neighborhood for about six months and don't know many people yet. I'm sure you need to get back to work, but let me know if I can buy you a beer sometime and learn more about your time in Mexico." It then dawned on me that what flew out of my mouth could likely be construed as a gay pick-up attempt in arguably the gayest city in the world. "And I'm not gay, by the way." Why not err on the side of clarity?

"My name is Hulises, and I'm not gay either," he said with a chuckle, shaking his head. "No offense, but you're a strange guy, Toby. Not in a bad way, but a guy who walks up to a stranger and starts asking all sorts of personal questions followed by a slightly homophobic exchange and an offer to buy you a beer seems odd, wouldn't you say?"

"Well, when you put it that way, I do sound like a bit of a whack job—sorry, man. I was just trying to be clever, but I guess it came out all wrong. I'm just looking to make some friends."

"Well, you ain't going to make a lot that way, pal. You seem harmless enough, and I can always use a free beer, but I'm not afraid to punch a freak in the face if you get my drift. I get done at five. Wife's out tonight, so I've got an hour to burn after work. Meet around the corner at The Tipsy Plow?"

I wasn't expecting a Mexican guy to want to grab a drink at an Irish pub.

"Sounds like a plan, and I'm buying," I said. He was right. I was a freak. And he was a bit of an idiot for accepting my offer, given the conversation. "See you there," I added and made my way down to the sidewalk as Hulises ambled back over to the job site.

The opportunity to have an actual conversation with the construction guy stranger was worth seizing. In this instance, I was determined to withhold further judgment as an attempt at self-improvement, if nothing else.

I've always been curious to learn other people's stories. San Francisco is an incredible walking town. Some of the world's most beautiful views and architecture, along with just enough human feces on the sidewalks to keep you focused and moving. My favorite time to walk in my current neighborhood, the Inner Richmond, is right after dusk when everyone's lights are still on, allowing you to peer into their inner lives for a few moments from the sidewalk under the cloak of darkness. Because about twelve to fifteen houses are pressed together on each side of a single block, you don't have to walk far to get your fill.

I would often see the unique art on a family's walls, 60-inch plasma TVs going, exotic plants, trendy paint colors, and people moving through rooms that looked like they were featured on the cover of Architectural Digest, with the bonus of a shiny red Tesla in the driveway. Then, right next door, another living room meticulously adorned with heavy metal concert posters and prayer flags, illuminated with black light and maybe a waft of bong smoke dissipating towards the ceiling from the red bong clearly visible on the window table. It's funny how, regardless of social status, people love to display their favorite red toy for strangers to admire.

That's when my mind fills in the missing pieces of the story. We have the hedge fund manager— enjoying a glass of his $200 scotch, loosening his tie after having increased his net worth by another $3 million this week— living right next to the five wannabe hippie roommates in their early twenties who moved to San Francisco last summer from some midwestern town to find themselves in a city that no longer remotely resembles the heartbeat of the 60's counterculture. Of course, they sleep on mattresses on the floor with clothes strewn all over. Unwashed dishes, surely filling the sink, and their bathroom would be filthy as all hell. Surely, people must detect my lowly situation when walking by my apartment at night, which is one set of prayer flags away from an opium den. However, I did need to consider what to display in my window. But I digress.

Discussing Hulises's work history rekindled my awareness that I needed to start "really" finding a job of my own. My entire net worth of about two thousand dollars would be gone in another month. Fuck. Maybe something in porn would be fitting, me being an experienced collector with professional references. My only path straight to the acting part of the industry would be if they were casting for 'Tubby Toby - Unchained.' Gina and the kids could be proud of my artistic talent and newly found fame and maybe even entertain bringing me back into the mix. But seriously, I needed to find a damn job. The downside of waking up without a hangover is the now more alert brain's grown-up voice reminding me of all the responsible things I wasn't considering doing, which was now being received like a steel-toed boot to the sack.

Luckily, drinks are at five—still time for my sack to heal.

Someone's black and white cat was strolling up the sidewalk and taking inventory of me as it moved to the side to create more of a buffer in case a getaway was required. I knelt and extended my hand with a "Here kitty kitty," accompanied by a little clicking sound. We always had cats growing up, sometimes as many as five. Back then, spaying and neutering cats wasn't as common, so there were always kittens running around too. Their unique little personalities and ability to sit and enjoy their surroundings made me feel more content just watching them.

The cat slowly made its way over and cautiously took a whiff of my fingers. After determining I passed the sniff test, it rubbed its cheek against my fingers and raised its tail.

"Hey, little guy. Are you out hunting?" It started rolling around on the sidewalk, giving me the message it now felt totally safe. After a few more minutes of petting and scritching, I attempted to pick him up. Cats either like to be held, tolerate it, or hate it. Therefore it's critical to look for cues during the beginning of the pickup to minimize panic. This little guy had no issues and was used to being held. God, it felt good to cradle this little critter and rub my face against his soft fur. It's incredible how cats have almost no smell. Sure, they are fastidious self-groomers, but you'd think there would be a general cat smell. This little guy was now running the risk of being over-petted. Drool was starting to appear on his tiny lips, and he was frantically rubbing his face against my hand and occasionally giving my index finger a lick. It felt plain good to have anything want my affection and return it. Two individual creatures crossed each other's paths and found love in the most unexpected places. That's how life is a lot of the time. Some of the most precious moments arrive just as unannounced as the most heinous ones. If there's one thing you can count on, it's that life doesn't fail to surprise.

The cat decided he had had enough, so I gently put him down. He walked a few steps into a sunny spot and started licking his back. Not surprisingly, I must have deposited an unacceptable filth on him that warranted immediate attention.

I felt less alone and sad than I had for some time. Cats accept us however we are—a luxury we seldom afford ourselves.

After all, I'd become a fat, unemployed, divorced man who's broke, living in a dilapidated crap rental with little to no motivation to do a damn thing about it. Although I wasn't happy with any of it, my actions didn't seem to care much anymore about what my mind thought should be happening. For this reason, more than anything else on my list of recent failures, I'd grown not to like myself very much. That had never been the case up until this point in my life, and it scared the shit out of me. There had been things about my life I wasn't happy with or things I wanted out of life that I didn't yet have, but I was always able to make changes or figure out a path to change things. The fuel in that tank had finally run dry, and there didn't seem to be a service station in sight. It was as if I wasn't so much choosing to be a complete tool of a loser but rather that it was being chosen for me, and I was being forced to watch it happen.

I returned home and got right to work on watching TV. After a few hours of channel surfing, I came to the conclusion there was nothing good on. I had about another forty-five minutes before I needed to head out to meet Hulises, but I needed to get out of the bean bag chair before it finished devouring what little hope I still clung to for a better life. When things aren't going well, boredom must be avoided, as it only provides ample opportunity to reflect. I decided to kill time by heading out and walking around to distract myself.

CHAPTER
FIVE

S tanding at the top of the stairs outside the front door, I noticed the local homeless guy was on the sidewalk next to a newly planted city tree playing tug-of-war with what appeared to be half shepherd half pit mix of a dog. The dog's euphoria escalated with each success as he repeatedly ripped the rag from his owner's hand. Either the guy's grip was failing him, or he was letting the dog win just often enough to bolster its resolve. Regardless, they were enjoying themselves with no concerns.

I could almost always smell this guy within a six-foot radius. It was an unusual scent as there were multiple contributing facets. I can best describe it as a compilation of stale beer, body odor, and rotting produce. He was sporting blown-out shoes, grimy-thighed jeans, and an unraveling stocking hat. I couldn't tell if he was bald and compensating with his shoulder-length hair descending from the bottom of his red San Francisco 49ers stocking cap or if he had a full head of hair. His mostly gray Santa Claus beard did throw an unshaven component into the mix, rounding out the picture nicely.

"Hey," I said as I ventured his way.

"Hey there. Hell of a day, eh?"

"Sun shining, no wind, and no jacket required. About as good as San Francisco can offer in June."

"Want to spell me?" he asked, handing me the rag. Why the hell not? I thought.

I wrestled with his dog for a few seconds, following his example, letting it rip the rag away after a few seconds. Apparently, I was doing it all wrong as the dog rushed over to repeatedly shove it into his owner's leg until the guy re-engaged.

"Don't take it personally. It's a game not easily mastered," he said, chuckling as he pulled the dog's head from side to side, teeing it up for yet another victory.

"No offense taken. How long have you had this guy?"

"Got him as a puppy two years ago. He was a rescue, although sometimes I think he rescued me. You know they won't let you adopt a dog without a home address?"

"Really?" I had never considered this, but it made complete sense. If the goal was to find a loving home for an animal, it's logical that a home should be involved somewhere in the equation. "So, how did you maneuver around that little hurdle?"

"Mrs. Parker, around the corner, let me use her address for mail so I could get Cowboy. Nice of her, huh?"

"I suppose so. Haven't had the pleasure of meeting her, but she sounds like a good lady."

"I'll introduce you sometime," he said as the corners of his mouth turned up a bit into what might have been the foundation of a grin. I had accidentally entered into an actual conversation with this guy, and for some reason, it seemed easier to go with the discussion than extricate myself. "Didn't catch your name?" he said.

"Sorry, I'm Toby."

"Nice to meet ya," he said, extending a filthy hand, which I shook anyway.

"Is it hard having a dog, living on the street? I'd be worried about him running away, biting someone, or getting sick."

"I imagine it would be if you didn't train him up right. He knows not to go farther than a few yards unless I OK it. Hasn't bitten anyone yet. Bet he would bite you if you tried to hurt me."

"Luckily for all of us, that's not part of my game plan. What made you decide to get a dog? Just lonely?" That I could understand. Petting that cat earlier made me realize I was pretty goddamn lonely. I suppose this could also be demonstrated by my chewing the shit with bums and immigrant laborers.

"Maybe a little, but mostly for protection. Ya know what a homeless person's biggest danger is, don't you?"

I could quickly bang out a list, but he was getting ready to tell me, so I set aside the list. "Embarrassingly, I do not. What would that be?"

"Funny you should ask. It's getting robbed or attacked by another homeless person when sleeping. Happens all the time, you know. Makes it hard to get much rest, as you could imagine."

"I imagine it would. But if I were going to rob someone, I'd break into a home or store. Seems I'd find more for the taking."

"And more of a chance of them taking your stupid ass to jail and impounding all your stuff," he countered. "Takes a while to get the right street gear, you know. Plus, it's easier to take someone else's gear and cash than find your own. A dog is quite a deterrent." His rationale did make sense.

"I reckon there's some logic there. How much cash does the typical homeless guy carry around these days?" I asked, becoming curious.

"Hard to tell; you don't talk about that on the street. Kind of the rules. Don't want people to feel you're sizing 'em up, if ya know what I mean."

"I've never seen you ask anyone for money like most homeless folks do. Why not?"

"Have enough. I can even buy Cowboy the good food you can only get at the vet, not the Safeway crap that dulls their coats."

"So you go to the vet, huh? How do they feel about a homeless guy with a shopping cart owning a dog? They ever report you?"

"HELL no! Dr. Osgood says Cowboy's the healthiest dog he's ever seen. Has all his shots, strong as an ox, and teeth look great," he said with a proud nod.

Dogs probably would fare better outside with the fresh air, plenty of exercise, and quality food. Interesting, the things I'd never bothered to consider. It would appear he took better care of Cowboy than himself. However, in all fairness, he probably took better care of himself than I had of myself lately.

"If you don't mind me asking, and I'm not sizing you up, just curious. Where do you get your money?" Bringing my voice down to create the hush-hush of understood secrecy. I'd been passing this guy daily for a few months, and this was the longest conversation we'd had to date, but so far, I did have a track record of not mugging him, which I hoped he'd noticed.

"Can I trust ya, mate?"

"You bet." I imagine anyone could spout that less-than-convincing argument out, but it seemed he was reading my eyes more than listening to the content of what I was saying.

"What's your name again?" he asked.

"Toby."

"So you are. Sounds trustworthy enough. About 15 years ago, I used to repair TVs and radios using Mrs. Parker's garage. I had all the tools and everything. I used to work in a repair shop once upon a time," he said with a wink, reminding me of the crazy storyteller outside the 21st Amendment the night before I lost my job.

He continued, "These days, they are too damn complicated with circuit boards and everything and cheap enough to throw away and get a new one when they break. I suppose the only thing that never changes is that nothing stays the same for long."

Who knew? I would never have expected an entrepreneurial homeless guy would make money by actually delivering a genuine service. If I were to become a gambling man soon, I'd put my money on the fact that he may not be your typical homeless stereotype. Sure, as realms of appearance go, but living in San Francisco, one accumulates many data points to drive an analysis like this. He had no apparent signs of acute psychosis; he didn't appear to be an addict and seemed much less miserable than the textbook derelict. And man, he loved that dog.

"Bookie during the NFL season nowadays," he tossed in.

"No shit? Seems like a good way to advertise you've got cash for those sizing up who to mug next."

"Clientele is critical. And so is Cowboy. Made $2,360 on Super Bowl Sunday." This time, he ripped the rag out of Cowboy's mouth, igniting another tug-of-war frenzy. "Please keep that on the down-low, partner." Great, we were now partners. Maybe I could fill the six-month employment gap on my resume with "Partner to a home-less guy."

Shit, he was having better financial luck than me. After Gina and I split up our assets, she got the house—that didn't have much equity—and I got the twenty thousand in savings. I invested it in an international high-growth fund that immediately went into the shitter to demonstrate how I could better my fortune more effec-tively without her guidance. I then panicked and withdrew the remaining four thousand dollars, which is now down to about two thousand.

"Well, I must say I'm impressed. And now I know where to go to place a bet. I don't gamble, but then again, I'm collecting vices these days, so stay tuned. I've got an appointment down at The Plow. I'll leave you and Cowboy to get back to the business I interrupted. I'm sure I'll talk to you guys soon."

"Have fun. You know where to find us. And my name is Eddie, in case you care."

"Pleasure to meet ya, Eddie."

"I'm sure we will talk again soon," he said with a big smile that revealed a few missing teeth. "You're a better man than you give yourself credit for."

"That would sure be great," I responded, turning and going South toward Clement Street, hoping he was right.

A few houses later, it hit me that I hadn't disclosed any details of what a piece of shit I had become. How did he know what I thought of myself or did or didn't give myself credit for? It must have been his idea of a joke or something. He probably says that to everyone.

CHAPTER
SIX

A few minutes later, I was standing on the corner of Arguello and Clement, outside *The Tipsy Plow*— referred to as "The Plow" by those who frequented the hole-in-the-wall Irish bar. It was staffed with real live Irish people, making it a nice escape from the streets of San Francisco right into the darker side of Dublin. It was a seedy bar, comfortable for seedy patrons to share a pint, some chips, or crisps. I was becoming a regular.

I strolled up to the Dutch door; the top part always remained open unless it was raining, as it was the only way to get any fresh air into the place. It was oddly sunny and warm for June at a tepid 75 degrees. I've developed a habit of checking my *Yahoo* weather app almost hourly to determine how comfortable it is outside, apparently, even when I'm already outside. I'd learned it's best not to trust myself or my own experience in any situation.

Luckily, no Irish band was playing tonight. Even in the right atmosphere and circumstance, the annoying shrillness of the tin whistle and flute still sounded like an elementary school band figuring out how to make real music while savaging the eardrums of all the parents in attendance. The accordion is unable to neuter the melodic sins committed by these more atrocious instruments, which always seem to be played louder than the limited dimensions of the establishment would support, making conversation a bitch. As an added dividend, I avoided a ten-dollar cover charge.

Upon entry, I was welcomed by the perfumed stink of cabbage, corned beef, and stale beer. I walked past the red-felted pool table on the immediate left of the front door; a dart board hung on the wall to the right. I navigated the maze of metal folding tables and chairs, making my way toward the bar as my eyes adjusted to the lack of light.

The bar itself was on the back right wall and was stereotypically simple: coffee pot in the corner of the back of the bar, always on; basket of individually portioned packages of chips (crisps) on the end of the bar, with a small sign clipped on the handle - $1.75. You had a nice choice of Nacho Cheese Doritos, Cool Ranch Doritos, or Cheetos, and about twelve different kinds of Irish whisky in the center of the shelf behind the bar, with no more than two varieties of any other alcohol.

Today, the lights and mirrors on the back of the bar beamed like a lighthouse in the dark seas of the long, narrow, windowless place. A jukebox was quietly sitting opposite the bar next to the stage in the rear left corner, which was wonderfully dark and instrument-free. The stage was a simple, black-painted wooden structure two feet high, maybe 8x10. As far as bars go, it was utilitarian with no frills. The Irish didn't bother trying to fool themselves. The place was there for people to drink, laugh, and occasionally fight, and nobody was trying to make it anything more than that.

"Hey, Toby! How's the day treatin' ya, now?"

"Pretty damn good so far," I responded.

"Well, that's a first, so it is. Glad to hear it, mate. What'll it be? The usual?" Connor, the proprietor, asked.

"The usual would be great, Connor," I answered, pulling out a bar stool. "Expecting a friend in a few, but let's wait to see what he wants. Don't let him pay, though."

"It'll be grand to meet a friend of yours, Toby. Didn't seem ya had any, now," he said, chuckling at his own joke.

"New friend, which might be using the word liberally. He's working on that project around the corner. I'm sure you've seen him here; it was his idea to meet here. Do me a favor and at least act like I'm less of a charity case than reality would counter?"

"Happy to lie for your arse, mate, unless ya stiff me on the tip." Conner laughed out loud at his joke this time. He fancied himself in rare form this afternoon, and it was always more fun when he was in a festive mood, as it lifted the energy of the place.

"Y'know, Toby, ya always be whinin' and carryin' on 'bout yer hard times, bein' a charity case and all. But it's the same bleedin' story. If ya ask me, which I know ya didn't—but 'cos I'm older, presumably wiser, and been there meself—I reckon ya need a checkup from the neck up. Matter of fact, ya need to stop fightin' life, mate. Ya are where ya are; accept things for what they are right now; trust things will keep changin' and start flowin' with it," Connor laid out.

"Fuck that *let go and let God* bullshit. Life kicked me in the nuts, or maybe I kicked myself. I let my eye slip off the ball, and now I'm paying the fiddler. I'm going to have to fight my way out of this shit-hole existence, and I just need some time to get my courage up. The good news for you is that I keep buying your beer and crisps," I replied.

Connor placed a Corona in front of me. "Speaking of crisps?"

"Not just yet. You still have the curry cheese chips on the menu?"

"Only if ya order 'em with the fish. Otherwise, we run out, and nobody can order the fish and chips combo, which is our most popular item," he explained.

"Fair enough. Let me get back to you in a bit," I answered as a young woman obnoxiously bumped into me as she arrived at the bar.

"Connor, can you break a twenty? I want to put some songs in the jukebox," she spouted. "Excuse me," she said, turning to face me. "I was trying to avoid the spilled beer on the floor."

"Not an issue," I said, scooting over to give her space. She seemed a bit excited and possibly drunk or just unnecessarily loud and reckless. She was attractive as hell and a tad full of herself. She was one of those ladies who had been told she was good-looking enough times that she started to believe she was special instead of just lucky. I wouldn't say I like those types. Beauty and innocence have but one enemy—time.

Connor had worked his way down the bar, checking on the drinks of the other two gentlemen, whom I estimated to be in their 70s, hunched over their beverages, insulting each other in a way only old friends can without the situation escalating. I didn't recognize either of them.

"Just hold tight, and I'll be right there," Connor yelled at her from the other end of the bar. I had turned to check the door just as RV Jeff strolled in, followed by Hulises.

RV Jeff, as one may suspect from the name, was indeed the kind of guy that's up to no good. The type of guy, in most stories, you were with when the problem started—a guy who makes no judgments and is the ultimate enabler and funny in an aggressive way. Before I could catch his eye, he was sidetracked by the pile of *Street Sheets*—a free neighborhood weekly attempt at a paper, stacked on a bench inside the door—detailing all the most recent week's crimes in the Inner Richmond. RV was undoubtedly looking for his name to ensure credit was given where credit was due.

I gave Hulises a quick wave as he began to weave his way through the contorted maze of a dining area towards the bar. He looked like a guy fresh off the job. Hulises had one of those thin body types with an isolated slight belly starting to develop, primarily evident when he sat down. His tan *Carhart* jeans were now filthy, as was his red sweatshirt. He had one of those cool, old-school black lunch boxes with the two silver buckles holding it shut. The kind with the rounded top that has a thermos held inside the roof by a thin metal thingy. He set it down on the floor next to his stool. I was envious, in a way. He had put in a hard day of manly work. Not having put the slightest effort into even thinking about finding a job, I felt like a complete pussy by contrast.

"What are you drinking, Hulises?" I said, greeting him with an open hand.

He returned my shake and said, "Guinness. Thanks. I see you prefer Mexican beer. You know, in Mexico, Corona is considered a shitty beer. People started serving it with limes just to make it drinkable."

"I appreciate that. With this new information, I can now relax and enjoy my drink. Hey Connor, can I get a lime down here? "

Connor recognized him immediately with a wave as he handed some five-dollar bills to the woman who hurried off towards the jukebox, again bumping me as she circumnavigated the spilled beer. "Shit, I'm sorry, I did it again," she said, barely breaking stride.

Connor was probably in his early to mid-fifties and beefy; he had a firm belly but not yet sloppy. He wore a medium-length light brown and gray beard, marginally kept, reminding me of an Irish wolfhound. His hair was mid-length, mostly gray, and well into its thinning phase on top. There was a good chance he could work it into a tiny ponytail with enough product to hold the strays in place if he felt a sudden crazed impulse to be hip. His skin was leathered with little checkerboard squares on the sides and back of his neck like he'd spent a good amount of time outside. Or maybe Irish skin didn't age as well. I didn't know his backstory, but I was curious. His eyes were either blue or green, as it was hard to tell with the reflection of the bar on his round wire-rimmed spectacles. He looked like a dad, grandfather, and farmer all smashed together. He was modeling the newest *Tipsy Plow* t-shirt they had just gotten in stock. It was classic black with white, almost cursive-like letters reading "Plow Like You Mean It."

He poured a Guinness for Hulises on his way down the bar

without inquiring as to what he wanted. Hulises must also be a regular; we just hadn't crossed paths yet.

"How's work, Hulises, me lad?" Connor said, expertly landing a beer in front of him without any foam spilling off the top.

"Getting close. We pour the new foundation tomorrow, and it should be done in a couple of weeks. Anything new to report?" Hulises inquired.

"Nah...but we finally got the new t-shirts in, ya know?" he boasted, pointing to his chest.

"Connor, what can I buy you?" I asked, feeling generous. Buying the owner a drink is really just a tip, as they can drink whatever they want at almost no cost. But it's a goodwill gesture that brings one into the inner fold or at least creates that illusion. Connor would occasionally return the favor and give me a beer on the house, especially if I'd been there for a few hours.

"Thanks, mate, that sounds bleedin' nice. I reckon a Jameson's would be a good stinger to kick off the night," he said mid-pour, turning around with his shot glass extended in our direction. "Cheers." Connor downed his shot and strolled back down the bar, leaving us to ourselves.

"Thanks for the beer," Hulises said, taking a sip and wiping the foam off his mustache with his sleeve. "I can put up with all your silly questions for as long as you keep one of these filled for me," he said, laughing.

"I insist. You must be a regular here. Connor seemed to know your drink," I said.

"Stop in here once every week or two. The guy is well-suited for his job," he pointed out.

"Speaking of line of work, you mentioned you were in Mexico and moved up here for work. Making bricks or something? What was it like growing up there? Do you miss it?" I asked, getting down to business.

"Curious George, here comes the interview. Look, buddy, happy to tell you whatever you want to know, but it's not going to be that exciting. Why don't you tell me what you do for work, why you're in San Francisco, and if you have a family and all that? I prefer a conversation to an interrogation, and you haven't said nothin' about you."

"Shit, I'm sorry. Honestly, my story is shit which is probably why I'm more interested in somebody else's. I'm local. I was born in the East Bay, moved to the city in my teens, and have lived here since. I lost my job about six months ago, my wife divorced me and took the kids, and I moved into a crappy little apartment around the corner from here around that time," I paused to take a swig of my beer and see if he'd heard enough. He gave me that "go on" look, so I continued. "I worked in high-tech and didn't realize quite how much I hated it until after stepping away from it, so I'm trying to figure my shit out right now. Sadly, that's the extent of it."

Hulises took another sip of his beer and chuckled. "Sorry, not laughing at you, just laughing because that's a lot of excitement, just doesn't sound like a lot of fun. But if life were easy, we'd all be retired and sailing around on yachts drinking Pina Coladas. It could be a lot worse," he pointed out, then downed the rest of his beer, perhaps dehydrated from a day on the construction site.

I caught Connor's eye and pointed out Hulises's empty glass; he wasted no time remedying the problem.

"I suppose it could be, but I seem more focused on how it used to be a lot better, which bums me out. Anyway, I wish I had something more inspiring to share. So tell me, if you haven't been in the States that long, why is your English so damn good? You don't even have an accent."

"Impressive, huh? I grew up speaking English a lot. An American family moved in across the street when I must have been about five, and their son, Jackson, was a couple of years older than me, and we became friends. His father was with an organization called *Save All the Children* or something like that. They were creating schools for towns that didn't have any to provide education for the kids that were interested. I'm sure they were living in our neighborhood because he wasn't making much money doing charity work. Regardless, they were a great family who didn't seem to mind that I was there about half my waking hours. Jackson was my hero. An American boy who was just enough older to be cool, and he treated me like an equal. I really wanted to be like him and decided that speaking like him was a good start. After three or four years, they moved to a different town, but I was speaking fluently by then. My reading and writing are still pretty weak, though."

"Sounds like you made the most of a good opportunity. What did your dad and mom do for work?" I asked.

"My dad and his dad made bricks. It was hard work, and we almost always had food on the table. My Mom took care of my two sisters and me and would babysit some of the neighbor's kids to make extra money. Even by Mexican standards, we were poor and shared a one-room apartment. But we were fortunate."

"Why was that?" I asked.

"My dad had work locally, whereas most kids' dads lived in other towns or in the US where they could find work and send money back. It could have been a lot worse, and we knew it because we saw how it was in other families. There isn't welfare, food stamps, housing assistance, or anything like the stuff you guys have up here. The families in the neighborhood had to help each other out through hard times."

"Is it hard being away from them," I asked.

"Yeah, it is. Sometimes harder than others. Birthdays and holidays mainly. I definitely miss my aunts, uncles, nieces, and nephews. Home is home, and family is family, regardless of where it is. But that's easy to say, as I had both growing up. Other stuff doesn't seem quite as important if you have the right people around you. That's one of the biggest differences between here and Mexico, in my opinion," he stated, then got right to work on his fresh beer.

"You lost me there. What's the biggest difference between Mexico and here?"

"In the US, the stuff you have is what everyone works for. That's also true for some people in Mexico, but I never grew up with that perspective. It didn't seem to run in our neighborhood. Thinking about it, a man's value wasn't his position or how much he made, but what kind of father, husband, and neighbor he was."

Clearly, Hulises was more thoughtful and self-aware than me. What he said made sense. His worldview was interesting—a far cry from mine.

"That makes sense. It almost makes too much sense. So what's next for you, Hulises, after this project wraps up?" I figured it best to take things back to the present before my questions wore out their welcome.

"Our crew has another job lined up already. I'll take advantage of that opportunity as long as it lasts. My wife and kids moved up here with me, so I feel lucky we were able to make that work. My wife works at a salon and brings in some money, so we aren't only dependent on my income. My mother-in-law, I think I mentioned earlier today, lives in San Jose and has been in the US for about eight years. My wife loves that. Whether we stay here or go back home, we're good either way. The schools are better here, and we'd like to stay as long as possible to give our kids a better education than my wife and I had."

"That's great, man. It sounds like things worked out pretty well for your whole family."

"So far, no complaints. Nobody is missing any meals; we have running water, can adjust the thermostat to whatever temperature we want, and have a toilet in the house instead of an outhouse. Most people that have ever lived on this planet would be thankful for all that, right?"

"I suppose they would," I confirmed. "I guess we mostly take that stuff for granted here."

"You have a lot to be grateful for here," he pointed out. "Funny, Americans live like kings but don't appreciate it. Most of you spend all your time focusing on what you don't have and are unhappy about it," he said, standing up. "Sorry to interrupt, but let's pause there. I've got to use the bathroom something fierce," he said, standing up and patting me on the shoulder as he passed my chair.

Suddenly, music began blasting from the jukebox, where the spirited young woman was now bopping around, punching in more songs to use up her credits. She was obviously a Ted Nugent fan, which, try as I might, I couldn't fault her for. Who doesn't like to hear a little *Whang Dang Sweet Poontang*?

She either wanted attention playing a song like that in a quiet and mostly empty bar, or she liked good music and couldn't give two shits what anyone thought. I'd known both types of girls and what they both had in common was they were a pain in somebody's ass.

A significant commotion at the front of the bar immediately commanded everyone's attention. To no one's surprise, RV Jeff was front and center. "Listen, fuck face, you try to cheat my ass, and I'll knock your dick in the dirt!" RV said, severely encroaching on some kid's space. They were both holding pool cues. A billiards dispute, possibly with a wager on the line?

This kid, maybe in his mid-twenties, similar to RV Jeff, looked like he had nothing to lose and took a step forward as the corners of his mouth turned up into what appeared to be the beginning of a welcoming grin. Being nothing funny was said, it seemed he was happy to let RV attempt to "knock his dick in the dirt." That's when all hell broke loose.

The kid slammed his pool queue down on RV's foot and shoved him backward into the pool table. RV stumbled back a step, immediately regained his balance and shot both arms above his head; still holding his pool cue, and in that onerous pose, he screamed, "COME ON!" With cat-like quickness, RV grabbed the kid's face with his right hand, crushing the kid's sunglasses beyond repair while they somehow remained on his face. I always thought wearing sunglasses indoors was asking for it, and this confirmed my suspicions. RV dropped his cue and smoothly transitioned into an attempt to muscle the kid into a headlock. The kid was having none of it and kneed RV in his naughty bits, and they were instantaneously rolling around on the floor in full grapple mode.

Connor was already halfway around the bar with "The Persuader" in his hand and nearly flattened poor Hulises on his way by, who was returning from the bathroom. "The Persuader" is what he called the bizarrely massive crescent wrench he kept behind the bar for precisely this reason. It was no less than two feet long. I couldn't see a happy ending to this debacle. Not certain if we should be helping to break this up before an ambulance was required or enjoy the show from a safe distance, I looked to Hulises, who had just returned to his seat, for a cue. He appeared perfectly happy to watch the show from his stool, so I followed his lead.

Connor was now hitting his stride, which was quite a sight. He looked like a pissed-off mama grizzly bear on her way to dismember the poor fucks unlucky enough to find themselves between her and her cubs. When you own a business, and someone disrespects it like that, I imagine you could feel a bit violated.

The kid let out a yelp as RV Jeff sunk his teeth into his ankle, and they rolled into the doorway. RV struggled to his feet, and the kid remained on the ground clutching his now bleeding ankle, "The fucker bit me!"

RV had transitioned into full WWF mode and was preparing to administer an elbow drop to The Kid's head, shouting, "You're done - Ass Clown!" Just as he reached his tiptoes to initiate his descent, he collapsed onto the ground. He remained motionless, stunning everyone into silence as Connor slid to a stop directly in front of the two bodies now littering his doorway. Nobody said anything for a few seconds as everyone tried to make sense of what had transpired.

In the doorway stood an overweight woman in her late thirties or early forties who looked like she was in desperate need of a shower. Her hair was half tied back and half clinging in greasy clumps to the sides of her face. She was dressed in an oversized white t-shirt, which was remarkable given the considerable body it had to cover. Below this sheet of a shirt were her dark blue knee-length athletic shorts and a pair of baby blue nubby felt slippers. She held a small cast iron skillet and appeared calm as a cucumber.

The Kid, trying to comprehend the recent turn of events, had scampered on his knees out of the doorway and was now seeking shelter halfway under the pool table. By this time, it was clear anything could happen, and he wanted to be well out of range when it did.

Connor's voice eventually broke the silence. "Get his arse back home, Big Sallie, where he can't fuck anything else up, or get him to the ER if his head won't stop leakin' soon."

Big Sallie handed the pan to Connor, grabbed still unconscious Jeff under his armpits, effortlessly dragged him out onto the sidewalk, and then came back in to reclaim her skillet.

"Dumb son-of-a-bitch took the grocery money to the bar again," she half yelled. "It's like having a toddler around the house. I've had enough of his shit, Connor, and you're an enabler."

"I'll enable the police to haul your hefty arse down to the pokey for assault with a deadly weapon if the both of ya aren't gone in five minutes. Now move!" Connor yelled and turned to The Kid, "Ya ain't the victim here, let's be clear. Ya picked a fight with the wrong bloke, and now ya can go to bed tonight knowin' Big Sallie had to save yer feckin' arse. Ya're welcome to stay if ya can blend in and shut up. I don't wanna see ya near that pool table the rest of the night." The kid made his way to his feet, taking inventory of possible injuries.

That was an educational experience. I was excited to learn that "persuaders" come in many shapes and sizes. I respected both Connor and Big Sallie's choices, but Big Sallie's persuader had a timelessness to it that I admired. I also learned that RV Jeff's significant other was an atrocity on many levels. I wasn't surprised he seldom spoke of her.

"Well, what da ya think of that, Hulises?" I said, somewhat relieved that nobody was seriously maimed. Well, maybe RV was, but I somehow doubted it. He was the kind of guy that was born to take a beating.

"As the Irish say, here's health to your enemy's enemies," Hulises answered, raising his glass.

Soon after the dust settled, Hulises announced he had to stop by and check on an elderly neighbor before it got too late. The few remaining patrons, the kid, and Jukebox Girl also shuffled out shortly after the entertainment ceased, leaving Connor working on receipts at the other end of the bar and myself. I wasn't in the mood to end what had been a good day up until now by being the lonely sole patron at a dive bar, so I squared up with Connor and stepped out of The Plow into the stark clutches of the crisp evening air. Plus, I was hungry for something other than bar snacks and fish and chips. The sidewalk was quiet and devoid of people for the time being. Big Sallie had apparently transported RV Jeff elsewhere, and there were no noticeable blood stains on the sidewalk, which was a good sign.

Before Hulises departed, I had told him I was looking for employment, which was a lie, but inevitably I would be, so I asked him to let me know if he came across anything.

I suppose I got what I wanted out of my conversation with him. I envied him for his childhood, family, and general contentment. I also envied his job—or at least, his gratitude for having a job. Most of all, I was impressed by his general outlook on the world. He took it as it came and took the good with the bad, not losing sight of what was important to him. Shit, I no longer had any clear idea of what was important to me or who I was becoming.

CHAPTER
SEVEN

I rounded the corner, taking a left onto my street, and ducked into the corner store in search of a passable dinner.

After walking all three aisles to examine my options, I settled on a can of Hormel chili and a 24-oz Tecate. In hindsight, I realized I could have done better at The Plow.

I walked out, saw Eddie and Cowboy down the street alongside my building, and turned back into the store. *"What the fuck?"* I thought and grabbed a second 24-oz Tecate and headed back out into the welcoming dark emptiness of the night, feeling an unfamiliar flicker of momentary contentment.

Eddie and Cowboy were sitting on the cement in the alcove on the side of my building alongside their shopping cart, each enjoying their respective hot dogs. Eddie looked up at me, a drip of mustard decorating his mustache. "Hey, Toby, already back from The Plow?"

"Yep, it turned out to be kind of a one-and-done type of night, but entertaining as always. Figured instead of having a second helping there, I'd rather share a beer with you and Cowboy if you're up for company?" I held out a Tecate.

"Our pleasure, Toby, and how much do I owe you for the beer?" he asked.

"It's on me. I bought it specifically for you, so if you weren't here, it would find its way to you sooner or later from my fridge. It seems like I'm crashing dinner."

"Shit, sorry. I would have got you one, too, if I knew you were coming."

"I brought some to-go food with me. Would you happen to have a can opener and a spoon? If not, give me a minute to run inside and get one."

"Fret not. We've got you covered." Eddie rifled around in one of the bags in the bottom of his cart and produced a spoon and can opener, which were both surprisingly clean. "Pull up a seat."

I plopped down on the sidewalk beside them and started working on my can. "Seems like Cowboy elected to go sans condiments tonight, huh?"

"He makes a mess of it, I've learned. Best to keep it simple, like a lot of things."

"How does the vet feel about this nutritional regimen?" I joked.

"Oh, it's Cowboy's cheat day," Eddie replied with a smile.

I assumed he was feeding Cowboy a small piece at a time to make it more of a shared meal than a spontaneous annihilation, and Cowboy appeared to be just fine with that. Opening my can had turned into a demolition event, but I finally managed to get the lid off. Surprisingly, most people don't eat chili right out of the can. I find it just as good but in a different way, like leftover cold pizza or baby-back ribs the next day. Eddie didn't seem to notice or care. Gina would have felt free to ensure I understood all the various ways why it's wrong to eat right out of the can, insinuating there was no doubt that she was, once again, disappointed in me.

Eddie thanked me again for the beer and poured some into a bowl for Cowboy, who eagerly lapped it up—it was unlikely that this was his first exposure.

"What else is going on, Toby?" Eddie asked.

"Other than my ruined life, no job, and post-divorce identity crisis—same old, same old." I figured there wasn't any reason to put up a facade. Eddie didn't pass judgment, and keeping the conversation real felt cathartic. Nothing was more real than two dudes, down on their luck, sitting on the ground eating canned chili and hot dogs with a dog next to a shopping cart. A year ago, I never would have believed this could feel natural and remotely comforting. "Oh, I almost forgot; a medical professional informed me I have the aging sphincter of a seventy-five-year-old."

"Some people take great pride in being mature beyond their years. Could be considered a badge of honor," he said, laughing at my expense.

"Well, it's staying under wraps. What about you? Is there anything newsworthy to report?"

"Well, I've got some bad news. I just learned that Mrs. Parker, from around the corner, was taken to the hospital in an ambulance today. A stroke, I think, or that's what the paramedic said. Not sure how she's doing, but keeping my fingers crossed. She is a good lady and the closest thing to family Cowboy and I have."

"Shit, Eddie! That sucks. Sorry to hear it, and I'll send her good vibes or prayers or something."

"Thanks. Nobody lives forever, but she's only sixty-eight. I like to think she has a few good years left," he said with a sigh. "She's a rugged one and will probably power through."

Eddie seemed to be doing a pretty good job of rolling with it, but I'm sure he's seen a lot and had to learn to roll with many things.

"Well, here's to enjoying what we can when we can," I said, toasting with my can of chili, which, for the record, tasted fucking spectacular.

Eddie held out his beer. "Well said, brother."

"Hey, do you think Cowboy wants to try a chili dog?" I offered.

He held out Cowboy's next bite, and I put a spoonful of chili on it, and he put it up to Cowboy's nose. It passed the sniff test, and he eagerly accepted it, but not with more or less enthusiasm than the previous bites.

"Cowboy ain't particular. Dogs seem to take what life offers without complaining. That's why I prefer them to people if I have a choice. No offense."

"None taken. Hey, you know if you and Cowboy want to sleep inside, you're welcome to my couch. It gets cold at night." I had unconsciously transitioned from disliking homeless people to eating with them and now offering them lodging. Uncontrolled lunacy was bursting from my mouth like water from a broken fire hydrant.

"Thanks, Toby. That's a generous offer, but we prefer to be outside. After thirty years, it's home. Cowboy feels the same. Hard to get him inside anywhere. We got a sleeping bag and tarp if it rains. Plus, I've got my inside overcoat if I need it." He held out a flask to me. "Want some?"

"Sure. What is it?" I inquired.

"Johnny Blue."

"Fuck Eddie! That shit is north of $200 a bottle."

"Yep." He handed me the flask.

I took a bump and closed my eyes as the smooth, smoky warmth eased down my throat. It suddenly clicked what he meant by an inside overcoat. "Thanks, man." I passed his flask back to him.

"It's my guilty pleasure. Keep it for special occasions like this."

I felt myself getting choked up, contemplating if I was just emotionally raw or touched. This homeless guy, who had almost nothing, was willing to share his best without a thought.

"You're a good man, Eddie. Thank you. What's your story, if you don't mind me asking? I mean, where did you grow up? How did you end up on the streets? Everything." I hoped I wasn't putting him in an uncomfortable situation, as it could be embarrassing, or maybe he didn't want to relive a series of unfortunate events by telling them. Then I remembered Hulises giving me a hard time for stranger interrogation. "Sorry, that's personal shit, and you don't even know me. I'm curious because I haven't had the opportunity to get to know a lot of homeless guys, but that's no excuse for crap manners."

"I don't mind. It's not a glamorous story."

"Neither is mine, and I don't care. Seems I'm just more interested in others lately than maybe I used to be."

"Well, I won't be offended if you interrupt when you've had enough. I ain't going to sugarcoat anything or add any revisionist history to pump up the drama or make a better tale. Might as well start at the beginning."

I intentionally interrupted. "That's enough. Thanks, though."

"I warned you it wasn't a glamorous story. Sorry to drone on like that," he replied.

"Just fucking with you, Eddie. Seriously, go ahead. I'm all ears."

Eddie continued with a chuckle. "Born and raised here in San Francisco. My dad was a union dockworker down on the piers and an alcoholic. Most nights, he came home drunk and beat up on my brother, my mom, and me as a matter of habit. Not unlike most families in Hunter's Point, I suppose. He was angry about a lot of things. That can happen to a guy when he realizes his life turned into the one he never wanted, and he never became anywhere near the man he hoped he would be. He was probably trying to determine if he failed at life or if life failed him." This last part hit a little close to home for me.

"Shit, man. Sorry to hear that. Must have been a scary house to be a kid in," I said, feeling horrible for him.

Eddie continued, "Correct. Eventually, I couldn't take it anymore and left home when I was fifteen—lived in friends' basements, mostly. Didn't finish high school. It wasn't my thing. Got odd jobs, sometimes for a couple of weeks, sometimes longer. Shortly after turning eighteen, I got drafted."

I interrupted, "Holy shit, man, that's a brutal start. Can't imagine how painful and hard that all must have been and before the age of eighteen."

"It was the hand I was dealt. I was more pissed off than anything.

I used to convince myself the world owed me more. Kind of the victim thing, which is a complete bunch of bullshit, but that's another story.

"The point is, it wasn't until the Army that I felt I was needed or wanted by anybody. You depend on each other to stay alive, and having a common enemy trying to kill you unifies a group of young men. Twenty-four of us went through basic training and, later on, some serious advanced training, and we got deployed to Vietnam. Knowing there were people who would give their lives for me—and for whom I would do the same in return—was something new to me, and I can't say I didn't value it. I am still thankful for that experience. Life was about something bigger than me for the first time, and people depended on me. Not surprisingly, I didn't miss home. Leaving these guys behind to return to nothing never crossed my mind. For most, getting drafted and sent to Nam was worse than hell. For me, it saved me from the hell I was trapped in. Sounds weird, huh?"

"Yeah, man, it does. I don't know whether to be happy or sad for you about all this." I was being honest; his perspective was one I wouldn't have considered.

"Seems like most of this play we're in is written for us, for better or worse. Most of the time, I reckon it's hard to make sense of things until they're in the rearview mirror."

"I reckon you're right. Listen, I don't want you to share anything too painful…"

Eddie interrupted me. "Toby, one of the few lessons I've garnered in my humble bumble around this planet is that suffering is a part of everyone's life. Just because someone isn't talking, texting, or tweeting about it doesn't mean they aren't wrestling with it. If you're afraid of diving in to meet it head-on in that cold black cave hiding deep in your soul, you can't walk out with the treasures hidden there. The suffering molds us and reminds us of what's important. It can free us—if we let it. I also learned in Nam that if you make friends with fear, you're never alone."

Eddie talked with a calm confidence that only a seasoned vet of life can wield with that kind of insight. As he spoke, he locked eyes with me, catching me off guard; his eyes were an icy blue that seemed to take in everything I was and would ever be in a single glance. It was as if he was looking at me from the inside out, and it was somehow as frightening as it was comforting. A rod had been thrust into the ever-spinning gears in my head, seizing them up, leaving me naked and eye to eye with an abyss that felt more familiar than anything I've known, yet refreshingly new. For a brief second, I could no longer discern where Eddie stopped, and I started. Then, reality unpacked itself, and we were back on the sidewalk. Eddie looked down at the last bite of Cowboy's hot dog and tossed it in the air. Cowboy leaped to catch it, which jump-started my mind. My first coherent thought was that I must have suffered a minor stroke. Feeling otherwise fine, I concluded there must have been more than just Johnny Blue in that flask.

"Sorry, what were you saying before I rudely interrupted you, Toby?" Eddie asked as if the last few seconds were a figment of my imagination alone.

"Uh....yeah. I was curious about what it was like over there. Nam, I mean. I also understand it's something most vets don't like to discuss and would prefer to leave behind. I understand if you'd prefer to talk about something else." I needed to think about the weird experience that had just happened, even if it was most likely my imagination, and make sense of Eddie's words, which seemed urgently relevant in some way.

"I don't mind talking about it one bit. Problem is, most people don't truly want to hear about it. People want trite platitudes like, 'It was horrible,' or 'I saw things I'd rather forget,' which are both true, but we all have horrible things that we'd rather forget, right?"

"Like my entire existence," I threw out as an example.

"Time will tell. If you're interested, I'll tell you what changed me the most over there. It will paint a pretty clear picture of what it was like," he offered.

"Eddie, honestly, I'd be grateful to hear anything you want to share." I wanted to get his take and perhaps better understand his experience. I was about to get a lot more than I bargained for.

"Well, as I said, my first tour started with our platoon, who had all been through training together, which was another flavor of hell that can bond men. However, we were about to find out what pure hell was.

"One night, we were ordered to advance our position and found ourselves crawling slowly and carefully through a minefield. I was scared as shit, and I could see the same in the eyes of my buddies. In an hour and fifteen minutes, give or take, I watched the only real friends I had ever known get blown up in front of my eyes, one after another. Worse than that, I heard the shrieks of buddies, their legs, arms, and large chunks of their bodies shredded. Some even remained conscious as their remaining lives bled out of them. I could smell their blood and flesh all over my uniform. The safest path forward was to crawl over those dead or dying bodies since we knew those mines had already been detonated. It was like swimming through a sea of fucking body parts. To see their faces and hands groping for anything to hold onto....death was dancing in its playground like a giant vacuum that night, hoovering up everything they had or would ever have. I crawled on, knowing I was in the final minutes of my life, beyond terrified, with an adrenalin-fueled hyper-alertness that's almost impossible to describe. Mine was the last living face most of those still alive would ever see as I crawled over what remained of their bodies, helpless to do anything but keep going. I just wanted the inevitable to hurry up. Death was in a cruel mood that night and tortured me by stringing it out. In the end, only two of the twenty-four of us who started made it across." He paused to stare at his hand as he slowly opened and closed his fist.

"Jesus, Eddie, you were one brave-ass son-of-a-bitch. I can't imagine...." What do you say after someone tells you that? It was all I could come up with, and I felt like an idiot as it rolled out.

"Call it what you will. I was terrified. Afterward, I wasn't right upstairs for quite a while," he replied. "Plus, it's easier to be brave, I suppose, when you don't have anything left to lose."

"Imagine so," I said. He had a point.

"I don't know if it was by design or blind luck that I was left behind on this earth. I honestly would have traded places with any one of my friends who died that night as they had a lot more to live for and left so much more waiting for them back home. Some had fiancées, some were married, a couple had very young children, and others had worried parents and good friends. I had nothing waiting for me," he said, shaking his head at the absurdity of it all.

"Well, that would be enough to make me pretty fucking bitter," I shared.

"Toby, every morning when I wake up, the first thing I do is look at my hand and move it, and I am just thankful I am alive to live another day. I am blessed. I can laugh, love, and cry. I can experience what these guys were robbed of, and I am lucky and owe it to them not to take it for granted."

Everything Eddie shared about his story indirectly applied to me as much as it did to him.

"I need to reactive my inside overcoat. Need a bump?" Eddie offered.

"Eddie, I'll pass this time. I need to go contemplate life. Today has shaken me up, and I need to try to make sense of it." I was now thinking of Hulises and his story as well as Eddie's and how they illuminated the tangle of my life in a new and bizarre light.

"It can feel impossible to find a foothold when everything you thought you valued, believed, or hoped for gets blown up right in front of you, Toby. A foothold, however, isn't always all it's cracked up to be."

"I don't pretend to know what that means, but I'll try to remember it. Eddie, thank you for sharing all that. You're a good man, and as good men do, you may have given me the shove I need to take inventory and figure some shit out."

Eddie laughed. "Don't try too hard. It can be a fool's game. Enjoy the rest of your evening, my friend."

"Yourself the same," I said as something jarred my leg. Cowboy was ramming his rag into me. We played tug for a few seconds, and I let him experience victory as he ripped it out of my hands. I turned to walk inside and felt another bump on the back of my knee.

"Cowboy seems to have a new friend," Eddie said.

I laughed, walked into my building, closed the door, and leaned against it. My mind was now spinning recklessly, and tears started streaming down my face for no one specific reason that made any real sense.

CHAPTER

EIGHT

The clock now showed eleven minutes 'til midnight. I had been in bed for two hours, and my mind must have crammed four hours of thinking through that tight window. How was it that Eddie and Hulises, who had nothing by my standards, were absolutely content? Hulises didn't own a home or car; he lived in a new country without the lifelong familiarity of anything. He had no significant successes or recognizable achievements to be enough for even cocktail party conversation. Neither one had any remote certainty of what tomorrow would bring nor much influence over it. Yet, each of them had no discernible anxiety about this. Both appeared to be accepting of pretty much anyone or anything. But what was most curious was their calm and even-keeled nature that conveyed the feeling they downright knew everything would be OK, and I'm not talking about that "The Lord has a plan for me" type of blind faith-based bullshit. They just knew.

By now, I had to piss and figured it would be wise to do something about it. On the way back from the bathroom, I stubbed my toe on the corner of the doorway and had to turn on the light to determine if I was bleeding. The exterior of the toe appeared to be OK, although I was now wide awake, so I just kept on ruminating.

Relative to the challenges Hulises and Eddie's lives had served them, they had come a long way. Maybe it's not where a guy ends up but how far he came from where he started that measures his success. But still, I'd known plenty of people that had overcome seismic obstacles and catastrophes who were still miserable as shit, full of regrets, and constantly fearful of what could happen next. How did these two find a sense of acceptance and peace that had eluded me for most of my life?

Even when I had a good job and successful career, what I thought was a good marriage, and enough money not to have to worry much about paying the bills, I was stressed and struggling to find a way to ensure it would last. Who knows—maybe it wasn't my efforts, work, or design that had been responsible for my successes. How much of it was just the right place/right time? Deep down, I felt my life was a charade and a fraud, faking it until I made it while secretly wondering if I had what it took.

And why was I having such a problem figuring out what to do next besides watching TV, drinking, and nursing the next hangover? Was I just in denial of my situation? Maybe I had broken something upstairs, and this is how society's stragglers end up strung out on their luck, fighting to hang on. It was easy enough to get fat, stop exercising, and develop a chemical dependency. Those achievements happened almost on their own with no master plan or vision, which supported my fears of what life would become without judicious management and a clear vision. Maybe, although I thought I saw causation patterns, there never really were any. Something always seemed to be missing. I felt what I needed was almost there, just around another corner, but still just out of reach. I had always believed that striving towards ever-shifting goals gave my life purpose. Now, I wasn't sure I had any goals that made sense, and I was lost, along with my purpose.

Just lying there, mired in circular thinking with no answers and only more questions, was kicking my beat-up ass, which reminded me of my advanced discoloration. I needed a visual on this; I was sure it couldn't be all that bad. After about five minutes of struggling through a series of yogic contortions, I ended up on my back with my legs splayed in the air, knees to my chest, and finally, my iPhone selfie mode gave me the view I was looking for. Holy Christ, the doc was right! This was a remarkably grim situation that took me to a new low. Seventy-five-year-old bung? What does eighty look like? I tried to convince myself that sooner or later, my luck was bound to change, and something good was bound to happen. Things would balance out sooner or later, right?

As it turned out, the tide turned, and the highlight of my night was an impressively long urination session, my PR (personal record). I assume most guys must have a process of determining, relative to their bladder size, what is a heroic piss. My methodology was simple. I would start counting at the first drop, one-one-thousand, two-one-thousand, and so on until the last drip before the shake. This one was seventy-five-one-thousand, crushing my previous best set on my wedding night of sixty-nine-one-thousand.

I think I got the first inkling that peeing would need to happen as Gina's Dad walked her down the aisle: nothing problematic, just a quick heads up from the bladder.

Then, as newly pronounced Mr. and Mrs. Toby Tenderhill—the name of a man destined only for a beer gut—reached the front door of the church, we were to immediately start the procession line and be viewed as husband and wife for the first time. I got the signal from below that we would need to start thinking of timing, as urination was imminent. We had only greeted the wedding party at this time, which seemed kind of dumb to me as they were right up there with us during the whole ceremony. Then came the family, each individual of which was on a mission to give us the longest hug of our lives, followed by hand-holding and good wishes with extended eye contact to ensure we understood the intensity of their sentiments.

I had just finished this little routine after an extended handshake followed by two much too firm back slaps from her father when the bride's mother stood there before me with a smile and tears in her eyes. It was quite possibly the moisture of her tears that triggered the first squirt of urine, which I effectively shut off with my young, virile prostate. We all know this only buys a guy five to eight seconds - tops. I needed to excuse myself politely at this inopportune time; the line was already backing up behind my new mother-in-law.

"How do you feel right now, Toby?" Gina's Mom, Shirley, asked. Stupid question, I thought.

The eight seconds had just passed. "Shirley, I'm pissing."

"What?"

"Yep, no doubt about it. I'm beginning to piss!" I said this louder than perhaps the situation warranted and abruptly charged through the crowd and back into the church. "Where's the bathroom?" I yelled. Someone directed me down the hall to the left, and I began to sprint, counting three-one-thousand, four-one-thousand. I finally hit the urinal at five-one-thousand.

The transition of my member out of my pants mid-pee was going to be tricky, but luckily, this wasn't my first rodeo. Just pinch the penis and block the flow. This is only a temporary halt, like kinking a garden hose, but it requires precision. The kinkage was applied from outside the pants and required a pause in the counting. Using my free hand, I unzipped the zipper, and the stage was set for the main event. I had my free hand through my fly, and I would need to release my kink and transition my member out of my pants as fast as possible, as urine would begin flying immediately. Something went horribly wrong as I executed the release with my left hand and started counting again. My right hand missed the baton, and the floodgates were wide open. Six-one-thousand, seven-one-thousand......

Now, with broad sweeping motions in my pants, my right hand was in rescue mode, ready to pull anything it found out the fly hole. The target erratically whipped around like an accidentally dropped fire hose on full blast. I scrambled to regain control, but not without consequences. My sweeper hand eventually found its target and wrenched it out, freeing me up again to focus on the counting. A short time later...sixty-nine-one-thousand... and it was over. In case you're wondering, twelve-one-thousand was the count when the escaping convict was finally beyond the gates. Yet, it was a personal record and the best of all possible gifts on my wedding day. However, urine-soaked pant legs and underwear were the sacrifices required for this bounty.

Luckily, I knew these woods well from past visits and was far from lost. After a quick disrobing from the waist down, a fist full of paper towels, some frantic blotting, and a fling of my boxers into the trash, I was as good as new. Black tuxedo pants can't darken with moisture, as they are already black. They can cling to one's legs, but that can't be helped and would go largely unnoticed. Plus, the guilty pleasure of knowing I was now free-balling at my own wedding gave me that feeling of superiority that only knowing something nobody else does can provide.

Upon my return, my dad was next in line, and I was now ready for whatever heartfelt words of praise and sage advice he may impart. We weren't close, but times like these, which ideally happened once in a guy's life, seemed like an excellent opportunity to open up.

"Why are your pants clinging to your thighs?" was the best he had to offer.

"Just urine."

He gave me a nod of approval and a pat on the shoulder and made his way down the line. We had connected, finally.

CHAPTER
NINE

I drifted off, reliving the highlights of my wedding day, and managed to snag a few additional hours of sleep before eventually waking up. I decided to get dressed and head out for a strong cup of coffee. I knew I would need it.

It was still early, about 8 a.m., and it was already crystal-clear outside, the sky a deep turquoise. Luckily, the ocean breeze in San Francisco blows our smog over into the East Bay, and we can enjoy our polluting ways without the risk of haze-induced guilt.

Eddie and Cowboy hadn't yet emerged from under their blue tarp tent, strategically connected to their shopping cart, creating a lovely covered porch addition to their home. I had asked Eddie why the tarp, which eliminated any view of the stars. He informed me that it wasn't to protect from rain or cold but to keep the dew off, which kept everything from becoming damp and colder than necessary. Funny how a guy never contemplates what later emerges as stunningly obvious outdoor survival basics when said guy has never not had shelter. Of course, I'm sure I would have known this if I had been the kind that goes camping or backpacking. I, however, preferred a controlled climate at seventy degrees, allowing me to remain comfortable in a t-shirt around the clock.

As I headed down to the coffee shop around the corner, I wondered when Eddie had last awoken to a warm cup of coffee placed in his hand.

I crossed the threshold of the *Blue Danube* coffee shop a few blocks from home, and Jimmy, the owner, was behind the register. It was a small funky place on Clement Street, painted royal blue with yellow trim. A few tables were outside on the sidewalk, facing the morning sun—a perfect venue for enjoying coffee and a pastry.

"Morning, Toby," Jimmy said with a smile.

"Hi, Jimmy. What's new these days?" I replied.

"Baby is due next month, and we're working on getting everything ready."

"That's right! I didn't realize how far along the wife is. Do you know the sex yet, or are you going with yellows and greens in the nursery?" I knew this from experience, as we elected to be surprised when Jacob, our first, was born. Every towel, onesie, rattle, little cap, and pair of booties we received at the baby shower were green or yellow. Luckily, those colors fit nicely with our yellow nursery with the green rug and changing table cover.

"It's a girl, so we are doubling down on the pink to reduce the chances of future gender fluidity," Jimmy said with a laugh.

Jimmy also owned the Thai restaurant across the street, bought The Blue Danube a couple of years ago, and did a great job fixing it up. Jimmy was one of those guys who always had a genuine smile on his face, and you never questioned if he was actually glad to see you. Unlike typical small talk about the weather, Jimmy would ask you questions about yourself because he was genuinely interested. Where were you from, what kind of work you did (or didn't do in my case), if you had kids, what you liked to do for fun, etc. I generally find small talk a complete bore; however, it was always refreshing and authentic with Jimmy.

"I'm stoked for you guys, Jimmy," I said, feeling a sense of loss, as this chapter of my life had passed and the evidence of it had also been confiscated. Since Gina and I can't respectfully talk about anything, we certainly don't reminisce about the shared highlights of our marriage, leaving me alone in my memories with nobody to fill in the missing gems I may have forgotten.

"Twenty-ounce americano?" Jimmy asked, remembering my usual, as I'm sure he does with all the regulars. He, like Connor, was in the right business.

"Make it two today. Bringing one to a friend."

"Absolutely!" he said, getting right to work on them.

We settled up; I wished him good luck and made my way back to Eddie.

"HEY, TOBY!" I heard someone call out. As I scanned for the source, I saw Hulises chasing me down the block.

"Hi there. How's it going, Hulises?"

"Great. Going to be a nice one today," he said, coming to a halt next to me. "I'm glad I caught you."

"Well, how can I help you, sir?" It felt good to have someone other than Gina's attorney or a bill collector seeking me out for once.

"Actually, I may be able to help you out. You asked if I could keep my ears open for any job opportunities," he said. I had already forgotten that, but was somehow proud of my initiative.

"Yeah...sure. Sounds like you may have found something?"

"My wife, who works at a salon, said they have an opening and need someone who is good with people. They don't need experience but someone dependable."

Dependable isn't the first or even fiftieth word that would come to mind when describing myself, but it was theoretically possible. Salon work was something I had no experience in, but I'm sure it wasn't rocket science either. Maybe I could specialize in hair removal. Just apply wax and rip it off while trying to seem compassionate. I'm sure I wouldn't be given the coveted bikini wax projects, but I wasn't yet familiar with how the inner gears of hair removal services turned.

"I'm sure it doesn't pay what you're used to, but it's money and something to do if nothing else."

Hulises was right. All my idle time was a breeding ground for rumination, resulting in more of a quagmire than a launchpad for constructive efforts. I was sure I had lost all high-tech options, plus this seemed more interesting than the pressure cooker of enterprise software. It may not impress new acquaintances or the ladies, but I wasn't doing much of that anyway.

"Call Babs, the owner, this morning before they find someone else. Make sure to mention I referred you." He handed me a piece of paper with "Babs" written on it and a phone number. "I'll talk to you later. I need to get back to the job. Figured I should catch you when I saw you."

"Thanks, Hulises, I really appreciate this." I specifically didn't say I would call Babs as I had to mull this career opportunity over. I suppose I was ready to assume some real responsibility again, but actually doing it required commitment, which wasn't so much my thing.

I reached Eddie and Cowboy's estate seconds later and heard some rustlings. "Good morning, sunshine," I said as he poked his head out of their makeshift tent.

"How are you? Wow, for me?" Eddie noticed I was offering him a coffee.

"Yep. Nice way to ease into the day, Eddie," I proclaimed as Cowboy gave me an approving sniff. "Top of the day to you, Cowboy."

"To what do I owe this kind gesture?" Eddie asked, accepting the paper cup.

"Honestly, I thought I might buy a few minutes of your time if you don't mind me joining you?"

"You're always welcome, and thanks again. What's on your mind?" he asked.

"Eddie, like I told you yesterday, my life is upside down right now. I lost my job, or maybe 'shit-canned' is a better description of what happened—caught with porn on my work computer. My wife left me far too eagerly, and I only see my children if she approves it, which is exactly never. I've been informed that no job and a porn addiction don't create a household where children will thrive. I'll be broke in another couple of months, and I think I'm drinking a lot. Oh, I almost forgot to mention I gained 40 pounds and have the anus of a seventy-five-year-old man." Figured I might as well roll out the red carpet.

Eddie raised his eyebrows and nodded as if this was not unusual. "Oh, is that all?" he said with a warm smile despite the sarcasm. "I do remember the aged anus thing from yesterday. Better than saggy man-breasts."

"I'd say maybe on par. There's more, but I wanted to give you the lay of the land first," I said.

"I'd love to help, Toby, but I don't know how I can. I'm not hiring anyone right now and don't know how to reverse anal aging," he said with a loud exhale. "Shit, I hope you didn't lose your porn collection in the divorce because I don't have any to lend you. Guess I'm not much help after all."

"I'm not looking for that kind of help. Let me get down to it. Wait, you just woke up. Do you need to take a leak or feed Cowboy or something? I feel like I caught you by surprise." Which is precisely what just happened, and it dawned on me that I was being rude and selfish. Maybe Gina wasn't wrong about all my faults.

"Let me hit the urinal real quick." He climbed to his feet and ambled over to the drain in the sidewalk behind his cart. The sounds of street pissing filled the fresh morning air. Luckily, I was upwind. Cowboy joined him in what I assumed must be a morning ritual.

He returned and asked me, "What's the real thing bothering you?"

"I can't quit trying to make sense of everything, and no matter how much I try to, I'm not any closer. I don't entirely know who I am now or even who I want to pretend to be, making it damn near impossible to know what to do next. I feel like I have been thrown into quicksand, and the more I struggle, the deeper I'm stuck. On the other hand, you have been through much more than this and seem to be at peace with yourself and life. I'm curious how you made sense of it and put the pieces back together into a picture you could live with?"

"I'm sorry to hear that, Toby; however, I suspected you may be in transition. Why are you trying to make sense of it?" he asked.

I was taken aback by his question. Wouldn't anyone try to figure out what went wrong and how to get back on track? "Well, I suppose I want to get my life back on track."

"So, you want a believable story about why these unfortunate events happened to you and to create a future story you can live with and pursue?" Eddie asked.

"More or less, but I want to understand the truth. Then I will feel like I've learned something that can help me not to continue to fuck my life up and help me find a more stable path forward. I'm looking for a different perspective." That was the crux of it.

"Toby, our reality is the fiction we choose to believe," he said gently as he raised his eyebrows with a smile.

"Yes but...fiction isn't real...I'm not sure I follow."

"How would you respond if I asked you who you are?" Eddie asked.

"I'm a guy whose life fell apart suddenly and dramatically, and I'm, quite frankly, lost. That's how I would respond," I humbly stated, feeling somehow completely safe saying that out loud in front of him.

"What does *fell apart* mean?" he then asked.

"What was there is no longer there, and I'm having a real problem putting anything in its place. I suppose I'm having an iden-tity crisis."

I had always had a passion for life and a promising future. I tended to dive deep into whatever I was into at the time. It was my career and, of course, hobbies for a while. At one point, I was into golf until I contracted a severe case of golfer's elbow from those stupid AstroTurf mats at the driving range.

I also dove into fly fishing, collecting old-fashioned church key bottle openers, and learning to appreciate the nuances of fine single-malt Scotch. Maybe I was checking boxes on a "how to be a man checklist," or perhaps these things were just fascinating, likely a combination. Then those passed, and I was on to something else. I liked to think that who we are is the sum total of our experiences, and I was always searching for a new and compelling one to add to my collection. In retrospect, I rationalized that I was curious and eager to explore, but I could have just been looking for distractions. I didn't know what from, but I've never been a good relaxer. Maybe I just needed to occupy my mind with something stimulating enough that I didn't have to face my thoughts and could prove to myself that I had dimension. Regardless, it appeared this collection of experiences hadn't aided me in knowing who I am right now, today, just who I used to be back then. I was starting to realize my approach to life may have been a fool's game all along.

The one thing that I stuck with the longest was running. Running was the only alone time that I enjoyed. Of course, with my active mind, I was thinking about my pace, heart rate, split times, water intake, weekly training load, and greater endurance achievements. It was goal-oriented and fulfilled my desire to attain another goal, demonstrating I was getting better at something than I was the day before. I would sign up for 5Ks, 10Ks, and the occasional marathon. Plus, I always felt calm after a run. Maybe it was the centering effect of the endorphin high that I was always seeking through these different pursuits. It was hard to be certain what drove me before, but whatever it was had taken an extended vacation.

For the past few months, I'd have flashes of interest or motivation, only to watch them fizzle out only hours later. Even paying bills required a few days of getting psyched up. Instead of swimming with the current of life, I felt like I was standing on the pool's edge, watching everyone else swim painlessly, effortlessly, and happily. I was on the outside looking in but feeling helpless to join the game. Life was choosing teams, and I was the kid left standing, unpicked, with a hollow feeling in his gut.

What I had thought of as life's purpose, collecting experiences, now appeared hollow and ultimately unsatisfying. Sure, it was temporarily fulfilling when an experience was achieved, but it faded fast and required another experience to get that moment of satisfaction back. I didn't feel sad; simply empty. I didn't think I was depressed, but maybe depression was different than I thought.

I needed focus, something to focus on, something bigger than myself to drive towards.

I decided then and there to call this Babs person at Hulises's wife's salon to try to make a little cash to bridge my search for a real job and maybe even go for a run. I hadn't run in over a year but still had my shoes and running shorts. Running is a sport that requires very little capital investment, which was right in my wheelhouse.

"Toby, I see your wheels turning. Let me throw a wrench in the gears. As best as I can determine, life is a series of interconnected patterns that continue until they don't. When the patterns break, doors open. That's the best part of this play, and a person can miss those doors if they're not paying attention."

Most of the patterns that made up my life had indeed been broken, if not violently shattered. Maybe the number that Hulises gave me was the type of door Eddie was referring to.

With that thought, something clicked, and finally, I felt I could shift out of neutral and into drive for the first time in six months. I hoped my newfound motivation wasn't just another flash in the pan. I needed a paycheck and self-respect and had decided that getting evicted from my shit-hole for not paying rent was a reality I wasn't eager to explore.

"I hope you're right, Eddie. Sorry to run on you. I've got a call to make. Catch you later, OK?"

"I'm always around," Eddie replied.

CHAPTER
TEN

I finally found the piece of paper Hulises had given me with Bab's number crumpled in the corner of my pocket. I had somehow missed it the first three times I checked. I punched in the number and hit the green button to dial it. After a few rings, a woman picked up, sounding young and chipper.

"Hello, this is Babs."

"Hi, Babs, Toby Tenderhill here. A friend of mine, Hulises (realizing I didn't know his last name), gave me your number. I understand his wife works for you. I'm looking for work, and he mentioned you may need somebody, and here I am," I said, trying to sound enthusiastic.

"Nice to meet you, Toby. Hulises's wife, Carlotta, mentioned you might be calling. One of our receptionists just returned to Mexico, and we are now down a person. The role is more than a typical receptionist, as we will train this person to help with the basic services we offer once they get up to speed. Does that sound of interest to you?"

"Sure, I'm definitely interested in learning more about it," I said.

"Wonderful. As a next step, I'd like to meet you and chat in person. If you can stop by the salon, we can get to know each other, and I can share more details. Then, we can determine if it might be a fit. What's your schedule like this week?" Babs asked.

"Babs, it's wide open. I'm not currently working and can work around your schedule. What works best for you?"

"If you could swing by around 5 p.m. today, that would be perfect, and there shouldn't be a lot of interruptions. Do you know where we're located?" she asked.

"Sadly, I don't. Even worse, I don't even know the name of your salon."

"Not a problem. We're a full-service salon offering a nice array of different services. It's called The Altered Ego Salon, and we're on the corner of Steiner and Divisidero."

"That's easy and within walking distance. I'll be there at five. What do I need to bring?" I asked.

"Don't worry about bringing a resume or anything unless you've worked in a salon before. Relevant experience isn't required for this role, and we can train you on what you need to know to be success-ful," Babs answered.

"Sounds good. Thanks for taking my call, and I look forward to meeting you later, Babs."

"Very well then. I look forward to meeting you in person as well, Toby. Bye for now." And she ended the call.

I felt oddly energized for a thirty-seven-year-old man getting an interview for a receptionist at a salon. A girly job. But shit, I had nothing to lose as I had no dignity left to protect at that point. I had taken a step in the right direction, which felt good.

What does a guy wear to a salon interview? I decided to dress for the interview and not the job, which I also read about once but can't remember for the life of me where or when. I rummaged through my closet in an attempt to find a pair of slacks and a button-down shirt. Eventually, I found what I was looking for, but they appeared neither clean nor pressed. A trip to the laundromat was in order. Luckily, I had plenty of time. It was only ten o'clock in the morning, and the day was still young.

Momentum tends to feed on itself, and before I knew what I was doing, I was wearing my old running shorts, which were more than a little tight and unfashionably short. Then I was lacing up my running shoes that I hadn't worn in months. Luckily, my feet had remained fat-free, and they fit in a nice, familiar way, like an old pair of shoes, which made sense.

I deposited my laundry in a washer at the laundromat two blocks down and decided to head out on a quick run instead of sitting around at the laundromat, wishing I had a washer and dryer of my own.

The clear blue sky had acquiesced, allowing a few clouds to take up residence, and there was a slight breeze coming off the ocean from the west. The temperature was now in the upper 50's, perfect for a run.

To reduce my body's potential shock due to my supreme lack of physical activity, I decided on a slow jog in Golden Gate Park, which was only four blocks away. I entered the park off Arguello near the botanical gardens. Three blocks later, I was already huffing and puffing, and my knees felt the impact of every step while my heart redlined. As I erratically lurched forward, I must have looked as if I had a severe handicap. The feeling was vaguely familiar, and then I realized it was the same feeling as crossing the finish line of a marathon when my legs were seizing up and nothing worked remotely right anymore. But that was at mile twenty-six, and I was barely five minutes into my run.

Perspiring excessively, it became clear I had no choice but to take a forced walking break. I want to say it felt good to get the blood flowing, break a sweat, and breathe the fresh air again, but that would have been a lie. Instead, I was worried about not being able to get back to my laundry. I turned around and alternated walking with running each block until I staggered back into the laundromat, but not before I heard a little girl, who couldn't have been over three years old, ask her mother, "Why are that man's legs so white?" At which point she was immediately shushed.

I hadn't thought about that until then, but it was an accurate observation. White, flabby, and now twitching and cramping. Jesus fuck, I was a mess. It was one of those gut-check moments where I realized my gut was impressive, but I had let myself go far beyond what I could have ever imagined. I was sure this was the "runner's low" I'd never actually heard of before, but there was now no doubt that it was a thing.

"Are you OK?" the laundromat attendant asked. She was an older African American woman, probably in her 60s, and appeared genuinely concerned, which she should have been.

"No. I don't think so, but if I sit down for a few minutes, I may have a chance of survival." The digital timer indicated I still had 15 minutes remaining on the wash cycle. I wondered if there was a chance I'd be physically able to transfer my load into the dryer by then.

I straightened out my legs in front of me to witness both quadriceps promptly cramp up. I let out a yelp that brought the attendant rushing back over.

"Should I call an ambulance?" she asked with saucer-like eyes.

"Help me bend my knees, please?" I asked, to which she obliged, and my seizing thighs reluctantly released. "I'm a little out of shape, I guess. I now understand the phrase, walk before you run."

She seemed to calm down and asked if I needed any water, to which I replied I did. I wasn't sure if I was proud of myself for attempting to exercise, or humiliated, or concerned I'd done some permanent damage. Likely, it was all of the above. After about ten minutes, my breathing returned to normal, and I thought I might make it after all.

"You're no spring chicken anymore," she informed me as if I had overlooked this critical detail.

"Yeah, I haven't exercised in quite a while. I assumed I'd have had enough residual athleticism to jog longer than five minutes before an involuntary shutdown."

"Life's a bitch sometimes," she informed me.

"More than just sometimes."

I made my way over to the washer, being very careful not to straighten my legs completely. Transferring my clothes to the dryer, I was relieved I had another 45 minutes to do nothing until I could return home. Maybe I need to stretch out some more, I thought. Then I changed my mind and started thumbing through a *People* magazine that turned out to be two and a half years old. Seeing pictures of young, fit, extremely good-looking, and most positively happy famous people was not my best medicine.

By the time my clothes were dry, I was feeling much closer to normal, although the muscle soreness was already setting in to remind me what a pitiful physical specimen I was for the next few days—life's cruel that way. The whole thing was funny when I thought about it, but at the same time, not so much.

I managed to fold my laundry and make it to my apartment stairs without incident; however, I was exhausted when I came up on Eddie and decided to chat with him while I built up the courage to navigate the six steps to the front door.

Eddie was working on what appeared to be a tarp repair project involving a healthy amount of duct tape. Cowboy felt compelled to lay down on the exact part of the tarp Eddie was working on, making it more challenging.

"A little home maintenance, Eddie?" I asked.

"Supposed to rain tonight, and I've been putting this off. No more time to waste," Eddie answered.

I thought how funny it was that Eddie's big project he had been procrastinating was taping up holes in his tarp, maybe a twenty-minute job. In contrast, mine was getting a job, finding a better apartment, losing a ton of weight, and eventually finding potential romance. Oh yeah, and cutting down on the booze. At that moment, I envied Eddie and began to feel overwhelmed by my own to-do list.

"Did your call go OK?" Eddie asked. It took me a moment to put two and two together and realize he was referring to the call with Babs. Funny he would remember that and raise the question.

"Eddie, I have a job interview later this afternoon. It's a stupid job, but at least it's a lead," I informed him.

"Stupid is a relative term. It may be just what you need right now, partner. Who knows."

I hoped so. I was starting to realize Eddie had a nasty little habit of being right about things. Maybe this was indeed the open door he was referring to earlier.

"Thanks, man. I'll keep you posted," I said as I left.

I had recovered enough that the stairs weren't an issue. I decided to spend a few cycles contemplating what questions Babs might ask and how much of my current situation was prudent to share without shooting myself in the foot. If she was looking for dependability, I wouldn't be able to produce a lot of recent examples other than being dependably lazy, which I somehow doubted she was looking for. Explaining the last six months could be difficult.

Then my mind drifted to something Eddie had said, "Reality is the fiction we choose to believe." Could our identity and our perceived reality really be nothing more than just that?

CHAPTER
ELEVEN

It was now 4:15 p.m., and I started getting ready for my interview. I hadn't considered that, since my impressive weight gain, my older clothes might no longer fit. I managed to get my pants buttoned and secured with a belt, which was now on the last hole, slicing like a knife into my muffin-top midriff. It looked like hell and screamed, "This guy used to be a lot thinner."

I was a mess and had to pivot to a different strategy that wasn't so excruciatingly painful and equally brutal for others to consume visually. I went with my jeans and a better-fitting casual belt, hoping my button-down and shoes could supply the minimum required professionalism for a passable first impression—nothing like surfacing body image issues right before a job interview. On the bright side, I was no longer in immobilizing discomfort.

I hustled out the door and headed towards Divisidero Street, appropriately named as it divided the city in half from East to West. I had calculated the walk at about twenty minutes and arrived a few minutes early, providing the much-needed opportunity to stop sweating. One of the many downsides of being borderline obese is that it leaves one well-insulated.

I managed to cool off in the shade, and my breathing slowed to a normal rhythm as the clock struck five. Then I headed on into The Altered Ego Salon.

It took a second for my eyes to adjust to dimmer lighting, revealing a very friendly and modern lobby with plush navy-blue chairs and light purple walls. Fresh yellow tulips were on the counter, and the place smelled faintly of lilac and lemon. Soft classical music was playing; I was pretty sure it was Pachelbel's Canon. I don't know exactly what I was expecting, but it was much less than that. I had to admit it did have an immediate calming effect.

The young woman with dark shoulder-length hair and thick, black-rimmed glasses behind the counter looked up and smiled. "Can I help you, sir?"

"Yes, thank you. I have an appointment with Babs at five. My name is Toby Tenderhill."

"Absolutely," she replied. "My name is Carlotta; nice to meet you, Toby. She is expecting you. Let me tell her you're here. Feel free to have a seat and help yourself to a water if you'd like."

"Thank you very much," I responded, moving towards the chairs.

Carlotta... that name sounded familiar, but I couldn't put my finger on it. I noticed the mini-fridge on the corner side table next to one of the chairs and helped myself to a bottled water. I greedily guzzled it down, then deposited the plastic bottle in the waste basket marked "recycle."

A few moments later, Carlotta returned and informed me that Babs would be right out. Sure enough, after a couple of minutes, a slight-of-frame woman, who appeared to be in her sixties, emerged from the hall behind the counter. She had straight, long gray hair midway down her back, contrasting nicely with her black sweater. She wore a pleasing smile, the kind where her dark brown eyes smiled right along with her mouth. I had been expecting someone much younger from her voice on the phone. I wondered how my appearance contrasted with her image of what I would look like. I saw no immediate expression of disappointment on her face, which was a relief.

"Hello, Toby, and thank you for coming right in today. I'm Babs, and it's a pleasure to meet you," she said, walking around from the back of the counter to greet me with a firm, crisp handshake.

I was already on my feet and extending my hand. "Believe me; the pleasure is mine. Is now still a convenient time?"

"Absolutely. Why don't you come back to my office, and let's chat," she said, spinning on her heels and leading the way. Something about her demeanor said this lady was a professional and no stranger to efficiency.

I followed her through the door behind the counter and down a nicely carpeted hallway. There were three doors on each side separated by framed black and white pictures of what appeared to be various outdoor farmer's markets, most likely not from the US, by the looks of the clothes people were wearing and some unfamiliar produce. The hall's lighting was slightly dim but not to the point that visibility was a problem. A small water feature on a table midway down the right side of the hall filled the air with a soothing sound. Babs opened her office door at the center of the far end of the hall, leading us into a small room with the sun shining through a window in the back. Palm-like plants sat on the floor in each corner, and there was a large mirror on the left wall with an ornate oriental wooden frame. Two sitting chairs facing each other were directly to the right, the room smelling faintly of sandalwood. Everything was neatly organized and very professional. This was a businesswoman, not someone fresh out of cosmetology school trying to make a go of it.

"Let's have a seat over here." She motioned toward the two chairs.

"Thank you," I said, sitting down, being extra conscious not to man-spread all over the place.

"I don't know if you know, but Carlotta, who you already met, is Hulises's wife."

"Oh. No, I didn't, but she seems very pleasant," I responded, now realizing why that name sounded so familiar.

"She's been a godsend; we're lucky to have her. So tell me more about what you're looking for, and I can then tell you about the job description, OK?"

"Well, Babs, in full transparency, I left my previous career in high-tech because it was insanely hectic and beyond stressful. I was going through a divorce at the time, moving into an apartment, and it was all a bit too much. What little money I was left with is running out, and I am looking for a job doing something completely different," I answered with selective transparency, realizing I had just told her I was desperate and weak.

"Well, this would be something entirely different," she said with a singsongy laugh. "Are you looking for full-time or part-time?"

"Full-time is preferred, but if part-time is all that's available, I suppose I could go that route."

"Well, what I have right now is right between the two. We lost one of our receptionists last week, and since we're open six days a week from 9 a.m. to 8 p.m., we need more than just Carlotta. She has young children at home and can't work sixty-plus hours a week much longer. I'm usually busy with appointments and walk-ins, and since our services are done in private rooms, I can't keep an eye on the front desk. We have two shifts, 9-3 and 3-8. Carlotta works 9-3, so we need someone to cover the 3-8, six days a week, which is thirty hours a week, plus it gives you the best part of the day for the rest of your life," Babs explained. "I firmly believe, as it sounds like you've discovered for yourself, a work/life balance is as important as enjoying being at work. We're better people for it, and our customers feel that."

This made sense and sounded good while simultaneously raising the internal question: What *was* the rest of my life? Somehow, I filled the hours but couldn't recall precisely what with. My days didn't start with intentions, task lists, or appointments. Time somehow passed, but in entirely unmemorable ways.

"That all works for me, Babs," I said. "However, what does a day in the life of a receptionist at The Altered Ego Salon consist of? The reason I ask is I want to make sure I have the skills to do what you need."

"I assume you can work a computer and organize appointments and things. Is that indeed the case?" she asked, maintaining a formal demeanor. She could have easily been a nun teaching in a catholic elementary school somewhere.

"Absolutely. I come from the high-tech industry, so no issues there."

"My assumption was correct then. Carlotta can teach you how to run our appointment application and the credit card machine. The most important thing, and why we are sitting here now, is your people skills, professionalism, and attitude. You seem professional, respectful as well as calm, and willing to listen when others talk. That sounds trite, but believe me, those are qualities you can't teach and aren't as common as one might suspect."

"Now that I think about it, I suppose you're right."

"That I am, young man, and I'm not afraid to admit when I'm wrong. That is another trait that's important to me. You have to be open to feedback, good or bad. I've been in this business for quite a while now and have seen what works, what doesn't, and why. If I see anything you need to be aware of to help you in your job, I'll speak my mind and will always do so with respect; however, a willingness to learn is what I'm looking for in return. Is that something you feel comfortable with? Taking feedback, corrections, etc.?" she asked, holding eye contact in a more curious than confrontational manner.

"Babs, I would view my role as ensuring that the customer has a good experience. I know that how my duties are performed are an extension of your vision and approach to running your business. I have pride in my work, and knowing exactly how I'm meeting or not meeting expectations is critical for me to feel I'm adding maximum value." Jesus, what a bunch of bullshit, I thought as I watched myself weaving buzzwords together like a wicker basket. But I wasn't saying anything I didn't believe. I would have to leave my previous workplace arrogance at the door. Since I could no longer think of anything to be arrogant about, this would be easier than it would have been a year ago.

"Tell me, Toby, how do you deal with stress in the workplace? You mentioned your previous job was intense. How long did you work there?"

"I was there for eight years total. And yes, it was very stressful at times." I considered telling her about the cathartic advantage of keeping a list of people you want to punch in the face but pivoted in a different direction. "It wasn't the people interactions that were stressful. It was the constant influx of projects and radical shifts in strategic direction that overwhelmed my team's limited resources. This workload could only be handled by working evenings and weekends. Although at times that's necessary for most jobs, week in and week out for years starts to take its toll. Of course, I'd try to take breaks, meditate, do breathing exercises, and work out at lunch. But ultimately, the sheer hours demanded and the constant whipsawing of priorities caused me to realize it wasn't sustainable. I'm sure, amongst other things, it contributed to my divorce as well." My response was hard to argue with, especially after she had just preached the virtues of work/life balance.

"Well, I don't blame you for making a change. However, it seems fair to ask why you left without finding other employment first. Did you leave on good terms?" Fuck. My mind froze. I don't know why I hadn't prepared for this question. It was, after all, quite logical, and I should have known it would come up. Babs seemed like the type of person who may not receive the truth of the matter well.

"To be honest, I didn't leave on the best of terms. Let's say I made a moral decision. My team was running on fumes, and one of my employees had suffered an anxiety attack two weeks prior. I had heard, through the grapevine, that another member of my team was interviewing with a competitor due to the constant unrealistic demands. My boss dropped another 'A1 priority' on our plate that involved a tremendous amount of detailed analysis on restructuring our entire pricing methodology. I decided I had to push back, or my team wouldn't be able to recover. Essentially, I laid out all our priorities and asked my boss which ones could be pushed out to handle this new urgent one. I was informed that all of these needed to be executed on their current deadlines, and we'd have to put in some heroic work. I had already decided I'd be looking for employment elsewhere, so I said I would turn in my resignation if we weren't given more resources or if the number of concurrent projects wasn't reduced. Let's say this ultimatum wasn't well received, and I ended up resigning."

"Toby, I respect that more than you may think. It appears you have a good business mind and probably good judgment and decision-making skills. I say we give this a shot. I predict it will work out well. And you may have fun at the same time! What other questions can I answer for you?" she asked, glancing at her watch. I was impressed with my spiel and marginally surprised she took it hook, line, and sinker.

"Well, thank you. I guess it would make sense to inquire about what the role gets paid. I'm assuming that working less than forty hours would mean no benefits?"

"The position pays seventeen dollars an hour, basically $510 for a thirty-hour week, and sometimes more with tips, which you would receive if we need you to cover any of the simpler treatment services from time to time. And you are correct; it doesn't include benefits."

I did some quick math and figured a little over two thousand a month, about a fifth of what I had been making previously. However, I'd be working about half as much, and it didn't seem that stressful, which would allow me not to stress out when I wasn't actually at work. Plus, this was a stopgap until I could find something that paid better, and the schedule would allow me the flexibility to interview during the day if I needed to.

"I can make that work, although it will be tight. What are the services The Altered Ego Salon provides?" I asked, figuring I'd need to know this sooner or later anyway.

"We don't do hair. Well, I guess we do hair removal but not styling. We also do manicures, pedicures, eyebrow dying, and things like that. And once a week, we have a massage therapist who comes in. Pretty traditional stuff, none of which is complicated. We have two people besides myself who perform all the services. You'll meet those two when you start. Jessica and Jazmine. Both are charming people, who I'm sure you will enjoy. I try to create a light-hearted, family atmosphere here. We joke around a lot and want our customers to feel welcome and cared for, not just objects to profit from. About 70% of our customers are regulars, who you'll get to know over time. A sense of humor is important and welcome. Does that sound OK to you?"

"Well, to be honest, I think families are overrated, and customers need to know their place," I said deadpan and waited a few seconds before adding, "Just kidding. Trying out my sense of humor on you."

Babs laughed out loud with a distinctive snort. "You wield the sword of sarcasm well. That will work just fine. How soon do you think you'd be able to start?"

"Anytime. My schedule is wide open."

"Well then, let's have you come in at 2:30 tomorrow afternoon, and I'll cover the front desk while Carlotta spends a half-hour or so teaching you a few things you'll need to know. This is great. Thanks, Toby. I like you already."

Whoever said, "Nobody likes a liar," was wrong. Although hard to believe, that was about the nicest thing anyone had said to me since I could remember. Babs was friendly and very professional, but not in a stiff way; it was more caring. She seemed incredibly sharp and was the type of person you didn't want to disappoint. Maybe it was because she had more confidence in me than I had in myself, and I didn't want to disappoint her. It also could have been that I needed approval, and receiving it from someone I respect means a lot more than from some dumb-ass boss.

"Thanks, Babs. I can say I like you as well, which makes a difference to me. Great then. I'll come by at 2:30 tomorrow unless there is more you want to cover now."

"I think I have everything I need. I have a good feeling about this and look forward to getting to know you more. Oh...I almost forgot proper attire—clean clothes, a tucked-in shirt with a collar, and no tennis shoes. Jeans are fine as long as they don't have holes—essentially, what you are wearing right now," she explained.

"Great," I responded, thinking I may need a couple of new pairs of pants that actually fit.

"Well, I have an appointment soon, so we'll need to wrap this up. We can do the basic paperwork tomorrow. I'll see you at 2:30, then. I'll tell Carlotta to expect you as I may be in an appointment when you arrive."

"Looking forward to it. I can show myself out if you need to get ready for your appointment," I offered.

"Thank you. That would be great, Toby. Bye for now," she said, standing up and extending her hand across her desk.

I shook her hand, said goodbye, and left feeling pretty good about myself—which struck me as humorous. I had just lied my way into a low-wage job with no experience required and had the impressive title of "Receptionist." Hey, at least I had gainful employment, would have money coming in, and had something to do other than wallow in my self-pity. I felt a flicker of genuine excitement and wondered if it might ignite a fire under my ass.

CHAPTER
TWELVE

"Cowboy, the neighborhood is going to shit. Here comes yet another yuppie to further gentrify the Western Edition. Kill, Cowboy! Kill!"

Eddie must have seen me coming, dressed as my recently altered ego. I was an illusion of responsible professionalism. Maybe a bit of a leap, but I felt things were starting to shift. As Eddie had suggested, a door had opened. I had finally caught a current after helplessly drifting sideways for so long.

"Oh shit, Toby. I didn't recognize you in that costume. Thank God Cowboy doesn't mind very well," he said with a wink.

"Very funny. I have good news, but I'm too cold to share it. Do you have dinner plans?"

It was starting to get dark and chilly. The wind usually dies by early evening, but tonight it had a different plan. The fog's tendrils were already weaving through the outer Richmond and would pick their way to us soon enough.

"Well, if I answered no, would I still have an opportunity to hear the good news?" he asked, smiling.

"Nope. I'm going to go in and get my jacket and run down to the corner store to pick us up a couple of cans of chili, if that works for you?"

"Only under one condition," he qualified. "Please let me open the cans this time."

"Fair enough," I laughed. I liked Eddie's gentle way of teasing. Who would have thought I'd have met what may have been my new best friend next to a shopping cart on the street? Who would have guessed many things would unfold the way they had?

I slipped into my crap apartment, ripped off my button-down shirt, which was operating as more of a corset, and replaced it with my go-to "This Guy Loves Bacon" t-shirt. A quick jaunt to the corner market, and I was heading back towards Eddie within ten minutes with two cans of Dennison's Hot Chili and a couple of 24-oz Tecates.

When I arrived, Eddie and Cowboy were playing tug with the same rag as last time, completely immersed.

We got a dog when I was a kid, and I was told I had complete ownership of naming it. This, like Santa Claus, turned out to be another lie. In the end, a family vote was ultimately required.

Initially, under the illusion I had ultimate decision-making authority, I had immediately caucused on this with my middle-school buddies, Matt and Johnny Vapor, the latter of which tended to have pretty bad gas. The three of us came up with a quick laundry list of potential names, but eventually settled on three that seemed to be damn good: Tit Dog, The Burning Erection Hound, and Spatch (short for spatula). Once I learned that a family vote was required, I presented the shortlist at the dinner table. I was outvoted, which was ironic, since I had been tasked with naming the dog in the first place. He was thereafter known as Spatch.

Since then, I have never been much of a dog person.

It wasn't all bad, but most assuredly, not that good. I preferred cats due to the minimum maintenance requirements. Dogs need to be let out to defecate, need walks, chew up shoes, need regular feedings, puke all over the place, have diarrhea accidents, need expensive medication, stare you in the eye when they beg for food, and frequently snore. Additionally, they require tremendous efforts to train, which mostly fail. A dog is a perfect surrogate if you are looking for a toddler substitute to make you feel needed.

"Hey guys, dinner is served!" I announced, approaching them. Cowboy dropped the rag and ran over, tail wagging, to greet me. I rubbed him behind his ears and patted him on the back, which seemed enough, as he ran back over to Eddie.

"Now that's the Toby I remember," Eddie said, acknowledging my change in attire. "Pull up a seat."

The ground around them theoretically had infinite seats to choose from; I took the one three feet directly across from the old man.

"You cook, and I'll clean," I offered, handing the cans to Eddie, who had the can opener out and ready for action. I opened both beers and handed him his.

"Thanks for buying. Tell me about the good news."

"I'm proud to announce I'm, once again, gainfully employed."

"Well, that's fantastic. I figured something like that might have prompted you to clean up your appearance. Income is important, especially if you are an apartment-dwelling type. What's the new gig?"

"I'm a receptionist at The Altered Ego Salon down on Divisidero. Seems easy enough, thirty hours a week, and Babs, the owner, seems cool. It turns out it's not one of those horse-shit nail salons we see on every other corner in this town. The place was nice and clean; appointment-only type of deal."

"I could see you being good at that. Not a bad career choice."

"I don't know about a career, but it's a start to reestablishing my life. I do finally feel motivated to start the rebuild."

"Strike while the iron is hot, right? Any other plans for your life reconstruction project?" Eddie had no issue opening the cans and handed me one with what looked to the naked eye like a clean fork.

"Funny you should ask, as I've been starting to give that some thought. I think financial stability comes first. It will be a big relief not to worry about when the money will run out. And I need to get back in shape, or at least stem the tide of the dilapidation. Shit, I tried to go on a run today and almost killed myself. I only got a few blocks and was forced to walk. I used to run marathons, for fuck's sake, not that I want to do that again. But being physically fit will go a long way in building back my self-esteem. Once I get the old confidence back, I may be able to engage with women without certain rejection. I'm starting with the basics."

"Well, that seems like a logical path back to your old self," he said.

"That's what I'm hoping for. Frankly, I miss being happy."

"So, were you happy before things started to fall apart?" he asked.

"Yeah. Things weren't perfect, but nobody's life is perfect. But I made a good life and had a family, car, and a decent two-bedroom flat. Hell, my clothes even fit."

"Well, there you have it: a vision, a goal, and a comeback story. I'm excited for you and wish you luck," he said, raising his beer for a toast as a genuine smile spread across his face.

"What's next for you, Eddie?" I asked, realizing that, as usual, the conversation had been all about me up until that point.

"I don't know. I guess we'll have to wait and see what happens," he said with a chili sauce-laden smile. "I'll just take it as it comes."

I felt kind of sorry for Eddie. He didn't have a concrete goal and, subsequently, no plan. The uncertainty of what could happen every day on the street must be pretty sucky and probably a bit scary.

"Would you say you are happy now?" I asked. It was a personal question, but he started it.

"Happiness comes and goes. I find it's relative to my idea of what's important to me at the time."

Interesting answer—maybe a copout. I mean, there's a lot a person, if properly motivated, can do to create their own happiness.

"I suppose you're right," I said, not trying to debate him.

"Good chili. I like it better cold anyway," Eddie said, digging in for another bite.

"So do I! As a kid, when I was on my own for lunch, if we had canned chili, I would always eat it cold out of the can. At first, I thought maybe I was too lazy to put it in the pan and clean up afterward, but I realized it just tasted better. It's funny how many people are appalled at the idea without ever experimenting with it."

"You could apply that to a lot of different things, I suppose," he said.

"You're probably right. What else is new?"

"There's a good chance Cowboy and I may need to move," Eddie threw out.

"You're shitting me. Why is that? Your choice?" I asked, concerned for selfish reasons. I was becoming used to Eddie and Cowboy and knew I'd certainly miss having them around.

"Wouldn't be by choice. Brian, your manager or whatever he is, mentioned it didn't look good for prospective tenants to see homeless people outside the building. Probably true, I suppose. Said one of the tenants complained." Eddie paused to scrape another bite of chili from the bottom of his can, popped it into his mouth, and continued, his mouth full. "People like to pretend we don't exist or, at best, are a necessary evil—as long as they don't have to look at us. A lot of deranged, mentally ill, and drug addicts are on the streets, all of which do tend to be unpredictable. He didn't say he would call the cops or anything, but now that he's thinking about it, it's only a matter of time. Usually, the way these things happen."

"Well, that pisses me off. Maybe I can try talking to him. Can't hurt," I offered, realizing that it very well could have been my complaint before meeting Eddie that contributed. "Worst case scenario, where would you go?"

"I'll try to stay in the neighborhood. It's not uppity and gentrified yet. I guess I'll have to look around," he said calmly. Cowboy walked over, sat down in front of me, and proceeded to stare me in the eyes at close range as I deposited another bite in my mouth. "Cowboy, leave him alone." Cowboy immediately scampered back over to Eddie and lay down beside him.

"How do you feel about that? I'd be a little nervous and pissed," I asked, noticing a sorrowful look on Cowboy's face.

"Well, the world is always changing, Toby. I can argue with reality all I want, but reality always wins out in the end. Like I say, when patterns break, doors open, much like one did for you today. People either get scared of the uncertainty or get curious to see what the next chapter will bring. I choose to remain curious."

"I suppose there's some truth to that, but you can always do things to affect the outcome," I offered up.

"Perhaps." He pondered a bit. "Or perhaps that's a belief we embrace because it empowers us with the illusion of control."

"Eddie, do you really think that's true? You're saying that life already knows how it will play out, and we're just along for the ride, for better or worse?" What a bizarre concept, I thought. Apparently, one that can leave you homeless. It seemed like giving up to me. Maybe he had, and that perspective helped him to rationalize it.

Eddie had already finished his chili and let Cowboy clean off his spoon. He then shifted his focus to his beer. After pausing for a few contemplative seconds and taking a swig, he said, "It's possible. How much of life doesn't happen the way people want it to, despite their rigorous efforts? People make huge sacrifices to force a future they think they want, and half the time, it doesn't work out that way in the end."

"Yeah, but what about the other half of the time when it does?"

"Maybe it would have worked out that way regardless."

"But maybe not. I'd say we can't rule out our ability to influence outcomes." I took a pull off my beer. "See, I just decided to have some beer, Eddie."

"I'd have been bewildered if you had decided against it. We tend to think that our actions shape the outcomes when things go to our liking. But when they don't, we blame external factors. If you tally it up, there's likely less than a coin flip's chance most things will go your way unless you never leave your house. Sometimes more goes your way than other times, but I bet it's roughly the same percentage for most of us over the long haul. Some call that fatalism, but it's hard to disprove. We create narratives about what caused this and that, the role of luck, and so on, but believing those stories doesn't make them true," he explained. "I bet you'll take another sip of your beer soon, too."

I thought he had a point, so I chugged some more beer. But his theory was depressing, and I wasn't ready to accept it.

"Eddie, there is obviously cause and effect. We can't always control every cause, but we can most certainly cause an effect a lot of the time. If we don't do anything, we've reduced our chances considerably," I countered.

"I'm not saying not to do anything. If we are moved to do something, great. Do it. However, much of our life is spent beating our heads against the wall to no avail until, sooner or later, we realize we have to accept reality for what it is. Everything is intertwined. For everything that happens, many causes affect the outcome, most of which we don't see. For example, you went and landed yourself a job today. Sure, you had to show up, but the job had to come to your attention. In this case, it was through Hulises." I wondered how he knew that Hulises had put me in touch with Babs. Maybe I had mentioned it to him, or possibly he knew Hulises.

"The job opening had to come into existence," Eddie continued. "The owner, this Babs, had to be willing to consider an applicant without prior experience. She had to determine if she thought you were a fit based on her criteria. The compensation and the nature of the job had to be acceptable enough for you to consider it. It just so happened that the timing of you reaching the end of your cash reserves, as well as your discomfort in your current situation, occurred at the same time as her need for a new employee. If Babs had eaten the wrong thing for lunch, putting her in a foul mood, she may not have considered you. Many factors affected the outcome, most of which were not in your control, although a few were. The percentages were against you. Maybe you got lucky. You were undoubtedly an active participant in the entire process, but it's possible that a significant portion of it unfolded independently of anything you did or didn't do."

"Well fuck. That's deep. I can't prove that's not true, but I've always had a different perspective, and I can list examples of times when I made decisions, took action, and affected the desired outcome," I said.

"If I have examples and data showing a bunch of interrelated causes all coming together to create an outcome, and you have data and examples where specific actions on your part were the cause of certain outcomes, which one of us is right?" he asked and took a generous swig of his beer, wiping his mustache on his sleeve.

"Well, if you put it that way, we don't know for sure," I answered.

"Exactly. It's a matter of belief at that point. We have different beliefs; maybe neither is true, and we're both wrong. Let's say that after a thorough review of the data, it becomes clear that I'm right. Would you be willing to deduce that just because you believed you were right earlier, that didn't make it true?"

"Well, in that particular example... yes," I acknowledged.

"Well, if it could be the case in this pretend instance, couldn't it be the case with other beliefs where you didn't have the data or experiences to show you that another one of your beliefs was wrong? Many folks think homeless people are scary, and guys like you don't think so. In reality, you are both wrong, but people don't want ambiguity. They prefer not to question their beliefs because they may realize they don't exactly know what's true, and that's an uncomfortable place to be."

This was a bit confusing to me, and my beer was having an effect —me no longer being in the mood for philosophical discourse.

"Do you think about this stuff a lot, Eddie?"

"I used to quite a bit, but not so much these days. I don't trust thought that much anymore... concerning these types of questions, at least. My point is that just because a person thinks something quite often, it doesn't make it true. Thoughts are often merely reflections of our beliefs, so just because we believe something, it doesn't make it true. But that's beside the point; it's a rathole we could get lost in for hours. We're celebrating your new job for crying out loud, and I don't want to rake your buzz. When do you start?" Eddie may have lost interest in more philosophical discourse as well, at this point, or felt the discussion futile.

"Tomorrow at 2:30. Even though it's a stupid job, I am excited, and that feels good, but I need pants that fit, or I'm going to be miserable."

"I believe that pants that fit are a good thing," he said and gave me a wink.

"Well, we can agree on that then."

At about this time, Big Sallie and RV Jeff stumbled around the corner in a very heated conversation. It appeared that there had been infidelity in the wind that night, which had resulted in Jeff being caught dancing with another lady back at The Plow.

"You better learn to keep your dick in your pants if you want to keep it," Big Sallie yelled.

Sallie was wearing another giant white tent-like t-shirt with the words "Fuck the Police" on the front in large black block letters. The thought crossed my mind that she'd make an excellent poncho model.

Jeff was dressed in cowboy attire, and I'm not talking like Eddie's dog. RV Jeff had the whole enchilada going on but, unsurprisingly, with a flair for the awkward. His hat was traditional western, a dingy gray that looked like it'd seen some miles. He also had a button-down plaid shirt with pearl snaps. (In the Wild West, a man didn't have time to fuss with actual buttons.) His jeans— they appeared to be Wranglers, because women go nuts for Wrangler butts—were tucked into his boots. He was obviously proud of his boots and didn't want any detail to go unnoticed. The bottom part of the boot that covered his feet looked like a normal tan leather with pointed toes. The top part had a red panel on the outside and a blue panel on the inside with a white stitched pattern intertwining both panels—they looked new. Unfortunately, he had overlooked a big rodeo belt buckle, resulting in a significant loss of credibility.

Let's just say Big Sallie had a more promising career modeling ponchos than RV Jeff did modeling Western attire.

RV Jeff was in an overconfident and unflappable state, most likely alcohol-fueled, or perhaps he had become immune to her verbal beatdowns. He burst into an old Bee Gees song. Something about how he walked made it obvious he was a lady's man; therefore, he did not have much time to talk. Or something of that nature. He was still slightly out of earshot.

Sallie was always within earshot and wasn't impressed. *"You ain't going to have no time to gawk 'cause you ain't going be no lady's man when I Bobbitize your cock,"* she sang back with authority.

They were now jaywalking to the other side of the street, and we couldn't make out much more of the conversation, but the tone didn't seem pretty.

After they were out of sight, we sat in silence for a few minutes. I was still mulling over Eddie not trusting thoughts much these days. What a bizarre concept. Thoughts are critical to get through the logistics of any day, learn from past experiences, figure out potential paths forward, weigh the pros and cons of big and small decisions, and whatever else. If he didn't trust them, how would he know to feed Cowboy, take him to the vet, get food, take gambling bets, etc.? After all, his thoughts about being so lucky to be alive after his combat experience gave him such a great perspective. I decided to probe him more on this, if for no other reason than to understand him better.

"Eddie, if you don't mind, can I ask you a question about something you said about trusting thoughts?"

"Sure, as long as you don't overthink my answer," he said jokingly.

"Haha. So, if you don't trust your thoughts much, how would you figure anything out, learn from past mistakes, plan for taking care of tomorrow, and stuff?"

"Thinking about basic functions of daily life, how to get to the store, making sure to drink enough water, keep an appointment, etc., are critical to survival. I use thought when necessary as a tool for navigating day-to-day logistics. What I meant is that I don't trust thoughts that create stories about who I am, or mentally reliving or lamenting something that's happened in the past or even worrying about the future."

"Why?" I inquired.

"They may be right, or they may be dead wrong. The past only exists in our imagination, and the same with the future, right?"

"I suppose....but there is a past and a future."

"Only in that they exist conceptually as thoughts in the present. Right now is the only thing happening each and every second. Unfortunately, we spend most of these waking seconds thinking repeatedly overused, worn-out thought patterns, whether it's how something wasn't our fault, how people perceive us, or what we want the future to deliver. It's all just our imagination partying and doesn't truly exist outside our minds. Thoughts will still happen, but what's the use of chasing them down the same ratholes every time we think them? Whether I sit on the streets because I'm an ex-convict who can't get my life together, a war veteran who prefers the simplest life available, or I just incarnated out of nowhere, what does it matter? I'm sitting here right now all the same, and if I don't realize that and experience that, I'll miss the only thing that's real," he explained.

"Well, if all that other stuff isn't real, what exactly is real?"

"Like I just said, this instantaneous, ever-changing present moment. It's magical that it exists at all, and it's gorgeous. We are a living part of this instant as much as the tree across the street, the clouds in the sky, and the black hole in the center of our galaxy. We are inseparable from all of life. Like Alan Watts said, "As an apple tree apples, the earth peoples." Just because we move around doesn't make us separate from the Earth. We need to take in its food, drink its water, breathe its air, and feel its warmth. Just 'being' with what's around you allows you to flow with right now. That is 'being,' not thinking, worrying, overplanning, or ruminating; all that's just content for an overactive mind."

"Well, that's interesting, but I certainly don't feel integrated with everything, so to me, it's just another concept. I might as well be honest."

"Now you're getting somewhere. You'll never think your way out of thought. It's the thinking that separates your awareness from actually being here now. If you haven't, you should pick up a copy of Ram Dass's book *Be Here Now* at The Green Apple Bookstore down on Clement Street. He has a beautiful way of illustrating what we're talking about."

At this point, I wasn't sure what to think. Eddie was talking gibberish that seemed like more of a rationalization to do nothing than anything else.

"Eddie, if it weren't for thinking about where I want to be, I wouldn't have gotten this job. Just like if I don't want to be lonely, I need to think about engaging with others. To get healthy again, I need to figure out an exercise routine. Those things don't happen without thought."

"Perhaps, or they might happen on their own anyway. You were thinking plenty of thoughts when everything fell apart and ended you up here. That didn't work out so well," he cleverly pointed out.

"Well, it turns out I was thinking the wrong thoughts, and I can learn from that by reflecting on what I did wrong. That way, I won't repeat those mistakes."

"You're kind of making my point," Eddie said. "You were thinking thoughts you believed were true that weren't. In retrospect, maybe you wish you hadn't taken them seriously since they weren't real. Now you are chasing different thoughts in hopes they bring you where you want to go to find happiness. How do you know these new thoughts aren't just as wrong, but merely different?"

"Well, that's the only choice I have, and I'll adjust along the way."

"I don't know if that's the *only* choice. That works sometimes, and things may unfold the way you want them to until they don't anymore. All I'm suggesting, Toby, is to *watch* your thoughts but not *chase* them. See what happens."

"Well, I've got a lot to consider and don't know if I have time for all of that right now. I'm finally just starting to make an effort to get my shit together."

"Times of change can provide the best opportunity to watch how this works, as the mind and beliefs are in flux," he added.

"Possibly. Well, I'm going to try to get a good night's sleep and be fresh for my first day on the job tomorrow. Thanks for hanging out and putting up with my questions, whether I agree with what you're saying or not." I stood up and handed Eddie my spoon, which he promptly handed to Cowboy to clean off.

"Hey, you can always just put those concepts on a shelf somewhere and then check back with them later if you feel the time is right. Or maybe not. In the end, none of it matters much."

"Well, that's good to know. I imagine I'll see you guys tomorrow."

"Not if we see you first," he said, smiling, and gave me a wave as I walked up the stairs into my building.

I was in bed by nine, but sleep didn't find me until around midnight. I kept pondering everything Eddie and I had talked about.

He did have a point. When I looked back at different stages of my life, what was important to me and why did it change, especially when I looked at five-year increments. I found quite a few thoughts and beliefs that were consistent, but many that were almost laughable now.

Like, in middle school, believing that my ability to ride a wheelie on my BMX bike farther than anyone else elevated my status among my friends and even strangers. I spent countless hours practicing, which was a central part of the story of who I was at the age of twelve. Now, looking back, I doubt anyone cared much except me. Then, at nineteen, I sank every dime I could earn into restoring my 1967 Mustang convertible. Again, it was almost a maniacal fixation, resulting in a beautiful car and a feeling of superiority. I was sure this car had skyrocketed my attractiveness with "the women folk," as my Dad called them, only to be followed by it getting totaled about six months later when I lost control around a curvy road, slammed the rear passenger side into a telephone pole, and ejected myself into a ditch. Luckily, I only broke my collarbone and a couple of ribs. In that crash, I had lost the most important thing to me and my self-image simultaneously. I was no longer unique, and this caused massive waves of insecurity and depression.

However, all the beliefs and thoughts motivating that behavior appear ludicrous now. Most recently, I had an excellent-paying job, a wife, and two kids, and I had become an up-and-coming, responsible grown-up. Of course, that is no longer the truth, and now there's a crater where my most recent identity once stood. However, I can work towards getting that back because that's real life, not just kid think. The bike and the car weren't really who I was when I look back; I just thought they were at the time. My career and family were real at the time, but not so much now. To Eddie's point, what other things do I not even realize I believe that might be nothing more than a mirage tomorrow?

I went round and round like a hamster on a wheel, thinking, debating, and generally becoming confused. It would be easier to contemplate these things once I stabilized my life or got out of survival mode. Maybe it was time to put Eddie's bizarre philosophy on the shelf for later and focus on getting my feet back on the ground.

THIRTEEN

I awoke the following morning well past dawn, nine-twenty-two to be exact. I ended up with plenty of sleep after all. My mind was unusually calm. Maybe I wore it out thinking the night before, and it was broken down on the shoulder of some two-lane road somewhere, waiting for a tow.

I'd developed a routine of taking a shower once a week, whether I needed it or not. As it was the first day of the new job, I made an exception. Coffee first, though.

The building was unusually quiet. Most of the other tenants, I'm sure, had already completed their morning routines and were either on the bus or in their offices by now. There was also silence where the usual construction sounds were supposed to be and a not-to-be-believed lack of sirens or other street noise. The morning sun streamed in the window sideways, creating a warm contrast to the shadows in the kitchen. It felt like someone had hit the pause button on the TV, and you could closely examine the frozen frame, noticing another level of detail you usually wouldn't before hitting play again.

Seeing the dust dance and swim in the sunlight was more fascinating than I'd have typically considered. A whole other world of activity like a massive school of fish moving erratically but somehow with unified intent. I was aware of the sound of my breathing and not because I was struggling to catch my breath. It was simply quiet enough to actually hear it. I wasn't thinking any of this at the time, but merely observing. I wandered over to the coffee pot and put in a new filter and a few scoops of grounds, again without even thinking, probably out of habit. The rich texture of the coffee grounds and their woodsy and chocolatey scent were oddly fascinating. It was a nice treat to be undistracted and just appreciate being a part of my morning routine.

I poured a cup of coffee, pulled a chair in front of the window, propped my feet on the sill, and closed my eyes, simply bathing in the warm, quiet light. The only thought that crossed my mind was how lucky I felt to enjoy such a perfect cup of coffee.

The caffeine slowly reengaged my mind, and by the time the cup was empty, I was going back for another. I then started contemplating what to expect on my first day. I had picked up a couple of used pairs of jeans and polo shirts at the thrift store the day before to ensure comfort wouldn't be a neglected part of the game plan. It's funny that regardless of the job, pay, or prestige, the nervous excitement of the first day is the same, maybe even sweeter, when it's a job you can easily do. I was looking forward to something different and meeting new people. Perhaps I'd find a new friend or two along the way.

After a couple of hours of reading sports and news headlines, it was approaching noon, so I decided to go for a walk to kill time. As I was locking my apartment door behind me, I looked up to see Brian walking down the hall, his back to me, exhaling a giant puffy cloud of what I assumed to be nicotine vapor.

"Morning, Brian," I said.

Brian coughed, swung around wide-eyed, and shoved his vape pen into his pocket. "Top of the morning to you, Toby. Haven't seen you in a while. How are things?" he asked, quickly moving away from the scene of his vice as the cloud disseminated.

"Good and bad," I replied. "I'm starting a new job today so I can continue to pay the rent."

"That sounds great, partner. Congrats. What's the bad?"

"My good friends Eddie and Cowboy will have to move soon, which is depressing. They've added some much-needed character to this place. I understand you may have had something to do with it. Is that true?" Might as well get right to the heart of it.

"Well, they packed up and moved first thing this morning; sorry to inform you. The landlord said the tenants didn't like the looks of having a homeless guy right out front," he somewhat sheepishly let me know. He didn't seem to imply an awareness of which tenant it could have been. I felt fucking terrible. I suppose there could have been other complaints, but I'm sure mine contributed.

"Well, it pisses me off. No one wants to see the reality of the issue and they all figure *out of sight, out of mind*, so that they don't have to feel like shit every time they walk by and don't say a word or do anything to help out a person having hard times. People are fucked. Do you know where he moved to?"

"I'm sorry you feel that way, and I get it. Eddie wouldn't hurt a fly and never bothered anyone. He actually kept an eye on the place. If it makes you feel any better, I told the owner exactly that, but it didn't change his mind, and I'm just an employee. It sucked telling Eddie that he was going to have to relocate."

That made my general anger toward Brian subside a little. If he tried to vouch for Eddie, maybe he wasn't such a douche after all.

"Do you know where he moved to? I'd like to visit him," I asked.

"He said he found a place just four or five blocks away on 7th Ave, off Clement, I think."

"Thanks, Brian. I've got to go. See ya later."

"Well, despite that, make it a great day!" he said with vape-infused gusto.

I set out to find Eddie and Cowboy. Luckily, it wasn't that far. Once I got down Clement to 7th Ave, I took a right, and sure enough,

I spotted them about four buildings down in the doorway of the currently abandoned rec center.

"Eddie, despite your attempts to hide, I've already found you," I chirped, being sensitive to his unfortunate turn of events and feeling every bit the cock that I was for my part in his eviction.

Eddie was busy spreading stuff out, rigging his tarp, and getting his new home in order. It must have been nice not to have to arrange a moving van, haul furniture up a flight of stairs, and unpack a truckload of crap.

"Morning, Toby. I figured you'd find me soon enough. What do you think of the new place?"

"Looks great, and the overhang on that doorway will provide some shelter," I said, trying to find something positive to say. "However, I hate that it's five blocks from my place. I enjoyed seeing you guys every time I came and went."

"Hey, at least we're still in the neighborhood. Always nice to appreciate it from a different angle. Beautiful day today, huh? Matter of fact, a great day for the first day of a new job. I'll be eager to hear how it goes," he said.

"Well, I'll swing by in the next day or two for dinner and tell you all about it, if that's cool?"

"You bet; nothing like a dinner party to break in the new digs, right? Plus, it would be good for the new neighbors to see me interacting with a housed person without causing any problems. The neighbors tend to get a little bit nervous when I first show up on the scene."

"Excellent point. I'm out for a stroll, so I'll head on and let you guys get back to unpacking," I said, kneeling down to scratch Cowboy behind the ears for a minute. He then gave me a lick on the face, which I didn't much appreciate, so I turned and started down the street.

"Toby," Eddie called out. I turned around.

"Cowboy's never done that to anyone before besides me."

"Well, I must be part of the family now," I said with a laugh and continued on my way.

I decided that dogs are much more fun when someone else has to care for them. I did like Cowboy a lot. Maybe because Eddie had something to love that loved him back, making his life less lonely. I was indeed envious.

When I got back to the corner of Clement, I saw a man rolling shelves out of a business onto the sidewalk. Then I realized I was standing in front of that bookstore, The Green Apple, that Eddie had told me about. I figured, what the hell, and walked in.

It was a used bookstore with a library-like smell of old paper and dust. The shelves were crammed like sardines, and the aisles were barely wide enough for two people to pass. Boxes full of donated books were waiting on the counter to be shelved. There were occasional chairs here and there for a person to sit and read if they were so inclined.

"Can I help you find something?" a tall older man said from behind the counter. I imagine I appeared a bit lost just looking around in the entryway.

"Sure can. Looking for a book a friend recommended by a guy named something Dass. The title was like....*Being Now*?"

"A classic. I'm sure you are talking about *Be Here Now* by Ram Dass. We always have a few in the eastern spirituality section on the left side of the back wall. They're alphabetized by author," he explained.

I worked past a few other patrons thumbing through their finds and eventually reached the far back corner. Apparently, I arrived at the end of the alphabet. Alan Watts's books were staring me in the face. I started towards the other side of the wall, looking for the D's, and then I recalled that Eddie had quoted this Alan Watts character yesterday, so I returned to that section. He appeared to be a prolific writer, and there were quite a number of his books. I grabbed one and opened to a random page to get the gist of what philosophy he was selling. I had heard that if you open a book to a random page, sometimes exactly what you need will be right there. I had serious doubts but gave it a whirl anyway.

"The art of living...is neither careless drifting on the one hand nor fearful clinging to the past on the other. It consists in being sensitive to each moment, in regarding it as utterly new and unique, in having the mind open and wholly receptive."

That was certainly right in the wheelhouse of what Eddie was preaching. Then it dawned on me that Mr. Watts was also describing an experience not at all unlike the one I had upon waking earlier, watching the sun stream in the window, illuminating dust floating around in the air. In retrospect, I was experiencing that unique moment with an open mind. Shit, maybe the random page technique had some merit after all. I decided to pick out one of Alan's books and settled on *The Wisdom of Insecurity,* as my entire situation and psyche had become more than a bit insecure.

I worked my way down to the D's and found an entire shelf of Ram Dass books, four of which were *Be Here Now.* What a strange purple book, handwritten on recycled paper with drawings and diagrams. It looked like kind of a hack, but what did I know?

Both of these used books came to a grand total of $13.75. I doubted I'd ever read them, but maybe an occasional random page check could be fun.

AFTER RETURNING to my apartment and glancing in the bathroom mirror, I was rudely reminded that I was still really fat. I didn't think of myself as a fat guy, but the visual evidence showed the contrary, which spurred a short burst of motivation. Before it faded, I grabbed my dirty shorts off the floor and pondered if running in dirty shorts could prematurely age a man's anus. Deciding it was unlikely, I changed and went out for a run, determined not to overdo it this time.

Of course, I was down the block and around the corner when it became clear it was much windier than I had anticipated. I was not only freezing but already needed to take a walk break. I had a choice to make, and I opted for braving the elements versus heading straight back home into the warmth and safety of my apartment.

I ran by a father trying to negotiate his screaming toddler into a car seat in the back of a sky-blue Honda Accord. I wasn't sure if I missed those times or was relieved they had passed me by.

Eddie had mentioned that happiness is impermanent and relative, and this was a convincing illustration of that. The youngster was not happy one bit, evidenced by cries that indicated he was likely being burned alive. I slowed to a walk to watch this wrestling match unfold. Not wasting time, the father expertly manipulated the child's flailing arms under the shoulder straps and quickly clasped the straps together. The child seemed to promptly realize the unthinkable had happened, and further resistance would be futile. Accepting his fate, the little man shifted focus as if nothing had happened. "Daddy, will Jeff be at the park too?"

"You bet he will be, buddy."

"Yay! I want to go to the slide first!"

I was now quite cold and not too happy about it. However, I was pleased that I got my butt out the door. So, was I happy at that moment or not? I guess it just depends on which vantage point I took. I decided to keep thinking about how great it was that I was out there doing something about my physical condition and tried to avoid thinking about hypothermia as much as possible.

After a few more minutes of walking, I started to jog again. My mind immediately began to rationalize that it was better to eliminate all doubt of freezing to death with cramping legs and go straight home. It's funny how the mind does that. Was my body using my mind to protect itself from a repeat of the previous trauma? Or was there lurking laziness rearing its ugly head? Shit, two minutes ago, I was thrilled that I had made an effort to get out and exercise. So, which thoughts represented the truth of the situation?

Eddie had said he didn't much trust thoughts or feelings these days. This is probably why. Just because my mind was thinking something didn't make it true. However, what can a guy trust if he can't trust his thoughts or feelings? And which ones are worth trusting? Hitler probably thought by creating the perfect genetic race, he was saving the future of humanity. He probably believed that as much as I believed I was being promoted the day I was shit-canned from my job, just thoughts of imagined futures that fate was in no mood to deliver on. I was already winded, and I began another shameful walking break.

Thinking about the future, trying to create the reality we want, and hoping it agrees to play along was, in a way, similar to thinking about the past. I used to think I was a family man with a bright, attractive wife and kids. Then, some events transpired, and reality no longer agreed with my story. Of course, I conjured up a new story to make sense of the new world I'd found myself in. The marriage had been kind of shitty after all, and I just didn't see the signs or maybe didn't want to. Now I find myself with a new story about my shitty marriage, me being an absentee father and a divorced single male. Maybe Eddie was on to something when he said the past and the future only exist as thought constructs. Thoughts are used primarily to build a narrative around what has happened, what is happening, and what we anticipate will happen.

I was startled out of my contemplation by an electric garage door opening to my immediate left and realized a car was waiting for me to get my ass out of the driveway so it could pull in—time to start running again. I was now heading west toward the ocean on Lake Street and, unfortunately, directly into the wind. Man, I hated the wind. It fucked up everything from smoking cigars at picnics to hanging out on the beach. And now it was fucking up my run and, without a doubt, taunting me personally. Just as I started to warm up from the exercise, the wind began to strengthen to ensure I was just as cold as when I started. Wind is always mean that way. I decided to accept what I couldn't control and focus on what I could. I just kept moving because I surely couldn't control the wind. But what could I really control?

I couldn't control that I was fired. I couldn't control that Gina divorced me. I couldn't control that I was aging. If I could go back in time, I could have possibly controlled some choices that contributed to those outcomes. But I was merely acting based on what I thought I knew at the time. Or maybe that's bullshit, and life was destined to dance to its own tune. Eddie had talked about free will versus predestination. What if, based on my experiences, how my mind worked, and how I had been conditioned up to any point in my life, my reactions and choices were the only possible ones that could happen? For lack of a better example, a mouse getting caught in a mouse trap. The mouse is a hungry animal foraging for food. It smells some cheese and has always lived by finding the source of the smell and eating it if it *smelled* safe. Of course, it tries to eat the cheese and springs the trap, snapping its little spine and killing it. That seems like predestination. Theoretically, the mouse had a choice and could have passed by the trap, but its genetics and experience led to one logical outcome.

If things are playing out by simple laws of energy, both physical as well as mental and emotional, then what we think of as a choice could, in reality, indeed be just the resulting outcome of the physics of what was already set in motion. Then, our thoughts weave a story about our contributing decisions to make sense of them and make us feel like we are driving the bus. Could the illusion of control be there simply to provide temporary peace of mind?

It also occurred to me that I was not a fan of this concept because the potential truth of it frightened me. If we didn't control our choices, nobody would be accountable for their actions or feel any real responsibility for anything. For example, maybe Eddie was destined to have to move, and my complaint was just part of his destiny fulfilling itself. Although that made me feel better, along those lines of thinking, a person's total life experience would be reduced to just plain luck. That's when the twenty-dollar bill blew past me along the sidewalk. I stopped, turned around, and sprinted after it, eventually claiming my prize four houses down. I stood there victoriously, holding it in my hand. Could there have been another parallel universe where I just let it blow on by and kept running? I didn't even think about chasing it; it just happened. So, was that a choice, or was that stimulus and response predestined by my prior conditioning?

My mind was now more tired than my legs, and I didn't care to ponder the topic any longer. Since I was already moving back in the direction of home, I decided to quit while I was ahead and return with my bounty before overexerting myself. I just got paid $20 to go for a run.

CHAPTER

FOURTEEN

I arrived at The Altered Ego Salon five minutes early to flex my promptness. Babs was at the front desk talking to Carlotta. After some brief chit-chat, Babs went back to tend to a customer waiting to get her nails done. Carlotta and I reviewed the day's appointments, and she gave me a quick tutorial on the scheduling application. She then demonstrated how the credit card processing procedure worked, where to make coffee, how to restock the bottled water, and how to maintain the restroom. She was sweet enough to stay for the next two hours to ensure she could answer any questions as they came up before throwing me to the wolves.

"Carlotta, what would you say is the hardest part of the job?" I asked.

"Honestly, the job isn't that hard if you can chat up the customers while they wait. The hardest part for me is seeing those customers who are desperate to improve their appearance and are racked with insecurity about their looks. I know that whatever service we offer will only provide temporary relief. Sometimes, they would be better off investing in a therapist than a new bikini wax or a manicure."

That I could understand, having packed on a few pounds. "I get that. I imagine treating them as if they are attractive and being caring goes a long way."

"Right. A simple compliment may be the nicest thing anyone's said to them all week. If they choose to share anything about their personal life that you can ask about the next time they come in, it will make them feel like more of a friend than a customer," she added, tapping her index finger against her temple.

"Is there anywhere I can add notes to their records to remind me? I may not be able to remember much of what they might tell me since they will all be new to me. It would be great to refresh my memory before they arrive the next time." She showed me how to work the scheduling application and where I could enter notes.

I briefly met Jazmine and Jessica, both violently hot, and I immediately wished they were giving me any sort of treatment in a private room. Jazmine was a tall brunette with shoulder-length hair pulled into one of those messy buns. I've always been a sucker for brunettes with green eyes. She looked fit and was startlingly sexy, and I sensed she might be well aware of it.

"Perfunctory!" Jazmine exclaimed after introductions had been made.

"Jazmine seems to be passionate about broadening her vocabulary, Toby. I imagine this is her new word of the day," Jessica informed me. I replied with a slight nod.

"Ha! Good job," Jazmine said, popping her gum. "I bet you didn't catch his perfunctory nod, did you, Jessica?"

"So it means nodding your head?" Jessica asked.

"No, silly. It means with minimal effort. He gave a very subtle nod without much effort. A perfunctory nod, some would say." Punctuated with another snap of her gum.

"I can appreciate good wordplay. I won the regional spelling bee in the sixth grade," I informed them. "That was definitely when my life peaked."

"You're funny," Jessica said. "Be glad you had a peak. I'm still waiting, but it seems mine flat-lined shortly after birth."

Jessica was shorter, in the 5' 5" range, with straight dark red hair in a pixie cut and a sweet smile. She had a gymnast-type body—athletic but not much in the chest department. She was built for speed, as they say. It also appeared her eyebrows had been drawn on. It didn't look that bad, but after noticing it, I found it challenging to stop staring and wondering how bad they must have looked before she had to make the call to eliminate them and settle on this strategy.

They were both pleasant but were rushed between back-to-back appointments, and there was no more time for idle banter.

The routine seemed easy enough, and I immediately knew I'd be bored to death. However, I'd challenge myself to remember the names of all the customers despite my tendency to forget anyone's name within the first thirty seconds of meeting them. Seeing their name on the computer should make it much more manageable. I would try to ensure everyone felt welcome and essential, both as a customer and as a person. I practiced making small talk and complimenting customers when appropriate, especially if they had their nails done. Complementing a woman on how great her upper lip looked after having a faint mustache waxed off was a poor idea, no matter how dramatic the change was.

I wondered: if a guy came in and asked to have his butt-crack waxed, would they oblige? Being a hairy guy myself, I knew that taking a crap out of an unshorn ass is like shitting out of the top of your head; no matter how many wiping attempts follow, it's never clean, and eventually, a decision must be made as to what's "good enough." Well, perhaps my idea of "good enough," in reality, wasn't "good enough" at all and had culminated in a severely shit-stained bunker. A huge underserved market was ripe for the man-crack maintenance program! I'd have to broach the idea with Babs—but maybe not on my first day.

Carlotta left around 5 p.m. and told me I'd be fine, offering me her cell number should anything come up while everyone else was in with a customer.

I had to admit that it felt good doing something, anything, to pass the time. Before I knew it, eight o'clock came around, and Babs showed me the closing routine, which took all of about ten minutes. It consisted of reviewing the next day's appointments and sending reminder texts to the customers, emptying the trash, watering plants, turning out the lights, and locking up.

I locked the front door behind me and inhaled the cold, misty evening air. Gusts of wind swept the fog down the street like a giant broom. And of course I didn't have a jacket. I thought about jogging home, but remembered I needed to either focus on recovering from my earlier run or prepare for more crippling soreness. I elected to freeze instead, shivering in the new reality of being gainfully employed.

FIFTEEN

During the walk home, I reviewed the names of the customers who had come into the salon that day and could not recall a single one. As a matter of fact, it seemed I forgot them the moment they introduced themselves. Apparently, a growth area had reared its dunce-like head.

Of the twelve customers who came through the door during my shift, I was able to recall that three were men. I don't know why it took me off-guard, but it was probably because I'd never thought about going to a salon for any reason. At this precise moment, I was passing The Plow and decided to pop in for a pint to celebrate being back to work and because I had a legitimate response when someone would undoubtedly ask me what I'd been up to.

It's funny how good news is relative. Two years ago, if anyone had told me I'd be noticeably energized after my first day as a salon receptionist, I'd have bet everything I owned against it. After everything I'd been through over the last six to eight months, it now seemed exciting. Kind of similar to Eddie waking up grateful on the street each morning and realizing he still had a hand to move around and a body that it connected to. I guess there's some validity to that old saying, "It's not where you end up in life but how far you've traveled from where you started." In my case, maybe not from where I started but from where I'd recently been vacationing from my previous world. Perhaps I'd merely taken a sabbatical to examine life and figure out the next chapter. It seemed as good a story as any to frame my current situation.

I walked in and right past two strangers playing pool near the door. An overweight older gentleman with an impressive double comb-over was schooling a younger gentleman who looked suspiciously like him. The older man was sighting in his eight-ball shot. At the same time, his opponent had all his balls still on the table. I figured father and son or uncle and nephew. The thrill of the older man's impending victory, or perhaps just walking around the table, had stimulated his overactive sweat glands, and beads of perspiration glistened on his forehead. Equally as impressive were the expansive pit stains on his blue button-down shirt.

When I strolled up, Connor was behind the bar, and RV Jeff was seated in front, hard at work on a pint of Guinness. The rest of the bar was empty, but it was a Tuesday night, and it was not unusual for it to be slow.

I caught Connor's eye, and he greeted me energetically, "Hey, mate. What's news these days?"

"Funny you should ask. Just started my new job today," I proudly shared, curious what the reactions would be.

"Let me guess, gay hustler?" RV Jeff tactlessly asked. I wasn't expecting that, but the wonderful thing about RV Jeff is his complete lack of predictability.

"Bingo," I said. "Actually, one step up from that: a receptionist at The Altered Ego Salon."

They both stared at me, then at each other, with expressionless faces that indicated they had no idea what a suitable reply was.

"Well, if that's the type of job you want, I'm sure it's great," RV Jeff finally quipped.

"Ya'd be lucky to land a gig like that, Jeff," Connor said to remind

Jeff of his budding career that didn't exist and maybe prop up my rickety ego in one well-orchestrated maneuver.

"I'll let you know if another position opens up, Jeff," I said. "Connor, I'll have a shot of Patron and a Corona with a lime." I have always believed it's a smart idea to start with a "stinger" when you arrive at the party late and have some catching up to do, and a shot of Patron is always eager to help get the job done.

"Fruit in your beer, meat in your rear," Connor said, and although it was at least the hundredth time I had heard him say it, somehow, it was always just as funny. One could say timeless, except gay jokes were no longer politically correct, which technically removed it from the timeless category, leaving it right in the middle of the "still really funny" category. I wondered when all jokes would no longer be politically correct or funny anymore. People were more sensitive now than in the entire country's history. I call it "The Pussification of America."

"Thanks for reminding me of that. Make it two limes," I said.

I sat next to RV Jeff, and he immediately asked if I wanted to see something that would blow my mind—kind of a rhetorical question as to who could ever decline such an offer.

"Sure, but you better not be overmarketing it," I warned. It turned out he wasn't.

RV Jeff started flipping through pictures on his phone and finally found the one he was looking for.

"Check this out," He said.

After looking at what appeared to be a happy couple in their mid-to-late twenties, I asked, "Who are these people, Jeff?"

"That's Big Sallie and me!" he proudly exclaimed.

"Well, that must have been before she took on the "Big Sallie" handle because she's pretty skinny, and so were you," I said, giving his burgeoning gut a poke. "You guys are a good-looking couple, or at least were back then," I added to ensure he didn't think I was implying he may still be anywhere close to his prime.

"Hard to believe, we were in that kind of shape...well, I've got this gut now, but Sallie...is...just...ah, ah, a... BEAST!" RV exclaimed, validating everyone else's suspicions.

I was somehow relieved that he noticed her reckless demise and even more relieved he hadn't initiated their relationship at her current fitness level.

"Well, so am I," I pointed out. "It can happen to the best of us. I've packed on forty pounds without even trying my hardest, and I won't walk in front of a mirror without a shirt on anymore. So I can't throw any stones at beasts. But if you don't mind, I'll be referring to you as "The Beastmaster" from now on. Besides, better to be with a beast than a bitch, I always say." Which I had never actually said.

"Sallie seems to have a corner on that market, too, I'm afraid," RV said solemnly, punctuating his statement by gulping down his remaining beer.

"Then why do you stay with her, RV?" I asked, genuinely interested.

"She, more or less, puts up with my bullshit, is loyal, and is a Tasmanian Devil in the sack," he unfortunately uttered. I shuddered at the visual of what that may look like. RV remained looking down at the ghosts of years past displayed on his phone.

"It's kind of sad how we are all ultimately on the same path to ending up old and funny-looking," I pointed out.

"Look on the bright side, me lads," Connor said.

"Enlighten us," RV demanded.

"We're the youngest and the leanest we'll ever be the rest of our lives right here and right now. And as an added bonus, we have more hair now than we'll ever have. Now that's something to celebrate, lads," as he raised his glass for a toast. Connor was unusually animated and engaged tonight.

Connor's comments immediately depressed me more than the idea of Sallie muscle-fucking poor RV Jeff, but it was a good perspective. He was right about the age part and maybe even the leanest part (with respect to Jeff), but I'd be damned if I was going to accept that I would forever be a "heavy" man. "Stocky," maybe. "Solid" would be OK, but I was "heavy" and not fooling anyone. At this rate, they'd be calling me "Tubby Toby" in another month or two if I didn't stick to my running routine.

"Cheers to that!" RV exclaimed, surprisingly enthused by Connor's idea.

"Whatever," I replied, throwing back my tequila shot and washing it down with fruity beer.

At this point, Connor looked over at another patron taking a seat at the far side of the bar, "I don't suppose you want a beer with fruit in it?" he asked the woman.

I looked over to see who had arrived on the scene and was disappointed to see the annoying girl who had been working the jukebox the other night. I immediately slid my beer closer to Jeff on the off chance she may derive that I enjoyed meat in my rear.

"Oh, God no!" she said. "Citrus in your beer, fistus in your rear." Connor looked over at me, nodding his head as if to prove his point about my latent homosexuality. She seemed to appreciate sophomoric humor, so at least she had that going for her.

"Despite popular belief, I am a confident heterosexual," I announced, which garnered a lot of laughs, for better or worse.

Although she was pretty, it seemed she knew it. Her hair was straight, dark brown, down to the middle of her back, and she had a blemish-free olive complexion and dark green eyes, all of which contrasted nicely with her white silk blouse. She wore almost no make-up, probably because she didn't need it. Why wasn't she down in the Marina with all the hipsters? Or some other happening place? I guess it's harder to be looked over when everyone else looks the same, so you might as well go somewhere where you can feel special. There was something about her I didn't quite trust.

"I'll take a Tanqueray and tonic, Connor. No lime needed, just the good stuff," she said.

"Our mate here, Toby, is celebratin' his new job," Connor informed her.

"Congratulations, Toby," she said with a nod and a smile. "Tell me about this new gig?" I then realized it wasn't going to sound manly or even remotely impressive. I was about to unleash the "R" word (receptionist), then thought better of it.

When you are single, there are three types of people in a bar. People that are acceptable targets, potential obstacles to said targets, and the rest are irrelevant. I was on a freight train toward irrelevant. An overweight man, out of his prime, just landing a big receptionist gig was not remotely impressive.

"Circus tumbler," shot out of my mouth. Why did I care what this bimbo thought? Then I realized that I still cared what I thought, and when a stranger who doesn't know me is forming their opinion of me, opening up with 'receptionist' isn't something I was used to just yet.

"Thank God," she replied. "It's hard to find a good tumbler these days." She was indeed witty.

"I'm sorry, I didn't catch your name?" I asked.

"Oh...Jackie, but my friends call me Jax," she said.

"So, Jax, what kind of work do you do?"

"I work at the fabric store a few blocks down. Ever been there? You strike me as someone who sews his own clothes," she chuckled, her laughter breaking the tension. It was a relief since the last thing I wanted was for my attire (my new, thrifted work clothes) to resemble a failed DIY project. "Oops, couldn't help myself. My bad!"

Thankfully, the conversation pivoted from my embarrassingly grim job to my equally gloomy wardrobe. You know you're not at the top of your game when that's a lucky break.

Then, I did something stupid in an unconscious move to ensure the conversation didn't work its way back to my next shortcoming. "Hey, I'm going to plug some money into that jukebox before someone decides to fill it up with Irish songs. You want to join me and pick a few songs you like?"

"Nah, I'm good," she replied.

This was embarrassing, which, out of principle, made me mad. I was left with little choice but to follow through with my stated intention. I stood up and began my slow, shameful journey toward the jukebox. Jax suddenly passed me by, "Come on, I was just kidding," she said, tugging at my arm.

It turned out Jax was a classic 80s buff. Men Without Hats, Blondie, Billy Idol, Tears for Fears, Bon Jovi, and even a Wang Chung kicker to finish off our credits. She couldn't have been any older than her late twenties, and she probably didn't consider that I was in college in the 80s and this was my era.

We rejoined RV Jeff and Connor at the bar, discussing our favorite 80's artists and hits. It appeared she might have the underpinnings of a real personality. Something was still different about her. She came across as too familiar for not knowing me, and that didn't make sense. She certainly wasn't trying to pick me up; she wasn't an idiot. However, she dished out friendly jabs as you do with friends you've known for a while, not someone you just met. Maybe it was this presumptive familiarity that sat wrong.

"This is an Irish bar, folks, not a gay bar. There are plenty of those in the Castro. Yer goin' to drive the regulars out with this rubbish," Connor exclaimed more than half seriously.

"Too late," I said. "Seems like we're about the only ones here, and we are the regulars. You should view this as a regulars' retention strategy."

And there, the four of us sat for another few hours and rounds of drinks, laughing, insulting each other, and having a genuinely good time. I had been so consumed with my internal drama that I had forgotten what it felt like to be lost in the moment, laughing with friends. It was now approaching 10 p.m., and Jax announced she had to excuse herself since she had to work in the morning.

I stayed another ten minutes or so, finishing up my Corona, and announced I should be on my way as well and squared up with Connor. Surprisingly, when I stepped outside, Jax was still standing out front.

"Here, take this," she said, gently pressing a slip of paper into my hand. "It's my number, in case you feel like grabbing a drink or coffee together again sometime. No pressure, really. I hope I'm not being too forward. It's just that I genuinely enjoyed our conversation, and... well, it was simply really nice." She smiled, her eyes sparkling with a mix of vulnerability and hope.

I just stood there with my mouth ajar, trying to understand what was happening.

"I'm sorry if I just offended you..." she threw in, her smile transitioning into what looked like concern.

"No...no," I interrupted. "I would like to have coffee. I mean, I enjoy your company, and the fact you are beautiful in a completely natural kind of way doesn't hurt either, but why would you be interested in me? Honestly, I've got to have at least ten years on you, and I'm an impressively out-of-shape circus tumbler." I have no idea why I said any of that, but I was honestly curious because it seemed suspicious, like I was about to be made the butt of a joke. Either that, or she was just plain drunk.

"Look, Toby, I'm thirty-three, and I couldn't care less about age when it comes to genuine connection. I've been through enough dating experiences to realize that most guys are just self-absorbed jerks. But you, you're different. You have an incredible sense of humor; you don't take yourself too seriously. You've got a full head of hair, and, let's be honest, you're good-looking. Trust me, that's a rare combination. And your taste in music? Spot on," she said, flashing a warm smile. "But above all, it's your transparency that sets you apart. You're what we women call a unicorn, and trust me, I know. I constantly get hit on. That's why I come here after work, knowing it'll be quiet and all the cheesy guys will be down in the Marina looking for hookups. But when I sat down tonight, I knew that wasn't your agenda. You were here for the same reason I was—to have a beer with friends and unwind. I suppose I should stop talking now. Sorry, just a bit nervous."

"Well, that's about the nicest thing anyone's said to me in a long time. I'd be up to having coffee with you and a few laughs. It's pretty bold to initiate a conversation like this. Frankly, I wouldn't have had the guts."

"I know. That's why I mustered up the courage despite being a nervous wreck. And you know what else I know? I don't give a damn about your occupation. I mean, I work my butt off in a freaking fabric store, making minimum wage, believe it or not, and strangely enough, I actually enjoy it. I've come to realize it's not about what a person does but how they do it that truly matters. You can fill me in on the real story over a cup of coffee. How does tomorrow sound?" Her eyes sparkled with anticipation.

"Sounds great," I said. She was now close enough to me that I noticed she smelled faintly of vanilla, but not the stripper kind. "This better not be a fake number." A cab rounded the corner, and she flagged it down.

"It's the real deal, don't worry," she laughed, got in the cab, and disappeared. I just stood there looking confused. What the fuck just happened?

CHAPTER

SIXTEEN

There I was in my bed, again unable to sleep, recounting every bizarre detail of the evening. In hindsight, I was impressed by my clever banter and how enjoyable the whole conversation with Jax, RV Jeff, and Connor was. It was great having friends again, Eddie included, although a motley crew we were. Shit, I even had a dog friend.

Sleep was futile at that point, so I ambled in the dark towards the kitchen, slammed my shin into the garbage can, lost my footing, and landed with an aggressive thump on the kitchen floor. Rethinking my strategy and now toting an adrenalin-infused hyper-alertness, I managed to get to my feet and turn on the light while deducing I may still be drunk.

As I gulped down my glass of water, I caught a glimpse of a white plastic shopping bag—the kind that always ends up in the ocean wrapped around a baby seal's neck with the words "Green Apple" on the side. Now that I was wide awake with no idea what to do next, I figured I could carve a minute out of my busy night to explore this purple Ram Dass book. I flipped it open randomly, landed on page 51, and read the last three or four lines aloud.

"Can anyone imagine that a woman as full and seductive as that is not going to teach something? Is not going to continue to teach something?"

Well, that was relevant. Working my way up the page, it appeared this was a description referring to some "Divine Mother Kali," which must have been a Hindu or Buddhist God or someone else worthy enough for a "divine" classification. The illustration of Divine Mother Kali left a lot to be desired. She was your basic National Geographic aboriginal-looking woman in a full-frontal squat decorated with a necklace of skulls and a grass-type skirt. Instead of grass hanging down, it was hundreds of severed human arms. Her breasts were entirely exposed and very disappointing. Her head was a gargoyle-type face, topped with a skull and feather-laden ensemble. And, of course, a giant gaping vagina wide open with nothing but darkness inside, shockingly reminiscent of my own incredibly dark orifice. The visual was utterly disconnected from the description below it, which had initially caught my eye—Jesus, what a weird book.

"Can anyone imagine that a woman as full and seductive as that is not going to teach something? Is not going to continue to teach something?"

After recovering from the horror of my first glimpse of Divine Mother Kali's impressively large and terrifying cooch, I pondered the words. "Full and seductive." This did seem to describe Jax, assuming full didn't mean fat. I suppose Jax had taught me that I might not be a complete loser, at least not when viewed in a dark, seedy bar after a few drinks by a woman with nobody else to talk to. I had that going for me.

I'm sure Eddie would find this an opportune time to remind me that when patterns break, doors open. This evening challenged my lifelong habit of avoiding rejection at all costs. This left me with an uncomfortable awareness that I could have developed a few blind spots in my beliefs about who I had become. Through the massive amounts of adipose tissue and minimal career promise, she had miraculously unearthed something that she found attractive enough to want to see more of. Then it hit me.

My initial reaction to Jax was disdainful for the type of woman she was. I didn't trust her, and her comfortable, casual nature bothered me. Had I been building a rationalization of why I didn't find her attractive to convince myself I didn't care if she disapproved of me? It's hard to feel rejected if you aren't attracted to the person in the first place—kind of a psychological preemptive preservation exercise.

However, deep down, I feared that once the actual pieces of the puzzle of my true self replaced the temporary pieces Jax had filled in to create the picture she wanted to see, her then-certain rejection would result in a powerful reaffirmation that I was still an unsalvageable wreck of a man.

I put the book down immediately to eliminate the risk of accidentally glimpsing any additional pictures of nude Divine Kali family members.

I retreated to my bed and, surprisingly, slipped into a deep and undisturbed slumber.

CHAPTER
SEVENTEEN

The morning sun on my face gently tugged me back into conscious awareness.

My clock said 10:32 a.m., instigating an instant panic, sure that I was late for something important. Then I remembered I didn't have to work until 3 p.m., and all was well. I felt uniquely rested and energized. After some quick math, I figured I'd gotten about nine hours of sleep, which was miraculous compared to my usual six to seven.

I then remembered meeting Jax along with the rest of the details of the prior evening and was relieved it wasn't just my dream world teasing me. Finally, I recalled that I told her I would call her for coffee and had missed that window. She had said she had to work this morning and was undoubtedly already there, certainly reconsidering having passed me her number by now.

Was it too soon to consider myself to be dating? I certainly hadn't thought about it. I was in transition and, undisputedly, at a low point in my life— not a good foundation on which to build any relationship. Well, shit, I had nothing to lose. I punched the number she gave me into my phone and hit the dial button without any consideration whatsoever as to what I was going to say.

"This is Jax," she answered.

"Jax, this is Toby. I'm sorry I didn't call first thing to meet for coffee," followed by an awkward silence as I contemplated what to say next.

"No problem at all. I'm just glad you're up for it. What is your work schedule today?" Jax asked, her voice filled with what appeared to be genuine interest.

"Three to eight."

"I've got an idea then. How about we grab a coffee and a quick bite during my lunch break at 11:30?" Jax suggested. Her enthusiasm was contagious.

"Sure, that could work. Where should I meet you?" It dawned on me that she was talking about 11:30 a.m., precisely one hour from that moment.

"How about The Blue Danube?" she suggested.

"Done. See you then."

"Great. Bye for now," she said, ending the call.

I rushed the shower like a possessed middle linebacker blitzing through an open hole in the offensive line. I began an overly aggressive lathering in a subconscious effort to scrub away my general inadequacies.

Shortly after that, I was at The Blue Danube. I arrived seventeen minutes early in an attempt not to be a minute late. However long her lunch break might be, I wanted to ensure she didn't piss any of it away waiting around for me.

I quickly briefed Jimmy on the situation, getting his buy-in to position me in as favorable a light as possible should the slightest opportunity arise. Third-party character validation could go a long way if she developed any early doubts that her drunken first impressions may have been merely wrong-headed thinking.

In my college days, my dating strategy would have been simply "Get her and stick it in her." My current approach remained still undefined, which was admittedly reckless. I had no plan nor time to iron one out as Jax entered The Blue Danube five minutes early.

"Well, there she is," I alerted Jimmy.

"Holy shit, Toby, that's Jax," Jimmy whispered.

"What the fuck does that mean, Jimmy?" I asked, figuring you don't just say that without any backstory.

"No time now; let's reconvene later," he whispered.

"Hey there, Jax," I said with a wave and a smile.

"Hi, gentlemen. How goes it?" Jax said, returning the smile.

"Pretty good, today being a shower day and all. Jimmy and I were just catching up. Have you two met before?"

"Oh, I come in here all the time. Jimmy is one of my absolute favorite people, isn't that right, Jimmy?" Jax turned to Jimmy, her eyes twinkling mischievously as she playfully put him on the spot.

"I'd hope so," Jimmy said, laughing.

"I'll have a soymilk cappuccino and breakfast bagel, please, Jimmy," Jax said.

"Breakfast for lunch again, huh?" Jimmy asked.

"If nothing else, at least I'm consistent, right?" Jax remarked with a chuckle.

"Nice to be able to count on something. What will you have, Toby?" Jimmy asked.

"I'm going to deviate from my usual americano today for this auspicious occasion. How about a low-fat caramel latte with an order of avocado toast? Might as well go with the fancy stuff while it's still trendy, right?"

"You never know. You may come in and find it off the menu any day now. All right, fun seekers, find a spot, and I'll bring it out as soon as it's ready." Jimmy then retreated into the back to begin preparations.

Jax looked every bit as naturally pretty as she did the night before. She had decorated herself with a cream-colored mid-thigh-length sweater over black leggings and stylish black boots. She identified an open two-top table by the window, and I followed her over, and we sat down.

"Great to see you again," I said. "You look great. How's your day going so far?"

"Oh, thanks, Toby. The store has been keeping me on my toes this morning, busy enough to make the time fly by but not so much that it becomes overwhelming. One of the perks of working in retail is the unpredictability. You never quite know what to expect. How about you? How's your day so far?" she asked, appearing genuinely interested.

"Truth be told, my day's just getting going. I've been awake for almost an hour now and am looking forward to my first cup of coffee. It took me a while to get to sleep last night, but shockingly, I was able to sleep in."

"Well, thank you for calling me first thing. You sure know how to make a girl feel special," Jax replied, her smile radiating warmth. "So, tell me more about yourself. You mentioned on the phone that you work at 3 o'clock today. Indulge me and share where you actually work and what you do. Not that it matters much to me, but I'm just curious about what a day in your life looks like."

Well, right to the test. That didn't take long. The drinks in the bar the previous night had cast a spell on her that was soon to be broken like everything else in my life. However, something about her unguarded sincerity made me feel open and willing to reveal my less-than-glamorous reality. She had said she appreciated my trans- parency. I figured now would be as good time as any to put that to the test.

"Well, Jax, I can't say I'm proud of this new gig, but it's a gig, and a gig pays the rent. I am now one of the two receptionists at The Altered Ego Salon over on Divisidero. Today is day two, so I can't say I know the ins and outs yet, but it feels right, at least for now."

"Well, that sounds exciting. Have you been in that line of work for a while now?" she asked with genuine curiosity.

"This wasn't a part of my master plan. I was in high-tech, which I was growing to hate. Since I left that job, not voluntarily, I'll add, I now wholeheartedly loathe the thought of returning to the soul-sucking drudgery of selling software to large businesses so they can increase their profits while doing absolutely nothing for humanity. Sorry, perhaps I'm still a little bitter. Regardless, I was searching for something different, and this opportunity fell in my lap. I realize that's probably oversharing, but for better or worse, that seems to be my style these days."

Fuck, what was I thinking? I'm sure it was theoretically possible to paint an uglier picture if I tried, but it would be challenging, that's for sure. Then it dawned on me. If I wanted to find someone I could deeply connect with, and whether that was Jax or not, I had to put it all out on the table, even if it was an ugly dish. She may not like the entrée, but it was reality I was serving, and that was what she had ordered. Or at least that was the rationale I was going with.

"That's refreshing. This is the first time a guy I've just met didn't use his career as a cornerstone of his identity, which I think is fantastic. You are comfortable being that unguarded out of the gate, which is refreshing. I mean, that's how old friends talk, right?"

"I suppose," I lamely responded, a bit taken back by her appreciation.

"Seriously, solid friends are real and genuine around each other. I need that right now. Well, I suppose I always value that, but this early in knowing someone, that comfort level is uncommon is all I'm saying," she said, gently patting my hand. "It sounds like you are in the middle of a significant transition and making some courageous moves, leaving your ego at the door. Good for you. I sincerely mean that."

At this point, I nearly burst into tears. The fact that I hadn't scared the shit out of her with that was more of a relief than I expected. I honestly didn't know what I expected. Maybe I assumed once I disclosed my reality, she would view me the way I viewed myself, which wasn't the most glamorous work of art in the gallery, that's for sure.

"That feels good to hear, Jax. To be blunt, I don't know exactly what will happen next for me, but it will be different than before, and I'm tired of hiding from life like I have the past six months. I might as well throw the truth out, and you can decide if you like it or want to sprint for the door."

Just then, Jimmy arrived with our coffees. "Here you go. The food should be just a couple more minutes. So, how do you two know each other?" Jimmy asked, masterfully playing the role of the guy who didn't know the answer.

"We met at The Plow last night, and things clicked between us, but now he's just trying to scare me away," she said with a wink and a mischievous smile.

"Well, that would be a crying shame. Toby is like the brother everyone wished they had but never did. You could go a lifetime and never run across another guy like this," Jimmy said half-jokingly but fulfilling his mission flawlessly. "Looks like a potential match made in heaven." He patted Jax on the shoulder, turned around, and returned to the kitchen.

"Did you pay him to say that?" Jax said as a joke.

"I did ask him to put a good word in," I said, not joking.

"Maybe you're the brother he always wanted, considering he grew up with only a sister. He can be a bit overprotective of me sometimes, but I suppose that's what you expect from a big brother," Jax mused.

"Jesus Christ, Jax! Jimmy's your brother? Why didn't you say anything? Not that it would have made a difference." I didn't see this coming. Thank God I didn't tell Jimmy I met some bimbo that I was looking forward to banging like a screen door in a hurricane or perhaps something far worse.

"I wanted to get his impression because, honestly, I haven't always made the best choices when it comes to men," Jax confessed, a hint of vulnerability in her voice. "After dealing with a string of douchebags, Jimmy insisted on screening any potential suitors in the future. I can tell Jimmy likes you, or he would never have said that.

And to be honest, his endorsement means the world to me. I promised him I would give him ultimate veto power from here on out," Jax explained.

"Well, I better leave him a hell of a tip then."

"Couldn't hurt," she said with a wink. "What else can I ask you about yourself as long as I've got you on the ropes?" she inquired.

"There's plenty more, and it doesn't paint a pretty picture, Jax. I'm scratching myself out from underneath the clutches of rock bottom here, but things seem to be moving forward now, and I'm starting to get excited about life again. So what about you?"

"What about me?"

"Well, for starters, are there any other undercover relatives I should know about?"

"I wish it weren't the case, but it's just Jimmy and me. Our mom passed away when we were very young. I must have been three or four, and I don't have any real memories of her. Just a few fragmented images that I'm not sure are genuine or simply figments formed from the stories I've heard," Jax shared, her voice tinged with wistfulness. "Jimmy was six at the time and has a few actual memories of her. Our dad raised us, which couldn't have been easy—trying to work, be a parent, and manage the entire household. Unfortunately, he passed away a couple of years ago from lung cancer. He had been a smoker for as long as I can remember, but sixty-two is relatively young to take that final journey, if you catch my drift," she continued, letting out a soft laugh laced with a touch of sarcasm.

"I'm sorry to hear that. Were you close?"

"We were all very close. To be honest, I'm still in the process of healing from the loss," Jax admitted, a gentle vulnerability seeping into her voice. "But you know what? There's something exciting happening soon. I'm going to be an aunt." A glimmer of joy brightened her eyes.

"That's right, Jimmy's baby is due soon. I bet you can't wait."

"Exactly! It feels like the month before Christmas when it seems like it's never going to arrive," Jax replied, her voice filled with relatable anticipation. "As for my family, it's just Jimmy and me now, as I mentioned earlier. We've had our ups and downs, but we've always been there for each other. Jimmy is more than a brother to me; he's my rock." She spoke with a mix of fondness and gratitude for the bond she shared with her brother.

I decided to go with my childhood family and back burner the story of the family I recently blew up. It might be too soon to unveil that little nugget. Of course, I'm sure Jimmy would responsibly apprise her of the situation in short order, so what the hell. She's destined to find out sooner or later.

"Well, I was born a poor black child," quoting Steve Martin in *The Jerk*. "OK, that part isn't true."

"I saw that movie. Very funny."

"Who doesn't love Steve Martin, right? I was actually born over in Piedmont in the East Bay and lived there until I was about fifteen, when we moved to the city—only child. My Dad and I were never close. He was a kind man but wrapped up in his work, and we seldom did things as a family. Weekends were for yard work, laundry, house cleaning, etc. He taught English at the University of San Francisco. I think it was just hard to relate since I had no interest in literature, and he had no hobbies we could share. Teachers don't make much money, and things were always tight—no family vacations, few dinners out, and the occasional camping trip, which my Mom hated. My Mom was very insecure and overcompensated by being a total control freak. As a result, I spent as much time out of the house as I could growing up."

"Awe. That's too bad. That must have been tough."

"Surprising, not so much. Luckily, I had a great group of friends and a generally happy childhood. Like your dad, my mom died on the young side in her late sixties. She had early-onset Alzheimer's. My Dad insisted on taking care of her well past when she should have been in a memory care facility, and it nearly pushed him to a nervous breakdown and absolutely pushed him into alcoholism. He probably needed something to look forward to each day, and the booze was more than ready to step up and help. He changed after that. Started drinking more and acquired an extreme disdain for humanity. He's hard to stomach these days, except in small doses. As a father, I suppose he was more of a reference point for who I don't want to become than an example. But I still love the guy. He worked hard to support our family and later took care of my Mom. And he's still my Dad. Let me guess, more than you wanted to know?" Suddenly it appeared; I couldn't shut the fuck up. Why would I expose all that?

"You know what I find particularly fascinating, Toby?"

"I haven't even taken a sip of my coffee yet?"

"Well, that too, but you seem to have accepted all that shit about your folks and choose to see the good alongside the bad. Most people find the need to categorize everything into a 'good' bucket or a 'bad' bucket to simplify their life story. You aren't afraid to play in the gray areas," she said with a sense of wisdom and openness that I found amazingly attractive.

"Jax, the gray is my domain. Nobody's as good as they appear at their best or as bad as they appear at their worst, I suppose. That's one thing my Dad always told me when I was young whenever I was talking shit about someone. Maybe everyone is doing the best they can, given their circumstances."

"I think your Dad was on point there. If he left you with that one perspective, he did something impressive. Most people don't think that way."

"Don't get me wrong. My tendency is not to think that way. Sometimes, I remember to, but most of the time, I don't. I suppose I aspire to believe that, but I'm still struggling. And for the record, Dad would say these things almost as if he believed them or read them somewhere in a parenting handbook, but he also judged me based on his values and not my own. One thing was always clear: success could be measured, and you either made something of yourself or didn't, but the choice was yours. He was a master of contradictions."

"Toby, if you don't mind me asking...." Jax was starting to say when Jimmy arrived with our food. I now felt awkward, waiting for him to whip a gavel out of his apron, pound it on the table, and announce, "Case closed – the defendant is guilty of not being good enough," which I wouldn't be able to dispute. Gina and I never once had a conversation about my past that she willfully engaged in. It was probably because I was busy, like now, talking about myself, my next step, the next goal for our family, etc. No doubt, she had to tune me out to keep from hating my self-centered ass.

"One breakfast bagel for the lady and a fancy toast for the gentleman," Jimmy said as he deposited our food on the table. Jimmy smiled, sat down beside me, and, surprisedly, draped his arm over my shoulder. "Jax, this is my brother from another mother. Don't break his heart." Then he got up and walked away, still smiling. That's when I realized I was tearing up.

"Toby, are you crying?" Jax said as more of an accusation than an honest question.

"Sorry. I guess I'm touched and feeling pretty damn grateful right now. Sorry. I realize my lack of emotional control must be off-putting," I replied.

"I think it's adorable. My hunch was right; you are a sweet guy, Toby," she said, putting her hand over mine. I didn't know why I was so emotionally raw. Maybe it was Jax's way of creating a safe space where I felt like I could say anything, and somehow, she would be OK with it.

"Jax, people often see what they want to see. I don't want to help you paint a picture of me that I won't be able to live up to. In the spirit of full disclosure, I had another family." The cat was now out of the bag. Nowhere to go but soldier forward.

"Not a growing-up family but a grownup family; real wife and two young kids. I blew that up, not intentionally, but in retrospect, my self-absorbed reckless behavior caused it. I got fired from my job for having porn on my computer and sending an inappropriate but very funny email to a male coworker." This clarification seemed important, like it would magically position me out of being a possible sex offender, leaving me just another fucked-up guy. "Then my wife found out before I told her, causing her to divorce me under claims I couldn't be trusted and was a pervert. I hardly ever see my kids, and I've gained almost forty pounds and am pretty much broke, living in a shitty one-bedroom apartment. So, there's all the ugly to offset the good you may see in me. Kind of shocking that I just said all that out loud."

"Wow, there's definitely a lot going on there. But hey, you're on the comeback trail. You have a new job, and although it may not be your dream job, you hated your old job anyway. And you know what else?"

"No."

"You have a girl sitting here who is genuinely interested in you," Jax declared, her eyes piercing with sincerity as she held my gaze. The intensity of her words made me feel vulnerable; a mix of naked-ness and fear washed over me. "And I understand that it must be difficult not being able to see your kids."

"Hell yes, it is! That's the hardest part. But the uncertainty around the kids is the worst part."

"Uncertainty?" she asked, leaning forward in her chair.

"Well, she's claiming I'm an unfit father with a porn addiction and no job, which is partially true. So she wants full custody of the kids for visitation and all decision-making about absolutely every-thing. Mediation didn't work out, so now we have to go to court to have a judge decide."

"Jesus, that sounds tough. I'm sorry you're going through all of that," Jax expressed, her voice filled with genuine sympathy. She reached out and gently patted my hand, offering a comforting gesture. "On another note, you're really into porn, huh?" she asked, her tone lighthearted and teasing, trying to shift the conversation to a lighter topic.

"Kind of... I was. This doesn't sound good. The reality is a coworker friend of mine and I would take turns trying to find exam-ples so offensive that we couldn't help but shock each other. It ended up becoming quite a competition over the years until we were caught because we were stupidly sharing our most recent outlandish finds on work email. So yes, I was into porn, but I wasn't jerking off to it."

"Kind of like Bill Clinton smoking pot but not inhaling?"

"OK, occasionally, I'd *inhale*, but not to the really gross shit. But, for the record, I gave it up entirely after I lost my job. I'm more of a recovered porn addict, if that helps?"

"Let's just say you're in transition, and lucky for you, regardless of who you were or may turn out to be, you're a remarkably self-aware guy," she said so sweetly that the whole thing suddenly smelled like a set-up, another cosmic joke at my expense. "I'm serious, Toby, and I have a truckload of my own shit too."

"I would certainly like to hear about it and take a break from unloading my truckload and talking about myself, which is a horrible habit I am trying to break."

"You got your seatbelt buckled?"

What could be that bad? Frankly, I didn't care. I wanted to humanize this woman to reduce the massive inequity in our overall goodness.

"Let it rip!"

"I have a habit of dating losers, present company excluded. And just so we're clear, this does count as a date," Jax clarified, her words carrying a mixture of vulnerability and honesty. "I was forward with you outside the bar because I sensed it might be a rare chance to have a real shot with a decent guy. In the past, I dated losers because, deep down, I knew it wouldn't last. I wasn't ready for a committed relationship. It felt like...I don't know... too much responsibility, especially given the other issues I was dealing with. So, I would let the relationship drag on until those losers would eventually annoy me enough that I'd end it, often causing them a great deal of pain. It's sick, really. I knew from the start how things would unfold, yet I went along with it. It was selfish and cruel." She paused briefly, staring directly into my eyes. "But now, with the help of my therapist, I've started to recognize these patterns. And you, you're breaking that pattern. It's both scary and incredibly refreshing. See, to avoid the risk of rejection from the type of people I truly wanted to date, I'd date the kind of men who I didn't care if it didn't work out."

"Jax, you seem to be awfully self-aware yourself. I get what you're saying. My friend Eddie says, 'Life is a series of interlocking patterns until they break, and when patterns break, doors open. That's when to pay attention, because it's the most exciting part, and you don't want to miss the open doors.' It's turning out to be the case for me, at least this last week, with the new job and meeting you."

"That's a great perspective. I'll keep that in mind. There's another thing I need to share with you because I owe it to you upfront. You need to be aware of what you might be getting yourself into. I'm impulsive by nature and crave new experiences. That sounds good enough, but it resulted in me dabbling in drugs, mainly cocaine and some molly. Then, I more than dabbled. Then, before I knew it, I was addicted to heroin. Jimmy saved my life. Three rehab appearances and two abortions later, I've been clean for eighteen months now. When Jimmy just now joked about not breaking your heart, he wasn't joking at all. It was a not-so-subtle warning because he seems to care about you. So, you are taking a risk here, and sharing this is very scary for me. If I were you, dealing with everything you're going through, I wouldn't want to take on any more risks right now. I would rather have you be honest and leave now. It's too easy to be nice, not say anything, and know it's a matter of time before you break the bad news to me." Jax's voice quivered slightly, her fears laid bare.

She then started to cry. What a broken and emotional pair we were turning out to be. This was turning into a hell of a surreal first date. Both parties share the depth of their neuroses in failed attempts to scare the other off sooner rather than later.

The place was now packed, and people were starting to take an interest, but neither of us seemed bothered by this. We were both scared, hopeful, and trying our best to break the patterns that had ruined our lives up to that point, which, I'm happy to point out, is way more difficult than one would think.

I felt like an asshole because I was relieved and a tiny bit happy to hear all this. In a way, it made us more equal, or at least we shared a similar journey. She was probably so compassionate and accepting because she was working to develop compassion and acceptance for herself as a part of her recovery. People who have been in dark places can meet other people there with a fundamental understanding. I think that's when I started to fall in love with her.

"Jax, everyone's got their shit, but nobody talks about it. People post pictures on social media of all the highs in their life and call up friends to share the good news, but nobody posts 'I'm lost right now' or 'I don't like who I am' or 'I'm scared shitless.' As a result, nobody knows anybody anymore because they don't share the inner half of their life, where the real struggles, sleepless nights, and fears live, waiting to seize the first opportunity to take control when we least expect it." I'd never actually thought about this before. I was again watching myself talk and surprising myself with accidental coherency.

Coincidentally, we also both demonstrated an impressive ability to talk with our mouths full.

"Hey, I know you've got to get going as it's almost 1 o'clock. I'll take care of the bill. When can I see you again?" I asked, trying to strike while the iron was still hot.

The demure smile on her face contrasted with the tears running down her cheeks as she tightened her grip on my hand. "I'd prefer sooner than later."

"Well, I get off work at eight and was thinking about surprising a couple of friends with dinner at their place. One of them means a lot to me, and if you're up for it, I'd like to introduce you. What do you say?"

"In!"

"Let's meet at The Plow for a stinger at 8:15, stop by the store for supplies, and head over to their place at, say, 9:00. Is that too late?"

"Works for me. I'm sorry I have to run, but you have no idea how much better I feel right now, Toby," she said, standing up. Then she bent down and gave me an intense kiss right on the mouth. Not any sort of tongue-waggling kiss. Just heartfelt. I could taste the salt from her tears on her warm lips and smell that same faint vanilla from whatever product originated it. The physical affection I didn't realize I'd been craving left me stunned, my head swimming in the details of our conversation that I knew I would be processing the rest of the day. "Can't wait to see you tonight, and thanks for lunch!" she said as she got up and departed.

Jimmy, of course, immediately descended on the table, helping himself to a seat. "Well, it seems you've already made my sister cry, but from over there, it looked like a positive cry, if that's a thing."

"Jimmy, an internal journey through hell can be a lonely one. I know that from experience, and it seems like Jax does too. The nice thing is, she's not afraid to talk about it."

Jimmy leaned across the table and administered a bear hug without saying a word.

"Check, please?" I said to provide levity. I looked up to realize that at least two-thirds of the patrons had now been sucked into all the drama and were eagerly awaiting what would happen next. I decided to add a final scene to their show, pulling them directly into the act. "And what the hell are you all looking at?" Which I thought was a fair question. And with that, everyone was, all at once, doing an excellent job of minding their own business again.

CHAPTER

EIGHTEEN

T t was now 8 p.m., and I was leaving work, which still sounded bizarre. My second day was a carbon copy of the first, but it went by fast, and I met a variety of characters, all dedicated to tidying up their appearances.

When I arrived at The Plow, Jax was already there, sitting at the bar with RV Jeff. It seemed absurd that having known her for barely a day, we both knew each other's family background, insecurities, and dark sides and had started to develop an empathetic affinity for each other's plights. That usually takes weeks, if not months. I was now beginning to second-guess everything I felt and how fast I had let things evolve. I needed to put the brakes on, or I would lament that I should have seen the warning signs early but was too reckless to avoid getting in too deep too fast.

Jax spotted me immediately and got up to greet me with a hug that terminated with her arm remaining around my waist.

RV Jeff had shaved his head, and he looked ridiculous bald. My eyebrows rose to maximum height and securely locked themselves in that position. I couldn't not acknowledge his makeover.

"Jeff, it seems you shaved your head. Is this a midlife crisis or what?" Not nice, but when you do something that rash, you must expect others to notice.

"Bald eagle, baby!" RV responded with confidence.

"Jeff, you have an impressively huge melon. I suppose that could motivate a guy to flex his cranial dominance," I exclaimed, curious if he would take it as a compliment or decide these were fighting words.

"Fascinating, huh?" he said with a sly nod, causing involuntary laughter on my part.

"If you ask me, RV, I'd say your new style is kind of like walking down a nude beach with a boner. You don't look quite as good as you feel," Connor added.

"I wouldn't know about that. Jackass!" Jeff blurted, rolling his eyes.

"Jeff, now you will need to wear hats to keep your melon warm. Of course, they will have to be specially ordered in your size and could be more expensive due to all the extra fabric required," I pointed out.

"Tell me about it. When I was a freshman in high school, the same thing happened in football. None of the helmets fit. They special ordered me an XXL, and I had to play the first three games without one while waiting for it to arrive."

"Well, that explains a lot," which it did. "What's the real story here, Jeff?" I inquired.

"Truth?"

"Why not, for novelty's sake."

"Large patches got ripped out in a scuffle with the garbage man this morning. It was unsalvageable, so I took it down to the studs," he said, patting the top of his head.

RV Jeff was a walking fistfight, looking for an opportunity to manifest. Somehow, I didn't doubt a word he said. His ridiculously large, exposed head left all his features crammed into the lower half of his face, gifting him an alien-like appearance. Jax and Connor appeared to be immensely enjoying this exchange.

"Toby, I imagine you're OK with anything with fruit in it?" Connor asked.

"The fruitier, the better, mate! How about a Mai Tai?"

"'Fraid not. Never served one. Never will. A proprietor must have standards."

"Fine then. Shot of Patron and a Corona with the juiciest lime you've got."

Jax ordered a gin and tonic and went over to pound credits into the jukebox, and I took full advantage of the opportunity to observe her perfect ass stroll across the floor. I collected myself and saddled up at the bar to see Connor and Jeff silent and staring at me, waiting for an explanation for how I had hoodwinked a woman of Jax's caliber, given my lack of anything to offer in return.

"I'm as shocked as you are. Believe me, guys. I think it must be my new high-power job."

"In that case, I'm stopping by to apply tomorrow," Connor said.

Jax returned as Spandau Ballet's *Round and Round* began to play. I raised my shot. "Here's to looking at Jeff's colossal dome," I offered and downed my shot.

"I'll drink to that all night long," Jeff said and chugged the last half of his Guinness, spilling more than a little down his shirt.

"Toby and I are one and done here tonight. Got dinner plans, so don't take it personally, boys," Jax said, imbibing a generous sip of her drink.

"Great, we have to sit here in the aftermath, listening to the garbage you just put on the jukebox?" Connor said, shaking his head.

"Connor, I truly think it's an exposure issue. Give us a few more weeks, and you'll be plugging the jukebox with 80's music. If you'd like, I can show you all the right dance moves to accompany it," Jax offered with playful enthusiasm.

"I'd rather take a beating than listen to another verse," Connor said, pouring himself a shot of Jamison's and downing it in one beautiful, seamless motion. Alcohol was Connor's medium; he worked with it like Michelangelo with paint.

I looked at Jax, "Shall we?" We pounded our drinks, and I told Connor to put it on my tab as we made our way to the door.

"Does he really let you run a tab here?" she asked.

"I don't know. Felt it was worth a try, and there didn't seem to be any objection."

We made our way down to the corner market to get the dinner fixings. "Jax, my friend Eddie and I are simple men. We usually eat chili right out of the can and drink Tecate because it's Eddie's favorite. You may want to veer from the menu to find something palatable, and I assure you neither of us will be offended."

"When in Rome," she said as we proceeded to the canned goods section, collected three cans of the Dennison's, and then grabbed three 24-oz Tecates. "I thought we were meeting a couple of friends?" she asked.

"Shit, you're right. Other guy's a bit strange," and I grabbed a box of Milk Bones while a confused look crossed her face.

I purposefully kept her in the dark about what she was about to walk into, just out of curiosity about how she would react when we sat down with a homeless guy and his dog for dinner. Maybe that was mean, but I was curious, and now she was too.

As we made our way down the block, she leaned into me and put her arm around my waist again; I responded in kind. We said nothing. For the first time since I could remember, the world was on my side again. Maybe I'd hold off pumping the brakes on the relationship a little longer.

A couple of minutes later, we rounded the corner onto 7th Ave, and I could see Cowboy sitting on some sort of makeshift dog bed. He spied us immediately, bum-rushed me, and excitedly started jumping up, his paws dangerously close to my crotch. I knelt down to his level and administered some ear scritches.

"Jax, this is Cowboy," I said and wrestled open the Milk-Bone box. Cowboy caught a whiff and immediately took on a textbook dog-sitting posture. Eddie had him well-trained. I gave Cowboy a

Milk Bone, and he hurried over to his bed/mat thing and began devouring it.

"Nice to meet you, Cowboy," Jax said, Cowboy paying her no attention.

A few steps later, Eddie came into view.

"Figured it was you, Toby. You're the only person Cowboy would leave our little camp to greet like that," he said.

"Honored by that, Eddie. So, Eddie, meet Jax. She's a friend of mine."

"Nice to meet you, Jax. How do you know this kind young man?"

"Nice to meet you too, Eddie. We met last night down at The Plow," Jax said, extending her hand to Eddie, who responded with a robust handshake.

"The Plow...where all good things begin and often end. I hope he was a gentleman and paid for your drinks," Eddie said as the edges of his mouth curled up into a grin.

"I squared up and left last night before he even had a chance. But just now, he did. We ended up celebrating his new job with Connor and RV Jeff. You know those guys?" she asked.

"Connor and I go way back. Hard not to know who RV Jeff is if you've been in this neighborhood for more than a few weeks. He has a way of being heard." Eddie was accurate. I was surprised to hear he had known Connor for some time.

"That he does. Got to love 'em," Jax said, shaking her head from side to side.

"Eddie, I'm not afraid to say, Jax and I only met last night, and I already feel like I've known her for years," putting my arm around her.

"Destiny is funny that way sometimes, isn't it?" he asked.

"Luck...destiny...to each his own, I suppose. We brought dinner from our usual place. You eaten yet?" I asked.

"Not since breakfast. Perfect timing. Dessert should be ready in about twenty minutes. I was going to forgo the entrée tonight, but not if it's our favorite."

"What's for dessert? Jax asked eagerly.

"Cinnamon rolls! Cowboy's and my guilty pleasure."

"How the hell are you cooking cinnamon rolls out here, Eddie?" I asked. He didn't seem to have a recognizable kitchen.

"Usually, the camp stove, but not tonight. We busted out the Dutch oven. Just fire up a small pile of coals and put some on the bottom and a few more on top of the thing, and bam!" he said, pointing to exactly what he described tucked back in the corner of the doorway. Luckily, the building was made of cinderblock.

"Seems reasonable," I acknowledged.

"Why don't you guys pull up a couple of chairs, and we can get started?" Eddie offered, pointing to an open area of cement. Eddie started rummaging for the can opener in a plastic bag that also contained plastic silverware and paper napkins. He eventually retrieved what he was after.

"I'll do that," Jax said, reaching for the can opener," which Eddie handed her.

Jax proceeded to open all three cans effortlessly and set them out in the middle of our little powwow.

"Why am I the only one that can't seem to use a fucking can opener?" I asked, honestly frustrated.

"Destiny is funny that way sometimes, isn't it?" Jax so kindly pointed out, to Eddie's visual amusement.

"Touché," was all I could say.

"Hot or cold, guys? We've got coals going," Eddie asked.

"I'll take mine hot," Jax said.

"I'm good cold, Eddie," I answered.

Eddie took two cans over and set them on top of the coals on top of the Dutch oven, stirring them every now and then. I cracked open the beers, handing one to Jax, and walked the other over to Eddie in the kitchen. What a funny situation. I was eating chili out of the can on the streets of San Francisco with my new possible girlfriend, whom I'd known for a day, my homeless friend, and his dog. Even funnier, there was no place I could imagine I'd rather be.

"Eddie, what are your thoughts on destiny?" Jax inquired, her voice filled with genuine curiosity. "You mentioned it being a funny thing a little while ago. I'm interested to hear your perspective." She leaned in slightly, giving Eddie her full attention.

"The only thing it can ever be. This very moment," he replied without taking his eyes off the chili.

"That's beautiful, Eddie," Jax said, smiling her sweet, sincere smile.

"Eddie, destiny implies a predetermined future as well. What about that?" I asked.

"Does it?"

"Well, of course, it does. Am I missing something here?"

"The future is a concept. Destiny is now. Sure, some patterns tend to repeat. But then again, as we've discussed, all patterns eventually break down, and things always change. That's the best part," Eddie said.

"That makes sense to me, Eddie," Jax responded. "But you have to trust that process, or you're always waiting for the other shoe to drop, right?"

"What's not to trust?" he asked.

"Oh...I don't know, Eddie," I said. "That life will kick you in the sack with a steel-toed boot if you aren't careful. My life came crumbling down just as I started to trust that everything was proceeding according to plan." Maybe a homeless guy has no choice but to trust or possibly hope everything will change and hopefully for the better. "Jax has had her fair share of adversity as well. For some of us, trusting life can be like trusting an abusive parent."

"Tell me about it. Toby, I know that's a hard concept. Everyone, especially the religious types, run around talking about God having a plan, surrendering to Jesus, and a lot of other horseshit. However, it mostly comes from a place of fear," he explained.

"Fear of what?" Jax asked.

"Most people seldom trust things will unfold how they want but want to feel there is a good reason for how things unfold. Let me ask you this, Toby, and be honest. If, by your definition, your life hadn't deviated from your plan, you hadn't lost your family and your job, would you agree you wouldn't have met Connor, myself, Cowboy, Jax, and RV Jeff?"

"That would be correct," I responded.

"Would you have been better off?" he asked.

I didn't reply. I hadn't considered this. Sure, I was broke, but my new job wasn't stressful. Jax was a blessing. Eddie was opening my mind like the can I couldn't open on my own, which was unnerving but at least drove a curiosity to explore different perspectives. Jax was looking at me, curiously awaiting my answer.

"Don't think about it, Toby. Just answer," Eddie said.

"No, I wouldn't have changed a thing. I could not happily go back to my old life." There it was. I hadn't thought it, but I said it, and it felt true. Jax reached over and squeezed my hand.

"So life took a surprise left turn for you down a dimly lit road that you'd never traveled before, and didn't particularly ask you what you thought about it. It dropped you into a different 'now' you weren't expecting. But, as you admit, it's a 'now' you didn't know you may be better off in. You experienced some pain, but what little you've learned so far allowed you to appreciate this specific moment, and you can't think of any place you'd rather be."

"I didn't say the last part, Eddie."

"But you were thinking it a minute ago," he pointed out.

"Yeah, but.... OK...so I was." Good guess on his part, but slightly creepy.

"Were you really thinking that, Toby?" Jax asked.

"Yes, in fact, I was." Her eyes were tearing up, and she hugged me and rested her head on my shoulder for a few seconds.

"Good," she whispered.

"What's not to trust?" Eddie asked as more of an exclamation point to end the conversation. "Our dinner is ready, Jax."

My mind, like a dead car battery, had become lifeless as well as useless. It needed a jump, and I didn't have any cables. I sat there staring at Cowboy, then at the Dutch oven, and over to Jax. I was not thinking, just being there, still remarkably content.

I dug into my can of chili, which tasted far better than usual.

"Eddie, I completely agree with everything you're saying," Jax said. "My path hasn't been all rainbows and butterflies, but it led me here, and maybe.... Well, actually, it feels right. But, for the longest time, I didn't trust things would ever be right. I almost drove myself insane trying to make sense of it all. Do you think I wouldn't have been so scared if I had trusted the whole process?" she asked with sincerity.

"Fear results from thinking you are separate from life and that life is something that happens to you rather than something you are part of. Trust is not for those with timid souls, Jax. To answer your question, yes. You wouldn't have been scared at all. You are life. It's all one inseparable thing," he said, holding up his index finger. "Or maybe I'm wrong. That happens occasionally," he said, giving her a wink.

I was now attacking my chili like a rabid dog, barely hearing what they were saying and still not thinking a damned thing—just eating chili. Then I came to.

"Eddie, I hope you don't mind; I gave Cowboy a Milk Bone," I informed him.

"Healthier for him than the Slim Jims he got into earlier today. It's fine, don't give him very many. I don't want him to get fat. The vet says dogs can get diabetes just like us if they gain too much weight. Plus, he needs to save room for dessert."

"Who knew? Dogs get diabetes," I said, tossing Cowboy another Milk-Bone.

Eddie went over to check on the cinnamon rolls and proclaimed they were also ready. He took the Dutch oven off the coals and removed the lid. "Smell that, boys and girls. Better let them cool down for a few minutes."

We finished our chili and continued to work on our giant beers. Jax got up and collected the chili cans, and Eddie pointed to a trash bag tied to the front of his shopping cart. "We keep the forks, even though they're plastic," he said, collecting them and setting them over by the Dutch oven.

"Eddie, if you don't mind me asking, and I don't know your story, are you happy with your life now? You seem like a very content soul," Jax asked. It was a personal question to ask a homeless guy, but she sounded very sensitive. I knew his answer already.

"Luckiest man alive," he responded.

We finished up dessert, and Eddie refused to let us help clean up, so we played tug with Cowboy while he scrubbed out his Dutch oven. Shortly afterward, we said our goodbyes and headed out.

CHAPTER
NINETEEN

"Thanks for meeting Eddie," I said to Jax as we walked down the street holding hands.

"Thanks for bringing me along. I can see why he's your friend, Toby—very insightful guy. I don't know what I expected when I first saw him, but it wasn't that. He gave me a lot to think about."

"He's always that way."

"How did you first meet him?"

"Cowboy and Eddie were living right next to my apartment building over on 2nd Ave. I'd say 'hi' as I came and went. Then, one night, I stopped by the corner store we were at earlier and picked up a couple of Tecates because I had seen him drinking one a day or two before. We shared a drink and got to know each other. He's one of those guys who hangs out with you because he wants to know you, not because he wants anything from you. He's never asked me for any money. Makes his own. I even offered to let them stay in my apartment, and he'd have none of it. I guess he grounds me, and I've needed that lately. Can't help but love the guy, and Cowboy's starting to grow on me too. Dog never leaves his side, except now when he sees me coming."

"Why did you decide to introduce me to him so shortly after we just met? Most guys wait until at least the third date to bring a girl into their homeless network," she asked.

"I don't know. Didn't think about it until I asked if you wanted to come."

"Well, I'm glad you did. Thank you," she said, leaning closer and putting her arm around me.

"Happy it worked out. Maybe I wanted to see how you'd react to me hanging out with the homeless. Subconsciously, I suppose, I knew, right now, I need Eddie's friendship, and maybe I thought if you were appalled, there was a risk to that friendship. Then I'd be in a tough place, and it would be easier to decide how to deal with that sooner rather than later. You surprised me."

"Why, because I adore the guy? He loves you, Toby. People don't talk about the nature of personal reality, destiny, and trust with just anyone. When we were walking away, I looked back, and he was sitting there, holding Cowboy in his lap, watching us, and smiling a big-ass smile. He is happy for you."

"I hope so because I'm happy for me right now, too," I said. "Some of what he says seems like a bit much, but I've never talked about that stuff with anyone before. I'd never even started pondering it until I met Eddie. In some ways, he's kind of Dad-like, don't you think?"

"I do think. The kind of Dad you wish you'd had, huh?"

"Yep," I answered, realizing how right she was.

"What about Cowboy?"

"Had a dog once as a kid. Didn't work out so well, but Cowboy's bringing me around. It's also different when it's someone else's dog."

"Well, I'm glad they have each other," she said, leaning her head on my shoulder.

"Me too."

"And Toby," she said, stopping and turning to face me. "I'm glad we stumbled across each other."

The next thing I knew, our mouths were smashed together, tasting each other as our tongues danced between our lips. Her hand found the back of my head, and she wasn't going to let me pull away, and I had no intention of doing so anyway. God, her lips were soft, warm, and welcoming. Her chest was now pressed aggressively against mine, and I could feel the gentle firmness of her athletic figure.

Unfortunately, at that exact moment, a kid on a skateboard rounded the corner and almost collided with us. "Get a fucking room," he yelled and proceeded recklessly down the sidewalk with his pants hanging halfway down his ass and, unbelievably, holding their position.

"Kid's got a point," Jax said. "I live all the way out in the Outer Richmond. How do you feel about showing me your place?"

"I feel like it's not clean, it isn't pretty, you'll be disgusted, and we better hurry up and get there as fast as possible."

We arrived at my apartment door after a five-minute walk packed with ass groping and excessive making out. It's a miracle we were able to find our way there. After what seemed like hours of rummaging around the full erection in my pocket, I was able to locate my key, and we were inside what could be confused with a college dorm room.

"Home sweet home. What do you think?" I asked. It was essential to get her reaction out of the way so I wouldn't wonder what she thought about my pathetic pad throughout whatever might soon transpire.

"It's bigger than my place. The furniture is dated, but it's much better than I expected from your description," she said, shoving her open lips against mine. She simultaneously kicked her shoes off and slipped her hand over my loins, igniting a fatal surge of excitement.

"Oops," I uttered as I pulled away from her kiss.

"Oops?"

"More of an 'over oops.'"

We both looked down to witness the darkening denim expand to about the size of a silver dollar, marking the precise location of where the sophomoric crime had just been committed.

"Wait. Jax...I haven't been with a woman for over eight months, and the dam holding back a river of pent-up lust just...well...failed, so to speak."

"Now that we've taken the edge off, kiss me while we wait for the recharge," she whispered with a pride-infused smile as she kissed me again, steering me towards the bedroom without breaking oral contact.

Within moments, her clothes had mysteriously vanished. Her dark complexion created a uniform full-body tanned look, accentuating her athletically toned thighs and flat stomach. Her white satin bra and matching thong-styled underwear remained on, leaving the main reveal for the second act. All that aside, I had always had a fetish for well-toned arms, shoulders, and back. An athletic woman in a tank top always did it for me, regardless of what was happening with the rest of her body. And Jax had been blessed with every aspect of these vital physical elements.

What I had failed to consider was that when she nuded up, it would only be appropriate to reciprocate and nude up, too, requiring me to unveil an impressive gut that I was sure would crush her like a bug. I figured I would go in, shirt on, sparing her the need to keep her eyes closed for her own psychological protection. I realized we weren't on the same page as she initiated a quid pro quo and began to wrestle with my shirt, to my dismay.

"Jax, I'm fat. I'm cool leaving the shirt on."

"Well, I'm not cool with it," Jax expressed firmly. "I want to feel your body pressed against mine, and that shirt is the only thing preventing that. It has to go," she informed me. My pants had already been deposited in the entryway, and she was right. It was the final barrier. "My attraction to you goes far beyond physical appearance and is largely led by everything on the inside and, of course, your rugged handsomeness. I don't want to get laid by a shirt. I want to get laid by you."

I thought those last two sentences would make fantastic song lyrics. She had flattered me into a false sense of body acceptance and ripped off my shirt before I could launch a second bout of resistance. And there it was, my white gut next to her tanned gym-toned abs, my 37-year-old broken-down jalopy of a body next to her 33-year-old Ferrari—a perfect visual for "when opposites attract."

The look of horrified shock I was bracing myself for never manifested. Instead, she proceeded to lead me through a master class in the administration of the pleasures of the flesh. Having taken the edge off in our little entryway fiasco, I somehow managed to present an impressive bout of stamina for the encore, which, from all nonverbal indications, didn't disappoint.

"Welcome back into the world of the sexually active," she whispered as we lay basking in the afterglow.

"Good to be back. Wow," a better response was no doubt available, but I didn't seem to have it in me to look for it. I had no business being in bed with a woman this kind, intelligent, and clearly a master of the erotic arts. Yet, there she was, still lying on top of me, looking down at me with a tear running down her cheek.

"Thank you, Toby," she said. "You have no idea how wonderfully perfect that was. Better than I could have ever imagined."

I had never considered myself a man of sexual prowess. I don't recall Gina ever thanking me, probably because she hadn't. As a matter of fact, this was the first after-sex thank-you I had ever received.

"Jax, I think I'm in shock," I informed her, watching the most endearing smile I had ever seen come across her face before she rested her head gently on my chest, allowing me to smell the wonderful scent of her hair as we laid there entangled for a very long time. She eventually drifted off to sleep. As she lay there on top of me in slumber, I hoped she wouldn't wake up anytime soon.

Only a week prior, I had laid in the same exact spot, a lonely, unemployed loser, sitting in the rubble of the afterlife of a shattered reality. I was now in the same room in an alternate universe, trying to make sense of it all. I had unexpectedly salvaged myself from the deserted desert island I had been stranded on. I had been able to begin to rebuild the foundation of another life—in many ways, a better life. I could see a return to self-confidence bubbling back up from the depths of its prison in my subconscious. It felt good to be back.

That's when I realized we had used no protection.

CHAPTER
TWENTY

Three weeks later.

I was a sweaty mess, standing with my hands on my knees, trying to catch my breath. I had been running every other day, tacking on an additional two minutes each time, lost five pounds, and finally had some momentum going. I had just made it three miles before my first walking break. My motivation was primarily to relieve Jax from the burden of maneuvering around my gut as we experimented with new and exciting positions while making love. You know you're in some sort of relationship when the sex references transition from "having sex" or "getting it on" to "making love." Two days ago, much to my surprise, she introduced me to her co-worker Tyra as her "boyfriend." We hadn't discussed our relationship status, but there was an unspoken shared understanding that it existed and was most likely monogamous, which was enough for me.

I was also relieved to learn that Jax had been taking birth control pills, so there was no need to fear any more unplanned pregnancy scares. In this instance, luck had been on my side yet again.

Jax and I were spending most of our free time together, and

things were going swimmingly. We had dinner with Eddie and Cowboy once or twice a week, hung out at The Plow, frequented the beach, watched TV, lazed around at my place, and humped each other constantly, like delusional rabbits on the first day of mating season.

Due to my new running routine, I developed an enviable farmer's tan. Men running around the city shirtless was a popular thing, and I had no intention of participating—at least not until I lost another twenty-five pounds; I would be sporting the "working man's" tan for the foreseeable future.

On one occasion, I did get to see my children because it was Taylor, my youngest child's birthday party. They didn't appear to be elated to see me, or maybe they were still traumatized by my abandonment of them, strictly enforced by Gina. God only knows how she was positioning my disappearance from their daily routine. I was betting that Gina's resentment would eventually start to subside, and the visitations would become more frequent. Time would tell; however, I was beginning to accept that I had very little control over this, and I wasn't sure of exactly what a father-in-exile's role is, but from what I was gathering, it was designed to be primarily a shame-based role.

All our old friends, who were now just Gina's friends, were at the party. I can only assume that she had told them I had leprosy since they were effectively avoiding any possible eye contact; upon my approach, conversations stopped instead of started. All of this made me hate them and Gina, but I no longer hated myself for everything that had transpired. Primarily due to Jax, my self-esteem had ascended back to pre-depression levels. Her unfettered approval was enough for me to survive on. Sadly, I was glad to get the hell out of the party as soon as Tyler was done opening her gifts, as she then had more than she could handle to distract her from the sad reality garlanding her cheerful little party.

Work was becoming more routine, and I was most definitely enjoying it. Recently, I learned a few very important things. First, a

French manicure wasn't just an unfinished nail painting job. The tips of the fingernails were supposed to be white, the rest unpainted, with just some glossy stuff on top. This was now fashionable. Secondly, a facial involves massage as much as it does cleaning, exfoliating, and moisturizing. Cucumber slices on the eyes aren't used that often anymore.

Thirdly, and most importantly, I learned the universe could take pity on a man, possibly due to the trials that the poor son-of-a-bitch had been forced to endure or perhaps just plain old great luck. In my case, I received this gift about a few weeks prior while chatting with Jazmine, waiting for her 2:30 p.m. appointment to arrive.

"So Jazmine, it says here your 2:30 is a lightening appointment. I didn't know we did hair lightening, but I guess I'm still getting the lay of the land," I said.

"Well, you are correct. We don't do any hair lightening. Babs doesn't want to compete with hair salons," she answered, popping her gum rhythmically between sentences.

"Michael Jackson type of shit? I suppose we probably keep 'race changes' on the down-low for obvious reasons, huh?"

"Toby, your naïveté is acute, although kind of cute in an innocent way."

"Sexy cute?"

"Maybe sexy-toddler cute, which sounds a bit wonky now that I say it. No, Toby. Skin lightening is what any lightening appointment refers to at The Altered Ego. But usually not faces—more like inner thighs, armpits, knees, elbows, etc."

"Who wakes up and decides I want bleached-out pits or knees? Is this really a fashion trend?"

"Wrong yet again, Toby. As certain people age, their skin can darken in areas with more friction or due to changing hormones. These areas include the inner thighs of overweight folks, parts of the armpit, knees, elbows, and labias, and...drum roll please...anuses. Usually, it happens...."

"Wait," I interrupted. "So a guy can do this lightening process to his overly brown starfish and return it to its youthful glory?"

"Or a woman. Men don't have the corner on the aging anus market, you know."

"This is great news!" I exclaimed with a guilty excitement. It seems my doctor wasn't abreast of the latest dermatological advancements.

"That women can also pinken their posteriors?" she asked.

"No. I mean that everyone can beautify their back door, should they feel so moved. How empowering! People can fight back against the horror of fate. Time may eventually win the war, but some battles can be won along the way. Even the smallest victories can have an amazing effect on morale."

"Well, Brigadier General Tenderhill, maybe you could lead the charge. We can call you 'Bleach-Master Double-T.'"

"More than happy to crusade for a good cause," I exclaimed. My work now had a purpose I could relate to! I could remove the suffering of these poor, beaten-down souls out there, having been forced personally to fight darkness with inferior posterior weaponry.

This revitalized my orientation around the possibility of a God. The universe had unveiled a path for people to take action against the evils of skin darkening. Even more shocking and empowering was that The Altered Ego Salon was ready and waiting to relieve their plight. Yes, we bleached the hell out of any and all of these renegade skin color misfortunes, which meant there was a path for me to turn back the clock precisely where time had ravaged me.

Jazmine informed me that the salon used a magical bleaching cream to accomplish these triumphs. I learned that chemical peels and laser treatments can also accomplish this; however, they can be more painful and much more expensive than the topical cream method that The Altered Ego Salon provides.

As I continued to hammer poor Jazmine for details, I was pleasantly surprised that the treatment was simple and straightforward.

Depending on the degree of lightening needed, a second or third treatment may be required, but a couple of weeks between treatments are needed to let the skin recover. A rectal recalibration was in order.

Of course, I secretly borrowed a generous sample of the lightening cream. I convinced Jax we should bleach our anuses later that very night to ensure we were photo-ready on a moment's notice. In a horrifying bout of self-disclosure, I shamefully admitted to her that I had a bit of a rapid aging situation down there that required some attention. She, of course, accused me of grossly exaggerating; however, after demanding an inspection, she reluctantly agreed there was a problem worth addressing.

Remarkably, it worked...for Jax. In my case, although she kindly suggested she noticed a difference, there was no visible evidence that my banana cannon had taken the time machine back to its 'youthful and fancy' state.

After seven more attempts over two weeks and seven more crushing defeats, I was confident it had gotten even darker. Even ever-optimistic Jax admitted that it didn't seem to be doing much, but she didn't care because nobody would ever notice. Nobody except me, I realized. I had spent what seemed like countless hours on my back with my legs over my head, snapping selfies on my iPhone in all sorts of new and creative lighting angles, determined to find encouragement, but all to no avail. I had permanently shit-stained my anus over the years while remaining blissfully ignorant that an unspeakable horror was manifesting.

At work, I was not allowed to help with facials, pedicures, or manicures because most customers, I was told, have a pre-existing belief that a man does not have the patience and attention to detail to provide an acceptable level of service. True or not, I was also informed a customer's belief is their reality, and we weren't getting paid to alter anyone's reality, just their egos.

Babs also educated me that "intimate lightening" when referring to the labia was not a treatment women wanted men to administer, which made sense to me. If I were to have my labia be the workbench for beauty, I'd much prefer a female to administer the cleaning. I found it ironic that rectal bleaching could be performed on a female by a male, but only if no female was available and the client didn't mind.

On the other hand, "basic lightening" could be handled by any fool, male or female. On more than one occasion, my talents were recruited to help administer lightening to knees, elbows, and armpits. This was usually when things got hectic due to people being late for appointments and backing things up or if a "specialist" was calling in sick, requiring whoever was available to chip in to handle their appointments. Calling customers to reschedule their appointments was not in the playbook. I was getting pretty damn good at the art of lightening, especially armpits and knees, but had yet to move to the rear of the center stage of the lightening arena.

I was checking off the boxes on my life's resuscitation to-do list and was getting it back on track. What a difference a few weeks makes. As Eddie says, the only constant thing is change; finally, things were changing how I wanted them to.

Jax had gone over to Jimmy's to assist with nursery prep and spend some quality time before the baby, due any day now, popped out and obliterated any further opportunity for relaxed and well-rested adult conversation.

By now, my breathing had returned to normal, and I had finished stretching out my calves on my apartment's stairs. I immediately concluded that I was bored. The thing about momentum is that a body in motion stays in motion, and, as a result, I lost my appetite for extreme relaxation unless, of course, I was relaxing with Jax. In that case, relaxing around was usually just a precursor to nudity and everything that goes along with that.

Plus, too much alone time away from Jax provided too much time to obsess about when the novelty would eventually wear off, and she would wake up, realize what a mistake she had made, and decide to leave me and my unbleachable anus in the rearview mirror.

Left with nothing else to do, I showered off and headed to work.

I was at my station, manning the entry to The Altered Ego Salon, feeling a little like cruise director Julie McCoy greeting the passengers as they boarded The Love Boat. Maybe a bit more like Isaac, now that I consider it. Jazmine, whose three o'clock appointment had been canceled, was killing time until her four o'clock waxing appointment arrived. I was grateful for the company and was busy working at maintaining eye contact to over-compensate for my lecherous sneak peeks at the fine chassis she was flaunting in her hunter-green spandex pants and sleeveless white blouse, generously revealing more cleavage than one could hope for in a work environment. She was recounting her back door bleaching experience from the day before. It was a man, and Jazmine has since refused to provide this service for the lesser sex.

"You've got to be kidding me!" I exclaimed in utter disbelief.

"I'm serious as a rattlesnake bite, Toby," Jazmine clarified with an emphatic pop of her gum.

"So he actually said, 'Trust me, this will be a workout for you,' as soon as you entered the room?" I validated.

"I shit you not," she replied, punctuating it with a firm nod. "He was fully aware of what was going on."

"What happened next?"

"He dropped his pants and eagerly separated his butt cheeks to reveal the most stunning display of ass-crack hair imaginable. I mean, it defied belief. I was sure it must have been a fake. Some sort of anal toupee. You know?"

"Jesus, Jazmine! Was it the real deal?"

"That's exactly what I asked him. He affirmed it was. He was looking for a pre-lightening wax as well. Claimed it was like shitting through the top of his head. But chivalry was not dead, and he made sure to let me know he had just showered, and I could relax."

"Well, that must have been a welcome relief. It's nice to relax," I said. "So what did you do then?"

"I literally threw up in the waste basket. It was too much for me to handle, and I told him we don't do that kind of waxing. There aren't words to describe the horror of that image, Toby. I may need therapy. He was none too pleased with my refusal to clear a path to the target. He filed a formal complaint with Babs and announced a scathing Yelp review would be coming shortly."

"Holy crack hair catastrophe, Batman!" I replied.

"You're telling me! Babs had my back and ineffectively tried to explain that he needed two separate services, one of which we didn't provide, but once he could find a butthole barber to shear his locks, we would be happy to brighten up his inner circle," Jazmine said, chuckling.

"She most certainly did not say that."

"Well, maybe I was paraphrasing a bit, but that was the gist of the rap she threw down on the guy. I'm sure we won't be seeing him again."

"I'd say that's a likely assessment. You have to admit that, although the humor was largely at your expense, for the record, it was fucking hilarious," I felt obligated to point out.

"Well, Babs also mentioned that now that we're down a head-count, you will be doing even more lightenings, if you know what I mean, so you better buckle up. It's time to go pro, big boy."

This was news to me. I felt relieved that Babs had drawn the line between butthole bleachers and butthole barbers. I was confident that the clean crack requirement could go a long way towards creating an endurable experience for the new bleacher-boy. I was about to expand my skill set.

"Jazmine, many people have latent talents. Fortunately, I've been training my whole life for this opportunity—my lightening borders on masterpiece. I work in bleaching cream like Picasso works in paints. Just wait for the Yelp reviews."

"Like a fish to water, huh?" she asked. "Or maybe a fly to shit?"

"Hilarious, young Jazmine. I'll let it slide only once because I like your outfit today. But no more." I felt it important to establish I liked how she looked because it opened a window for her to retaliate with an articulation of her intense sexual interest in me, which, if it were the case, forever remained her best-kept secret.

Yet another attempt to validate myself to myself, I thought. I was using a flanking move to manipulate a third party into validating I was attractive enough for consideration. First of all, that's sick and quite possibly pathetic. Secondly, it was surprising that I needed that to bolster my body image. I had always considered myself a moderately attractive guy, currently in more of a dad bod type of way, and it seemed I wasn't yet ready to cast off that ego requirement. I suppose I could replace that component of my identity with being a master bleacher of the anal underworld, but that didn't seem like a fair trade.

Just then, as fate would have it, my text notification went off, and I was surprised to see it was Babs.

> Toby, are you upfront?

> > Yep. Where are you?

> I'm in the back. My appointment is running late. I hate to do this, but I need you to cover my 4 o'clock lightening appointment.

> > NP. I'm kind of a big deal in the lightening community these days.

> So our Yelp reviews have confirmed.

> > Really?

> Yes. 2 positive reviews on you. But this one is a bit different.

> > ??

> Anal

> > I love anal.

> Good to know, I suppose. I think your client might as well.

> I mean, I would love the opportunity to expand my repertoire to include anal lightening.

> Great. Jazmine can walk you through the protocol. This is her second treatment.

> We've got this covered.

> Thx Toby.

This was synchronicity at its best and an excellent opportunity to expand my expertise in the discipline of the bleaching arts. And positive Yelp reviews already, just in my first month! Finally, something I could be recognized for and master outside the trench warfare of high-tech operations.

"Jazmine, we have a situation."

"Do we now?"

"That was Babs texting me. I need to cover her 4 o'clock anal lightening appointment. She said you can give me the rundown on what to do. Can't be that hard, can it?"

"The hardest part is expelling any residual fecal matter from inside the anus as it's challenging and painful for the customer, so you have to be authoritative," she started to explain.

"What! Are you fucking with me?"

"Of course I am. That would be ridiculous, Toby. It's easy-peasy. Come back to room three, and I'll help you get set up and walk you through the drill," she said, conducting a dramatic about-face, leading us down the hall and into the first room on the left.

"OK, Toby, first, a towel is placed over the massage table to avoid the postoperative wipe down to rid the table of unacceptable germs that could kill the next customer if gone unaddressed. Then, the baby wipes. When used by adults, they are branded as Wet Ones.

Wet Ones need to be housed in 'the wipe warmer,' which takes a little time to do its job."

"I wouldn't have considered warming the wipes; however, I suppose it seems more professional that way."

"Most likely, it seems that way because it is. Now, while waiting for the bleaching agent to administer its thrashing to the deviant skin cells, a client risks extreme boredom and possibly some vanity guilt. Taking other senses offline will blunt this unpleasantness at worst or eliminate it at best. Headphones, scented eye masks, and a dimly lit room provide a sense of anonymity. This cabinet is where we keep these things, and as you already know, the dimmer is on the light switch. Some people will elect to wear headphones and eye masks, and some won't. The important thing is that they know their options. Got that?"

"Yep. What else?"

"Classical music ensures feelings of sophistication and a sense of superiority to other less cultured musical genres. Oh, and the flannel gowns. Basically, a robe that allows tasteful access to the areas you will attack. You know how to work the music, and the gowns are in the closet; clean ones are hanging, and dirty ones go in the bin. Just have the robe ready on the massage table over here and tell them you'll be back and will knock in a couple of minutes after they've had a chance to change."

"OK. So far, so good. What's next?" I asked.

"Then I say something to them about it being wise to address this early before the condition continues to explore adjacent areas or, even worse, continues to advanced levels of darkening. Everyone likes to feel smart. Let's be clear: we are at war here. War is ugly, but we humans have had thousands of years of practice rationalizing it and instigating it without regret."

"So what then, I say something like 'Put your ass in the air and let me wipe you like a toilet bowl?'"

"Exactly...No! Of course not. You tell them to roll over onto their elbows and knees and that you are going to ensure they are wiped, and then you will do a light exfoliation with the exfoliating cream, which is right here," she said, handing me a tube. "You bring a warm damp washcloth back in with you and put the exfoliating cream on it and work it around there real good to ensure there is nothing between their skin and the bleaching cream you'll be putting on next. Rub the exfoliating cream around for a minute or two and then wipe it off with a second wet washcloth, dab things dry, and put on the magic bleaching cream. Easy-peasy!"

"Bleaching cream is in the cabinet with everything else?"

"Yep. You leave it on for exactly twenty minutes, then wipe it off thoroughly, and they are ready for life's next adventure! Got it?"

"Got it," I answered as we heard the bells ringing, indicating someone had entered the lobby from the street.

"Oh, and we send them home with some petroleum jelly to apply afterward if the area becomes sensitive. It's all in the cabinet," she informed me as we exited towards the front.

"OK. Hey, what are the most sessions that you've seen a person need to get things 'right' down there?"

"Oh...glad you asked. Sometimes, people need to come back for a follow-up session or maybe two. But I've never seen anyone need more than three. But if you think someone might want to come back, make sure to mention that it can take more than one treatment." This was discouraging news. I wasn't about to mention that I'd tried seven or eight treatments and gotten absolutely no results.

We arrived in the lobby, and Jazmine's next appointment had arrived to get her cheeks, chin, and upper lips waxed. This Italian woman was the George Michael of chicks. She was sporting an authentic four o'clock shadow that teenage boys prayed they could claim for themselves one day. From that perspective, by waxing this off, this woman was a complete ingrate.

Jazmine took the she-man down the hall while I waited for Amber, the four o'clock anal bleaching appointment, to arrive. This couldn't be too tough, and I was bound and determined to be damn good at it. Technically, I'd already bleached myself and Jax, so I did have some experience, with a fifty percent success rate. Just remember to make them feel comfortable and smart about taking care of their derriere and be professional.

Moments later, a striking Asian-American woman in her mid-to-late twenties blew through the front door like a warm ocean breeze, announcing, "Amber has entered the building, and Amber and her Shining Star will soon exit fully restored to her former glory."

"Pleasure to meet you, Amber. My name is Toby, and I've been given the opportunity to de-tarnish your star. I hope that's not an issue. Babs got double-booked as we are short-staffed, and she didn't think you wanted to reschedule your appointment, but if you do, I totally understand," I replied, intrigued that she would discuss herself in the third person.

"How do I know you know what you're doing? I'm a public entertainment figure and I do demand only the highest quality practitioners."

Amber had a sass and confidence that was as enchanting as it was entertaining. She wore her yellow and white sun dress well, revealing an impressively fit set of shoulders and arms, nicely tanned, and her black hair was in a perfect bob. She moved like a runway model; her make-up was applied flawlessly, although a bit thick for my taste. Normally, I'm not a fan of fake eyelashes, but anything less would have been out of place next to her larger-than-life persona. If I had to sum her up in one word, it would be 'intriguing.'

"Amber, I'm happy to announce that I'm the bleacher boy you may have probably read about in our Yelp reviews. I'm damn good at what I do and not afraid to share that I've even bleached my own back door." Which was technically accurate, results notwithstanding.

"Well...well...well. Today must be my lucky day. We may need to take a little peek at that later," she said with a wink. "Lead me to my destiny, Toby," she said, moving towards the hall. She extended her hand, which she then draped over my forearm as I led her to our room.

"So, you say you're an entertainer. Are we talking singing, dancing, stand-up, or what's your playground?" I asked.

"All of the above, and thank you for inquiring. I provide levity to the lives that need lifting and a life raft of lust to those cast away on sexless deserted islands. Amber's performance art is unique and never the same, which is why they keep coming back for more."

"Where is this palace where you fuel your patron's addiction to your special medicine?" I asked.

"I'm a mysterious girl, Toby, and I prefer to keep my fans curious and intrigued. I perform randomly at different parties, bars, festivals, and the like. Once I put out the word on my Instagram story, we sell out any venue in hours. No show is ever the same, so nobody wants to miss a unique performance that is literally a once-in-a-lifetime experience."

"So you really are a big deal, huh?"

"Toby, I'm merely a shepherd, leading my flock on an intimate journey to meet and greet their inner naughtiness," she said, slapping my ass as we entered the room. Her confidence and charisma had cast a spell on me. At that moment, if she had handed me a chocolate milkshake and told me to pour it over my head, I probably would have done so without hesitation.

"OK, Amber, I'll give you a few minutes to change into the gown. I'll be standing outside, so holler when you're ready for the bleaching artist to begin his magic show."

"I know the drill, sister. I won't be but a minute," she replied, waving me towards the door.

To say I was a bit aroused was an understatement. I was also a bit nervous, as this was my first official anal bleaching appointment, and I may have overmarketed my prowess a tiny bit. "Just play it cool; you got this," I told myself.

"Ready and waiting, big boy," rang out from the other side of the door.

"Let the games begin," I announced, entering the room. Amber was on the table on her hands and knees with her jaw-dropping derrière pointed skyward. I took a deep breath as I crossed the room, thinking of dead rats and vomit in an attempt to quell my emerging erection.

"How's that for an onion butt?" Amber asked.

"Onion butt?"

"Brings tears to the eyes, Toby."

I grabbed the exfoliating cream and a washcloth from the cabinet and stopped dead in my tracks a couple of feet from Amber and her onion butt. "Whoah!"

"See, I'm not making that up. Feel free to take a minute to dab your tears, my dear boy."

"Amber, that's quite a nut sack you have there," I stammered, trying to make sense of what I was seeing.

"And nicely shorn too, I must add," she proudly announced.

"I suppose so.... I just... Well, you know...."

"Weren't expecting that? Damn, girl, I figured Babs had given you the full back story, pardon the pun."

"Um...no...I mean...I...I admit, I feel a little blindsided, but that's OK, I suppose." Holy fuck. My potential erection had been rendered as lifeless as a wilted flag on a windless day. I was trying to decide if my initial attraction qualified me as gay, bisexual, or something in between that I didn't know the proper word for. Babs was going to get an earful from me about this little surprise.

"Let's get me ready for my soon-to-be-famous move, 'Amber's Ankle Grab,' where I plunge into an aggressive straight-legged ankle grab, winking my little soon-to-be pink eye at..."

"Too much detail, too much detail," I interrupted.

"No such thing. The attention to detail separates the good from the great in any profession. A master bleacher like yourself can surely appreciate that."

"I suppose that's true. This is just my first experience with a..."

"World famous drag queen is what you're reaching for there,

sister," she said, patting her ass or his ass. "Like my partner always says, 'the show must go on.'"

Quickly changing topics and trying to regain focus, I asked, "So what's your partner do for a living?" realizing I asked a question I may not want to hear the answer to.

"Jeff is a powerlifter and power-top, honey," she replied as I began the exfoliation process, forcing an air of professionalism through involuntary revulsion. "Let's clear a visible path to the target, sister."

I was now immersed in ass crack exfoliation and contemplating why I was so mentally shaken. The idea of bleaching a man wasn't horrifying, but this was remarkably uncomfortable for some reason that I couldn't quite put my finger on. "Well, Jeff is a lucky guy, I suppose," I said in an attempt to make small talk.

"Yes! Yes! Oh, that's the way, Toby. Sorry. I got a bit carried away. I mean, yes, he is. Let's just say he grounds me."

"Well, that can be important in a relationship, right?"

"Toby, my dear, I'm a complex girl, and Jeff's a simple man. We balance each other out. He's boiled life down to two simple values, and he lives true to those values," she explained.

"What would those be, if you don't mind me asking?" I inquired as I exfoliated.

"To quote Gandhi, 'Life heavy. Eat ass.'"

"Gandhi said that, huh?"

"I may be paraphrasing, but that's essentially what his message was. No, really, get in there, Toby, and get rough if you have to. We can't lose sight of the goal here, sister."

"Right. We don't want to lose sight of the goal. And what precisely is the goal, to make sure I don't lose sight of it?"

"I want people to feast their eyes and demand to eat my ass 'buffet style,' wondering how many licks it takes to get to the center of this tootsie-pop," she explained. "We want them to fantasize about trying on my little raspberry beret, if you know what I mean. There you go! Just like that. That's what I'm talking about."

Somehow, she had taken control, and I was getting butt-bossed by a drag queen. Somehow, my new career path had taken an scary turn down an unfamiliar dark alley.

"You're creating the American Dream down there, sister," she uttered in a breathy voice that left me even more unsettled. At this point, it was all about getting to the finish line and getting the hell out of there. I was the one working on a defenseless man's anus, yet it was *I* who felt remarkably victimized.

"Well, that's one way to look at it, I guess," I said, removing the last of the exfoliating cream and walking over to get the bleaching agent.

"For those seriously into analingus, 'Lickin' spokes' is no joke, my good sister," she said.

"Probably more than I need to know, Amber." I began a reckless attempt to apply the bleaching cream with as little skin-to-skin contact as possible as if, at that point, it really mattered. But at that point, it mattered a lot.

"Yes. Yes! Yes! Put that shit on there like you mean it, sister!"

That pushed me over the edge. "Amber, can we please keep this professional? I'm a professional bleacher here, not a sex slave. And please stop calling me sister."

"Oh, I like a man not afraid to take control!"

"Amber!"

"OK, fine. Sorry, Toby dear. I don't know what came over me. Amber needs to be reminded of personal boundaries from time to time."

"OK. So, we'll leave the bleaching cream on for twenty minutes. I need to head up to the front desk for a few, and I'll come back to check on you," I said, making a beeline for the door.

"Sounds good. I'll use this opportunity to activate my parasympathetic nervous system with my breathing exercises."

I had no idea what she was talking about, nor did I care to know. I reached the front desk in a now abandoned lobby, and it hit me. I couldn't care less about bleaching a man's anus or a woman's anus, for that matter. I had no issue with people having various sexual orientations. What I didn't care for was being obliged to touch a man's anus knowing he was loving it. Frankly, it made me feel gay to be doing gay things. And that most certainly didn't jive with my self-image. And I had been booby-trapped into the whole thing. Of course, being physically turned on by her prior to the trap being sprung still left some irreconcilable gayness swimming around in the back of my subconscious.

In an effort to clear my head, I spent the next twenty minutes doom-scrolling through reels on my Instagram feed, which provided a nice reprieve and helped me gather enough courage to reenter the bleaching arena.

I gave a quick knock on the door, and Amber responded with, "Entrez! Time to get back in the crack and pick up the slack, my fine feathered young friend."

"Let's get cleaned up and see how we did, Amber." I had settled on the philosophy that if I didn't really look Amber's anus in the eye, so to speak, then I was technically one stage further removed from gay butt play. It wasn't the sturdiest crutch, but the only one I had to lean on.

"Well? Can you see a difference? What's going on back there?" she asked.

I was determined to cling to my teetering heterosexual identity and wasn't about to give up my vow not to look directly at her/his rusty starfish. "Even better, let me get you the hand mirror so you can see for yourself," I offered, fetching the hand mirror from the shelf and handing it to her.

"OH MY FUCKING GOD!" she screamed. I must have left the cream on too long, but this could be a trick to get me to look.

"Is it that bad?" I inquired.

"Haha. It's fucking brilliant, Toby! As young and fresh as in my baby photos!" She hopped off the table and gave me a bear hug. "You weren't kidding about being a master bleacher. Amber owes you a great debt. I'm literally and figuratively tickled pink."

It was at this time I realized Amber's penis was touching my leg. Technically, it didn't count since she was still wearing the robe, but I wasn't excited about it. Luckily, Amber released her embrace and pressed her palms together in front of her chest, "Namaste."

"I'm glad my talents weren't wasted on an unappreciative patron," I exclaimed, feeling a calm wash over me as the stress began to evaporate. I'll be damned if I wasn't a bit excited about an epic first bleaching outcome. Another feather to put in my bleaching cap.

I left Amber to get dressed and waited for her upfront. Eventually, she emerged with a triumphant smile plastered across her face. "Toby, I am at your service. I had doubts about how far back we could turn the hands of time, but now I can sleep at night again. How about a private show, just for you, to show my appreciation?"

"Well, Amber, I'll have to pass on that. I have a girlfriend and remain a confident heterosexual. That would feel a bit like cheating. Although it's a generous offer," I added, wondering how to avoid appearing a total ingrate. "I am trying to become the best bleacher in San Francisco. I'm making a comeback in my life and taking things in a new direction, professionally speaking. Any chance you may feel so inclined to spread the word?"

"I'll do you a solid, sister. Give me a stack of your business cards. I'll rock my fancy-ass up and down Castro Street, handing them out like the Easter Bunny with a basket of golden vibrating butt-eggs," she said with a wink and another embrace.

"I bet the bunny outfit is a sight to behold," I said.

"You have no idea, young man. Toby, you're making America great again by returning the lost twinkle to all the dirty stars out there. It's the least I could do."

Amber paid and left a generous tip and took about a hundred of my business cards. "Bon voyage, my badass bleacher boy!" she said with a gentle wave as she disappeared through the door.

What I'd failed to think through was that a hundred of my business cards were about to be distributed with a credible endorsement to a hundred gay guys with broken down, beat-up bungers with miles of wear, and these shabby sphincters were going to end up on my bleaching bench for restoration. If there was no such thing as free will and life was truly unfolding on its own, the universe had a hell of a sense of humor.

Although I was proud of what we had been able to do for Amber, deep down, I was resentful of her bleaching success. Thank God I was off at five and could close up, get out of there, and distract myself with a change of scenery.

As I locked the door to the salon behind me, with confidence still surprisingly high, I decided to see if Eddie and Cowboy were up for dinner.

It was another cold, windy, foggy, perfectly classic San Francisco day. A damp cold is bone-chilling and requires one to dress in layers. On a moment's notice, the fog can burn off, and you are either suddenly roasting or stranded in between, where a t-shirt isn't enough, but a jacket is too much, making comfort impossible. On the other hand, on a beautiful sunny San Francisco day, one should also bring extra layers, as the fog can come in, changing the temperature by fifteen degrees in ten minutes or less. Either way, preparation is vital. I was bundled up with enough layers to be mistaken for the Michelin Man, my pear-shaped foundation perfecting the look. Scarfs, gloves, and hats are not at all uncommon, and the worst of this unsettling "fog uncertainty" always occurs in the summer, surprising unsuspecting tourists who are entirely unprepared. Tourists are sure that California is nothing but Baywatch-worthy beaches from top to bottom. My favorite place to catch a view of these disappointed visitors is on the Golden Gate Bridge, which seems to be on everyone's must-see list.

When driving across the bridge on a foggy summer day, you see these poor sods with new Alcatraz or Fisherman's Wharf sweat-shirts, purchased in a panic to address the climatic assault, trying in vain to capture a picture of the glory of this man-made masterpiece through a white veil so thick they can barely even see the cell phone in their hand.

This doesn't deter them from trying; however, few of those pictures ever make it onto Facebook, Snapchat, or Instagram. Social media is strictly for flaunting epic experiences to make the rest of us jealous in contrast to our sad, lonely, and un-epic lives. Ninety percent of what's posted shows people winning the game of life without a care in the world, even if it's just a snapshot of a plate of sushi. People flex their experiences to impress others and gain approval, which must be constantly reaffirmed with the next post and the post after that. Their social media feedback appears to be the mirror through which their self-image is now created and sustained and, sadly, constantly challenged.

However, in all fairness, even before social media, we did pretty much the same shit to prop up our egos. We would call friends when life was good to share the highlights but grow suspiciously withdrawn when things were shitty. We'd look at photo albums of our peak experiences, set goals, and celebrate achieving them with others, but we wouldn't talk much about our failures. It seems we all want positive attention, to be liked, and to be viewed as leading "successful" lives. I guess that's how we support an identity we can live with. Social media replaces the live one-on-one component with electronic one-to-many communication to get more and faster validation.

Regardless, it was cold out, I was energized, and I was about to spend time with a friend who didn't seem to want to see me any less if my life was in the shitter or more if it was peaking.

CHAPTER
TWENTY-ONE

"Hey, Toby!" Eddie yelled from down the street with a mouth full of toothpaste working its way through his beard.

"Tooth brushing day, huh, Eddie?"

"Once a week, even if they don't need it," he replied, spitting white foam into the gutter. "Cowboy is next, but he's not a fan."

It appeared laundry day must be just around the corner. Eddie's jeans were stiff with grime, and the putrid smell of rotting garbage was emanating from his estate. However, I knew my olfactory senses would adjust in a few minutes. I'm sure Eddie had no idea what he smelled like and could probably care less if he did. It must be nice not to worry about all the little shit we all spend a good chunk of time trying to control, day in and day out.

"Just don't forget to floss," I reminded him.

"When you've lost as many teeth as I have, there's not many nooks and crannies remaining for stuff to hide in. But I got to hold onto what I have left, or I'll have to fork over some cash on a blender to get my meals down."

"Hey, speaking of meals, you guys had dinner yet?" I inquired.

"I reckon we're due. Haven't eaten since breakfast. But this time, you sit your ass down and relax. Cowboy and I just went to the store for supplies, and I picked up a few cans of my favorite childhood meal, corned beef hash, in case you and Jax came around. You know, the good stuff with the tiny, cubed potato bits? We'll throw on a little Tabasco and be eating like kings. Your timing is impeccable. We just got back, and the beer is still cold."

"What can I do to help?" I asked.

"Sit down and open your beer," he said, handing me one. I thought we'd try Modelo. A Mexican guy recently told me they don't drink Tecate or Corona much in Mexico, and I should try Modelo. It's worth a shot, right?"

"I guess we're just before finding out," I said, cracking open the can.

It tasted indistinguishable to me. "Tastes good. What do you think?"

Eddie opened his, sniffed it, and took a sip. "To be honest, I can't tell the difference."

"You're right. Maybe our taste isn't yet refined enough."

Eddie was now screwing the tiny green propane can into the end of the little black hose, connecting it to his camp stove. "Got to eat this shit hot, Toby. Need to brown it up," he said, reminding me of Julia Child with the play-by-play, as he dumped it into an old copper pot. "You want an egg in yours?"

"Sure, if you got one."

"Got a half dozen. Can have two if you like?"

"Only if you do," I said.

He nodded and cracked four eggs into the pot. "Better fried and put on top, but only have one pot, so I'll mix 'em in. Hope ya don't mind."

"Not at all."

"Got some relatively sad news, Toby," Eddie said. "Mrs. Parker, you know the neighbor that let me use her address to adopt Cowboy?"

"Yeah, I remember you talking about her going to the hospital."

"Just got word that she passed exactly three weeks ago today. Her sister had been trying to find me, but I had moved here and failed to tell them."

"I'm sorry to hear that, Eddie; I know she was an old friend of yours."

"Death is as much a part of life as anything else. Guess she learned what she came here for. I'll miss her nonetheless."

"Well, still sorry to hear it."

Cowboy dropped his rag in my lap, his request to play tug, to which I happily obliged. My favorite part was his erratic head-whipping from side to side to rip it free. I usually let him win. He liked knowing he was dominant. He would then immediately drop it in my lap sympathetically, allowing me yet another chance to prove myself a worthy opponent. After five to ten minutes, Eddie decided I needed a break.

"Cowboy, leave it!" he commanded. Cowboy immediately took the rag over to the shopping cart and dropped it. I made a mental note to stop by the pet store to get him a more durable tug toy.

"I honestly don't mind, Eddie."

"He'll go on all day if ya let him," Eddie informed me, which I could see.

"So, how's the comeback going, Toby?" Eddie asked, intensely working the hash and eggs in his pot with the focus of a mad chemist.

"Eddie, I gotta say, it's going well. Jax is fantastic and, for some unidentifiable reason, seems to think I'm the best thing that's happened to her. Work has been interesting. Although I've personally failed to bleach my own anus back to its aesthetically pleasing prime, I am now officially providing this service to other poor souls afflicted with the same grotesque misfortune I have been saddled with. I'm removing darkness from people's lives, Eddie, and it appears I'm about to be specializing in homosexual sphincter restoration. Although horrifying at first, as I'm saying this aloud, maybe I've found a niche I can own. Oh...and I'm now up to running three miles and have already dropped five pounds."

"Sounds like the hero is making money, getting fit, and got the girl," Eddie said with a couple of huffs. Eddie's laugh was more of a staccato series of rhythmic exhales without any other discernable sound: "Huff, huff, huff," as his whole upper body participated. Even though you could barely hear him, it was a joy to watch him chuckle.

"Hardly a hero, but better off than a couple of months ago on all *fronts*—but not so much the *back*, unfortunately."

"The hero indeed! And all heroes have a weakness. You happen to have an Achilles anus instead of a heel. Aren't we all the hero or sometimes the villain of our own story, anyway?" he asked.

"I suppose, in a way, we are. I never thought of it like that, but I like it."

"Hero is winning at life, things go south, and the hero is now losing. Then the hero rebuilds his life and has ascended again. That's a story, and it revolves around you. What a wonderfully creative thing."

Well, here we go again. Eddie always makes me think; this time, I had the energy and relished it.

"I'll bite on that one. Love the analogy, but how is it creative? It seems like life is always changing, as you've pointed out before, for better or worse, but not always by our own doing. I guess we create what we want to do next once we get clarity around whatever that is. Right?"

"In a way, yes, but I was referring to something slightly different. The creative part I was talking about is the story we wrap around it and why it's important. Life is creative in how it unfolds, but once it's in the review mirror, we wrap it up in thought paper with a big bow, right? Then we look at possible futures, pick one that bolsters our story, and tuck that under the bow for a little flair to add dimension to the package and make it more convincing. It's our package, and we create the wrapping. You following me?" Eddie was in good form today, and what he was saying made sense.

"You're right. We create a lot of the story but not always the foundation. A brick falls off the roof up there and lands on my foot, causing a shit-ton of pain. I can look back and create a story like 'one more example of how unlucky I am,' right?"

"That's pretty much it. Are you happy with your story as of late?"

"I'm thrilled with the direction things are moving in. I still have a way to go, but I'm at least moving in the right direction. Right?"

"Can't stop from moving on or escape from things changing, depending on your word preference," Eddie said.

"Can't argue that." We appeared aligned, which was nice and not all that common.

"Are you happy?" he asked, turning up the burner on his propane stove.

"Of course, I just told you all the good stuff going on," I said, wondering if he was even listening. "Sadly, despite multiple bleaching attempts, I still have the hauntingly dark anus of a seventy-five-year-old."

"Life stains sometimes," he said with a chuckle. "So what's next?"

"Good question. I suppose I'll get a better-paying job once I save up some more money. There is little to no chance of moving up at The Altered Ego unless I became a specialist, but I've been told those aren't men's jobs. But once I get a better gig, then I can afford more rent and get a better apartment. That's the immediate financial plan. The physical plan is to keep running, run longer, and get down to fighting weight. And on the relationship side, try not to fuck things up with Jax." I hadn't defined my immediate goals. Just random thoughts coming together. But articulating it out loud has a way of crystallizing it.

"Well, it sounds like you aren't 'totally' happy because there are a few things that aren't quite where you want them yet, and one thing that is but could go away?"

"I do spend time ruminating on those things. I'm not unhappy, but I need to keep my eye on what's next."

"When you brought Jax by to meet me a few weeks ago, you mentioned that you were happy now and wouldn't have wanted your old life back, so I assume you weren't too happy back in your previous life either, huh? Why don't you consider it while I get ready to plate up our meal," Eddie said as he pulled plates, a couple of forks, and the Tabasco sauce out of the bottom of his cart like a mechanic in a messy garage, knowing exactly where to reach to find the right tool without even looking.

"Yeah, I wasn't completely happy back then, and in some ways, I'm not now either, but things are moving in a good direction. So what's the point of the original question?" I asked, wondering where all this was going.

"I can give you my opinion, which happens to be like an asshole. Everyone's got one."

"Sure. An asshole isn't that bad, especially if it's bleached," I joked.

"My opinion is that, like your dirty asshole, YOU may need a good bleaching."

"Very funny. What exactly does that mean, Eddie?"

"Upon further reflection, what you had that you thought you needed to be happy didn't make you all that happy. Then, you lose all of that and become even more miserable. Then you got a job, met Jax, and were quite happy for a few weeks, right?"

"More or less, I suppose," I answered, seeing where this was headed.

Eddie continued. "Of course, the luster of the new job started to fade, as it always does, and insecurity around your relationship with Jax surfaced, and that caused your happiness to start to tarnish, much like your butthole. You then build an idea of what to chase next that will bring back the elusive happiness you've been stalking. But if history is any indication of where you'll end up, you most likely will find only fleeting happiness as a best-case outcome."

"Yeah...in a way, yes, but in a way, no," I interjected. "It's valid that most people in my situation would entertain a better job or be concerned about maintaining a relationship they value."

"Or, that could be complete horse shit," Eddie kindly pointed out. "Many people would be sure they could be happy in any of the phases you've moved through and jump to trade places with you. Then, of course, there are also different people who would likely be more miserable than you have been. You're chasing your ideas of possible futures in hopes of finding a brief respite of temporary happiness," he said, sticking his finger directly into the hash, testing the temperature.

"I'd say I'm chasing goals that lead to a more stable and predictable life. A life with less uncertainty tends to leave a guy in a generally happier place," I clarified and took another pull off my Modelo. I still couldn't taste any difference between the Tecate we usually drink and the Modelo. Still, knowing a real live Mexican had made the recommendation, I figured I might as well appreciate it.

"But those goals are just ideas that we already know won't all too often manifest as reality. We have glimpses of happiness now and then because happiness, like absolutely everything else, comes and goes. Unfortunately, there is a delusional concept of a permanent state of happiness, and these days, that idea is stronger than ever, fueled by the media solidifying that illusion. If you look under the hood, this is only another belief in a potentially permanent state of contentment, a belief that provides almost no examples of success. It's a fool's game with insanely low odds."

Eddie paused as he forked in an impressive mouthful of hash. It must have been to his liking as he plated it up and handed me one, along with the hot sauce, and I took a bite. Damn, it tasted good.

I realized that what Eddie was laying out for me was entirely rational. Eddie went into more detail than in our previous conversations because, in retrospect, he likely realized I needed it spoon-fed to relate it to my specific situation.

Over the last few weeks, I had gotten so wrapped up in my comeback and things going how I wanted them to that I forgot to contemplate my thoughts and my narrative. I had forgotten that "happiness," along with almost everything else, is temporary. My mental idea that things were going well squashed my desire to search for objective truth.

"Wait, there's more, and I'm on a roll," Eddie said, having successfully fought another mouthful.

"That's a relief. The silence was becoming unbearable."

"The sad thing is that, deep down, where most people aren't willing to go to explore their psyche, there is full knowledge that thought-based happiness is fleeting at best. And that scares the shit out of them. People fear that being alone with their thoughts could accidentally lead them to the doorstep of this realization: that there is nothing but fleeting happiness surrounded by thoughts we don't actually control. So, what do we do? We distract ourselves with everything we can. Thrill-seeking, sports, TV, fiction, travel, Zoomba classes, recalculating our net worth, having sex with our spouse, or worse, someone else's. We ruminate on the past, fantasize about the future, whatever it takes, but never allow ourselves to be alone and intently look at what's happening right in front of us. We get so used to hiding from ourselves that we don't even realize we're doing it anymore. Then it becomes an unconscious habit. We get completely lost in our illusion and mistake it for truth."

"I'm pretty sure I get what you're saying, but sometimes it's just fun to travel or watch sports, maybe even read a book now and then," I pointed out.

"Sure, and in some cases, it's as simple as that, but that's more uncommon than most people think. Usually, in the end, each time the thrill of attaining a goal or having some novel experience starts to fade, we experience a knee-jerk response to immediately do or achieve something else because we don't know who we are without our experiences and achievements to define us. Therefore, we must always fortify our sense of self to maintain the identities we've built out of all this. And even more bizarre, it's a bundle of thought that we are terrified could be challenged by life at any moment." Eddie quickly scooped a couple more bites of hash into his mouth.

"So we're building our identity through actions and achievements as well as working to prove to ourselves our self-concept is true by seeking more proof from more and more achievements. To me, it sounds like the process of becoming and possibly growing, Eddie."

"I can see why it would seem that way. Ironically, while all this identity-saving, building, and escaping are spinning our brains around like tops, we aren't paying attention to the journey. As a result, we miss almost everything valuable the journey has to offer. For most people, their journey is primarily a means to prop up a self-image they can live with. In reality, Toby, life is 90% the journey, and most people miss it all. Then, on their deathbed, they realize the journey was all they had. Then they wish they had their journey back more than anything but can't buy it for any price, and it's game over. Am I making any sense here?"

"Too much sense. Which scares me, as it's pretty depressing."

"Why is it depressing?" he asked. "It's just the way it is, the way it's always been."

"I guess it's kind of discouraging to think about and will likely raise more questions than answers," I replied.

"Don't overthink it. But that's like telling a thirsty man not to drink the glass of fresh water you put into his hand. Think about this question, which will lead you to the next pit stop on the journey. 'When do you stop having to prove yourself to yourself?'"

"OK, Eddie, I'll mull that over and report back."

Just think, this morning, I thought things were going damn good. Then, in the last ten minutes, I realized I was already falling apart. I was never that happy, and I was chasing the ghost of a future life to an imaginary destination. But if the fiction I'd spun about my past, present, and future was just that, thought-created stories, then what was the truth? What are we, aside from a bunch of conditioned thought patterns, fears, desires, and attempts to make sense of our experiences?

We finished up, Eddie let me do the dishes, and Cowboy closely supervised this exercise. Who knew dogs are concerned that chores are done correctly? Cowboy was a character just like his owner, that's for sure.

There was no more talk of happiness, just refreshingly idle chit-chat.

"Eddie, I know leaving your belongings unattended doesn't make sense. I'm happy to stand guard anytime you want to take Cowboy for a walk, or I'm happy to take him for a walk myself if you want."

"OK, Toby, I'll ruminate on that question and report back," he said with a wink.

Shortly after a quick game of tug-of-war with Cowboy, I went home and contemplated when I'd no longer need to repeatedly prove myself to myself. I drifted off into slumber before I figured anything out.

TWENTY-TWO

After fumbling in the dark for my phone on the nightstand, I eventually located it and realized it was still pitch black out. Nothing good is usually on the other end of a ringing phone in the middle of the night. "Hello?"

"Toby, Jimmy's wife is having her baby. I'm in the waiting room now. Jimmy is in there with her," Jax's almost yelled into the phone.

I looked over, trying to focus on the clock, which read 2:18 a.m. "Holy crap, Jax, that's awesome! Any word on how they're doing?"

"Not yet. They've been in there an hour and a half. Her water broke in the parking lot. They got there at just the right time. I just wanted to talk to you because I'm so excited and nervous. I know there is no reason I should be nervous, but shit happens all the time during childbirth. Kind of like that old saying, 'It's not over until it's over.'"

"Do you want me to come down there and wait with you?"

"Sure...I mean, no...it's the middle of the night. I wasn't trying to ask you to come...I just wanted to tell you...YES, get down here; I'm freaking out, but a good freaking out, ya know?"

"Been there twice, and you bet your gym-toned ass I know. I'm on my way. Wait...where am I going?"

"CPMC is just down from Laurel Village. It's on the third floor. I'm excited you're coming. Bye-bye, sweetheart."

My head was still idling in neutral. I stumbled around, trying to find something clean and somewhat respectable to wear. I didn't want to look like a total bum, especially if there was a chance I'd meet Jimmy's new baby and possibly his wife for the first time. Then it registered as my mind began to rev. She had called me first, in the middle of the night, and wanted me by her side to share the experience of this glorious event in her life. I had started falling in love with her on our first date at The Blue Danube. Sure, the puzzle of her true persona was blank at that time, and I was filling in all the missing pieces with some I'd fabricated to depict a masterpiece of a woman. However, the more time we spent, the more pieces were validated as correct, and the more beautiful the picture kept getting. As a result, I was getting increasingly more attached and, at the same time, more uneasy that I was falling too hard and too fast.

Neither of us had uttered the "L" word yet, most likely because it implied a type of responsibility, especially if we both let this declaration slip out. When a couple says, "I love you" to each other, they are really saying, "My heart is now vulnerable because I'm super attached to you. You now own my heart, and with that comes the responsibility to take care of it." It's the next level of dedication, not just on the physical level of monogamy but on a mental and emotional level. A commitment that leads to either a devastating break-up or getting married, the latter of which will end in either a happily-ever-after or a crushing divorce.

This was a sticky wicket. At some point, one of us would have to test the waters here. However, if I was reading it wrong, brazenly pumping out the "L" word could result in an awkward silence if not reciprocated. The "no response" always shakes the foundation of the developing relationship because the first person who coughs up the "L" word is forced to a decision point if it's not reciprocated. I would be risking having to determine if it's just a matter of timing and Jax would eventually come around, or I'd need to scale back my emotional involvement to protect myself. That would surely thrust the relationship into a tentative position, at best, but would likely cause things to unravel in the throes of insecurity, spurned by the newly found relationship inequity.

I was now dressed and on the sidewalk. I was about eight blocks from the California Pacific Medical Center and thankful for the walk, as it gave me a few moments to evaluate my next steps.

The critical question was, is she also in love? After the divorce, I wasn't letting myself REALLY love anyone or anything. Life had become too tentative to risk committing to anything, only to have it ripped away again. A short while later, I was walking up the stairs to the hospital's front door, and the momentum of the pending birth was transforming my excitement into budding raw courage.

Something told me now was the time. In the excitement of choosing to share an intimate family event with me in the middle of the night, she validated she must indeed also be in love.

Walking through the waiting room door, I saw Jax sitting directly across the room.

She sprang up, charged across the waiting room, and enveloped me in an aggressive hug before I could even say "Hi."

"Thanks so much for coming here in the middle of the night. You're the greatest!" Jax uttered.

While still in her embrace, looking more at the back of her head than into her eyes, I let it rip: "Jax, how could I ever not want to be there for the woman I love during such an auspicious event?"

There. I had done it and worded it casually. I wished I could see if her smile had just melted into a wide-eyed expression of shock and horror or if there was a pleasant, peaceful relief that, finally, she knew I felt much more than a fun experiment was going on between us.

Jax eventually pulled away and maintained what appeared to be a forced smile, but maybe I was projecting that. A hollow vulnerability had temporarily caused me to stop breathing as the anxiety clawed its way from my stomach up my throat, rendering me unable to speak. She took a few steps back, retreating from the situation, and tilted her face slightly.

"That's sweet, Toby." With three words, she neutered my self-confidence and left me to flail in the dark abyss of uncertainty. I had been in her shoes before. I knew how painful it was to burst another person's hopes for a future that would never see the light of day.

Compounding the crushing feeling of rejection, I realized I had tried to seize this special moment of pending childbirth for my agenda. I was, once again, all about me, raking the buzz of her evening. I felt like a complete asshole.

"Good," I uttered with as loving a smile as I could muster. This implied I was selfless, not an asshole, and confidently OK with the concept of us being at different places emotionally concerning our relationship. "Have you heard anything since we talked? It seems weird to have no idea what's going on, doesn't it?" A question ensures she has to answer and take the conversation to that topic, which, by design, would end the awkwardness and provide us both some needed relief. I was fucked. From almost the highest of highs to undoubtedly the lowest of lows, and believe me, I was no novice at navigating the lows.

"No! Not a damn thing. I mean...I'm sure it's going well, or we would have heard something, right? Or maybe it's not, and they are trying to save the baby. I hate just waiting," she said, exasperated. It dawned on me that I was the guy who had been through two birthing events and should be providing some comforting insight.

"Waiting is OK. The labor often stays at the same dilation and contraction frequency, which can last for hours," I informed her. "The baby won't be coming out right away, and I'm sure things are fine. Let's sit over here, and as soon as we spot some medical person in the hall, we can accost them for information. Or we can start going into every room we can find, valiantly fighting security along the way, until we eventually burst into the delivery room and satisfy our inquiring minds," I said with a wink.

"I'd actually do that if I wasn't risking spending the rest of the night in a holding cell getting to know drug dealers, drunks, and gang members. Normally, that's fine, but not if it means we have no idea what's going on," she said, contemplating the pros and cons of the direct route to information.

"Good point. Best we wait it out."

I had risked fucking up Jax's building excitement and possibly her whole night, for that matter. Why was it that critical to hear that she loved me back? I needed to validate the reality of what I wanted to believe her feelings were, but why now? I guess I needed that next level of relationship achievement. Having a girlfriend with whom I truly connected on many levels and had so much fun was no longer enough. Why? Why did I need it to be more than that so fast? Eddie's question unexpectedly popped into my mind. 'When do you stop having to repeatedly prove yourself to yourself?' I guess it's relevant. I needed validation that I was lovable or maybe that my hopes were valid...realistic...or possible. If she were to have responded in kind and followed my plan, my concepts of the relationship's present and future would have been legitimatized. So, where did that leave me now? I realized I needed to get out of my head and back into the room.

Why were the lights always so damn bright in any waiting room in America, except, of course, at The Altered Ego Salon. Weren't there options other than the massive rectangular ceiling tile-sized fluorescent boxes that only released the most unnaturally colorless light possible? Perhaps my grieving over the conversation that should have been but didn't manifest was migrating from denial to the anger phase, like the start of a bar fight when the argument has just escalated from the final "Fuck You!" to a fist landing on the side of your nose.

I still had my wits about me, enough to know that Jax didn't deserve to deal with my emotional instability at a time like this.

I needed to redirect, so I refocused my irritability on what was available. There were only a few other people in the waiting room, all solitary individuals, in each separate corner of the room, maximizing the space between themselves and each other, as one does in the middle of the night and you are attempting not to interact with others in hopes of nodding off. Repeated failed attempts to conquer the cruel, hard-edged furniture's limitations always resulted in a futile struggle for temporary comfort. I think it's downright mean-spirited to furnish any room this way, let alone a room where anxious people had to sit for hours.

Waiting in hospitals always sucks, but it could have been worse. I suppose I could have been in an emergency room. In an emergency room, people are all miserable and there because they or a loved one are fucked. In a maternity waiting room, there tends to be a lot of positive excitement, and people are waiting because they love someone who was fucked nine months ago and is now about to be a parent. In an emergency room, people are generally pissed and pissed that they have to wait for hours with no rhyme or reason for how patients are prioritized. In a maternity waiting room, the waiting time is dictated by the mother's body, and nobody hates a pregnant mother, friend, or family member for taking too long.

In the ER, there are crazy, high, and drunk people whose revelry has gotten them into a nasty pickle. In the maternity waiting room, people are generally sober, sane, and have homes. In the emergency room, anything can happen at any time. Tempers flare, outbursts are common, and everyone is on edge, wishing they were anywhere else. Almost everyone is glad to be there in the maternity waiting room, brimming with anticipation.

After further examination, it became clear that an emergency room may have been more fitting for my situation. I felt any remaining enthusiasm for the future of our relationship draining out of my gut, leaving an empty vacuum in its place. Sure, I was just moments into the fallout, but something had popped in my head like a child's new shiny red balloon, knowing it was too good to be true in the first place. The thought occurred to me that I may have been catastrophizing, but one couldn't be sure, as there were unanswered questions that I certainly wasn't willing to risk asking. At this juncture, my only play was to portray an unshakable self-confidence by appearing unfazed. Like everyone else in the waiting room, I was now gambling on the waiting game, my baby, a budding unstable relationship. Any future initiation of sharing feelings or relationship dialogue would fall solely on her, along with any uncomfortable guilt associated with choosing not to address it. It was the only chip I had left to play.

It then dawned on me that I didn't even know Jimmy's wife's name.

"Jax, what's your sister-in-law's name?" I asked.

"Summer. Have you met her before? I somehow assumed you had."

"Nope. I hope it's OK I'm here, being I'm squarely in the complete stranger category."

"No, you're not. I've talked incessantly about you to the point I'm sure she wishes I'd shut the hell up. I had assumed you'd met her, but I don't know why. Anyway, she's awesome. Just like a sister to me and, next to you, my closest friend."

The wonderfully close family Jax was embraced in brilliantly illustrated the sharp contrast with my lack of anything remotely similar. Why would she need to rush into loving me when she had plenty of others to laud with her affection? She didn't have all her relationship capital invested in a single person and was probably content to let things flow without clinging to or rushing anything.

Luckily, Jimmy burst into the waiting room, providing a welcome reprieve from my torment. He was dressed like he had delivered the baby himself in blue scrubs, a matching blue hat, and a mask lowered around his neck. He rushed over to us at an adrenaline-fueled clip.

"Jax! Holy shit, Toby! No way are you here in the middle of the night, but I'm stoked you are! I'm a Dad! And Jax, you are now Aunt

Jax! And Toby...I guess you are now Aunt Jax's boyfriend?" Jimmy spat out in staccato fashion.

"I'm cool with that," I said, shaking his hand, transitioning into a full man-hug, although I thought "Aunt Jax's boyfriend that she's not in love with" would be a more accurate moniker.

"Jimmy!" Jax almost screamed as she threw her arms around him, forcing me to disengage and ensuring the others in the waiting room were now wide awake. "That was fast! How is Summer doing?"

"I was sure she was dying despite the doctor telling me everything was going fine. However, as soon as Jade popped out, Summer was the happiest I've ever seen her. She says she's feeling great, and the doctor says things couldn't have gone better! I've got to head back in as they are probably done cleaning Jade up, and I want to be there for the first breastfeeding. I guess, for some reason, it's a big deal."

"Jade! I love that name. She's so lucky to be born into this family, Jimmy, and to have you as a Dad. When can we meet the little angel?" Jax was losing her shit in the excitement of it all.

"Summer already asked if you can come in. The doc will let me know as soon as it's cool to have a visitor. I don't want you guys to have to wait until Jade is in the viewing area with all the other babies since that could be a couple of hours or whenever Summer needs to sleep next. I'm going to head back in, but stay tuned; I'll be back as soon as I can."

Jimmy shot out into the hall, unintentionally shoulder-checking an approaching nurse right into the door frame. He blurted out an apology as he accelerated down the hall. Having been in his spot before, I knew exactly how he felt, valiantly charging into a new and still loosely defined future, armed with a seemingly bottomless well of hope, love, and excitement. I took a moment to remember the feelings of the inner warmth and tenderness associated with those memories, followed by the sobering reality that I was not currently traversing a single one of the hope-filled futures I had so vividly imagined.

For Jimmy's sake, I hoped he would enjoy living those child-rearing realities that I now only experienced as ghosts of what no longer was. I had successfully compartmentalized my thinking about my children, how my relationship with them may never be what I visualized, and how I would reconcile all this. It was just easier that way. I wasn't ready to process these regrets and start the grieving process. Luckily, I was a master at stuffing my emotions and being very selective in which compartments I spent my time in. I felt the seed of contempt for Gina sprouting again, knowing it wouldn't be long before it broke ground. As Eddie said, these are just more ideas and blindly accepted beliefs, the bars of my personal jail cell. This was an area where I wasn't trying to justify myself to myself because I simply no longer could.

It was now 4 a.m., and I was fucked out of a good night's sleep. I needed to get out of there and away from this living example of the life I had once believed was my reality. I needed to reevaluate my relationship status with Jax, which just took an unexpected wrong turn. I realized I needed to build a narrative for all this that I could live with, which would take a little time. I also knew that whatever I came up with would be nothing more than just another manufactured story I would tell myself until I believed it, and in knowing that, it probably wouldn't be all that believable anyway.

It must have been about fifteen minutes later when Jimmy returned to fetch Jax to head back to meet Jade and see Summer, as she was allowed just one visitor at a time. I leveraged the opportunity to excuse myself to head home and get some sleep. Jimmy and Jax were more than thankful I had come. At least I was a better guy than before I arrived, in their eyes, for whatever that was now worth.

I ARRIVED BACK in my hovel actually happy to be home. I plopped down into my beanbag chair and kicked off my shoes, rubbing my temples. Sitting there in the darkness seemed like a perfect metaphor for my life. Why hadn't I let myself think about or process the loss of my children? Ironically, a baby was born tonight; however, I felt like mine were dying concepts. Maybe that would change over time; who knew, but why was it I hadn't been willing to go there? It felt as if I went down the stairs into the dark basement of my mind; whatever was lurking down there was eager to eat me alive. Plain and simple, I was scared shitless.

I flicked on the lamp on the side table to pull myself out of the darkness and noticed my copy of *Be Here Now* sitting there next to the lamp. Why not? I thought, picking it up and opening it to a random page, zeroing in on the words in the center.

"And suddenly I realized that he knew everything that was going on in my head, all the time, and that he still loved me. Because who we are is behind all that."

Eddie was the first thing that popped into my mind. On more than one occasion, he had said out loud what I was thinking but wasn't saying. The first time I had beers with him, I recalled that instant he stared me in the eyes, feeling him looking into my brain from the inside out. I knew Eddie wasn't your typical homeless man, but could he be more than your average man? However, maybe I was reading more into it. After all, it's not uncommon for someone to say something, and someone else replies, "I was just thinking the same thing."

Reading a bit further, I deduced that Ram Dass was referring to his guru, whom he accidentally stumbled across in India. Maybe more was happening with my relationship with Eddie than just a couple of guys eating chili and chugging cheap beer. Guru translates as "teacher," and I suppose, in a way, Eddie was a teacher to me. He exposed me to different ideas and concepts and asked questions about things I had never considered. He seemed to know my answers before he even asked his questions. It's like they were all rhetorical but designed to get me to think. I didn't believe in any magical beings performing Christ-like miracles. Hell, I considered the Bible another version of Aesop's Fables.

When I opened my eyes, it was starting to become light out, and my neck was killing me. Apparently I had dosed off. Bean bag chairs are called chairs and not beds for a reason. I needed coffee and needed to see Eddie.

Still bruised from the lack of reciprocation of shared loving feelings, I shifted priorities and elected to start the day with a much-needed endorphin release and changed into my running attire.

Time was of the essence to get out the door before waves of sleep deprivation washed me back into rationalizing that a run didn't make much sense. The sun was rising, and I wanted to be in Golden Gate Park when the warm morning light cast its magical golden glow on the trail through the trees. I was determined to find beauty, if it was out there—I deserved a dose of that medicine.

After about five minutes, I passed through the Arguello Gate into Golden Gate Park, enjoying the silence of the windless air. My nostrils filled with the smells of dirt, flowers, and grass at their zenith when the morning dew was still fresh on the ground. I descended towards JFK Drive from behind the Conservatory of Flowers, a vast, majestic greenhouse well worth the price of admission.

I turned right on JFK Drive, heading west, passing the DeYoung Museum, feeling rather proud of myself for dragging my butt out of my apartment first thing in the morning. I wondered if this run counted as an effort to justify myself to myself. Was I running because it was healthy or to add "being fit" to my list of self-descriptive adjectives?

Eddie had a hell of a point. How much of the effort we apply towards life is an effort to support a story we want to believe about who we are? Stories to support identities we hope are true, but which, at a deep level, we suspect may not entirely be. I suppose we're all either running towards something we don't yet have or away from something else we don't want.

I was doing both. I wanted a better job and more money, and I wanted Jax to love me because those things seemed vital for me to be happy with myself. I didn't like the feeling of being a schmuck loser for the last however many months after life took a few unanticipated turns. I was trying to collect thoughts I could live with to invalidate and squeeze out those I couldn't. My mind was most certainly working hard to validate myself to myself. I was not working, running, or enjoying time with Jax purely for the sake of the activities and whatever joy or pain came along with them. They were a means to an end. An end where I would find myself relatively more successful than my peers by my laughable definition of what a successful guy my age should be. Sure, moments of joy accumulated along the way, but the attainment was largely more important than the experience itself. And all this was happening unconsciously. Ah... the unexamined life.

I had now run under the 19th Ave underpass and took a slight left to continue onto Middle Drive towards the polo fields when the pondering of my mind was interrupted by an urgent warning that I was about to begin shitting. More advanced notice would have been appreciated. After frantically considering my options, my only real shot was to make it down to the polo fields and hope that the bathroom on the far side was unlocked this early in the morning. That was a quarter to a half mile away, and the situation's urgency appeared to be increasing exponentially. About a hundred steps later, I realized it was time for Plan B. Plan B was the only plan still available at this point and involved identifying the closest place to drop trou and crap next to the sidewalk I was now on. I'm sure every runner has had these instances, although I couldn't recall anyone sharing their experience.

A grove of trees was on the right, and I decided it was my best shot since I couldn't see exactly where the path would end up when it curved to the left shortly ahead. Plan B was unfolding nicely, as not a soul was in sight. Unfortunately, about five feet off the sidewalk on my way to the trees, Plan C launched on its own. The turtle was poking his head out and wasn't about to retreat, as they say. I found myself in a full squat with my shorts around my ankles, in active excavation mode, keeping my eyes peeled on the sidewalk ahead in case of the unthinkable: someone appearing from around the bend. I wasn't entirely sure what to do if that happened, but I decided to cross that bridge when I came to it. As quickly as it began, it was over. I started looking around for anything remotely adequate to wipe with and immediately concluded there was nothing but gravel. This problem was immediately combined with an equally unfortunate problem: a man that had just rounded the corner was looking at me and stopped in his tracks, trying to figure out what kind of protocol might be appropriate in a shituation like this.

"LOOK AWAY!" I yelled at the top of my lungs without thinking. Luckily, he was good at following orders, spun around, and remained as motionless as the park bench next to him.

Since I had been relegated to complete my run with a shit-spackled ass-crack, I pulled up my shorts and jogged right past him. "Coast is clear now."

"You're a complete jackass!" the stranger yelled, now behind me, as I rounded the corner only to see no less than forty Porta Potties in a row.

The tents and temporary fencing indicated that they had been set up for an outdoor concert, and I had been about fifty yards from complete salvation without even the slightest clue. What a perfect analogy for life, I thought, laughing at the humor of it all as I entered the nearest one to clean up.

If the run didn't get the endorphins going, the humor at my expense sure did. Fortunately, the rest of the journey home was far less eventful and my farthest run to date. I estimated I made it at least four miles and didn't feel worse for the wear.

———

I ARRIVED HOME, showered, and headed out the door to grab coffee for Eddie and myself.

It was a quick transaction, as Jimmy wasn't working, assuredly enjoying his first morning with Jade and Susan as a family.

Eddie and Cowboy appeared to have just woken up. Eddie was fumbling under his cart for something when Cowboy barked and rushed me, startling Eddie. Cowboy slammed his rag into my knee, nearly launching the two coffees out of my hands. Luckily, the lids performed as advertised.

"Cowboy, get off of him and get back over here," Eddie hollered, and Cowboy immediately rushed back to him.

"Eddie, you know I don't mind Cowboy's enthusiasm. Makes me feel good that someone or something is that excited to see me these days. And if you're rummaging around for your coffee pot, don't bother. I've got yours right here."

"Will the miracles never cease? I just woke up and said, 'Please, God, don't make me brew my own coffee again this morning. Just have a messenger bring it to me for a change.'"

"Eddie, that's a lie."

"So. It makes for a good story," he replied, accepting his cup. "Thanks, brother. To what do I owe this pleasure?"

"I was hoping to chat with you to gain some perspective, perhaps."

"I'll give you as many different perspectives as you like, but it doesn't mean any of them are worth a shit," he said, smiling.

"Somehow, I think one or two of them may be. You seem to have a nasty little habit of being right about most things."

Eddie did seem insightful, albeit his insights weren't always easy to digest. His beard had been trimmed tight against his face, leaving about a quarter inch of stubble that took about ten years off his age. His eyes appeared even more icy blue than before without the distraction of a tumbleweed hanging off the lower half of his face.

"Eddie, it appears you may have trimmed up your beard. Makes you look like more of a gentleman."

"Lost a bet with RV Jeff. I bet my beard against $10 that I could beat him in a foot race. Son of a bitch won by a foot and a half."

"You must have looked like two criminals fleeing a crime scene."

"I told him I wasn't running my fastest because I needed a trim, but he knew I was lying," Eddie confessed.

"What in God's name possessed you to race Jeff?"

"Because I'm fast as fuck, and he looked slow. He didn't mention that he was second in the state championships for the hundred-yard dash in high school. He may have had a genetic advantage on me."

"Or the fact that you are about twenty-five years older than him and, I'd wager, haven't been training much lately," I added. "Well, looks good all the same, and beards have been known to grow back."

I sat down, and Cowboy took the opportunity to rest against my leg. It was still cool out; he was short-haired and took warmth where he could get it. Eddie was stretching his hamstrings, no doubt addressing some residual tightness from his athletic endeavor.

"What's on your mind, Toby, my boy?" Eddie asked.

"Had a rough night last night, and it got me thinking, which didn't help much."

"It often doesn't unless you're trying to remember which one of the four things on your shopping list you forgot when you notice only three things are in your cart."

"Eddie, before I get into last night, how do you always know what I'm thinking?"

"I don't always know. I'm just a good guesser sometimes," he said, giving me one of his trademark winks.

"No, seriously, you seem to either say what I'm thinking or ask me questions you know the answer to but know I don't and need to think about." I wasn't going to let this go. "Am I right?"

"Partially. What are you getting at, anyway?" he asked, pausing to look me straight in the eye.

"Well, Eddie, it seems your perspective is...let's say...unusual yet brilliantly insightful. Also, you seem to accept me for better or for worse without judgment, and you kind of chip away at my world-view in a way that leaves me with more questions than answers."

"Introspection tends to work that way. Hard and slow at first. Gets easier and faster after a while. Not for pussies, I'll add."

"See! Now I have more questions than when we started. First, how do you know what's going on inside my head? Second, how do you know all the shit that I somehow need to know to make sense of things? Third, what's this process of introspection, and why does it speed up?" I was in the mood for more clarity, not more confusion. "Can you directly answer those questions, please?" I had become overly impatient and immediately felt guilty for my directness.

"I admire your directness," he said, almost taunting me with another example. "I'm happy to answer your questions to the best of what the English language can muster, but first, I have one question for you."

"Fair enough."

"Are you ready to hear the answers? I mean, actually understand them? Because this shit can get deep fast, and I don't want you to get the bends if you get scared and try to come back up to the surface too soon."

"Eddie, God damn it, I'm confused. I realize, in many ways, I don't understand myself or why I think the way I do and...I guess...I trust you and want to learn," I said, without anticipating what would fly out of my mouth. Suddenly, I felt vulnerable and exposed.

"The old saying is pretty much true. 'When the student is ready, the teacher will appear.' Until now, you were most interested in propping yourself up, getting on track, and doubling down on your beliefs about what a success or failure you were. That's a constructive exercise. I am willing to bet you are now starting to question what you believe and are curious about what you truly are underneath all the bullshit of shifting thoughts and beliefs. That, my friend, requires a destructive process."

"Well, you asked me when I will stop trying to justify myself to myself. And yes, I have been mulling that one over. And my answer is it seems like almost every thought is doing just that. The problem is, when I do see that happening, the thoughts about who I am or who I want to be seem more fragile in that I don't know if I buy into them as much, which scares the hell out of me. If those thoughts aren't true, I'm not sure what is. Does that make sense? I guess, now, I'm looking for answers as to how this all works."

"You now want to learn. Your mind is open to alternative perspectives: 'The beginner's mind,' like a kid eager to explore reality, except now you have about forty years of baggage holding you back."

"I imagine you're right, but what are the chances I meet you and you end up, kind of...you know...being there at the right time?"

"I'd say the chances are high. Seems to be how it works."

"What do you mean—how it works?"

"I mind my own business, and now and then, people cross my path at what seems like the right time. I tend to give them what they want until they eventually seem to want what I have to give them. You wanted validation, support, and someone to connect with while trying to get back on track. You wanted happiness, which unfolded in a way you hoped would bring you back to a confident state—job, girlfriend, fitness, etc. Recently, you realized maybe it didn't give you what you wanted, and now you are having a problem making sense of it all because your paradigms didn't account for that outcome. Am I right?"

"As usual, yes." He had accurately summed up the last month of my life in just a few sentences.

"Hey, I don't ask for this stuff, by the way. It happens on its own. At this point, I assume that's why I didn't die that night in Nam. Although I had nothing to return to like the others, I ultimately had a purpose in serving others. That night was a horrible experience, and it shook my core to rubble. I was never the same because everything that I thought mattered disappeared. Once I got home, I started questioning everything and couldn't find the answers. All I found was more bullshit that I didn't quite buy into anymore. The more I looked at my bullshit beliefs, aspirations, and thoughts about life and who I was, the more they all kind of burned away, leaving just the smoking embers of what 'I' once was."

"Well, Eddie, I kind of feel like that's happening to me right now, and it's more than a little unsettling, I'm eager to report," I retorted.

"As unsettling as it may be, it's great luck. In my case, a part of me wanted to find a new belief system that explained all this, but I was starting to realize more beliefs were just more illusions that would ultimately fade away. Eventually, there was no 'me' left by our normal standards of identity. Of course, my body was still walking around and needed to eat and sleep, but the deconstruction of my ego, identity, and personal narrative was complete, and all that was left was the only thing that ever was."

"And what was that?"

"The totality of everything, right here and right now. This exact moment is all there ever is. The history of all the change since the beginning of time has left us with only this exact moment, which will morph into the next exact moment, and so forth. Eternity all takes place exactly right here and now in the ever-changing present. The question is, how does one meet eternity here and experience it— not just think about it conceptually?"

"I'm not the guy to ask," I said, feeling lost and confused again.

"The answer is to give up on the mind as your vehicle to get there. Just watch reality for what it is."

"So just watch; that's the assignment?"

"Watch it all come and go, and try not to search, classify, or fortify. Stay simply aware and curious about what will surface next. Thoughts and emotions never entirely stop, but your belief in them and identification with them will."

"OK, fine. But I'm sure many people arrive at the same place as I am right now when enough shit goes down that everything starts to get questioned. Is there always a teacher that appears?" I asked.

"Yes and no. For some, it's the right book at the right time. For others, it's the right experiences that unfold at just the right time. People may find themselves at the right lecture, and others come across the right friend. Some find God, a Bible, whatever. The next step usually appears when it's time. Not everyone follows the path as far as it goes. Most never sincerely want to question our culture's beliefs about reality, or even their personal beliefs, for that matter. Most people are just looking for a little relief, and once they get it, they lose interest. Which is completely fine."

"Well, this introspective excavation of the psyche never occurred to me until we started talking," I pointed out.

"There's always a trigger. It all happens how it's supposed to for everyone who wants self-understanding; the path is there. For those that don't want it, their lives have different meanings obtained through experiences, although they eventually get lost chasing new experiences. Their happiness is intermittent, and they need more experiences like an addict needs another fix to connect with their ideas of who they are and what life is about," he explained with a sympathy that bordered on melancholy.

"Toby, there are a lot of events in this circus we call life," Eddie continued. "In the center ring is accumulating wealth and financial security. Of course, it is born out of fear and distrust for life. Then, in the ring on the left is being accepted, loved, and validated. In the ring on the right are experiences, status, and power—all different games in the circus tent of life. Any fleeting attainments in any of these circus rings are like waves briefly appearing on the top of the ocean, appearing, in a way, separate from their source, the vast body of water beneath it all. But our culture doesn't teach free diving into the depths of our consciousness. It teaches us to find boats, surf-boards, and fins to play with in the waves. But the thing is, the waves always disappear. Most mistake the temporary for the permanent."

Eddie paused and, after a few seconds, put his hand on my shoulder and started up again, "Toby, in this experience of life, not many people are brave enough to ride the big ride. The one outside the circus tent. The one that throws you up, down, and upside down. But it's the only real thing happening. Everything else is foreplay. You must ask yourself whether you want to directly experience true reality or chase the illusion of experiences and ideas. You don't *kind of* ride the biggest ride in the park. You *commit* when you get on and surrender to where the ride goes once it takes off."

"Eddie, I'll ride the ride if you ride it with me and let me know what the fuck is going on when everything no longer makes sense," I said, knowing I was too scared to ride alone.

"Toby, at this point, if you need to think about something, think about this one question. What are you willing to give up to get off this wheel of illusion?" he asked. "If the answer isn't everything, don't get on the big ride. The 'you' that steps on won't be around to step off in the end. Now get out of here and get on with your day. I've shared too much already."

"Hold on. You never answered my question. How do you know what I'm thinking? Once or twice may be a coincidence, but it happens a lot. Do you have some kind of magical power or something? Does anyone that attains a certain level of self-awareness have the ability to do that?"

"I don't know," he calmly replied.

"What do you mean you don't know?" I wasn't about to accept another copout.

"Toby, admittedly, sometimes I know things. I'm not thinking about them, trying to read your mind, or trying to violate your privacy. I'd say the consciousness behind the mind, persona, or whatever you want to call it, is one interconnected whole. I get a sense of what you're feeling or ruminating on, and occasionally, I'll mention it when it happens. I wish it were more glamorous."

"It's kind of cool though, right?"

"Not always. Toby, there are yogis, saints, and teachers like Neem Karoli Baba and Bhagawan Nityananda, to name a couple of many, who are reported throughout India to have performed miracles that make Jesus look like a toddler learning to walk. And not all of them are even enlightened souls. If those things happen, great, but for many of the most holy saints, nothing like that ever happens. Mostly, these experiences become traps that seekers chase with a desire for power or recognition. They become a goal versus a guidepost along the way. Once you become attached to producing things from thin air, being in two places at once, reading minds, healing, or God knows what else, you are trapped and building a spiritual identity for the sake of an ego. Please, don't get caught up in chasing that bullshit. If it happens, let it come and go on its own. But I hope, for your sake, it never does. Chasing experiences of any sort takes you down deep holes that can be very challenging to find your way out of. No more talk of distractions. Be on your way, my good brother."

"But wait, Eddie. I have to tell you about some stuff that went down with me and Jax," I said, realizing that the reason I originally came had yet to be discussed.

"Nope. That shit's good. It gives you fodder to bring up deeper thoughts, emotions, and beliefs to watch. But what are you willing to give up to get off the wheel? That's enough for now. See you soon, brother."

I took the hint and left with another assignment. What was I willing to give up to get off the wheel? Life was a wheel, spinning around and around—different fears, desires, goals, and experiences carrying us round and round. Fleeting happiness is replaced by inevitable anxiety, moments of depression, and then round and round all over again. Now my thoughts were sounding like one of Eddie's sermons. I had already given up most of everything in my life, but not by choice. Eddie was referring to what I was ready to give up internally, as that's ultimately what I thought we were talking about. I was now more curious than ever about what, if anything, remained the same through all this. But that wasn't the question. The question was, what was I willing to give up?

I had no idea.

CHAPTER
TWENTY-THREE

I exited the salon at the exact time of the day when the warm sunny afternoon stillness of San Francisco transitions into a stiff wind carrying the cold and shitty fog in to rake your buzz by dropping the temperature twenty degrees in a matter of minutes. It's as remarkable as it is discriminatory for anyone who appreciates a nice day. As it turned out yet again, I had no jacket.

The thing about the human mind is that hope sneaks into your brain just like a shot of tequila, immediately reducing your ability to make good choices. I had contracted amnesia and completely forgotten my twenty-two years of foggy San Francisco afternoons. Why would I need a jacket if it was sunny and warm when I left the house? I was as guilty of rampant stupidity as the tourists on the Golden Gate Bridge.

I broke into a slow jog because I was now a regular slow jogger and knew what I was doing. I was running away from the fog, as the unmanly tend to do. As it turns out, this cut my commute time in half, and I was soon in my apartment, debating if it might be a good idea to put on socks. Now extra cautious due to almost being taken down by a fog bank, I went with the socks, jacket, and Candlestick Park 49ers scarf.

It had been over a week since I'd been in The Plow, and I wasn't sure why I wasn't drinking more often. I had accidentally put my hard-earned alcohol tolerance at risk, which scared me. What other vices might I be losing without even knowing it? Maybe this was an example of something I was willing to give up to get off the wheel. However, technically, if you don't even consider giving it up, does it count? It just snuck out the back door while nobody was looking. I would take credit regardless. But who knew? Maybe it didn't always require effort to let something go.

I rounded the corner, wondering if anything had changed since the last time I patronized the establishment. Taking inventory upon entry, I deduced that absolutely nothing had and most likely ever would. Regulars wanted familiarity, and the Irish didn't give two shits about what the general public might like or not. Pubs were places to get drunk and maybe indulge in fish and chips. People either came to the pub because they liked it or didn't come at all. To each their own. No pandering to the masses. To me, it felt like coming home. The smell of brewing coffee and stale beer and disinfectant was as intoxicating as the spirits served. Seeing the fog blow down the street through the open door increased the coziness factor of this sanctified refuge.

"Connor, looking good, as usual. What's the word?" I asked, making my way over to the bar.

"Hey, mate! We've missed ya 'round here, but I'll deny ever sayin' such a thing. Ya look like ya've lost weight. That new girlfriend keepin' ya on the move?" he said, waggling his bushy eyebrows.

"Moving straight towards my grave, but that's another story. I'd fancy a Corona with a lime. My meat on the side, please," I said. Then, feeling a stinger was in order, "I'll have a shot of Patron as well. Can I buy you one?"

"I'll need one to ease the pain from yer Mexican orderin' tendencies. Ya know, ya are the only bastard who orders that garbage, which isn't a real beer, by the way. Just sayin' I'm concerned about yer choices. I ordered a twelve-pack over a week ago just for ya, and there are still twelve left. Although ya don't make sense, I've still got yer back. I'll deny it if ya mention a word of it to anyone."

"Over the years, with a lot of dedication, I've become quite adept at making and executing poor choices, and now you want to demean me for the only superpower I have. Your words are hurtful, Connor."

"Welcome back, mate. I think I'll pour meself a shot of Jameson's to toast old friends and questionable decisions," he said, reaching across the bar to give me a couple of affectionate pats on the shoulder.

"Good to be back. Have you had to use the persuader lately?" I asked.

"Not in a while, mate. No fights in almost a month. Maybe a record. Somebody took a shite in the urinal last week. There's still ongoing debate as to whether that's funny or just fucked up," he said, shaking his head, clearly indicating which side of the argument he was on.

"I think it's funnier than shit. I'm just bummed I didn't think of it first. Any clue as to who the perpetrator was?"

"Big Sallie is my guess due to her shite-slingin' nature. RV wasn't initially thrilled about the suggestion, but eventually came 'round to a respectful pride that she may have been the culprit. Funny what people value in a partner these days."

"Speak of the devil," I said as Big Sallie and RV sauntered in, hand in hand. "She must have done it." Although horrific to visualize, it wasn't hard to picture.

"Toby. Connor," RV howled across the bar, announcing his presence in proper form. RV had on a black and white do-rag, Axel Rose style, and his go-to t-shirt with the sleeves ripped off down to the waist, revealing what he was sure was an impressive set of lats, but in reality, were excessive love handles that jiggled like a perfectly cooked brisket. However, next to Sallie, he was ripped to shreds.

Sallie was smiling, which I had never seen before. Surprisingly, she had a beautiful smile—the kind that started with her eyes and consumed her whole face. Maybe RV had just given her the high, hard one, and we were basking in the afterglow.

"You two look stunning this evening," I said, getting off my stool to give them a handshake and a hug. Jeff reeked of Brut aftershave, and Sallie smelled of sauerkraut and baby powder, the baby powder losing the battle of the scents.

"Well, we're all dressed up for a reason tonight," RV announced.

"Thank God, lad. We were tired of seein' those old torn-up t-shirts," Connor said, not wasting the opportunity to get in the opening jab.

"Speaking of fashion, good call covering up the melon with that do-rag. It's damn chilly out there. But the real question is, are you showered as well or just riding on your good looks and sense of fashion?" I said, piling onto Connor's lead.

"Very funny," Sallie chimed in. "Today is not a shower day; however, due to the occasion, I made an exception. I have severely dry skin, so I have to put on a ton of lotion afterward, or I get super uncomfortable," she added. Nobody could determine why that variable was important enough to include, nor were we willing to probe.

"Doesn't anyone want to know what the occasion is?" RV asked.

"We just assumed Sallie's unscheduled shower and yer over-application of cheap cologne are both impressive enough achievements to qualify," Connor retorted.

"We are engaged!" Sallie blurted out, extending her meat hook of a hand and raising a sausage-like ring finger to reveal the smallest diamond anyone had ever seen without the help of a magnifying glass.

From behind the bar, Connor, operating without a magnifying glass, announced, "That's a beautiful band, Sallie, me darlin'."

"Well, the diamond's damn nice too," Jeff proudly threw out.

Leaning over the bar, squinting, Connor raised his eyebrows, "Sure as shite, there is a diamond there. I just saw it sparkle." A respectable backpedal.

Sallie's face blushed as she wrapped both arms around Jeff, beaming with pride. I tend to get emotional during life's poignant events, and I felt myself getting choked up. "Connor, you cheap ass, I think a round on the house is in order here."

"Alright. Ya three and nobody else," Connor clarified. "Ya can have one of anythin' you want, as long as it's Irish," he said, looking right at me with an evil squint.

"Maybe a bar of Irish Spring for Jeff to wash off some of that cologne," I playfully suggested.

"Just wait. It's aftershave, and it wears off fast and will settle into 'sexy' pretty soon," he reassuringly replied. "Connor, a shot of Jameson 18 and a Guinness for both Sallie and I."

"That's two each, RV. The offer is one per person, which will expire momentarily," Connor quipped.

"I'll pick up what Connor's too stingy to provide. As long as I'm here, RV and Sallie can order whatever they want on my tab and save their money for their honeymoon."

"Or the bachelor party, which is tonight," RV proclaimed. "We're going clubbing on the strip, boys, if you know what I mean." It appeared we were now included in the bachelor party, a jujitsu move RV had executed in a way that left one no choice but to acquiesce.

"Who's all going?" I inquired to provide myself with the necessary mental preparation to begin conjuring up the courage required for such an event.

"Just the inner circle. You, me, Sallie, and Connor." The guest list was short and unfortunate in many ways.

"Wish I could, but I've got a business to run here. I'll be there with ya in spirit," Connor replied. I suddenly wished I had a business to run.

"Looks like just us three, then, Toby," RV said with a deal-is-done tone. "Unless, of course, you want to bring Jax."

This was actually a brilliant idea. With Jax there, no matter how tense, awkward, and uncomfortable the air would be (with unsaid words still hovering), it couldn't be as bad as "just us three."

"Sure. Let me see if I can get ahold of her," I said casually.

I grabbed my phone and headed to the front of the bar to talk privately. I had no idea what to expect and figured I was most likely creating a more sinister series of possible outcomes than could exist in reality. Hope for the future of our relationship had been swapped out with concern for the relationship's current state, casting a web of doubt over everything.

But, ultimately, she hadn't said it back! I had provided her with the perfect open door to express her true feelings, but she didn't walk through. I was either further along than she was in my budding affection, or she had reversed course along the path somewhere and was now heading in the opposite direction. Regardless, this recent unfortunate turn of events had taken our relationship to the "Y." We had been moving along in perceived unison, and now we were at the bottom of the "V" section in the middle of the "Y." We would either decide to take the same turn or separate paths. Let fate run its course, but there were more immediate issues to address— namely, the possibility of my pending and likely incarceration along with RV Jeff and Big Sallie. I dialed the phone and listened to it ring. Jax thankfully answered on the fourth ring before it went to voicemail.

"Hi, Toby. You caught me on the way home from the hospital. Summer's sleeping, and Jade's in with the other babies in the infirmary, so I figured I'd use this opportunity to shower," she said.

"Well, no sense in wasting a good shower. How would you like to join me in celebrating RV Jeff's and Big Sallie's engagement tonight," I said, realizing that at least those two had both taken the same turn at the "Y."

"That might do me good. Let Jimmy, Summer, and Jade have their first crack at family time, right?"

"Great point. So you're in?"

"Yep, give me about a half hour to primp. Where are we going? I want to make sure I'm dressed appropriately," she asked.

"No idea," I stated, realizing I hadn't considered this. "I'll put it this way: Jeff is wearing his signature t-shirt style, although claiming it's new, and Sallie is wearing an article from her tent collection."

"That's mean, Toby, but pretty funny. I guess I'll pick out one of my tents then," she said.

"We are at The Plow now. I'll stall the migration elsewhere until you arrive, OK?"

"Perfect. See you in a few, hon," she said, ending the call. I liked being called hon. It implied existing affection, which indicated hope was not unwarranted; however, I decided to plan for the worst at this point, so it didn't take me by surprise when it manifested. It's funny how the brain does that—getting used to the worst-case scenario to better prepare us for it when it comes to fruition. The downside is spending a lot of time living through imagined painful scenarios that may never manifest. And if they do, I can't say if thinking about them in advance helps or simply increases the duration of the painful experience.

Returning to the bar, I couldn't help but notice a round of shots that looked suspiciously like Jägermeister being distributed. I also realized that it had been liberally added to my bar tab. It was sweet watching Jeff and Sallie banter with the excitement of elementary students on the first day of school.

This brought up a memory of my proposal to Gina. I had the advantage of not having to pony up for a diamond, as my mother had promised me that I would receive my deceased grandmother's ring, which had a beautiful one-karat diamond and a hideous band, crammed with too much detail for it to look like anything but a twisted nest of old wire. I thoughtfully decided to remove the diamond from the band to spare Gina's disappointment and avoid ruining the moment. I would let her pick out her band to save her the silent grief of living out the rest of her life saddled with the ongoing embarrassment of people's creative phony compliments when observing her hideous ring for the first time. So I acquired a traditional black velvet ring box and placed the beautiful diamond inside.

We had gone out of town and were spending the weekend in

Monterrey at a house on the water lent to us by a fraternity brother. I was waiting for the perfect moment, which never came. Adding to the pressure, I had confided in my two closest friends, Jack and Big Dong Don, my plans for securing a commitment to holy matrimony. I would now have to admit my spectacular failure to execute.

I was awkwardly silent while driving home, which was why Gina asked me if something was wrong. Without thinking, I pulled the car over on the shoulder, produced the box, opened it, and presented her with Grandmother's beautiful diamond, forgetting to speak out loud. This creative proposal technique was thereafter referred to as "the rock in the box" approach, which I was immediately informed —right there on the shoulder of the road with cars and semi-trailers whizzing by—was unacceptable. Somehow, it wasn't a "story-worthy" proposal and therefore didn't meet her expectations. Upon later feedback from multiple women I shared this story with, she was entitled to send me back to the showers. My second attempt, with said diamond mounted on a band, on my knees on Pier 9, over-looking the San Francisco Bay one starlight night, cleared the methodology hurdle, and the small tragedy of our marriage was set in motion.

As I suspected, the chosen shot was Jägermeister, which didn't taste any better than it ever had before. Sometimes, you need to earn your buzz. In an effort to take the revelry to the next level, I ordered another round of the same.

"You're a good man, Toby," RV said. "Sharing this day with you guys in our favorite place is like a sore dick. You just can't beat it."

"Scientists design special gels to navigate those situations, Jeff," I quickly informed him.

"So, is Jax coming?" Sallie interrupted.

"She wouldn't miss it," I replied, stretching the truth. "Should be here within half an hour."

To effectively secure the information needed to ruminate on worst-case scenarios, I asked, "So, what's the plan for the evening?"

"We were just discussing that, and to keep Connor in the mix, we will be enjoying dinner on Connor right here, saving money for our next stop later," RV said with an approving nod levied at Connor, who looked at me with an "I'm not such a cheap-ass after all, am I?" kind of look.

"I like that plan. What's on the agenda for later on?" There was still a possible risk that needed mitigation.

"For that, you're officially on a need-to-know basis, and right now, you don't need to know," Jeff informed me. The unknown was now all I could think about.

"Well, please let me know when I've earned the key to unlock the next level. Connor, let's line up a couple of shots for Jax because she'll have some catching up to do. Plus, it's more fun when everyone is operating with the same level of impaired judgment."

A short time later, Jax arrived carrying a small succulent plant in a green-blue glazed ceramic pot. She was wearing a short white skirt, accenting her toned, tanned legs, which, like kryptonite to Superman, immediately rendered me helpless. Up top, she had decided to go with a black tight-fitting tank top, partially covered by her unzipped leather motorcycle jacket. I realized I should say something instead of just leering with my expressionless face hanging out.

"There she is!" was the best I could come up with as she finished navigating the maze of brown metal folding tables and chairs and arrived at the bar.

"I hope I didn't keep everyone waiting," Jax said, approaching the bar. "Congratulations, you guys! Toby told me the good news. This is for you, Sallie," she said, placing the small plant on the bar in front of Sallie, which appeared to make Sallie quite happy. A plant gift to me was akin to getting socks for Christmas but with less functionality. Why women gift each other succulents is still beyond me to this day, but it's a real thing. Maybe, similar to RV Jeff, succulents are hard to kill.

"Top of the evening to ya, Jax," Connor said, pointing to the seat next to me, which was adorned with two shots of what could easily have been mistaken for dirty motor oil.

"Seems like you have a little catching up to do," I said as Jax saddled up next to me, taking a shot in her right hand and rubbing my lower back with her left. It appeared as if everything was normal in her mind, a stark contrast to mine. It occurred to me that we were just sitting in a bar. Nothing else was going on, but we were each having different experiences purely due to the thoughts playing in our brains. It was kind of funny when I considered it. Just like Sallie and Jeff, over the moon, but still just sitting at the bar as usual. However, their new engagement context made just sitting here special for them. Hope can make some folks happy, and fear makes others scared or sad, while all are having the same physical experience. It was a matter of perspective—picking one potential set of thoughts over another.

Jax slammed back her remaining shot and announced, "All caught up! Let the celebration begin," with genuine enthusiasm. I liked how her brain operated much better than the poorly coded program mine was running.

"What's the plan tonight?" she asked, eager with anticipation.

"First of all, we're splurging on a complimentary meal at The Plow, followed by an agenda that I've been informed I don't need to know," I said.

"I love surprises. This is going to be so much fun. Thanks for including me, guys." Jax, always the optimist. "Give me the story already. How did he pop the question?"

Sallie chimed in. "Well, we've been together off and on for sixteen years now," she explained. "A couple of weeks ago, I may have said something like, 'Listen, jackass, we've been together off and on for sixteen years. Are you going to shit or get off the pot? I do have other options, you know.'"

"That's exactly what she said," Jeff clarified. "Kind of got me thinking."

"Well, it must have, because today he made me breakfast in bed, which he'd never done before, and lo and behold, right there, wrapped around a Jimmy Dean sausage link, was this ring that fit perfectly, and here we are."

"Let's not gloss over the savage post-proposal sex, Sallie," Jeff felt compelled to include.

"Thanks for filling in the blanks, Jeff. Savage, huh?" Connor, unfortunately asked, giving Jax a playful wink.

"That's putting it mildly. He had never popped me in the chops mid-act before, and I've got to say, it's worth a try, guys. Takes it to a whole new level. Some type of survival lust kicks in."

"That's great," I interrupted before more details could be revealed. "Hey, should we consider ordering?"

Jax whispered, "It might be fun to pop you one in the chops."

"Traditionally, the man is supposed to do the chop-popping," I whispered back.

Connor grabbed menus for us as if we weren't fully aware of the extent of our fine dining options. "Whatever ya want, folks, but no more than one side. After all, margins need to be protected in any business."

"Generosity apparently has its limits," I responded, taking a menu anyway. "Speaking of generosity, who's up for another drink?" Four hands shot up at once. It was going to be one of those evenings. "As they say, the best times are the ones you can't remember."

People ordered their various drinks, thankfully migrating away from shots. I couldn't expunge from my mind the visual of RV Jeff jabbing Sallie in the face mid-coitus, causing me to wonder what transpired post-contact that defined "taking it to the next level." I guess I was still on a need-to-know basis and decided I didn't need to know that after all. I wondered if Gina and I would still be together today if I had popped her in the face more.

After an array of fish and chips, crisps, shepherd's pie, and cheesy tater tots, complemented with the finest of Guinness and Corona, everyone confirmed they were hovering around a seven on a ten-point scale of drunkenness. I was admittedly enjoying myself more than anticipated. It was now dark outside, and the place was slowly starting to come alive, dissolving the privacy of our little shindig. A few minutes later, we had finished our latest round of cocktails.

"On to bigger and better things," Jeff announced, returning his recently emptied glass to the bar.

"What's next?" Jax and I asked simultaneously.

"Well, we've decided to combine our engagement party with our bachelorette and bachelor party to keep costs down. We have reserved a table up front at the world-famous Tube Steak Boogie strip club! Buckle up for a wild ride, my little buckaroos," Jeff explained.

There it was beyond my wildest nightmares. I had sworn off strip clubs after a drunken escapade about ten years ago. I'd worn out the ATM in the lobby to buy multiple bottles of shitty champagne at exorbitant prices, in sneaky bottles with hollow bottoms, for girls with fake names and breasts, who were compelled to tell you about the trials of being a single parent and how this "temporary" job was helping them through school to get them back on their feet. In short, it is a palatable justification for fleecing you out of every cent you have in return for record-setting sexual frustration. In my case, it was an $875 evening. Blue balls and a crippling hangover were my only return on the investment.

"It'll be a shame to miss this, but I can't wait to hear all about it," Connor said, relief evident in his voice.

"Wait a second, Jeff. How does that check the bachelorette party box?" I asked, thinking this technicality may necessitate a last-minute revision of strategy.

"You just wait and see," he replied as a creepy smile worked its way across his face. Not the answer I was hoping for.

"I'm game," Jax said. "Never been to a strip club before. This ought to be interesting." I was the last holdout, but I wasn't willing to acquiesce just yet.

"This all sounds beyond fascinating; however, I must be honest. After this little drink fest we've just had, I'm a tad light in the wallet for such an excursion." Playing the poor card in order to manage expectations—I wouldn't be chipping in for everyone's lap dances, champagne, and VIP room visits. That was the best I could hope for at this point. This was happening, and now my only possible response was to mitigate the fallout.

"Fascinating you would mention that, Toby," Sallie interjected. "Wait for it...," she said as Jeff emulated a drumroll on the bar. "My uncle manages the place and has offered us a $750 credit to be applied at our discretion. And, NO cover charge." This was a counter-move I didn't expect. Further resistance was futile at this point. Jax clapped, RV Jeff and Sallie high-fived each other, and I contemplated how long the $750 might last.

"I'll throw in another $100," Jax said.

"And I'll give ya a $50 for good measure," Connor said, piling on. I figured we'd be good for a couple of hours at best.

"I'm in," I announced, and we were out the door.

The universe is an unpredictable creature. It could have been worse, and my wallet now had a fighting chance. Sure, it would be horrific enough to see tattooed women with heroin addictions dripping with body glitter grinding their muffs on Jeff's loins, but to what level Sallie would participate was the wild card I wanted (and dreaded) to see played. I had to admit I was curious in an apprehensive sort of way.

My new plan, which I called "The Long Shot," was to try to manage Jax and my level of intoxication to around an 8. This would allow decision-making to remain compromised while ensuring puking and losing consciousness remained at bay. Jax would either be revolted or unexpectedly turned on by what she saw. If the nudity and visuals activated her sex drive, we would both arrive back at my place ready to unleash a sexual fury down the yellow brick road to Naughtyville. If, on the other hand, she was disgusted, I would be masturbating alone tonight. It was indeed a long shot, but one worth taking.

"Let's establish a new baseline here. Where is everyone now on a scale of 1 to10?" I asked. I wanted to establish a pattern of regular check-ins. "I don't want anyone to accidentally slip below a seven and put their merriment at risk."

"I'm cresting on an 8," Jeff announced with pride.

"7.3," Jax informed.

"I'm a disappointing 8.4. Let's hurry up and order an Uber. Transportation time can rake a good buzz," Sallie said, making an astute point.

"What about you, Toby?" Jeff asked.

"Cresting on a 7.5, with my last beer still working its magic."

Jeff reserved an Uber and, not out of character, jumped right in the front seat, leaving Jax, Sallie, and me to shoehorn the equivalent of four people into a back seat constructed for three. I deduced there was a good chance I had fractured my hip trying to get my door shut. By the time we arrived, the compression exercise had taken me back down to a woeful 6.3.

There were two lines out front. The VIP line was more of a sign than an actual line, implying no wait for the elite. Then, the lonely and about-to-be-broke guy line stretched down the block, circumventing the corner of the building. Jeff had instructed the Uber driver to drop us off at the end of that line, which was unfortunate news, as we would be on public display for at least 45 minutes, waiting to patronize a well-known and seedy establishment while anyone we knew could drive by and easily recognize us. I suppose it was a fitting look for my current lifestyle.

"Now, the fun part," Sallie said as Jax and I took inventory to ensure we hadn't incurred any serious physical damage from the ride. "Follow me," Sallie said as we slowly walked past the entire line, straight to the VIP Entrance sign. "Nothing is more important than everyone else's jealousy in situations like this," she pointed out.

The doorman, a burly character with arms resembling Christmas hams and a short-cropped black beard, asked, "Name?"

"Big Sallie," Big Sallie said in an authoritative tone.

"So I see," said the doorman, not appearing to realize, or maybe just not caring, how what he had just said could be insulting. "Your name is right here on the list with special instructions from the manager. Follow me, please." Sallie was unphased by the initial fat shaming. Good for her. It must be nice not to care a lick what others think. As I'd come to realize, our thoughts are so often untrue; why the hell would anyone put stock in someone else's random thoughts? With a smile, making eye contact with everyone she could in the general public line, Sallie strutted through the door with a distinct air of royalty, her entourage following behind.

I envied her complete acceptance of her body type, with her self-confidence no worse for the wear. How much easier every phase of my life would have been just being OK with who I was, what I looked like, and whatever situation I was enduring at the time. RV Jeff and Sallie just flowed with life like a raft taken by the current down a river, enjoying the view as opposed to my fruitlessly persistent efforts to paddle my raft back upstream. It seemed it was just their nature to accept. If life was measured by who logged the most happy hours, I could make a fortune betting against myself.

Once inside, as is the case when entering these types of places, it takes a while to get used to what is pretty much complete darkness. My eyes began to adjust, and everything slowly came into focus. The place was still pretty dark except for the brightly lit stage. The idea is that guests can see the stage action from anywhere, but others can't see your private interactions with the ladies while they hustle your money in dark corners. It's always preferable to get shaken down in semi-privacy.

The place didn't reek of beer, body odor, or general bar stink. I'm sure this was intentional, as one feels dirty enough just walking into a strip club—no sense in validating the dirtiness of your ways with nasal confirmation upon entry. Intriguing scents emanated from the servers and dancers when they walked by, leaving an almost visible haze of lavender, vanilla, and cotton candy. The help was intended to be as pleasing to the olfactory senses as to the eyes. Of course, they were ready to ensure your sense of touch wasn't left out of the mix.

As far as taste goes, you were basically on your own, which is why they were happy to sell you any liquor you wanted as long as you overpaid for it.

Big Doorman Guy led us to a table right up front by the center of the stage, with a "reserved" sign on it. Sallie again enjoyed walking by all the other patrons to a spot the others weren't privileged enough to access. The downside of being that close to the stage is that the stage lighting guaranteed everyone could also keep an eye on us. For RV Jeff and Sallie, this was a best-case scenario. I'm sure Jax didn't care one way or the other. I was scanning the dark corners for open real estate.

As we were seated, the shoe model on stage made her way in front of us to ensure we were properly greeted. This was one of those clubs where complete, unabashed nudity was allowed, and any hint of clothing the girl entered the stage wearing was discarded almost immediately, much like a used condom. I was not a big fan of this approach. First of all, I want to imagine what I'm not seeing because it leaves me curious and paying attention. Secondly, nipples and vulvas don't always look attractive on a well-lit stage. Third, looking at anatomical details from every possible angle makes me feel a tidge dirtier than just looking at pretty women wearing bikinis. But hey, it wasn't my celebration.

As is the custom, we sat in a semi-circle around a ridiculously small round table with all the chairs facing the action. Sallie and Jeff sat next to each other on the left, Sallie closest to the stage, and Jax and I on the right, Jax closest to the stage, putting Jeff and me next to each other in the middle. As we settled in, a server wearing a tight tank top extending just below her breasts with no bra and cut-off jean shorts asked us what we'd like to drink. I always found the servers much hotter than the strippers. Their outfits left more to the imagination, and I still harbored the prejudice that their decision to be servers and not strippers made them higher-quality individuals. Although you were never going to take a stripper home with you, there was always that feeling that you may have a chance with a clothed server. It didn't make sense when you thought about it, which is why I usually didn't.

Sallie and Jeff ordered a bottle of champagne. After all, it was a celebration. A creature of habit, I stuck with a Corona and lime, and Jax, interestingly enough, changed direction and ordered a Moscow mule. A handsome enough gentleman, who must have been in his early to mid-fifties, approached the table, and Sallie leaped up and hugged him before he could get a word out.

"Everyone, this is my Uncle Pete!" Sallie said and introduced each of us by name.

"Well, you all better take good care of my niece tonight and you, Jeff, for the rest of your life," he said, exchanging the hug option for a fist bump to keep things hetero.

"That's the whole idea, my brother from another mother," Jeff replied.

"Now, this is for you to use however you see fit, Sallie," Pete said, handing her an envelope stuffed with cash. "Enjoy yourselves, and let me know if you need anything. You understand?"

"Thanks so much, Pete. Will you be able to join us for a drink?" I offered, figuring it was the courteous thing to do.

"If I get a chance. Pretty busy tonight, but I'll sneak away later if I can," he answered.

Now the whole room was focused on us. Hugs and fist bumps from the manager, an unmarked envelope, plus Sallie and Uncle Pete were blocking the view of the tables behind us, so the other patrons had little choice but to pay attention. As our server arrived with the drinks, Pete excused himself. Sallie was much too excited for a woman in a strip club. She started an intense conversation with Jax. It was hard to make out what they were saying over the Guns & Roses blasting through the sound system, but it was clear the topic had to do with the upside-down girl rotating around the pole on the far end of the stage.

"Toby," Jeff said, raising his glass to toast mine. "This is fantastic. Thanks for joining us. This place is like a sore dick...you just can't beat it." Jeff was already putting good mileage on his new clever expression.

"Well, we better be careful with the lap dances tonight, or we may find ourselves in that exact dilemma," I cautioned, clinking my beer against his glass of large-bubbled champagne.

I was mainly at risk because I was wearing jeans. All guys know denim doesn't offer freedom of movement and bunches up in the wrong places, making a friction-free environment for stump grinding next to impossible. I was hoping Jax's presence would not only reduce the chances of Sallie or Jeff buying me lap dances but, more importantly, provide me with a reasonable incentive to not splurge on them for myself until I could get a read on how Jax might respond to seeing me fantasize about penetrating a stranger straddling my loins.

At this point, three things happened simultaneously. We were all watching the stripper on stage who was now on her back, legs splayed, right in front of Sallie, aggressively humping an invisible partner lying on top of her. Sallie stood up, licked her finger, and touched it to the stripper's calf, yelling out, "I've got dibs on this one." Everyone knows you are not allowed to touch these professionals with your hands, and the bouncer on the side of the stage was now frowning in our direction.

A tall Swedish-looking blond with green eyes and a lovely thong bikini kneeled down next to me to inform me that she was willing to bet the cost of a lap dance that she could grind me to completion in one song. An intriguing offer.... Her glitter was tastefully applied, and she exercised responsible restraint in her use of vanilla perfume, which, for the record, is my favorite. I never liked that candy-scented stuff, but I'd been out of the circuit for a while now and was pleasantly surprised that classic vanilla hadn't gone out of style.

Looking over to see if Jax was watching this and get a feel for her general attitude, I was surprised to see her transferring a $20 bill from the envelope on the table into the hand of a woman who was quite fetching, in a Halle Berry type of way, with cartoonishly large bolt-ons. Halle then straddled Jax's lap backward, facing the stage, and began to twerk. These girls were honed in the art of surrounding, separating, and then flaying their victim's wallets. I feel better about myself when I exercise the discipline not to take the first proposition thrown my way. It shows I'm not there because I'm desperate.

Of course, I'm there professionally because I'm researching an article I'm writing for *Rolling Stone* called "The Art of Seduction," and I need to stay focused. That's my strip club identity. Then, I show them my fake business card to certify my legitimacy. This is a psychological play bordering on brilliance. Most likely, one of my top three most extraordinary accomplishments in life, although I can't remember the other two. What will then transpire is this dancer will immediately tell the others about me because they like a challenge. This often triggers a competition to demonstrate who is the most seductive. I immediately tell them not to waste their time with me as I'm there to research, not spend money. About 80% of the time, they insist on providing a complimentary lap dance to assist me in my efforts in exchange for a possible mention in my article. My business cards had been criminally discarded with most of my other single-guy possessions shortly after moving in with Gina. This included my Nagel prints, childhood beer can collection, BMX bike, and a collage of hundreds of sporting event and concert tickets, all of which I would give my right arm to have today.

"I'm sorry, and by the way, you are gorgeous; however, I'm here researching an article I'm writing and not directly participating in the establishment's fine services," I said, baiting the trap.

"Ah...a writer. What kind of article are you writing?" she asked, putting her arm around my shoulder. She carefully ensured her enhanced left breast made direct contact with my side, a classic opening gambit.

"This one's called 'The Art of Seduction,' which is why I'm here. You ladies are the masters of the art, and I'm just watching techniques and approaches to see if I can identify and document the best of the best. Seriously, I'm not spending money, and I would be a tragic waste of your time," I said, establishing enough eye contact to show sincerity but not enough to show interest.

"Do you mind if I check back with you later to see how the project's going?"

"Not a problem," I said as she started to walk away, hypnotizing me with the pendulum effect of her yoga instructor's ass shifting gently from side to side. The game was afoot.

The stripper working on Jax had now turned around to straddle Jax face to face and had determined it was time to reveal the totality of her breasts for Jax's consideration. Watching Jax enjoy a sensual interaction with another woman had an effect on me. Or, I should say, on mini-me. Jax shifted her attention briefly to see if I was catching this event, her eyes settling on my lap. She then wiggled her eyebrows in a 'we'll need to address that later' manner. Upon inspection, it appeared I was fully erect. I hadn't realized until that moment that maybe I was "the guy that likes to watch." I wondered if that guy had always been locked down in my subconscious and was finally released on parole or if maybe I wasn't too old to develop a new fetish.

Then I contemplated how a lap dance these days required a $20 down payment. Just ten to fifteen years ago, a lap dance was, if my memory served me, $5. But hey, it wasn't my money. What did I care? If people were willing to pay that, it was the market rate. Maybe it was harder to find action on your own these days, so a premium was justified. Or perhaps I was just getting old. I once again realized I was struggling in my raft where everyone else seemed to be unconcerned with these details and were happily floating downstream. I suppose I could have, over the years, unwittingly developed EDD (excessive detail disorder).

Jeff had excused himself to seek out Sallie's uncle for some reason. He didn't appear to be "the guy that liked to watch" as Sallie was now standing in front of the writhing lust bucket lying on the waist-high stage. That's when the shimmy started. Sallie must have hit a tipping point on her arousal spectrum, triggering her to take action. She slowly moved her shoulders back and forth, gaining speed until the momentum of her monstrous breasts maintained the shimmy entirely on their own, validating Newton's first law that an object in motion does indeed stay in motion.

A strip club is, in reality, just another "out." When people's lives become overly stressful, routine, or depressing, they want a break from themselves. Some people fire up a "J" and get high. Others have shots of Jägermeister, beers, and cheap champagne. Then some drop acid and others binge-watch Netflix. And finally, there are those that go to strip clubs. For a man, walking into a strip club is like stepping into another universe. A universe where the only time women will boss you and coerce you is when they are eager to grind on you. A universe where only the hottest of the hot are attracted to you and love to initiate sexual interaction. A place where you are in control, make the decisions and are blissfully at choice. I imagine video games offer the same feelings of escape into a parallel universe for the younger generation. We crave alternate realities, I suppose, mainly because we're bored with our own.

The strippers also have alternate-universe personas, usually named Chrystal, Amber, Brandy, or Trinity. Most patrons are not afraid to use their names from their base reality. I, however, alternate between Lance Erickson and Gary Davlin because, in this universe, women love to be banged by a Lance or Gary, not so much by a Toby. This alternate reality provides a guy an open window into the real-life experience of movie stars, rock bands, and superstar athletes who effortlessly backstroke through endless rivers of trim on a daily basis.

And the best part is, in this universe, no other guys ever cock-block you, because you are the king, proving that money can buy happiness. It's fleeting happiness, but isn't that usually true with happiness anyway?

We write these alternate narratives the same way we create our real-life identities, except, as I had been recently taught, we are convinced our real-life identities are real. After all my conversations with Eddie, I grew much more suspicious of who I believed I was. Or I was starting to think about it for the first time. Who we think we are is a collection of recurring thoughts based on unquestioned beliefs we've acquired about ourselves and the world. This raised my awareness that most of my assumed world may not be any more or less real than Lance's, Gary's, Chrystal's, or Brandy's, for that matter.

Things were getting exciting on the stage. The dancers who had just wrapped up their song collected their string bikinis, which had been carelessly discarded upon arrival, and their small sequined coin purses, which were jammed with newly earned one- and five-dollar bills. As they slunk away, the next shift entered Bon Jovi's "Living on a Prayer" with fresh pulsing energy and smiles, saying, "I will break your pelvis open like a piñata."

Jeff returned, holding a laminated piece of paper under the table, flashing a giddy smile.

"Jeff, would you have any issue with calling me Lance tonight?"

"Nope. Would you have any issue with helping me peruse the secret menu here?" he asked, flashing me said menu for a gander.

"They have such a thing? I thought secret menus were only at In-N-Out Burger and Taco Bell for those in the know," I asked. I hadn't heard of such a thing in an adult entertainment establishment being formalized enough to have its own documentation. Usually, the strippers try to lure you away from the safety of your pack into a private VIP room and rape your wallet. This appeared to take that to a whole new and exclusive level.

"They do for family and friends. A special upstairs section is seldom used except for those in the inner circle. Check this out," he said inconspicuously, sliding the menu my way. I wasn't sure how I felt about being part of the Tube Steak Boogie's inner circle, but Lance Erickson, on the other hand, had already embraced the concept. Jeff had Lance at "special upstairs section." This was beyond the VIP room, and I was confident the naughtiness level would not disappoint.

Jax had passed on extending her lap dance another song and scooted her chair back closer to mine, eager to discuss the shenanigans that had just transpired.

"That was interesting, to say the least," Jax whispered.

"Oh yeah? Was it enjoyable?" I figured, why beat around the bush, so to speak?

"Oddly, yes," Jax responded candidly. "At first, it felt weird and awkward, and I was self-conscious about what I should be doing, how I should react, and all that. Once I settled down, it was kind of fun seeing another woman up that close doing erotic stuff to me. It turned me on, which I wasn't expecting."

This was exciting news, bolstering my hopes of executing on "The Long Shot."

"They are professionals. Seeing you enjoying yourself with her like that totally turned me on."

"I could see," she replied, gently rubbing my crotch, triggering a re-emergence.

"Sallie seems to be having a nice celebration. I think she's 100% bisexual," Jax said. Sallie was now on her knees in front of a dancer's uncloaked anus, securing the optimal viewing angle to observe this woman contract her unmistakably lightened sphincter to the driving rhythm of ZZ Top's hit "Gimme All Your Lovin'".

Jeff was conversing with a husky entertainer with a white-blond crew cut and a noticeably large, hooped nose ring. At least he had a "type." RV Jeff was a chubby chaser. Jeff was willing to see the sexy where he found it, regardless of society's magazine-cover defining examples. I felt a slightly jealous respect for him.

"Check this out, Jax, and keep it discrete. We are beyond VIPs here tonight. Jeff has arranged for us to go into the "secret" invitation-only area upstairs, which has its own menu of options, and I happen to have that menu right here," I said, sliding the menu onto her lap. We perused it together. "We are now part of the 'inner circle,'" I proudly informed her.

THE SECRET SERVICE MENU

1. *Nude Encounter* / Nude up for your private and clothing-free interaction with the companion of your choice.
2. *Touching Without Touching* / Intimate and private personal pleasuring at shockingly close range.
3. *Tickle Me Pink* / Feathers are forever. Tickle your companion anywhere and everywhere with the finest feathers of all lengths and sizes.
4. *Contortion Distortion* / Experience the shock and awe of Perla the Human Pretzel as she shows you the limits of what the human body is capable of with an unobstructed view.
5. *The Extended Dance Mix* / That's right, no sad endings as the song concludes, because this lengthy lap dance's unique mix appropriately prolongs your ecstasy.
6. *The Director's Cut* / We're not talking circumcision here. You are in charge and will direct two strippers on how to perform together in creative and provocative ways.
7. *The Puss Circus* / The name says it all.
8. *The Anal Intruder* / It's essential to have the right tool for the right job. We supply the gear.

"I think we should pick one and do it together. This is the chance of a lifetime, Jax," I suggested.

"In that case, the only real option is the Puss Circus, as far as I'm concerned. I'm pretty sure we could participate in the rest of the menu at your apartment anytime," she said, continuing to rub my mini-me, who was again at full attention. I loved Jax's bold curiosity for the discovery of the unknown. I didn't have to compartmentalize my inner psyche when I was with her, leaving the lusty or unmentionable thoughts locked away to avoid offending her. Gina wouldn't have considered walking in the door, let alone initiating a trip to the

Puss Circus. It was genuinely refreshing to connect with a woman sexually, from thoughts to action. She was curious and not afraid of new spaces or places. Jax was the ideal partner for exploring life. Gina was equally as proficient at engaging in the art of predictable routine, which, due to the definition of "routine," sucked the novelty out of life like jelly filling out of a doughnut. Gina didn't love sex; she tolerated it. Jax needed it to feel physically and mentally connected, as did I. Then I remembered the inequality of our shared feelings in the arena of verbalized love and again wondered where her head was concerning our long-term compatibility. Mine was lost in imaginary best- and worst-case scenarios that may or may not even exist, instead of being right here with an amazingly sexy girlfriend in a strip club about to see a Puss Circus. What was wrong with me?

"The Puss Circus it is!" I declared.

Now that Sallie's anal inspection had concluded, Jeff shooed away the butchy blond girl, and we all returned to our respective spots to caucus on the situation and develop our plan.

"Did you get it?" Sallie asked Jeff.

"Fuck yes! We're in whenever we're ready. Toby has the menu." I passed it to Sallie, who studied it like she was analyzing a suicide letter.

"Shit, I can't make up my mind. Let's head up, and we can figure it out up there. Our choices could be dictated by the talent level available," she said, making an excellent point. Luckily, for a Puss Circus, anyone would do as we were looking to be awed by the sheer atrocity of the acts, primarily for storytelling purposes. However, with the more erotic choices on the menu, the perceived attractiveness of the companion would be paramount to creating the experience.

Jeff caught Pete's eye and swirled his finger above his head, indicating, as Ted "The Sledge" Nugent would say, "We're cocked, locked, and ready to rock!"

Pete led us up the backstairs into a minuscule waiting room with three plush red velvet chairs and the same menu we had already received blown up and on the wall behind a delicate art deco desk. An insanely attractive woman sat behind it, wearing a white collared shirt, a dark blue blazer, and a matching miniskirt. Her dark hair was pulled back in a bun, and her dark-rimmed glasses perfectly framed her icy-blue eyes. It was a classic secretary fantasy look, I thought, and she wore it well.

"Welcome to the secret suite," she said. "My name is Tabitha, and I'll be your host up here tonight. First things first. Would you like to order a round of drinks?"

"Does the pope shit in his hat?" Jeff answered. "Another bottle of champagne. Make that two, one for Sallie and one for me. What do you guys want?"

"I'll take a shot of Patron with a Corona backer, and don't forget a lime, please." I was back up to a firm 8.25 and felt the sudden urge to get to a 9 as fast as possible.

"I'll follow his lead," Jax said.

"Quick check, gang. Where are we on a scale of 1 to 10 right now?" I needed to ensure nobody was falling behind.

"7.25," Jeff said.

"8," Sallie.

"7.5," Jax.

"I'm winning. 8.25," I proudly announced. "About to be a 9. Jeff and Sallie, it seems like you may need penalty shots for unacceptable sobriety levels."

"So four shots of Patron, two bottles of champagne, and two Coronas?" Tabitha confirmed. We nodded in agreement, and she called in our order on a walkie-talkie.

"Can we see the available talent before ordering from the menu?" Sallie inquired, wasting no time getting down to business.

"Absolutely. They will be in shortly," Tabitha confirmed. It briefly occurred to me that I could love and care for Tabitha for the rest of my life if things didn't work out with Jax.

We began to carefully debate the different menu choices, as making the wrong choice with such an impressive variety of offerings could result in long-term biblical regret. Of course, Jax and I were firmly set on the Puss Circus, so most of the discussion centered on what RV Jeff and Sallie should do.

"I think I could benefit from the Director's Cut," Jeff exclaimed and continued. "A controlled porno, every aspect at our whim? How awesome is that?"

"I hear you, Jeff, but the woman-on-woman thing, although fascinating for men, seems frustrating as hell to watch from the side-lines," Sallie explained.

"Why don't you each try a different one, and we can reconvene and share the highlights of three different events?" Jax offered as Jeff and Sallie silently pondered this for about six seconds.

"OK," Jeff said.

"Good idea, Jax," Sallie responded.

"OK, Jeff's taking The Director's Cut, and Jax and I are going to the Puss Circus. Sallie, what's the decision?"

"The Anal Intruder," Sallie blurted out without hesitation. Initially surprising, it made sense after watching her extreme fasci-nation and shimmying to the dancer's rhythmic expanding and contracting rusty starfish. Sallie's penchant for butt-play had made the decision a no-brainer.

"Fascinating," I couldn't help myself.

"I can't wait to hear about 'the gear' they provide," Jax said earnestly.

"I can't stand not having the right gear," I threw in for good measure.

Jeff was now off in his head, no doubt, working out the details of his first self-directed porno. To arrive on set without having thought through the ins and outs of the act would be downright irresponsible and result in a woefully blown opportunity.

The door opened, and seven ladies, in costumes ranging from a nurse to a construction worker, entered the room. We were informed that only two possessed the elite training required to perform in the

Puss Circus, which was fine, as they were attractive enough if you didn't mind tattoos on a heroin addict.

Jeff immediately called dibs on the heavy-set, bleached, buzz-cut-wearing, seasoned strip club vet with whom he had already formed a relationship downstairs. In a hushed tone, he leaned over and unabashedly informed me, "I like the big fluffy ones."

"I'd like to inquire if there are any others not present that have a similar body type to this one?" he asked respectfully.

"We can arrange this," Tabitha replied, picking up her walkie-talkie and requesting "Trouble" to report upstairs. Likely an earned nickname.

This was fascinating to me. A peak into the mind of RV Jeff's sexual fantasies. "Fluffy." I had never remotely considered it, but it made perfect sense. Soft, full-figured, more to engage with but in a pleasing way. I imagine he would consider a petite, hard-bodied figure to be more like the pit of a peach—what's left over when all the fruit has been stripped away—less than the whole enchilada. Jeff was a "more is better" guy, and I respected that. He wasn't afraid to play in that mental space. And he had cast a wider net within a population prone to less ego, better-developed personalities, and undoubtedly a more appreciative population. My tastes were blindly spoon-fed by pop culture. Jeff was willing to consider all angles and decide what he found attractive, regardless of how it fits into what the current media was peddling.

Sallie, on the other hand, had decided that taut was hot, picking the fitness model naughty construction worker, whose devious smile, upon being selected, confirmed a dark side ready to be unleashed.

Jeff bumped the side of my thigh a couple of times with his fist and opened his hand to reveal a tiny white capsule, which I immediately grabbed and popped into my mouth. One could argue I was caught up in the moment. "What did I just eat, Jeff?" I asked, assuming that was a fair question.

"Just a little molly," Jeff answered. "Good for your bones and teeth. That's the last one, so keep it on the downlow."

"A vitamin then?"

"Basically. It's good for appreciation."

I had taken "molly," known as "X" back in the day, a few times before, and the experience ranged from slightly nauseous to astounding ecstasy, depending on the quality. I felt a little sheepish going behind Jax's back to basically drug myself. However, that quickly passed—I had just set sail into the "anything can happen" zone. It was not a night prone to making good choices, but I may have impulsively made a great choice. We were just before finding out.

My favorite cocktail waitress, or "server" for those bent toward political correctness, arrived with a tray containing four shots of tequila, two bottles of champagne, and two Coronas.

"Here's to Jeff and Sallie's past, present, and, most importantly, future!" I said, taking a shot from the tray and holding it in the air as one does. "And here's to the freight train to 9."

Jeff popped a bottle of champagne, sending the cork ricocheting off the ceiling and onto Tabitha's desk. The overflow spilled down the sides of the bottle and onto the carpet, which didn't seem to bother Jeff in the least. "And here's to Connor, who is with us in spirit!" Jeff proclaimed, holding the bottle over his head before downing his shot and taking a generous swig directly from the bottle. He then passed it to Sallie, who took an even more impressive swig.

"Trouble" had arrived, and Jeff's two "handlers" took him by the arm and guided him down the hall into one of the rooms, but not before he chugged half of the remaining champaign and told Sallie to keep the rest. Big Fluffy #1 was holding a clapperboard, ready for first-time director Jeff to yell "Action!" And "action" was what, I'm sure, they had in store for him.

Sallie and her THOTH (The Hottest Of The Hot) were next. As they turned to enter one of the rooms, I could see Sallie administering a firm slap on her ass, establishing precisely who would be calling the shots, whatever that entailed.

"Let the circus begin! On to the center ring," one of the heroin addicts announced, marching in rhythm while thrusting a baton up into the air and then down, setting the tone. I could still feel the assuring warmth of the tequila in my throat—the feel that usually proceeds either the best of times or a giant mistake.

The room we were taken to was reasonably large, with a small semi-circular stage on the far wall. We were deposited in the two chairs right in front to ensure we wouldn't miss a thing. A box was produced from under the stage and taken behind a screen, where both circus performers disappeared for a few minutes as Jax and I waited in nervous anticipation for what we were sure would be a journey into a brave new world.

"Jax, Jeff gave me drugs, which I ate only to find out it was his last one. I feel kind of bad that you aren't able to partake. I just thought you should know in case I seem out of sorts." I had cleared my conscience.

"Toby, do you really feel bad that you couldn't give a recovered addict drugs?" she asked.

"Oh shit, I forgot about that. I kind of regret eating it now. I may have been a tad caught up in the moment."

"What drugs do you suppose you consumed?" she asked.

"That's what I asked after swallowing it. Come to find out, it's molly, which we called ecstasy in my day."

"Well, that's better than heroin or meth. Now you are prepped to appreciate the finer details of the circus and to let me know all the ways you appreciate me," she said with a smile, apparently without issue, patting me on the thigh.

About this time, I discerned a slight wave of nausea and felt a bit sweaty, realizing it was starting to kick in. The circus performers emerged in sequined G-strings carrying a small table that held a few objects we couldn't quite see. As they set it down on the back of the stage, "New Sensation" by INXS began to fill the air, and the lights dimmed. There was some dramatic strutting around as one of them blew up a red balloon and taped it to the brass pole in the center of the stage.

"And so it begins," Jax whispered.

"Is it wrong to be truly excited?" I asked, feeling a second wave of nausea wash over me.

"If it is, we're both bad people," she informed me.

The second girl had already discarded her G-string and was spread-eagled on her back, crotch facing the balloon. She produced a tube that looked like a giant straw and, without hesitation, inserted it into herself. Then she produced a dart, waving it in our direction to ensure we understood exactly what we were dealing with. The nausea dissipated, and I felt exceedingly relaxed despite my elevated heart rate and flushed face.

At this point, it was no mystery what was about to transpire. The dart shot out of the tube, popping the balloon as we all clapped. Although it was inspiring, it left unanswered questions about propulsion. If the world knew the answers, I realized everyone would be doing it. A second dart was fired from a greater distance. Lo and behold, a third dart had appeared, and another balloon was taped right above the head of the other performer. The suspense was palpable as we were now entering a life-or-death scenario. Luckily, life won out as the balloon popped, and the shooter sprang to her feet and took a bow. This was serious stuff and not to be tried at home. Suddenly, I REALLY appreciated it and the amount of work that must have gone into honing such a skill. I felt a twinge of compassion for these two and knew their lives were not all glamor and respect. They did what it took to get by and, likely, get their next fix. Somehow, that was admirable and wonderful all at the same time.

The next act had just gotten underway. A beer bottle was produced, and the lousy acting conveyed a sense of frustration that it was unopened.

"Do either of you have a bottle opener?" the blowgun girl asked.

"Sorry, we don't," Jax answered.

"Oh well," Blowgun Girl said and handed the bottle to Balloon Girl, who inserted the top of the bottle into her bajingo and opened it effortlessly, leaving Jax and me speechless and stunned. I was now "rolling" from the drugs, as the kids say, and had reached the point where I was simply along for the ride. This was when Balloon Girl decided to chug the entire beer and, with her thirst quenched, announced, "We will be taking a small intermission to prepare for the next and final act."

"Jax, is this as remarkable and unexpected as I think it is, or is it just the drugs?"

"That wouldn't be the drugs, as I'm speechless too and feel a sudden sense of vaginal inadequacy," she said, appearing to be sincere.

"Hon, I can only imagine that, at this point in their career, having sex with one of them would be like throwing a hot dog down the hall. I can't imagine how beat up and vacuous they must be down there. I wonder if these are standard Puss Circus moves or if these two are the creative force driving this artistic masterpiece?"

"Maybe there's a wizard behind that screen who's the master-mind," she postulated.

"Well, in that case, I'd be the scarecrow because I'm terrified of what the final act might be."

The star performers returned, appearing as nude as when they left. However, I was distracted by how perfectly shiny, healthy, and sexy Jax's hair looked. "Can I smell your hair?"

"Absolutely. It appears the molly seems to be the real thing," she said, leaning over to position her head for my olfactory pleasure. It was a wonderful, clean jasmine scent that seemed important to keep smelling until Jax interrupted me. "It seems you may not want to miss this."

Both women were now pulling yard after yard of what appeared to be ribbon out of themselves, then taking hold of each other's ribbon and backing up in opposite directions to ensure the length didn't go unnoticed. I imagined I was a Roman emperor at a sexually exotic feast, viewing entertainment only fit for a king. I didn't know if it was the drugs, but the ribbon appeared to be never-ending. At least thirty or forty yards had been extracted from each of them, and it didn't seem to be ending any time soon. Every so often, the color would change. We had passed through red, green, and purple and were now in the orange phase.

I decided to check in with Jax on this. "Is that a lot of ribbon, or am I just high?"

"It's not to be believed," she answered.

The ribbon extraction continued for another couple of minutes, followed by an unnecessary amount of bowing and an offer to examine their vaginas up close, which we respectfully declined. My current state of complete gratitude left me feeling exceedingly fortunate to have witnessed such a talented display and gave me a renewed appreciation for the vagina and its potential. The show had concluded, and they seemed excited that we were impressed.

Within a few minutes, we were back in the now vacant lobby area, and Tabitha had either moved on or taken a break. Jeff and Sallie had either returned downstairs or were still in session. As we discussed our next move, we heard a female voice shout, "I didn't need to see that!" from one of the rooms in the hall, and I felt compelled to investigate. While standing outside the door, listening to Quiet Riot's "Come on Feel the Noise," I raised my hand to knock on the door when Jax pulled my arm away.

"I don't think we should disturb them; it could kill the moment," Jax said. "After all, it is a movie set."

"How about we just sneak a tiny peek?" which seemed harmless enough to me.

I opened the door a few inches, and Jax peered in, immediately removed her head, eyes wide open with shock, and said, "I don't know if you want to look in there." Which, of course, solidified my resolve to investigate. I pressed my face against the door frame to peer in, and low and behold, she was right.

Jeff was directing the two soft and fluffy actors in a scene involving live one-on-one oral pleasuring; however, they had taken a slight break to convince him that he may have crossed the line between acceptable and unacceptable viewing behavior. Jeff was wearing only his boxers with his scrotum hanging out the fly, which was timelessly funny. However, what happened next was unexpected. Jax was now on her knees, also peering through the doorway.

"Want to see a dove breast?" Jeff asked them. Before they could answer, he had grasped his scrotum up high, forcing his nuggets to pop out below, amazingly looking precisely like a dove's breast. Jeff was not only a talented director but also a solid porn actor with a unique humorous bent to the erotic. I decided I was proud to be Jeff's friend; however, I had seen enough. We quietly closed the door, remaining unnoticed.

"Want to see a hummingbird breast?" I asked Jax.

"Give yourself more credit than that. Maybe Robin or even Blue-jay, I'd say," she said with a laugh. "Jeff never ceases to amaze. He doesn't ever disappoint, does he?"

"He's his own man. I'll give him credit for that. Can't help but love him, even when I'm not blissed out on molly. I think our next move is obvious at this point."

"Find Sallie?" she asked, as I nodded in agreement.

There were two more doors besides Jeff's and the Puss Circus. A peek in the first showed it was empty. As we approached the second, I steeled myself to be ready for anything. Mötley Crüe's "Girls, Girls, Girls" rocked its way through the door into our eardrums, signaling that we had arrived at our destination.

"I have butterflies in my stomach," Jax admitted.

"I'm just plain scared. You do realize that unimaginable things are going on in there, and whatever they are, butt-play is a certainty? Her experience is called 'The Anal Intruder,' for Christ's sake," I clarified.

"Just to be clear, we could be about to see something that we will never be able to unsee the rest of our lives. We don't have to do this and may forever lament it if we do," Jax prudently warned.

"Yes, we do. If we don't take a gander, we will be forever mired in regret. Just approach it like you would if you were the first on the scene of a gruesome car accident. Something horrendously fascinating lies just on the other side of that door," I said as she nodded, unable to find fault with my logic. It turned out to be far worse than a car accident.

Jax slowly eased open the door about four or five inches, which was adequate as the stage was off to the left, giving us a remarkable view. Sallie was on her knees and elbows on a stage, revealing a maze of intricate red arrow tattoos, pointing, you guessed it, towards her sting ring from every angle. That alone was more than enough fodder for cocktail party conversation, but that was the least of it. The construction worker babe only wore a tool belt, hard hat, and leather work gloves. Work gloves are vital so you don't lose your grip or get blisters when wielding your battery-operated jackhammer equipped with a miniature fist replica and savagely penetrating someone's sphincter.

"How about that, honey!" the girl yelled, giving her a hearty slap on the ass to accompany the rapid-fire penetration.

"That's not getting the job done! Now do it like you mean it!" Sallie yelled. The construction worker welcomed the challenge and replaced the small fist attachment with a life-sized one.

She went back to work on Sallie in a manner that was anything but gentle and kicked her in the gut for good measure.

"Now we're getting somewhere, you dirty whore!" Sallie yelled. We all learned a little bit about the stripper lexicon that night, as Sallie had chosen her words poorly.

Sallie didn't see the angry grimace spreading across this woman's face as she impressively managed the jackhammer with one hand while reaching down with her free hand to pick up her bottle of Bud Light. The light beer must have kept her figure so trim, I thought to myself. As she raised the bottle, it soon became apparent that she had no intention of taking a drink. She was now holding it by the top upside down over her head, beer spilling all over herself, the jackhammer, and Sallie. She then thrust the bottle down, breaking it over Sallie's head.

"Go ahead! Call me a whore again, and I'll slit your throat," she said, giving the jackhammer an extra rough push. Sallie was now frantically attempting to crawl away but, in her dazed condition, was not fast enough to break contact with The Anal Intruder, as the girl obviously experienced in wielding this instrument easily kept up with Sallie and kicked her knees out from under her, leaving her defenseless and flat on her stomach.

Now, it's common knowledge head wounds bleed a lot, and this was no exception. From where we observed, it was hard to tell the extent of the damage, but Sallie had either lost consciousness, was playing dead, or was, in fact, dead. All three of these potential scenarios were not good. Jax, without hesitation, rushed the stage and took down Whore Girl before she knew she had visitors. The first mover's advantage had enabled Jax to free Sallie temporarily, and the stunned perpetrator was now taking a repeated kneeing to the back of her head as Jax held her firmly by the hair from behind.

Determining that the situation was beyond fucked, even from a molly-infused state of bliss, it was clear that we needed reinforcements. "Jeff, Sallie needs help! Jeff, Jeff!" I screamed from the top of my lungs down the hall. Jeff, who must have had acute hearing, shot out the door and into the hall, his bald head whipping from side to side, trying to determine where this cry for aid was coming from. We then locked eyes, and I screamed, "In here!"

Jeff was at full sprint, his scrotum still hanging out his fly, swinging pendulously from side to side as the two Big Fluffies poked their heads out the door to see what all the commotion was about.

"Zen as Fuck" Jeff shot through the door and into the room without considering what type of mayhem may be waiting for him on the other side. RV Jeff was a man of action, not prone to dawdling. I bravely followed Jeff back in, feeling that the three of us had the attacker outnumbered and the situation would be quickly diffused. By this time, Jax was now in a headlock and was losing hair by the fistful. Jeff masterfully assessed the situation en route and knew exactly what was required. In four strides, he was on stage, sack still wild and free, and had commandeered the jackhammer, immediately activating it on whore girl's face, facilitating Jax's release and sending blood gushing from Whore Girl's nose. Sallie was beginning to stir, which thankfully ruled out death. I then realized I was lying face down on the hunter-green shag carpet.

The Big Fluffies had come to their colleague's rescue, and I became a logistical casualty as they rushed the stage. Jeff was testing the battery life of the jackhammer on Whore Girl's face when Big Fluffy #1 leapt onto his back and started choking him. As I staggered to my feet, a quick assessment of the situation revealed that Sallie was still on her face and groaning with minimal movement, Jax was sitting on her butt with legs extended in front of her, holding the side of her head, Whore Girl was holding her nose in a clouded daze, and Jeff was spinning around in circles frantically trying to shake off his assailant to no avail. Big Fluffy #2 now had one knee on the stage and was wrestling the rest of her girth up over the edge, preparing to add more fuel to the fire.

It's funny how the body can respond to danger entirely on its own without any assistance from the mind. Call it survival instinct, divine intervention, or blind rage. All I knew was that I had shifted into autopilot and appeared to be having an out-of-body experience. First, I watched myself grab Big Fluffy #2 by the face from behind, ripped her off the edge of the stage she was summiting, and slammed her onto her back on the floor. I immediately jumped up in the air and landed on her well-protected stomach with both feet, providing a springboard to propel myself onto the stage, causing Big Fluffy #2 to let out a guttural cry. Jeff was facing me with Big Fluffy #1, who was still taking the choking quite seriously, as Jeff's face produced a purple hue. I bum-rushed Jeff, lowering my shoulder into his chest, sending them both flying backward, Jeff landing heavily on top of her and myself on top of Jeff. The impact forced her to release her choke hold long enough for him to push me off, roll over, and begin repeatedly head-butting her, which was quite dramatic and very much in line with the entire situation.

Jax, having assessed her scalp damage and determined she was no worse for the wear, rushed over to tend to Sallie. Realizing the jackhammer was unattended and conveniently within arm's reach, I leveraged the opportunity to put it back to use on the back of Whore Girl's head as she was traversing the few feet between herself and Jax's back, who was now huddled over Sallie.

Whore Girl was not pleased. She whipped around, uttering a battle cry that sounded something like, "Fucking die cock sucker!" Apparently, she had no idea who she was talking to. In a fortunate twist of fate, her head conveniently rotated her squashed tomato of a nose directly under the pulsating jackhammer's fist, providing about thirty direct blows in less than four seconds, which was all that was required to leave her heaped in a bloody mess, which surprisingly, caused me to yell "whore bitch" into her face at close range. I wasn't proud of this, but without a doubt, she brought it on herself.

Jeff's head-to-head jackhammering exercise had severely disabled Big Fluffy #1, who was now crawling away the best she could, in full retreat mode. Jeff was demonstrably establishing his niche as a violent porn director, which suited him well. Meanwhile, we redirected our attention toward Sallie, whom Jax was consoling while examining her head wound. That's when we heard the pump of a shotgun.

Tabitha had a bead on the stage, and everyone froze except Jeff. "Put that down, you piece of shit, or I'll wrap it around your head. One of your sluts cut my woman, and we are acting in self-defense," Jeff said, with no fear of escalating the situation.

"One move, and I'll shoot your balls off," Tabitha warned as we all looked at Jeff's exposed scrote centered in the middle of his boxers like the bullseye on a target.

I'd been in fights in high school and seen bar and parking lot fights more than a few times, but I'd had yet to experience gunplay at close range. I began to panic, ending my out-of-body experience, and begged Jeff to stand down, but he would have none of it. He walked straight over to Tabitha, ripped the gun out of her hands, and threw it on the floor. "Where is fucking Pete? I want to talk to him now!"

Now defenseless, Tabitha sprinted out of the room to get Pete or to avoid the same fate her coworkers had suffered. Big Fluffy #1 and #2 were right behind her. Whore Girl had now collapsed onto her side, her bleeding face in her hands, doing her best to appear invisible.

"Fuck, Jeff! You could have been killed! We all could have been killed! What the fuck were you thinking?" I more scolded than asked as I contemplated if I might be going into cardiac arrest.

"Toby, cocking a shotgun dislodges a spent shell. No shots had been fired, and no shell had been ejected. The gun was obviously empty," he calmly explained, picking up the gun and opening the chamber to illustrate his point. It was indeed empty. "See!"

"Jeff, what if it holds more than one cartridge?" It seemed logical.

"Excellent point, but no longer relevant," he said with a dismissive wave.

"Sallie's bleeding pretty good, but she's awake and seems alert," Jax said. Sallie was sitting up and observing the blood on her hand, which she had just removed from her head.

"She's fine," Jeff said. "If it were worse, she'd be bleeding a hell of a lot more than that, and you wouldn't be struggling to find the wounds. A couple of stitches, and she'll be good as new. Maybe a concussion. What kicked off this shit show?"

"Well, Jeff, the key takeaway here is there is a fine line between being a stripper and a whore," I responded. "Where a whore may not take offense at being called a stripper, a stripper doesn't much appreciate being referred to as a whore. There is a pecking order, and apparently, Sallie was confused about where that fine line was."

"I was lost in the throes of ecstasy and did some dirty talking, as one is prone to do. Nothing turns me on more than when Jeff calls me a filthy whore, and I thought it was appropriate. Why is everyone so God damned sensitive these days, anyway?"

"Sallie! Jeff! What in the name of Old Hairy Jesus's balls is going on? Pete asked, having entered the room while we were educating Jeff on the finer details of stripper/whore nomenclature.

"The Aristocrats!" we all answered in unison.

"Very funny. And, speaking of balls, why are yours hanging out of your fly, Jeff?"

"Pete, I'd ask you if you've ever seen my dove breast, but I'm not in the mood," Jeff said, tucking his impressive nut bag back into his boxers. What we have here, Pete, is an assault charge or charges we'd like to file. This one," he said, pointing to Whore Girl, "apparently broke a beer bottle over your niece's head and ripped out a bunch of Jax's hair. One of the other girls tried to choke me to death, and Tabitha pulled a gun on us and threatened to kill us all. What the fuck kind of ghetto establishment are you running here? As a matter of fact, who has a phone? I'm calling the police."

"Hey now, everyone settle down for a minute," Pete said, pulling up a chair and taking a seat to demonstrate what settling down looked like.

Whore Girl was now on her feet, tool belt still around her waist, her hard hat lost in the tussle, and her face looking like a decomposed jack-o-lantern.

"Sarah...I mean, 'Delilah,' go downstairs and get Jill to take you to the ER to get this looked at before these guys press charges and you spend the night in the clink," Pete said, and Sarah left, a bloody, humiliated mess, the hotness knocked right out of her.

Pete didn't want the police in his club or charges filed. After a lengthy negotiation, he offered to pay for any medical bills Sallie required and let her keep the envelope of cash without paying for any drinks or exotic experiences. Although my molly high had now worn off, likely due to excessive adrenaline, I still felt pretty damn lucky and grateful, kind of like when you wake up and realize you were dreaming and don't actually have to take a final exam for the class you forgot to attend all semester.

Pete escorted us out the back door to minimize panic and general awareness that heads were cracked, guts stomped, hair ripped out, and guns were drawn upstairs. In these types of establishments, violence begets violence, and Pete had already had his fill.

As Jeff predicted, shockingly, Sallie was, for the most part, OK—nine total stitches. The most noticeable damage was where they had to shave parts of her head to sew it up. In retrospect, this should have been a pay-per-view event. "RV Jeff, Big Sallie, Toby, and Jax take on Whore Girl, Big Fluffy #1, and Big Fluffy #2; weapons and construction equipment encouraged."

We exchanged pleasantries and departed from the ER to go our separate ways.

"Thanks for the evening, guys. Quite an adventure," Jax said.

"Sallie, nice tattoos," I said, feeling the need to say something kind.

"Fuck you, Toby," Sallie answered, not feeling the need.

"Nice scrote, Jeff," I said, trying again.

"Thank you, sir," Jeff replied as they got into an Uber and disappeared.

CHAPTER
TWENTY-FOUR

I was already starting to feel hungover. Exhaustion quickly backfilled the adrenaline leaving my system, and I was sure our Uber ride back to my place would never end.

"Is that a rug burn on your forehead?" Jax asked.

"Probably. Regardless, that was more fun than I expected when we were leaving The Plow," I confessed.

"I would imagine Whore Girl and the Big Fluffies aren't saying that right now. We administered quite the bully beatdown. I guess we can say we run with a rough crowd these days, huh?"

"Yep. People should know better than to fuck with us," I said, and we both busted up laughing as we finally reached our destination. "Let's get some ice on your head to keep the inflammation down. Does it hurt where your hair got ripped out by the roots?"

"Not as much as you'd think, but at the time, it sucked. Remind me to pack a helmet next time, just in case."

"You know what was weird?" I asked, unlocking the door to my apartment, relieved to finally be safely home.

"Sallie's tattoos? Or maybe Jeff's scrotal display? Possibly the jackhammer, complete with various fist attachments? Or are you talking about how strippers have an extreme disdain for being called whores?" she offered up. "Or, this could be a stretch, but maybe the Puss Circus?"

"All of the above. That's for sure—Jesus, what an insane series of events. The weirdest part for me was, as that shit show was unfolding, I was entirely aware of everything, like watching a play, but I wasn't thinking about anything I was doing or going to do next. It's like I was watching through my eyes, and my body was engaged in the mix, but my mind wasn't thinking a God damned thing. Everything was happening on its own, and I was a part of it all, of course. But it was like I had disassociated from being me at the same time and was hanging out in this calm place, witnessing all of it, but at the same time detached from it all. Does that make any sense?"

"I can't fully grasp the experience since I haven't ever had it myself, but it does sound intriguing," Jax responded, her voice filled with curiosity. "It's weird you were throwing people down, fighting, and not even thinking about what you were doing or going to do next. Maybe you're just a natural brawler. It's very attractive," she said, giving me a bro-like pat on the back, reaching out, and taking hold of my hand. "Don't forget, you were on mind-altering drugs at the time."

"Maybe, but it had been wearing off noticeably before the scuffle. However, I'm sure there must have been enough in my system to have altered my awareness."

I loved that Jax was open to any concept, whether she could personally relate to it or not. In her own way, she accepted what life served up, didn't judge it, and could pretty much flow with whatever happened. She was cool with not having to know, understand, or dispute new things, whether they were concepts, beliefs, or experiences. I felt this constant need to make sense of everything, whereas she didn't seem to need to. And she appeared better off for it. I was always cerebral, with an active mind, but somewhere along the way, I had determined it was crucial to fit everything that transpired in my life into my belief systems or points of view. This wasn't a conscious decision. It just became a habit, like drinking Diet Coke. It was a part of how I operated, and after a while, I didn't remember what life was like before the addiction set in. Maybe I had a general fear of the unknown, and part of me felt that by understanding what was happening and why, things became known, and with that came a sense of predictability, which felt safer.

"Jax, do you believe everything happens for a reason or that life's events are random?" I asked, curious to see what general beliefs enabled her to willfully accept life on its terms.

"In a way, I believe that things happen for a reason, if I consider it," Jax replied thoughtfully. "But ultimately it doesn't matter, because life seems to have its course, regardless of what I do or don't want. Life has given me incredible blessings, like a wonderful brother, a caring sister-in-law, and a beautiful niece. It has also presented me with challenges, such as drug addiction and a lack of long-term vision. And amidst it all, it has given me you," she continued, her voice filled with sincerity. "I suppose I've grown from all these experiences, often the most from the most painful ones. So, even though I don't fully understand the journey I'm on, I've chosen to trust it," she replied.

"OK. Let's say you generally trust life. Does that trust eliminate the need to understand what's happening and why?"

"I suppose in a way it does. I still worry about stuff. I definitely have pieces of my life I want to turn out in certain ways, and I assume I have some influence on that, but if I'm losing a battle, I don't feel the need to die on every hill. I try not to spend much time attempting to redirect the ship after it's changed direction," she explained.

"That's well said. So, what are your preferences for the future?" I asked, hoping I might be included.

"General stuff, I suppose, like being healthy, having enough money to get by, staying clean. I want a family someday: a couple of kids, maybe three, and a husband with whom I can share that journey. Possibly a person like you," she said with a sweet yet vulnerable smile. "Seeing Jimmy and Summer and how having Jade created such a loving experience for the three of them triggered something in me. It cemented that having a family with kids also needed to be a part of my life. Toby, with your two kids, was your experience similar to Jimmy and Summer's?"

"Initially, they were a hell of a lot of work, but it didn't seem like work. You love them and would take a bullet in a second for them if that's what was required. I've stuffed all that, I imagine, because I know Gina's largely taken it away." I wasn't prepared to go deep into repressed emotions, but we had unexpectedly landed there like a golf ball stopping right in the middle of the cart path.

"Do you ever think about starting another family someday?" she asked.

The truth is, I hadn't. And I just assumed I wouldn't. I don't know why, and this was a rare instance of me not having dissected and classified something, but it was probably out of fear. However, I knew where this question was leading; regretfully, I didn't know the answer. I owed her one, however. Maybe this was why she hesitated to say the "L" word. Knowing that being in love with me could lead her into a life she didn't want if I wasn't up for another family.

"Honestly, I haven't thought that far ahead, so I can't say I know right now. Parts of it I undeniably miss. However, losing those two has been more painful than I thought. Maybe it's time I start working through that." I could have said "absolutely" and given myself time to reconsider and an opportunity to cement my relationship with Jax, but that was too manipulative even for me and would have been cruel.

"Probably not a bad idea," she said, followed by an uncomfortable pause as I contemplated exactly what she meant by that, knowing full well the future of our relationship was hanging in the balance.

It was now almost 2 a.m., and my brain was frazzled. Jax spent the night and insisted on screwing my brains out, a welcome distraction from the quicksand of uncertainty sucking me down. The Puss

Circus, Director's Cut, Anal Intruder, and an ER trip had gotten her hot and bothered. If only I had known years ago that was all it took to get a good-looking woman in the sack; my sex life would have been way different.

But now I had something a lot more serious to figure out.

The following day, Jax had to get up early for work and departed with a kiss on my cheek as I groggily tried to sort out what day it was, drifting off again before figuring it out. I eventually woke up for good around nine-thirty and spent the next twenty minutes replaying the previous night's events. There was a lot to process, and it became clear that I didn't have the energy to keep trying.

Still somewhat dazed with an alcohol withdrawal-sponsored shakiness, I checked my hidden grommet for further darkening and was relieved that things hadn't taken a turn for the worse. In fact, and it was hard to tell for sure, but it didn't seem quite as monstrous as usual. Laying on my back upside down was causing my hung-over head to throb, so I abandoned any further inspection and chalked it up to an illusion due to my severely swollen and puffy eyes.

I bypassed the shower, got dressed, and made a run for the border.

After waiting for my order at Taco Bell for at least four minutes, finally, an employee held out a bag, "Order #751. Four breakfast sausage burritos and two cups of coffee." Although not deliberate, I appeared to be on my way to see Eddie and Cowboy yet again.

"Toby, me boy! I hardly knew ye," Eddie said after putting down his newspaper to see what had rousted Cowboy. "You're looking a little rough around the edges. Everything OK?"

"Sure. Just riding the struggle bus today. Late night last night," I said, offering him a coffee.

"Got after it, huh?" he asked.

"Unplanned. Started at The Plow, where all good things begin or end, right?"

"As rumor has it."

"RV Jeff and Big Sallie are now engaged, and it turned into a celebration, complete with a visit to the emergency room. Sallie's going to be fine. Just a few stitches. I'll spare you the details."

"Just sounds like partying to me," Eddie said, taking a sip of the scalding coffee without any indication of seared flesh.

Cowboy had now transitioned from his butt-scratching position onto his back for belly rubs, which I willingly provided. He was a tremendous no-hassle dog—a real unicorn.

"Is that a new bracelet you're sporting there? I didn't take you for the jewelry-wearing type," I said, noticing a mildly tarnished half-inch wide silver band that contrasted starkly with his sun-worn brown skin. What language is that?" There were letters wrapped around the band that didn't appear to be from the Roman alphabet.

"I found this in a box of junk left on the curb for people to pick through. It's Sanskrit, the ancient language in which the Vedas were originally written. Sanskrit was developed in ancient India. It is no longer a spoken language. Supposedly, the vibration of the words translates the meaning."

"How would you know that, Eddie?"

"Don't exactly remember," he said.

"Any chance you know what it says?"

"*Om Nama Shivaya*. It means I honor Shiva, one of the main three Hindu Gods. It's a popular mantra, and when repeated, it is supposed to mitigate the worries of a burdened mind. It also means 'Universal consciousness is one.' I am not a huge fan of Hinduism or any organized religion, for that matter, but I like its philosophy."

"Seems like there is some confusion around the meaning," I pointed out.

"Not at the highest level. Their concept of God is complex, like the universe. They believe that the experiences of God can be very different, like looking at a house from different sides. The front porch looks nothing like the back porch but is still part of the same house. You just can't see both sides at the same time. Like not being able to see your own eyeballs, but they are an active participant in everything you see. In nondualist philosophy, everything is all one thing.

The eyes, the looker, and what the eyes see are all a part of an interdependent event called 'seeing.' The division is in our mind as we label objects, seemingly dividing the single act of seeing into separate pieces. Thus, the illusion of dualism. The opposites require each other to exist, but at the highest level, it's all one unified thing. Our language is divisive and requires duality. Subject, verb, object. Sanskrit is different."

"Fuck, Eddie. Why do you bombard me with this when I can't even think right now? Seems kind of like psychological bullying."

"That's exactly why. With the thinking out of the way, you might be able to hear what I'm saying," he said, pausing to take in the aroma of his coffee.

"So if I repeat this mantra..."

Eddie interrupted. "*Japa. Japa* is what you call the repetition of a mantra."

"Sure. If I *japa* the shit out of this, my mind will stop worrying?"

"That's the idea."

"Well, I'll take all the help I can get in that area." It couldn't hurt to try it, I supposed.

"How's all that thinking working for you?" he asked.

"It's still a work in progress. I'm at the "Y" with Jax. She ultimately wants kids and a family. I've been down that road and don't know if I want to do it again. Kind of qualifies as a potential irreconcilable difference if I decide I don't."

"Why wouldn't you?" he asked.

"I don't know. Sometimes I do. Maybe it will give me a second chance at regaining the family I lost. Maybe even a better one in the long term. Who knows?"

"Maybe. Maybe not. Can't tell what the future holds," he added.

"That's exactly it. That's what I've got to figure out, I guess."

"Let me ask you this, and feel free to think it over, as you're prone to do. What's the best decision you've ever made?"

"There's not a lot of them to choose from. There were what I thought were good decisions at the time. Marrying Gina, a career in high-tech, going to college?"

"In retrospect, were they good decisions?"

"Maybe. Or maybe not. They felt good at the time and I had no regrets about college. Then, I felt bad when my marriage and career fell apart. Now I feel good that I'm free from them."

"Do you think you grew from them?"

"Yes. I did, I suppose," I contemplatively answered.

"So, at the time, you had no idea how those decisions would turn out, but they took you on a journey. Isn't that what life is? It gives you what you need—not always what you want, but usually what you can handle."

"Good point. Maybe I need to think about it some more," I said.

"Or maybe you don't," he suggested. "Isn't that where the suffering comes from? You and Jax are having fun and enjoying each other, and you're excited. Then you start thinking about what if that pleasure disappears, and you get anxious. You're scared your happiness could be lost. People can give you pleasure, Toby, but not happiness. You're on your own there. It comes from a place inside you don't spend much time in because you think you are what's going on in your mind. But the mind is just patterns of thought—a process running like a computer program based on inputs or memories. In 'what' is all of that taking place?" he asked.

"What does that mean?" I said, getting frustrated at my successful failure to follow him.

"What part of you is aware of your thoughts? Your mind is running like a locomotive, but there's something that notices that every now and then—that same something that's always been there watching. Maybe you should get to know that part of yourself. Set your mind gently aside and play in the nonthinking awareness between the thoughts. Bow to Shiva. *Om Namah Shivaya*," he said, laughing.

"*Om Namah Shivaya*," I said, holding up my cup to toast Eddie.

We dove into our burritos, and I walked Eddie through the

details of the night before, and we laughed at the absurdity of it all. We also laughed at the absurdity of our lives. A vast universe with billions of galaxies, each of which would take tens of thousands of light years to cross. In one of those galaxies, one of a billion suns was our sun, with a tiny blue planet orbiting it. Such a small piece of the whole universe that it's arguably insignificant. Almost microscopic. On that one microspeck of the universe called Earth, there exist even tinier creatures you can't see from twenty-thousand feet above. These almost sub-atomic flecks snapping in and out of existence in just a few years. Those flecks come with a sense of feeling separate from the totality, believing they can understand the scope and meaning of it all through such an unstable thing as fleeting thoughts. The absurdity of it all. Yet, those thoughts are all we know, like a single cell on your fingernail struggling to grok the entire experience of being a human being. It seemed utterly ridiculous. We are nothing in the bigger whole, but we believe we are the only thing of importance. How is that not the grandest illusion of all? But because we all share that same illusion, it's seldom questioned. But it causes so much angst. It occurred to me that thinking we can know anything for certain could be a fool's errand.

I eventually bid them farewell for the day, turning to walk away, still chuckling to myself.

"Toby," Eddie called as I was walking away.

"Yeah?" I said, turning around.

"You can't think your way out of thinking."

I nodded and continued, not thinking and just laughing my way home.

CHAPTER
TWENTY-FIVE

L ater that day, on my way to work at The Altered Ego, I practiced trying not to think. It wasn't going well as I was so absorbed in thinking about not thinking that I failed to notice the red hand signal, indicating it wasn't an opportune time to cross the street. Luckily, the bus was coming to a halt and skidded to a stop about a foot before taking my life. Eddie had mentioned witnessing thoughts and not trying to fight with them, so I decided to take a step back, follow Eddie's advice, and be aware of thinking versus suppressing it, all while keeping an eye out for things that could kill me.

By this time, I had accepted that Eddie had a good handle on human nature and how our psyches worked. Everything we discussed appeared to get right to the root of the problem. He wasn't a teacher, per se, or if he was, he didn't seem to have many students currently enrolled. I had at least stopped trying to challenge everything he said and looking for flaws in his logic. This may have been due to the exposure of so many flaws in my own paradigm. However, I was starting to wonder which was worse—being oblivious to our manufactured mental reality or being aware of it but helpless to change it. The flip-flopping between these orientations was doing an outstanding job of boosting my sense of mental instability. I wasn't willing to go back to leading an unexamined life, but I couldn't seem to experience the reality behind my mind except for a brief glimpse here and there, unsure if it was imaginary and I was on a fool's errand. I had a foot in both worlds and no traction in either. I concluded that I was fucked up, lost, or, more likely, both. I'd need to add that to my resume of current inadequacies.

"What's news, Jazmine?" I said, entering the salon.

"Hi, Toby. Good you're here, as we're fucked at 3 p.m. today. Babs is double-booked, and you will need to help out and take a lightening appointment. And by the way, we've been inundated with back-door bleaching appointments, requesting you by name. What's up with that?"

I replied. "Oh yeah, I guess to say my customer satisfaction scores are exemplary would be an understatement. Glad to be bringing some new referral business into the Salon," I said casually. "And, of course, I'm happy to help with the 3 p.m. lightening appointment."

Jazmine was visibly relieved and more than visibly roasting hot just standing there wearing her perfect body and pouty red lips; I observed myself thinking, followed by my thinking about what was wrong with my lecherous self. Why was every woman either hot, fluffy, a whore, or basically non-existent? What was underneath was most important. However, I often couldn't get beyond the wrapping. How much of that was just lousy thinking habits? More thought patterns to watch and not get caught up in, I guess. Hopefully, those patterns would break one day, and I could see people purely for the beauty and magic within them.

Three customers were waiting, and sure enough, we were overbooked, resulting from someone's failure to leverage the scheduling software, and I was just happy that I wasn't to blame. Luckily, I was there and able to manage the front and 'back office,' so to speak.

Today, I was the solution, not the problem. If I had a nickname, it would have indeed been "The Swiss Army Knife."

"Just give me a second, and I'll be right with you," I said, pulling up the computer to see who was there to see who. "Tom?" I asked as if it was necessary since there was only one male and the two women didn't look like tomboys. He quickly raised a hand, indicating he was indeed Tom. "Babs will be providing your pedicure today and should be done with her current appointment momentarily. Angie?" I asked, and the younger of the two women gave me a nod. It said Angie had a waxing appointment. This was an instance where we wouldn't say the treatment name out loud. Some people were embarrassed about others being made aware that they may have out-of-control pit, lip, or undercarriage issues that needed professional taming. "Jazmine will be with you shortly for your appointment."

By process of elimination, I had deduced that the geriatric old lady was Eunice and my three o'clock appointment. The computer said she was here for anal lightening, which was clearly an error. I was pretty sure Eunice had not signed up to have a strange man prod around in her ass-crack, exfoliating and dabbing cream on her aging sphincter. In a timely turn of events, Babs emerged from her appointment, looking marginally frazzled from the day's chaos. I motioned for her to look at the screen, pointing to my appointment so she could understand the issue without creating any inadvertent alarm. With a quick nod of understanding, resting her hand on my shoulder, she leaned in and whispered, "Thanks for pitching in on short notice, Toby," and then in a louder voice, "Angie, great to see you again. As usual, you look fantastic. Follow me back." And she was gone.

My mind was racing in circles like a Hot Wheel car rocketing through the loopty-loops of its track. First, I would have to witness the horror on Eunice's face when she realized I, a man, would be bearing down on her anus while splashing toxic chemicals around. Then I was worried about Tom witnessing whatever reaction Eunice might have. Both Tom and Eunice were now looking at me.

Eunice was not yet aware of exactly who her appointment was with. The computer indicated it was her first time in, so it was doubtful she would have requested a technician by name. Tom knew he was with Jazmine and wasn't paying close attention anyway because he was likely bored as shit.

There weren't a lot of options at this point—just two. Walk out that door and never return or bleach Eunice's eighty-something-year-old anus.

Unexpectedly, I found myself reflecting on my now-deceased grandmother. After migrating into adulthood, we became a lot closer. She was on the front end of the baby-boomer generation and had lost my grandfather as the casualty of a long and painful battle with prostate cancer twenty-five years before her own passing.

They had opened and operated a hardware store on Third and Clement Street in San Francisco around the same time my mother came onto the scene and were content to live in the small apartment above it. After my grandfather's death, she continued to manage the store, working long hours without complaint, up until the day she died. She was among the most even-keeled people I'd ever met; she never complained, argued, or offered unsolicited advice. She accepted me without any expectations or judgments, or at least not any I can remember. As I got older, we transitioned from a grand-parent and grandkid relationship into two adults, getting to know each other. We would discuss adult topics like the ten-day weather forecast, funny stories, the latest town gossip, hopes, bucket lists, fears, regrets, blah, blah, blah. We started gently teasing each other about things, and from then on, we just hit it off, laughing, crying, and realizing the good fortune that we both had each other, and neither of us took it for granted.

She said I reminded her of her older brother, whom she lost in a tragic furnace explosion when she was eight and he was fifteen. The one that took her along on any date that involved a movie. Who took her to every school dance because she loved to dance, and he loved her more than anything else in the world. The brother who insisted she join every family poker and gin game before she knew the rules, to the dismay of the other siblings. And God damn if that woman could play gin. The kind of brother we all dreamed of having but none of us were ever capable of being. I can't imagine how that loss must have impacted her at such a sensitive developmental age, but I was glad I could help her reconnect to where she felt someone was in her corner she could always count on.

By then, she had outlived her remaining four siblings, her husband, and almost all of her friends, which was hardly a prize for a well-fought life of hard work and compassion. There are no golden years. It's just a concept that provides a mental escape to an imagined happier future. It delivers us from the unspoken truth that life has its own agenda and our destinies are often decided by what we have the least control over.

In her later years, I had been her best friend, and it dawned on me how much I missed being there to support her. Maybe the idea of reconnecting with this part of me motivated me to do an exceptional job of lovingly bleaching Eunice's anus. Or perhaps it was a newfound determination to see beyond a woman's appearance.

"Eunice, I'm Toby, and you'll be with me today. If you're ready, we can head on back?"

"Ready as I'll ever be," she retorted, hopping up as if she expected nothing else. We made our way down the hall while exchanging brief pleasantries.

"Does it make you feel uncomfortable, Eunice, that I'm a man and not a woman?"

"Only if it makes you uncomfortable," she calmly responded as I ushered her into the bleaching lair.

"You are here to get your neither region bleached, and I'm here to bleach that nether region. I want to ensure you have a positive experience and the outcome you are expecting." I don't know why I said that or where it came from, but I couldn't have come up with anything better if I'd made a project of it. "Is this your first time with this procedure?"

"Toby, I'm a bleaching virgin, and you'll be the only one that can take credit for stealing my virginity, so to speak," she said laughingly, putting me at ease.

I walked her through the details of the drill and gave her the special hospital-like robe to change into. Respecting her privacy, I left the room for a few minutes, which was slightly ludicrous as we both were fully aware that privacy wasn't a part of this process.

I knocked on the door to ensure she had completed her costume change and entered to find her lying face down on the table. "Ready for action?" I asked.

"As ready as I'll ever be. Do you think it's weird that an old lady is sprucing up her back door?" she asked, her nonchalant demeanor surprising me.

"Why would I? You get your hair done, probably exercise, put on make-up, and buy nice clothes, right?"

"Of course."

"So if someone at any age is taking care to present themselves at their best, why would this be any different than other even more obvious tactics to optimize appearance?"

"Young man, you make an excellent point. We do the best we can with what we have. Why not?"

"Why not," I confirmed.

We got her comfortably situated with her lily-white derriere pointed skyward and her head on a pillow as I gave a Wet Wipe the full tour of Eunice's keister. Surprisingly, it didn't look much different than anyone else's, likely a result of excellent genetics or good hygiene. However, there was an opportunity to take it to the next level with a little touch-up. I gently exfoliated the region with a wet cloth and gritty cream and administered the active agent.

"So we'll leave this on for twenty minutes. I can either leave and come back or stay and keep you company. Whatever makes you more comfortable."

"Might as well stay. It will pass the time faster," she said.

So I pulled a chair up where I could see her face, and she could be assured her anus was not under further scrutiny.

"Eunice, do you mind if I ask you a personal question?"

"Well, under the circumstances, it only seems fitting as it appears I've already revealed something quite personal," she said, laughing.

"What motivated you to get your bum lightened in the first place? I can't imagine people have been telling you for years to take better care of your rectum."

"I've got a new boyfriend. He's a passionate man, and I'm a passionate woman, and it seems we both have some residual naughtiness still left in the 'ol tank. It's only a matter of time before we take things to the next level, which I've never had an issue with, if you know what I mean. Anyway, he's a sixty-five-year-old man, willing to deal with making love to an eighty-year-old lady. I don't want to make it any harder for him to maintain an erection. It's out of compassion, I guess. It's not like I will be looking down there myself."

"That's as good a reason as any. He's lucky to have a woman like you, Eunice. A twenty-five-year-old adventurous woman with a great sense of humor who is disguised as a classy eighty-year-old. That's role-playing if I've ever heard of it," I said.

"Now that you put it that way, he is a damn lucky bastard, isn't he?" she said as we both chuckled. "I don't see a ring. I assume you aren't married. You seeing anyone?" she asked.

"I was married, and that was a tragic story. I do have an absolutely fantastic and relatively new girlfriend, except for one thing," I replied.

"Probably needs her butt bleached, huh? Let me know if you want me to talk to her." Eunice had a charming yet confident sense of humor that I respected. Her guy was lucky, and I was surprised to see myself thinking I could understand what he saw in her.

"In the spirit of full disclosure, we bleached each other shortly after I started here to see if it worked. And I'm happy to say the results are noticeable." I decided against detailing exactly whose results I was referring to so as not to discredit the very procedure she was taking part in by revealing I was sporting an impressively unbleachable anus. "But we are kind of at a junction point in our relationship. She really wants kids and is waiting to see if we are on the same page before letting things go any further."

"Do you want kids?" she asked, not beating around the bush. Of course, when you're eighty, you don't have much time left for beating around the bush. It did make for efficient conversation.

"I already have two that I no longer appear to be allowed to see. That's another story. But I can't say I'm excited to have more. That sounds messed up, as I enjoyed being a Dad, and one would assume a second chance would be a welcome opportunity to fill that void. It just seems that I don't know what I want or who I'm becoming at this stage, and it's not responsible to Jax, myself, or any potential offspring to figure that out after starting a second family. That's asking her to take a big leap of faith. As I'm talking about this out loud for the first time, I feel like I don't want to go down the path to parenthood again, even though I can't articulate exactly why. I owe her an answer, and I'm just procrastinating the inevitable," I said, feeling even more naked and exposed than Eunice was.

"Toby, if you don't want to have more kids, you don't want to have more kids. Two may be enough. You could spend months figuring out why, but does it make a difference? Most of the time, we don't know why we do what we do anyway. Trust your gut, and you can figure out why afterward. If you change your mind and she's still available, it's meant to be. If not, you were true to yourself at the time. If you aren't willing to know and accept yourself as you are, you certainly won't be able to accept anyone else. That's the key to relationships. If you have an honest and sincere relationship with yourself, it's possible to share one with someone else. Maybe your gut is telling you that you have other internal work to do before you make any long-term commitments to anything, and because you care for her, you owe her that honesty. It will surely be a painful conversation, but not one to avoid. And that's just the two cents of an eighty-year-old woman getting her butthole bleached, for whatever that's worth."

"God damn, Eunice! That's it! You nailed it. I couldn't begin to articulate that, but as you said it, it became crystal clear that's exactly right. I'm in process and need to surrender to that process first as my number one priority. Otherwise, I'll be making decisions from a place of reckless abandon, which could be cruel to those I care about."

"Toby, the good thing about being old is you can see the shit rolling downhill from a mile away before it squashes you. Your situation isn't that uncommon."

"We'll it feels uncommon for me. Thanks for the insight. I sincerely appreciate it," I said, meaning every word. The conversation shifted to her childhood, interests, and various other topics until the timer's chime rang out, signifying it was time for the unveiling.

"It's been twenty minutes. How are you feeling down there?"

"To be honest, I don't feel a thing. I'm curious if it worked, though. The suspense is killing me," she said with a tinge of sarcasm.

"Eunice, you are going to be happy with this. Night and day difference," I proudly stated, handing her a hand mirror to inspect things for herself.

"Damn. I'm amazed at the dramatic difference. I guess I expected it wouldn't yield such noticeable results. Toby, you've restored my back door confidence." It was starting to seem like my pooper was the most stubborn pooper on the planet. I was thankful that someone as kind and sweet as Eunice didn't have to bear my burden and could enjoy the results of a successful bleaching of her anus.

"I'm a professional Eunice. I laugh in the face of discoloration, and I'm glad I could brighten your day, amongst other things." And I was. "Often, people will need a follow-up treatment or two to obtain the desired shade of lightening, but it's advised to wait a couple of weeks between sessions so the skin can recover. If you feel you need another session, give us a call for round two, but initially, it appears you could be a one-and-done type of gal."

I left Eunice to get dressed and told her to meet me up front and to take her time.

"How did things go in there? Sorry to spring that on you, Toby, and thanks for being a team player," Babs said, having just finished her appointment as Tom, her pedicure customer, closed the door behind him to bestow his well-manicured feet upon the world.

"It was a delightful and 'enlightening' experience," I joked while, at the same time, not joking at all. I didn't even find myself mired in jealousy of Eunice's optimal results. I was simply happy for her.

"Well, glad to hear it didn't leave you in a dark place," Babs said, exchanging puns.

I had just enjoyed bleaching the anus of an eighty-year-old lady and, in the process, obtained clarity around a relationship-ending dilemma. Job satisfaction can rear its head in the most unlikely of circumstances.

Why wasn't I revolted and sickened and wallowing in self-pity for the exemplary life I'd worked so hard to unsuccessfully build? I realized the switch flipped once I had thought about my grand-mother. In connecting to those memories and feelings, I opened up enough to connect with Eunice in the same way, from the heart. It wasn't just me having to go through this uncomfortable experience with a complete stranger; I had connected with her and, as a result, felt a level of compassion, which felt good. Why would I be surprised, I thought. After all, I was regularly eating out of tin cans on the street with a homeless guy and, as a result, becoming more self-aware, for better or for worse.

At that point, it dawned on me that I was quite possibly going mad. I was starting to feel I didn't know who I was anymore, like the first few seconds after waking up in the morning trying to make sense of what day it is and why I'm looking around a shitty hovel of an apartment. Maybe this is how it happens. Suddenly, a cog or two falls out of place, and we lose perspective and happily, without even knowing it, wake up one day in an alternate universe we would never have considered, wondering what the fuck happened. And even worse, no longer caring. Maybe this was where life gives up on a person, who, in return, just gives up on life.

Carlotta arrived to cover the late shift, as I had taken the early shift today upon her request. This left me with the rest of the afternoon and evening to plunder as I pleased.

AFTER RETURNING HOME FROM WORK, I decided to get a run in. For a change of scenery, I would run down Lake Street West to the Park Presidio green belt and then take that north into the Presidio through the Mountain Lake Park entrance. Then, I would run up Mountain Lake Trail towards the golf course and see how I felt before circling back or continuing up a nasty hill to the top of the Lyon Street stairs. If you've never been to San Francisco, that means nothing, but it's a beautiful run all the same.

My timing was glorious. The sun was about an hour from setting, weaving a lemony orange veil of warmth between the trees and houses. It must have been sixty-five or seventy degrees and not the slightest wind. These evenings were few and far between in The City.

Now that I had built up to running a bit farther, it opened up opportunities for piecing together some scenic routes. I was lucky enough to live between Golden Gate Park and the Presidio, two beautiful green spaces bravely fighting off the sidewalks, streets, and houses to let nature thrive amidst man's progress.

I passed a father on the sidewalk, acquiescing to his toddler's demands to ride on his shoulders, as he negotiated holding onto her leg with one hand while pushing the vacated stroller with his other. I painfully reminisced about my own paternal experience. Children's fresh curiosity towards life and a strong desire to remain connected to their parents while experiencing it all was enchanting. Finally, it dawned on me. It wasn't necessarily more children I didn't want; it was grieving the suppressed loss of my own that I wasn't prepared to address. Ultimately, I would have to reconcile that loss, which terrified me. I suppose that those memories, hopes for their little futures, and the desire to be there to protect and prepare them would need to be given up if I wanted to move on. I ran past them, realizing I was running from a reality I couldn't yet reconcile. How symbolic. At one level, this was a pain that defined me, and yes, I was willing to give this up; however, the void replacing it scared me more than the pain itself.

I was now at a point where I was ready to release my professional identity. I could let go of financial stability. I was OK with letting my marriage go. My sense of certainty over how the world and my mind worked was falling away on its own. But yet, I was clinging to my deepest fears and pains like a life raft. Why? Maybe it was one of the only familiar pieces of myself I had left. What would remain of who I believed myself to be without even those? Sure, the future was uncertain, but I was becoming accustomed to living with that. But letting go of the most meaningful pieces of my past felt like letting go of the only thing still tethering me to feelings of love. With Gina, my resentment and anger powered me through the disconnect, diffusing or maybe transforming love into a mere husk that could be comfortably discarded. But this was something else entirely, and it felt callous to move on, although I didn't have an option. The only choice was how long I wanted to harbor these feelings of loss, these memories, and what I gained from doing so.

Opening up and being willing to let it play out on its timeline without resistance was all I could do. Just accept what is—what a conflicted concept. Life is something you are supposed to manage, control, and bend to your preferences. Then suddenly, to accept it on its terms, when I'd been trained to never accept anything less than desirable, felt like surrendering. In life, at least in America, surrender is synonymous with failure. Maybe Ram Dass or Alan Watts would say surrender is ultimately the only way to achieve any significant freedom. I was clinging to my past, most likely as a way of continuing to validate myself to myself. Could I find a space where I could live without any validation? Was it possible to watch this play and this Toby Tenderhill character evolve on its own terms and be OK with it? That seemed almost unthinkable.

I had chugged up an impressive hill on the Mountain Lake trail, distracted by these questions, and was now passing the Presidio Golf Course's driving range on my left. A voice in my head rattled, "You can't think your way out of thinking, Toby." Maybe it was the exhaustion from the hill I had just climbed or the mental fatigue from what I had been churning over the last ten minutes, but my mind, at that moment, just involuntarily gave up thinking.

There was just running, breathing, seeing a little league game on the softball fields on my left, with parents cheering encouragement to their kids. I was smelling the eucalyptus grove up ahead and simply being there as a simple part of this masterpiece. I was the guy running in this movie set. Looking back, I would describe the experience as just being part of a whole symphony playing out. A musical fabric into which I was inextricably woven, and simultaneously, I was simply one of many such vantage points. Things were flowing, and in a way, "I" wasn't there because "my mind" was on pause. Maybe this could be called the flow state that athletes refer to, although I was far from an athlete. I can only describe it as the complete absence of resistance on any level. It was all simply happening—all on its own.

A few minutes later, after ascending another steep grade, I emerged from the trail out of the East side of the Presidio, precisely at the top of the Lyon Street stairs. Two other runners were summiting the top stair from below, and one of the guys warned, "Be careful, dude. Those are a real ass-kicker." He apparently didn't think I looked up to the task.

That jump-started my brain, and I realized I had gone farther than anticipated. I was looking down a multi-tiered cement staircase, transcending a couple of city blocks, running parallel to the eastern edge of the Presidio. As it turns out, 332 stairs, to be exact. I know this because I counted as I descended them, depositing myself at the bottom to muster up enough motivation to turn around and run back up.

I was now back in the spin cycle of my thoughts, worrying I may have made a foolish decision to come this far. After all, I hadn't incorporated these stairs into any previous runs. I would pay the price in the morning. The shortest way back was the way I came, putting me at the halfway mark.

I was where I was and had only one option: to keep going. The guy who warned me at the top was right. It was a total ass-kicker; however, after stopping to catch my breath twice, I eventually summited the last step and enjoyed a blissful downhill recovery as the setting sun injected crimson life into the clouds framing the horizon.

My legs were heavy on the way home, but there was a twisted relief brought by the clarity that I knew I had to traverse the grief of losing my children if I wanted to move on with whatever my "new life" would become. What I didn't know was if this would result in me entertaining the idea of starting another family in the future, but one way or the other, if I wanted to give up this grief and pain, I had to move through, not around it. Just directly acknowledging this made me feel about twenty pounds lighter.

However, what troubled me the most was that I could see my mind trying to validate myself, spin narratives I could live with, and hide from the pain and fear. But I didn't trust its volatile gyrations anymore. And even more concerning, what else remained if I wasn't just these repetitive thoughts, pockets of lingering emotional pain, and largely unquestioned belief systems? I could create a new story, strive for a new goal, and seek happiness, but it all was starting to seem so thin.

I finally arrived home, realizing I was still lost.

TWENTY-SIX

My lack of clarity led me to Eddie's doorstep after my run, which provided a fifty percent chance of more clarity and a fifty percent chance of more confusion—better odds than I had on my own.

"I can tell you what you want to hear or what you need to hear. It depends on if you are looking to feel good or if you are looking for truth. The menu is simple; it just depends on what you're in the mood for?" Eddie asked as he focused on shaking out Cowboy's mat.

"Eddie, it seems you're getting a little meaner about sharing your insights these days," I said, only half joking.

"Just holding you more accountable," he replied. "You can find yourself hopelessly lost in the no man's land between your previous unquestioned perception of reality and the unknown on the other side. You may or may not realize it, but you can't go backward. Reality, as you knew it, just got a lot less convincing, right?"

"Shit, I'm starting to question everything. Next thing I know, I'll find out I'm a woman trapped in a man's body."

"Unlikely, yet entirely possible. However, I imagine the truth lying unexposed underneath it all has yet to become convincing enough to have faith in. A little guidance can go a long way if you are willing to investigate versus struggle to justify."

"Eddie, lately, I think I'm potentially going insane. I see all this happening like I'm watching my life through a window. But I am on the outside looking in and I miss being on the inside. Does that make any sense at all?"

"Complete sense," he said, sitting there pondering his hand.

"Well, it's a shitty place to end up mentally, Eddie—questioning everything, not knowing what to believe in or what's just another perception based on unquestioned ideas. Then I meet people like you, Hulises, RV Jeff, Big Sallie, and even Jax, who all seem to derive contentment from lives I would have felt only a hollow pity for only a few months ago. You know... the unfortunate, the unlucky, the lazy, or the recovering drug addicts. But in reality, you are all content and enjoying the same things we all strive for—love, connecting with people, helping people, and laughing. I'm wasting time worrying about potential futures that in all likelihood may never manifest. Then I think maybe my belief about what freedom is may not entirely be correct. Then I worry about what other beliefs are potentially wrong that I'm not even considering."

"You've got to clean the mirror to see the reflection of what you are. And honestly, you have a mirror as filthy as your butthole. So your reflection, self-image, identity, or whatever you are in the mood to call it, is distorted, as it simply reflects a picture clouded by the filth of your remaining beliefs, ideas, and fears. You are starting to remove the first layers of gunk, but you still can't yet see a clear reflection."

"Then who or what am I underneath it all, Eddie?"

"Get the rest of the filth out of the way and see for yourself what remains. Until you experience what's behind words and thoughts, you will think they are 'you,'" he said, poking his finger at me.

Eddie continued, "Most people don't investigate their beliefs, or at best, only at socially acceptable levels. People feel safe arguing over politics, debating the best knot to use when tying a fly on a line or if it's better to pan-fry or grill a steak. We know it's relatively safe to be wrong or change our minds about these things."

"Well, it's always better to pan-fry a steak if you know what you're doing," I clarified.

"Agreed, but what about the rest of it all? Questions like, 'Is who I am just a collection of memories, thoughts about the future, and cyclical patterns that repeat themselves enough to add a sense of permanence?' Or 'Who was I before I had any beliefs, memories, or coherent thoughts?' Or even 'Am I just this body and this mind?' Why don't we feel comfortable asking these questions?"

"Because they threaten the foundation of what we believe about who we are and what's really going on here?" I suggested.

"Bravo!" he yelled, jumping to his feet as if his team had just scored a touchdown. "It's funny. People will free dive one hundred feet underwater, leap out of a plane with only a piece of material to slow their fall, run marathons, work eighty-hour weeks, and initiate other very dangerous or painful experiences. Still, they aren't brave enough to spend *any time at all* inquiring into the underlying nature of themselves."

"So you're saying people are basically scared pussies?"

"I think subconsciously, yes. People's worst fear isn't death, loss, or poverty. People's worst fear is that they, as they know themselves, are an illusion based on unexamined thoughts—that who they believe themselves to be doesn't really exist. Ego death is scarier than physical death. We fight to protect our illusions and, in doing so, earn the right to keep them. And they, in turn, become the bars of the jail we find ourselves in. A jail we are familiar with is often preferred to the freedom of the unknown. As I said, Toby, deep intro-spection is not for those with timid souls."

"For the sake of argument, suppose my soul is not timid. How do I obtain some additional clarity here instead of remaining stuck in these so-called 'illusions' and just swapping one out for another, pretending to be making some progress?"

"Again, it's not an additive process. What's required is a destructive process. Identify everything you are not. That's the filth on the mirror. When we don't clear away the filth—our ideas of what's important and what we can achieve—we are building stronger fortresses that make it harder to escape. Tear down the fucking walls and see what things look like. But the real question is, what are you willing to risk? If the answer isn't everything, you'll always be clinging to something. And clinging to anything will always bind you."

"Eddie, that seems like dying, in a way."

"No. It *is* dying! It's waking up from a dream we were positive was real, only to find that who we thought we were all along was never real at all. What's always there beneath it all?"

"I don't have a God damned clue. I can't stop thinking my life is spinning out of control, and I'm going crazy sometimes."

"Well, then, don't think about it. Just be right here, right now. Don't think about being right here right now; *be* here. That's all that's left when there aren't any more ego goals to fulfill. Spiritual goals are just more ego goals. Creating more thought-based reality, which will eventually erode into more rubble."

"Well...it seems like you are telling me to strive to get rid of a false reality I created and, simultaneously, not to strive for anything. That makes no sense, Eddie."

"I'm saying, let it all fucking burn and *be* what remains, and you might find it's far more than you ever imagined."

"Fine. Just watch what's in front of my face and let it all fizzle into nothing," I said, still suspicious that I was errantly boarding a rocket train to Crazy Town.

Cowboy was now standing on my lap in a masterful way that allowed him to force his entire body weight through his two front paws directly into my thighs, which hurt, but he was cute enough to make it endurable.

"Most importantly, don't get frustrated. It's not easy, but nothing of real value ever is."

"Eddie, I bleach old ladies' asses."

"See, you're already observing things," he said with a barely perceptible smile beginning to work its way across his mouth.

"But don't analyze it, right? Observe the old lady's ass and then observe what's next?" I said, asking for some clarification.

"That's the practice. If you forget and get sucked back into your mini drama that you call 'yourself,' focus on what's happening in front of you. Nothing to do but be here and be aware. And it's OK to suck at it."

"That's a relief. That seems to be my modus operandi these days. Well, I think I'll observe myself getting on my way, Eddie," I said, gently ushering Cowboy off my lap as I stood up.

"Then I guess I'll observe you leaving." Then he stood up and, shockingly, hugged me and looked straight at me with his ice-blue gaze. "It'll be OK. It always is."

"I'll assume you're correct," I said and made my way down the block, dialing Jax's number to see if she was up for a beer. It was time to rip the Band-Aid off.

CHAPTER
TWENTY-SEVEN

"Hi, Toby!" Jimmy yelled out from the kitchen.

"Jimmy, you're back at work already? How are Summer and Jade doing? More importantly, how are you doing? It's the Dads that nobody realizes need the most support," I stated with a wink.

"Ha. Mom and baby are doing great. There was initially some latching issue, but that's resolved now. Jade is only getting up a couple of times in the night. I've been informed that it's much worse usually, so no complaints here. How are you doing?"

"Things have been damn interesting," I said. "Jax is on her way here now to have a beer."

"She's here now," he said, pointing to the doorway as Jax strode through, wearing a bright yellow fleece jacket and a scarf. Appropriate for what was transitioning into a blustery San Francisco evening. The wind had now picked up, administering a chilling frontal assault that had advanced from the open front door to the back counter where we were standing.

"Hello, boys," Jax said, joining us at the counter.

"Hi, Jax," Jimmy and I said in unison.

"Beer or wine tonight?" asked Jimmy.

"I'll go beer," I responded.

"The usual Corona with a lime?" Jimmy asked.

"You got it, Pops!" I answered.

Jimmy had remembered my go-to beer even though I was almost exclusively a coffee customer. I always marveled at his ability to remember details like that, especially with hundreds of regular customers. Jimmy made me feel like one of his favorites.

"Jax, same for you?" Jimmy asked.

"Yes, sir!"

"Grab a table, and I'll bring 'em right over," Jimmy said.

We sat down on the coveted oversized brown leather couch that was miraculously available, providing comfort that the naked wooden chairs couldn't compete with.

"How was work today?" I inquired only because it was polite and a nice way to start a discussion that would soon take a turn for the not-so-pleasant.

"Nothing newsworthy. At the end of the shift, there was a bit of a kerfuffle when the drawer was exactly $100 shy of the day's cash sales total. For a minute, everyone was sure one of us had decided it was a good time to go rogue and start dipping into the well until finally, our manager remembered she tucked a hundred-dollar bill under the money tray in the register. I wonder if she thought that if we were held up at gunpoint, the robber wouldn't think to look there, and we then wouldn't be totally cleaned out? Anything exciting at the salon today?"

"Just the usual. Manning the desk, answering the phone, bleaching an eighty-year-old anus, and keeping the restrooms clean."

Jax laughed. "How did the eighty-year-old anus come out?"

"Glorious. I'm damn good at what I do," I said with a splash of bravado.

The thing about waiting for the right time to transition into a topic like, 'I don't want to have kids, and you do, so I get it if you leave me,' is that conversations tend not to flow in that direction naturally. The longer I waited to force the conversation to this topic, the more intense the dread would become, possibly resulting in a complete abandonment of the mission. So I quickly (and with as much tact as a non-tactful guy could muster) initiated the beginning of the end. "Ripping off the bandaid" was the perfect analogy.

"Jax, you ever hear that expression, 'ripping off the bandaid'?" I opened with, realizing how dickish it sounded as the words left my lips. At least I was aware of my present lameness right here and now, which didn't make things any easier.

"Did you injure yourself?" she asked, knowing fully what I meant.

"Well, I'm pretty sure I'm about to. I've been thinking a lot about our conversation regarding long-term family planning. Jax, I wish I could tell you that children are in the cards for me, but I honestly can't. It would be much easier to tell you what you wanted to hear, but if I owe you one thing, it's complete transparency, which has been the bedrock of our relationship. Sure, people change their minds, but there's a good chance I might not. A child needs both parents to be excited to be parents and to feel truly loved and supported. Maybe I'm gun-shy after losing two kids and want to avoid any chance of more of that pain. I've realized I haven't even processed what I've just lost. Or maybe all along I wasn't cut out to be a motivated father. I can't say I know for sure, and maybe it's some of both. Regardless, given what I've just said, there's a big risk on your part: waiting around to see if I ever figure it out. Plus, there is an opportunity cost. You don't want to wait for years only for me to decide emphatically that I don't want to go that direction when you could have moved on, gotten over me, and met the right person for that particular journey." Jax didn't say a thing and just looked at me, silently processing my words.

"Toby," she said, finally ending the excruciating silence. "I love you for being honest, and at the same time, although I had a feeling this could be the case, it's heartbreaking to hear it. Regarding children, we are in different places right now, but I also understand how important it is not to start a long-term relationship with such a major disconnect. 'Begin with the end in mind.' Is that what the Seven Habits guy says?"

"Stephen Covey is who you're talking about. Yes, I suppose he did say that."

Jimmy arrived with our drinks, sensing we were in a serious conversation; he respectfully didn't linger any longer than necessary. I then began, as a guy about to go through a breakup does, to wonder if I was ever going to have sex with Jax again. The idea of going from a partner who expected, initiated, and almost demanded regular coitus back to a marginally fulfilling self-pleasuring protocol seemed like a shitty payback for putting Jax's long-term happiness first. It did amuse me that my mind would go there, but sadly, it didn't surprise me either. I don't think, possibly outside of hookers and one-night stands, that anyone is aware that the next time will be the last. The universe can be cruel that way.

"Toby, I hate this, and I suck at getting over relationships. Knowing it's ultimately the best for everyone involved doesn't make it any easier. And it wasn't until I saw up close how going from a couple to a family created such joy and love for Jimmy and Summer that the importance of that experience in my life was solidified. I had loosely considered it, as everyone does now and then, but I didn't have a strong feeling one way or the other. So don't think I knew I felt this way all along and figured I'd spring it on you once we were in deep. That wouldn't have been fair and was never my intention."

Tears are required for a breakup of any significance, and they were now flowing from Jax's emerald eyes; tiny little streams creased her olive complexion. Regardless of the circumstances, a woman crying in your face flips a genetic switch in men to make it stop. However, I was preoccupied with wrestling back my tears before audible sobbing commenced. You can plan a breakup as tediously as you want, but, like losing a loved one that has been on death's door for months, it hurts just the same when it happens. Anger began to slowly emerge from my subconscious. Not anger at Jax or myself. Anger at life for being a sneaky fucking thief. If horse shit luck were a currency, I'd have cornered the market and been a millionaire by now. But it's not, and I was just a casualty of life's heartlessness. Maybe trusting life, destiny, God's plan, or whatever other clichés are used to make us feel better about eating a shit sandwich is, as Karl Marx said, "the opium of the masses." I'd have plenty of spare time soon to drown myself in Self-Pity Lake, so I decided to be right there, right then, and in the moment, mainly because it was likely the last moment I'd share with Jax, possibly ever.

"I know, Jax. The thought of any clever manipulation on your part never crossed my mind. That's not who you are or who you will ever be. You are the kindest, most level-headed, and sexiest person I've had the pleasure of knowing and sharing a part of my life with. The pain goes both ways here. This may sound scripted, but it's from the heart when I say that you'll find the right guy, and, if you don't mind, I'd like to refer to him as 'the luckiest bastard alive.'" I said, smiling through tears. I must have been sick the day they handed out lives with happy endings. I swallowed a gulp of my beer, the carbonation providing a welcome distraction as it passed over my tongue and down my throat.

"The hardest thing about this shit," Jax said emphatically, "is the person you need to lean on the most is the one you're losing." I reached out and put my hand on hers as she sobbed into her other hand, knowing full well that the gesture wouldn't make anything OK.

"Jax, even now, knowing how this would eventually end, I'd do it all over in a second. You pulled me out of a dark place, gave me hope and laughs, reminded me of what it felt like to be cared about, and reminded me how to care about someone else again. I'll always be thankful for that. I'd say let's try to be friends, but we both know that will only delay the healing process. I'm sure it may be possible one day, but, in my case, it might not be for a little while yet."

"You're making total sense," she said, the tears taking a reprieve.

"I have Jimmy, Summer, and Jade to lean on, Toby, but you don't have anyone, and that makes this even harder for me."

I hadn't considered this. I had been through the loss of my entire former life alone and knew things would eventually get better with time, but when I considered this, a sense of dread surfaced. I was aware of that emotion, my breath becoming more shallow as an uneasiness filled my abdomen. It soon passed, and I was out of my mental and emotional turbulence and calmly dropped back into this room, this table, and this now.

"You are partially right. But I have Cowboy and Eddie, who I can talk to about almost anything. Not so much RV Jeff or Sallie," I said to inject levity, which went unnoticed. "I should probably go now, as saying anything else at this point will only give me more time to consider the loss of the wonderful woman I'm parting ways with. Plus, there's nobody else here right now, which will make it possible for you to have a little time with Jimmy before the late evening rush." It felt like life had unleashed a knockout blow and was standing over me, sprawled on the mat, reminding me, yet again, that I was not a worthy opponent. Wondering where that thought originated, it faded away, gently dropping me back into the present with alarmingly peaceful clarity.

"How about we plan to check in with each other in a month or so, so that I can know you're coming out the other side, OK?" she offered. A month seemed like forever, but I was willing to follow her lead.

"I'd like that," I said, standing up, going over to her side of the couch, and embracing her in our final hug. "I still love you. Right woman, wrong time, I guess." And I walked out, making my way toward my apartment. The fog enveloped me, walking me back into a familiar and unwelcome solitude.

I LAY in bed in a state of surreal shock. The fuckering had, once again, penetrated my increasingly more unstable life, carefully ensuring any perceived sense of control was squashed, leaving my fate again to the wind. Life doesn't negotiate. It plays on its terms, and for some of us, it's just varying degrees of bad hands we're dealt as a hostage at the table, just waiting, hoping we may buck the odds when the next card is revealed.

I watched my thoughts flip and twist like a gymnast in the air, unfortunately failing to stick the landing and all the while wondering who was watching this mental circus right now. "Don't process; just watch," Eddie had said. I watched myself eventually drift off to sleep, nervously wondering what the next act would bring when I awoke tomorrow.

CHAPTER

TWENTY-EIGHT

After a restless sleep, I woke up the next day and checked in on my little brown starfish. By God, it was a shade lighter. Nothing dramatic but noticeable. More diligent wiping may have influenced it, but that seemed unlikely.

Enthused, I migrated to the kitchen to start the coffee pot. The residue of slumber had evaporated just enough for the previous night's events to swim up to the surface of my awareness and rake my buzz.

I reached into the cupboard for a mug, blindly pulling out one that said, "A new day brings new opportunities." "Fuck you," I said out loud, putting it back, searching for a substitute without letters. As I waited for the coffee pot to drip out enough for a full cup, it became clear that I could fill it faster with the tears running down my cheeks. Today, the smell of morning coffee provided no comfort that the day would offer any new potential.

Knowing that only time would eventually melt away the icy feeling of despair in my chest, I decided to speed it along by binge-watching old episodes of The Office until it was time to go to work, another welcome distraction from being alone with my thoughts.

I considered that maybe, ultimately, it's all just a game of hide and seek with ourselves. If so, at that moment, I was probably the most victorious "hider" ever to play the game.

I arrived at work to find the salon lobby to be precisely the opposite of relaxing. Carlotta was running from room to room, assuring clients that Babs would be right back. Babs, looking harried, emerged from the first room, caught sight of me, and changed course for the front desk.

"Toby, I've never been so glad to see you. Well, I'm always glad to see you, but especially right now. Jazmine had to leave an hour ago because her Mom got her foot run over by one of those little meter maid vehicles while arguing over a ticket. Anyway, she's with her at the ER, and we didn't have time to contact her 2 p.m. appointment. We've got customers in three rooms, two waiting for manicures and one mid-lightening session. Oh crap, the cream has been on for 25 minutes now. Can you finish the lightening appointment while I attempt to manicure the other two simultaneously?"

"I'm on it. What room?"

"Number 2," she said, hurrying off down the hall.

I knocked on the door, already apologizing for the wait, to find an anal lightening in mid-session, butt in the air, face in a pillow, and a cream-filled woman's butt crack—a nice looking crack, at that. As I made my way across the room, I noticed a vaguely familiar small pink birthmark on top of the upper left butt cheek, where the lower back transitioned into the upper hip. Her purse was on the chair, a brown and goldish Gucci bag, just like the kind Gina always carried. Now I was only a few feet away and realized why the birthmark seemed oddly familiar. I was staring at my ex-wife's ass.

If there was any written protocol or best practice for situations like this, I certainly hadn't come across it. Shockingly, she hadn't recognized my voice as she lay motionless, not seeming to mind a man spontaneously appearing on the scene, viewing her ultimate exposure. As with most men, an attractive ass staring you in the face, regardless of circumstances, was always a turn-on, even while being mildly horrified at the statistical impossibility of the situation I had stumbled into.

"Good afternoon, Gina. It's nice to see you again?" I felt a casual approach was best so as not to make a big deal out of it.

Gina's head launched off the pillow and executed an owl-like twist. She somehow looked me straight in the eyes while remaining flat on her stomach. I gave her the double eyebrow waggle, nonverbally saying, "Weren't expecting this, were you?"

Gina began a fruitless scramble to her feet while grabbing the towel under her, trying to cover herself from view as if she still had a fighting chance at privacy. This tricky move ended up being too advanced for her to execute. She was now flat on her back on the floor, legs spread, providing an unencumbered view of her now intentionally hairless vagina. It appeared she was a waxing customer as well. "Nice look," I said, punctuated by another double-eyebrow waggle. Although arguably a shocking and traumatic turn of events on many levels, I couldn't help but appreciate the brilliant cosmic humor of the whole thing. Gina, on the other hand, did not.

"Jesus fucking Christ, Toby! Who let you in here?" she asked at a Who concert decibel level.

"I kind of let myself in as one does when they are a lightening specialist employed by The Altered Ego Salon," I replied smugly.

"Not at all surprising for a porn-loving scumbag. You must be so proud, you son of a bitch. I see you've landed well and made quite the pathetic life for yourself."

"You're a fine one to cast judgment with your prepubescent lack of patch and newly pinkened sphincter. It seems like you're getting your own porn prep cycles in. Dare I say 'slut,'" or maybe 'whore'? Did you know strippers hate to be called whores, it turns out?" I couldn't help myself, as trying to diffuse the situation honestly never crossed my mind. "You're a fine example for the kids," I tacked on for good measure.

Gina was now on her feet, frantically wrestling her clothes on like a teenage girl busted by her father in mid-coitus with her boyfriend on the basement couch. Always the multitasker, she was well trained to issue declarations while simultaneously executing against her own immediate challenges.

"The kids? The kids? Well, you may be disappointed to know that you aren't the biological father of either one of them! I have DNA tests that confirm this, and their real father's name most certainly isn't Toby Tenderhill, the butt bleacher," she informed with a smug nod.

This was unexpected and required immediate retaliation.

"This revelation proves two of my points. First, you are a whore, and second, your whoring ways are a despicable example for the children," I said, exercising superhero strength to appear nonchalant. "And sadly, if said DNA tests are confirmed, you can kiss any child support goodbye. Might be a good time for you to track down their real fathers if you can remember their names." The adrenaline seemed to fuel my mouth while also quarantining any potential interruption from the cold shock numbing my brain.

"Get the fuck out of here, you asshole! You're a God damned waste of human existence. I FUCKING hate you and always will. My attorney has copies of the DNA results, and yours will too soon enough!" she screamed, maintaining her near-deafening volume. "How ironic that the proud owner of the most heinous dark and scary butthole known to man is somehow qualified to take care of anyone else's?"

The shouting didn't go unnoticed by anyone within a mile radius. Babs then burst in, eyes wide open, trying to get a handle on what was transpiring. Other clients were now out in the hall with little pieces of white foam still separating their toes as their newly applied polish dried. "Toby, what's going on here?"

Gina opportunistically jumped in to capture the first mover's advantage and began to position the situation. "This asshole, son-of-a-bitch, snuck up on me and...and...," her ability to speak suddenly failed her before she could mention that I had knocked first, apologized for the wait, and pleasantly greeted her by name.

"Babs, I'd like to introduce you to my ex-wife Gina. She's always been a tad emotional." A proper introduction was the gentlemanly thing to do.

Having reactivated her vocal cords, Gina picked up right where she had left off. "Fuck you, Toby!" a less than witty reply. She shifted her gaze to Babs. "What the fuck are you doing sending a man in here, knowing a naked woman was vulnerable?" Now fully dressed, Gina shoved me out of her way as she collected her purse and angled towards the doorway.

Gina continued, "Maybe you didn't know your bleacher boy was fired from his last job for pornography on the company computer? It seems like there should be some screening during your hiring process. And I'm going to sue you for...emotional trauma...and other stuff! And a devastating Yelp review is on the way!" she threatened, looking at Babs.

Gina made her way to the door, flipping me off with her left hand while wagging a threatening finger at Babs with her right, like a cowgirl, unloading her guns as she backed out of a saloon, or in this case, a salon. She always had a flair for the dramatic.

"You know you should consider removing that bleach from your anus before it starts to blister," I said in a helpful and compassionate tone as she entered the hall. A few seconds later, the jingle of the front doorbell confirmed her exit.

"Babs, did she just leave without paying? I can chase her down if you want." After all, we weren't operating as a charity at The Altered Ego.

"Toby, you need to leave. I don't have time to make sense of all this, but you appear to be an active participant in this catastrophe, and I need to settle things down," Babs said. As I quickly found out when I returned to my post upfront, she didn't mean to leave the room. She then sent me home for the day.

In retrospect, although it was an unfortunate incident, I cannot dispute that I did receive a dirty satisfaction in watching Gina scurrying around like a trapped squirrel, unquestionably humiliated and psychologically pushed to her breaking point. I didn't have the gratification of seeing her in any real anguish during the divorce, and this was a definite step toward justice. Suffering can be a relative thing. I suppose that's where the phrase "misery loves company" originated. It's not as bad if everyone is dealing with a calamity versus just ourselves, but today, both sides had incurred heavy casualties, mine quite likely the worst.

Today I had pulled out the linchpin and watched Gina's tower collapse while I stood triumphantly on top of its rubble. I'll take the most minor victory where I can find it, even in the most pathetic of places.

ON THE BRIGHT SIDE, I had the afternoon off, which allowed me to launch an escape attempt from my new reality by watching a few more episodes of The Office. However, their ridiculous jobs reminded me of my absurd job that Gina had so nicely pointed out was laughable. Like one of the comic scenes with Dwight and Michael, today's work scene verified that my life had been reduced to a sitcom, where I was once again the butt of the joke.

My suspicions of Gina's cheating ways, however, were validated. I also learned that not having access to your children is horrible. Not even having children when you thought you did is horrific. It was too surreal to imagine, but her lowdown, slut-laden ways somehow validated that I was less of a schmuck by comparison. Everything I thought my family ever was ended up being a total mirage, no more real than The Tooth Fairy or Santa Claus.

I escaped again into another imaginary reality and was watching Dwight explain the rigorous family upbringing that had resulted in the powerful man he had become when my phone rang. The caller ID let me know it was coming from The Altered Ego Salon. I muted the TV and answered the phone, eager to clear things up. Instead, Babs took control of the conversation and informed me, "Toby, your behavior was inexcusable. Regardless of who the customer is, their satisfaction is the utmost priority in building this business. You seemed to revel in escalating the situation instead of considering options to diffuse it. I'm going to need to relieve you of your duties. I'm sorry, as you were a promising manager candidate, but you have lost your coworkers' and my respect, which is critical for anyone's success at The Altered Ego Salon." I hadn't considered this outcome, but after hearing it aloud, I had to admit Babs had a point.

"I'm sorry, Babs. It had been an ugly divorce and came with a lot of pent-up baggage and anger. In the heat of the moment, I lost my better judgment and...well...I made a poor decision."

"I'm sorry, Toby. I'll mail you your final check in the next few days. Goodbye."

Stunned, I was glad I was sitting down, or, even better, lying down, as was the case. It then dawned on me that I had lost my girl-friend, children, and job in less than twenty-four hours. I was gaining an awe-inspiring mastery over the sport of self-destruction and appeared to have now advanced to the playoffs. It reminded me of the intro to The Wide World of Sports on Sundays as a kid. Not "the thrill of victory" but, more specifically, "the agony of defeat." You know, when the downhill skier totally eats shit at an ungodly speed, skis and poles flying everywhere as he helplessly tumbles and slides down the mountain. I was that guy, wondering where I would finally come skidding to a stop and what condition I'd find myself in.

Lately, I had been making progress in observing what was going on around me, even if it was my largely self-created chaos. Now, not only was I busy watching my bizarre thoughts, but I was still watching myself thinking about my thinking these thoughts, all the while failing to bolster the few remaining pillars of my life. Another failed relationship, job, and the additional failure to remain present. I pondered if this type of emotional jail was where all the other complete fuck-ups out there logged their hours.

More concerning, my thoughts and actions appeared to play out on their own accord, leaving me again watching my life like a slow-motion car crash. And while contemplating that, I had yet again utterly abandoned being here in the present. This dance didn't seem that enlightening. What it did illuminate was that I could no longer trust anything I ever thought might be true.

I was successfully losing my grip on what made sense and what didn't, begging the ultimate question. "What really was the point of it all?" This seemed like a good question for know-it-all Eddie.

CHAPTER
TWENTY-NINE

As it was now beyond the dinner hour and starting to get dark, I decided to head out, and I dipped into the corner market to procure chili and beer for Eddie and myself. Upon exit, I inadvertently inhaled the diesel fumes of the city bus pulling away from the stop in front of the store as the skateboard bastard almost ran me down again, unleashing in me a healthy desire to smash him in the face.

"Hey asshole, slow the fuck down when you are passing an open door!" I yelled, old man style.

"See you soon," he said, flipping me the bird over his head. His black baggy jeans, magically defying gravity, remained adhered to his hips, providing me with an unobstructed view of his underwear. I watched him almost gracefully weave in and out between the other pedestrians on the sidewalk, pulling away from me as my anger and I marched our way, hand in hand, toward Eddie's camp.

SOMETHING about that kid rubbed me the wrong way. I couldn't put my finger on precisely what it was—possibly a combination of ingredients. He was always in a hurry, as if his services were in high demand. He exuded an air of either inflated confidence or not giving two shits about anyone. "See you soon," he said. "You'll see me beating your ass if you almost hit me again," I thought. It's easy to be brave when standing alone in your thoughts, in the same place where it's just as easy to feel the most frightened.

The post-twilight darkness of the night was starting to settle in as the streetlights and neon signs in the mom-and-pop shop windows gained luminosity. The sidewalks were still full of people returning to their respective home bases to wind up their days, eat their dinners, and get ready for bed. Then, wake up the following morning and repeat it all over again.

I turned the corner onto Eddie's block, trying to shift my focus to how much I truly loved canned chili, when halfway down the block, I saw a raggedy man in a mid-calf length khaki overcoat bolt across the sidewalk towards the street. "No, come back!" It was unmistakably Eddie's voice. Then, the screeching tires drowned out all the other sounds playing in the dusk. "Stop!" again from Eddie at the top of his lungs. The man, moving as if his life depended on it, just cleared a moving car's far side front bumper. The dust and smoke from the skidding tires had created a haze, obscuring the finer details of the chaos. However, I could see his pace and direction had suffered no impact.

What appeared to be a small duffle bag was illuminated in the spotlight created by the now motionless car's headlights. Eddie was now crouched over it, oblivious to the crowd forming as the driver frantically exited the car, rushing around to inspect the damage. I was running myself, having dropped the chili and beer, as whatever Eddie had almost been robbed of was suddenly much more important. Coming to a stop behind Eddie, I could make out over his shoulder that what initially appeared as a duffle bag was, in fact, Cowboy, twitching and yelping in anguish.

"Put him in the back seat. Let's get him to the hospital," the driver yelled as Eddie gingerly lifted Cowboy close to his chest, making his way towards the back door of the navy blue Prius. I opened the door, making sure they were safely inside, closed it, and hopped in the front seat. The driver floored the gas, and another shrill squealing of tires filled the night air as we sped off. "God, I'm so sorry. Holy shit! They just ran out in front of me. I tried to stop," the hyperventilating gentleman, in his late sixties, pleaded. "I know where the emergency animal hospital is in The Mission." Unfortunately, that neighborhood was at least fifteen minutes away, without traffic.

Cowboy had quieted down, but his chest's rise and fall signaled he was still alive. Eddie stroked his head, his falling tears creating a small dark circle on Cowboy's gray furry neck. "It's OK, buddy, it's OK. I'm here, buddy," Eddie quietly whispered in his ear. Cowboy was lying motionless, looking into Eddie's cool blue eyes. "Thank you, Cowboy. Thank you for looking after me." I felt utterly helpless, with no idea what to do or say. The three of us, in our respective mental worlds, still sharing a gruesome reality in utter silence as our bodies rocked violently back and forth as the driver weaved in and out of traffic. He seemed to know what he was doing, so I turned my attention again to the back seat. Although it was dark, I could make out the silhouette of Eddie's shuddering body. Victim of a stop sign, the car suddenly stopped as the bright intersection lights filled the vehicle. Cowboy's chest was no longer rising and falling. Eddie looked up at me, his eyes swimming in tears, his chin quivering in staccato contractions. "He's gone, Toby."

"Are you sure? Maybe he's just calming down," I offered, unwilling to accept what Eddie already had. My shallow, irregular breaths gave way to explosive tears. It selfishly occurred to me that Cowboy was the only dog I had ever truly loved. Thoughts filled my mind of him nudging me with his rag to play tug, hitting me with his paw for more pets, and laying down next to me on the sidewalk with his back pressed against my leg. And most of all, his unfailing and protective love for Eddie, his sole companion around which his entire doggie life revolved—Eddie was his everything. If there was a God, he had taken the night off.

The driver was frantically weaving through traffic again, trying to reverse fate or outrun the guilt of delivering the fatal blow. "It's too late," I said, patting his forearm. Thank you for trying."

"What do we do now?" the driver asked, slowing to a more reasonable speed.

"Eddie, what do you want us to do?" I asked.

"Take us back, please," he listlessly responded, his eyes unwilling to release their gaze on his dearest friend as he rhythmically caressed Cowboy's head, the dark gray spot on Cowboy's neck expanding with Eddie's tears. If Cowboy had been bloody or mangled, it would have made it somehow easier to accept he had passed, but seeing him without any external injuries made it seem like he was asleep and would spontaneously wake up at any moment, releasing the noose of shock and sorrow that grew relentlessly tighter around our necks.

The driver returned us to the scene of the crime, profusely apologizing. The reality was—there wasn't a happy ending available. He had taken Cowboy and his owner's heart along with him. Life had taken a wrong turn, and unfortunately, he was the one behind the wheel, guilty of simply being in the wrong place at the wrong time.

After a few more apologies and feeble attempts on my part to absolve him of his guilt, the driver finally left us on the sidewalk in front of Eddie's cart, Cowboy wrapped in Eddie's jacket, cradled in his arms. An unwelcome silence descended on us, perfectly analogous to what had just befallen our friend Cowboy.

Without any forethought or contemplation, I started putting Eddie's camp stove, sleeping bag, and other assorted possessions into his cart. "What are you doing, Toby?" he asked.

"You are spending the night at my place tonight. You don't want to be alone right now, and neither do I. We can figure out what's next in the morning," I said, pushing his cart out towards the sidewalk;

Eddie merely nodded without objection. I pushed his cart, and he carried our friend in a heavy silence that was neither awkward nor comfortable, just raw. When we arrived, I opened the garage to push his cart into my parking spot, which was more of a storage area since I had no car. This way he wouldn't have to worry about leaving it unattended outside, nor would we have to wrestle it up the stairs into my apartment.

"Toby, do you mind Cowboy's body in your apartment? I understand if you do," he asked as we neared my building.

"Eddie, I insist on it. A body isn't going to decompose overnight. Shit, you can keep him in my freezer for a year. Whatever you want is completely fine with me."

"I'll bury him tomorrow in Golden Gate Park in a special place where we used to go and play fetch each day in the woods. It's right off Fulton and 12th Ave," he said, almost whispering.

"Well, I'd like to help and be there unless you want it just the two of you."

"Toby, you're the only other human he loved. Cowboy would have wanted you there, as do I."

I felt my throat tighten as I tried to hold myself together. Losing a loved one is horrible enough, but losing them prematurely to a random accident wraps a layer of shock around the pain, adding that extra gut punch for good measure. "Eddie, do you prefer a bed, couch, or floor? Whatever you want, man."

"Just some privacy and quiet to process," he said.

"Yeah, I think that would do us both some good. You guys take the bedroom. Put him in the bed with you if you want. I need to wash the sheets anyway. I'll get the coffee pot ready, so you just need to turn it on if you get up before me. I'll be here in the living room if you need anything." Eddie's blue eyes stared into mine as he stood before me, holding Cowboy. My emotional state shifted from sadness to love. Love for Eddie, his friendship, and Cowboy. A wave of unexplained gratitude washed over me that I couldn't make sense of. Without a thought, I extended my arms and embraced the both of them, group hug style, melting in a confusing soup of emotion with far too many ingredients to isolate any single one. This was my only family now, and I was just thankful I could be there at this exact moment with the two of them, hoping Eddie felt he was loved despite the significant loss.

Eddie shuffled into the bedroom with our friend as I got him a toothbrush, towel, and the extra pillow from the closet. We said our goodnights, and I closed the bedroom door and stood motionless in the kitchen, trying to wrap my mind around what had just happened. I realized that the adage that bad luck came in threes must be bullshit because, with Cowboy's death, I was at four and counting.

Thoughts of Jax flooded my mind; how I wished she was here to hold onto, and how I missed feeling a part of a team, knowing we would somehow make it through everything together. My attention then shifted to the stark realization I now had no income and had been living paycheck to paycheck. Then, back to Cowboy and knowing there would be no more games of tug, dog treats handed out, belly rubs, or excited greetings as I neared their camp. That thought was interrupted by the settling realization I had lost my identity as a father along with the two little people I loved the most. It's only through loss that we learn to appreciate what we have. I felt hollow, and at the same time, I felt thankful that I still had Eddie.

My fitful mind finally yielded to a fitful slumber close to midnight. I found myself standing there, shivering naked in a glass prison cell. Jax, Cowboy, Babs, and my kids on the other side yelled at me, but I couldn't hear them. As I approached the glass, they began to appear farther and farther away, almost as if an invisible force field was pushing them. "Please come back! Don't leave me here alone!" I yelled, pounding on the thick, cruel glass yet rendering no noise. They gradually faded out of sight, leaving me crying on my knees, overcome with a sense of complete hopelessness.

"You created your cell; you have the master key," came from behind me. I turned around to see Eddie standing there with a smile on his face. I was sure he hadn't been there before, or I would have surely noticed.

"Eddie, there's no door, no lock, nothing. We're trapped."

Eddie was now suddenly outside the cell, looking in, still smiling. "We only appear to be trapped," he said clearly through the glass as his smile broadened across his face, his labradorite eyes twinkling.

"Please don't leave me, Eddie. I can't find the fucking door and don't want to be trapped in here alone. Tears were streaming down my face as I beat on the walls, looking for an invisible trigger to open the door that Eddie had magically slipped out of.

"You are the jail, the prisoner, and most importantly, you are the door," Eddie said, shimmering and fading into nothingness, an evaporating mirage. I felt myself drowning in horrific loneliness, the oxygen expiring from my lungs, unable to get to the surface in time.

I suddenly awoke with a sincere urge to piss, realizing I was in my living room and the bathroom was off the room Eddie was sleeping in. With no other options available, I opened the living room window and urinated through the screen down onto the driveway. Luckily, a stream of urine can pass through a screen, unaltered, which I knew from experience. It was a crude plan B but effective unless someone was standing below in the driveway, which, come to find out, Brian happened to be that night.

WITH A CUP of morning joe now in my hand, I had settled into a deep funk, continuing to fixate on the multiple beatdowns life had administered in the last couple of days. My mind couldn't get through a coherent thought about Jax without interrupting itself to worry about my job, only to yet again shift to Cowboy, my kids, and around and around it went, as the mind is prone to do. After forty-five minutes of successfully failing to gain any insights, strategies, or the slightest concept of what my next steps would be, Eddie mercifully emerged from the bedroom to break this useless pattern.

"Morning Toby! Thanks for the good night's sleep and shower," he said, wearing a towel. "Mind if I get some clean clothes out of my cart?"

"You bet. Here's the key to the garage from the inside door downstairs," I replied, handing him the key. "And you know you can keep it there and stay here as long as you want. I like the company."

"Thanks, Toby, but I'll head back to my spot later. It's just that I prefer to be outside, maybe because it's familiar," he said, taking the key.

Eddie was again his usual self. I peeked into the bedroom after he left for the garage to see Cowboy wrapped in a blanket, with his head on the pillow, looking like he would spring up at any moment, wag his tail, and want to play.

"Thanks," Eddie said, tossing the key back as he reentered the apartment, carrying what did appear to be clean clothes. "You still up for coming with to bury Cowboy?"

"Definitely. Whatever time works for you, as my schedule appears wide open today," I responded.

"Well, let me get dressed and have a cup of coffee, and then let's set out. You wouldn't happen to have a shovel, would you?" he asked.

"I don't, but I know for a fact there is one in the garage with the other garden stuff they have for the backyard. I'm sure nobody will miss it."

Eddie emerged from the bedroom a couple of minutes later, helped himself to a cup of coffee, and sat on the couch, noticed my copy of *Be Here Now*, and started thumbing through it while I took my turn in the shower. A few minutes later, we headed out. Eddie put Cowboy in the cart and covered him with his tarp to avoid the unwanted attention of wheeling a dead dog down the street, while I carried the shovel. Eventually, we came to the corner of 12th Ave and Fulton and descended the hill into one of Golden Gate Park's many small forest areas. This one was ironically called *Hero's Grove*.

"Here's the spot," Eddie said, navigating his cart through the dirt and overgrowth to a small open and level area between two massive trees, surrounded by bushes, a place that would remain undisturbed. "We used to camp here a lot when Cowboy was a puppy until the park police decided to clear the park of all the homeless establishments. Cowboy always remembered it when we returned. He would immediately come right over here and sit down. This was where he felt most at home," he said with a big smile.

"Quite a peaceful place. I can see why he liked it." We took turns digging and eventually had a Cowboy-sized hole. Eddie wrapped him in an old shirt, placed him in the hole, and stood up to grab the shovel. "Wait, did he have any personal effects we should bury with him?" I asked.

"Good point." He rummaged through his cart and produced a mostly empty box of Milk Bones and Cowboy's tug rag, which elicited in me an unexpected surge of emotion and accompanying tears. Cowboy and I had enjoyed many moments with that rag as the glue connecting us.

Eddie placed the two items next to Cowboy and proceeded to fill the hole, patting down the top and covering it with leaves and pine needles. "Thank you, my old buddy, Cowboy. Thanks for everything," he said and returned to his cart. "Damn nice day for a funeral, huh?" he asked, pointing to the blue sky, sprinkling beams of sunlight here and there through the canopy of redwood trees onto the forest floor. The smell of pine and dirt reminded me of the few camping trips we spent in the Redwood Forest as a child—calm, peaceful, full of life, and simultaneously silent.

"Where to now?" I asked Eddie.

"Back to the usual spot, I figure. I could use an assist to get this cart back up the side of the bank if you don't mind?"

"Sure. I'll walk you back to your spot. It'll give me a chance to spend some more time outside. It is indeed a pretty epic day. Must be seventy degrees already, huh?"

"Seems about right," he said. We eventually emerged on Fulton Street with his cart, realizing we'd forgotten the shovel. So I made another trip down and back up the steep bank, which, as far as I was concerned, qualified as that day's workout.

We started to navigate our way down Fulton toward 6th Avenue in silence. Eddie was smiling big and humming a tune I couldn't make out. He appeared admirably calm and peaceful, given that we had just buried his best friend, whereas I was well back into my funk after only a couple of blocks.

"What seems to be the problem, Toby?" he asked, breaking the silence.

"Well, to start, I already miss Cowboy, who was the only dog I ever loved. I miss Jax, too. We broke up. It's complicated. I was fired from The Altered Ego Salon yesterday; another story. Found out my own kids aren't mine after all. That kind of sucked. By common definition, I've had my dick knocked in the dirt repeatedly over the last couple of days."

"Could be worse," he said.

"Not much."

"Could be Cowboy," he responded, laughing.

"I don't know. I think I want to trade places with him right now."

"Aw, bullshit. Who gives a fuck about that stuff. You think things are good, then that shit happens, and you think things suck, and then, pretty soon, something else good will happen. Hard to tell what's good or bad. That's why they say, 'shit happens.'"

"Well, you seem quite chipper, considering everything," I said, slightly annoyed.

"It is what it is. You can't change the past by brooding over it. Plus, it's a nice day, and I'm hanging out with my friend. And most of all, still alive to see what happens next."

"Well, that's an impressive perspective. Don't you feel sad about Cowboy? I mean, what a horrible thing," I pointed out, feeling he had no right to be content.

"Sure, I'll miss him, but hey...I got to share a few years with him, which was great. He died saving my life, which was his mission: to protect me. He accomplished his goal, we shared some great times, and most of all, we got to love each other. That's cause for celebration. Most people get lost in the emotional lows and forget the highs."

"What do you mean he saved your life?" I asked.

"I don't know what you saw or not when you arrived on the scene last night."

"I saw him chase some guy out into the street, and then he got hit. That was it."

"The guy he was chasing moments before had a knife to my neck, demanding I return the money he had lost a few days prior betting against the Giants. It was a straight win or lose, no odds, and he lost, but that didn't sit well. Once he snuck up on me and threatened to kill me, Cowboy attacked him, bit his arm that was holding the blade, causing him to drop it, and then started chasing him. Instead of stopping at the curb, he decided to chase him farther away to protect me, which, it turned out, cost him his life. His life was basically in service to me, and I'll be forever grateful. I'm sure all the love we shared gave him a rich life, too. I'm thankful, and the love won't leave my heart just because he's left his body," he explained.

"That's a great way to look at it, but...man...it's a shame he had to die for it, Eddie, and experience so much physical pain. What a shitty way for the little guy to go."

"How many people, or animals, for that matter, don't die a shitty death? Maybe one in twenty? Death, on the physical level, usually sucks. The reality is simply that he has passed. He suffered in the end, so it seems like he's stuck there, but it's over, and he's not suffering. Like Ram Dass says, 'Now is now. Are you going to be here or not?'"

"Well, here we are, so I guess the answer is yes," I said in a less-than-enthusiastic tone.

"Physically, you are, but mentally you're not. You are in the past with Jax, your job, Cowboy, your previous concepts of what it meant to be a father, or past hopes you had of a future that never really existed anyway. You're living in memories—shadows of a reality that is no more. You're missing this nice day and don't even have to go to work. It might do you good to enjoy it while it lasts and not feel guilty doing so."

"Maybe, but it's not that easy for me, Eddie."

"If you argue for your limitations, you earn the right to keep them," he said, smiling.

Happiest man alive. Life must be easy if you want nothing. That may be the difference. I wanted a lot of shit from life. Jax, a job, an apartment, to lose a few more pounds, my friend Cowboy. I wished those things weren't important to me, but they were, although they caused me angst when I didn't have them and caused me angst when I did because I feared losing them. It's easy not to want to give a shit about stuff, but that doesn't mean you don't. It just means you wish you didn't.

"So how do I stop wanting things to turn out a certain way and fearing bad things might happen? Sadly, it seems part of who I'm destined to be," I added, feeling defeated. "Hell, I am still woefully lamenting my seventy-five-year-old ass-crack fiasco, and that's not even something I can do anything about."

"Remember what Alan Watts said?" he asked.

"No."

"You are under no obligation to be the same person you were five minutes ago," he reminded me. "Ponder the totality of what that means," he said, stopping to adjust some things in the lower part of his cart that had shifted in the descent and ascent from the burial.

"I get that, but I'm afraid it's not so simple. Just wanting to let go doesn't make it so," I said from recent experience.

"Don't get me wrong. It's not easy, but the first step is admitting it's possible. The fear is that it isn't possible to change your core nature, as it's been a part of you for so long that you're tremendously invested," he said, now retying his beaten-up Stan Smith sneakers.

"I wonder if it is possible. I see the same patterns repeating themselves but only see them after the fact. I like to think I'll do things differently, but it ultimately ends up more of the same or just a temporary adjustment at best. As much as I'd like to, I just don't think I get it, Eddie."

"If you want, I can explain it all to you again to give you a map that will give you a sense of where you are; however, don't confuse the map with the territory. You can study a map of Golden Gate Park all day, but it will never give you the experience of marveling at the rose garden or watching the toy boats race around Spreckles Lake. You get my drift?" he asked.

"OK, lay it out, and I'll try to follow, but don't be pissed if I don't accept it all hook, line, and sinker," I said.

"Well, as we've discussed, you have basic beliefs that your identity and worldview rely on. Examine those beliefs to ensure you know what they are. Things like needing a fixed amount of money to be financially safe, having a job that people respect, enabling you to be seen by others as successful. Also, things like making smart decisions or being perceived as intelligent or meditating, chanting, and chasing gurus to validate you are spiritual. Even trying to be humbler than others is just a way to flex your exalted status by differentiating yourself. For some, it's chasing experiences to validate an image of being the adventurer or having more comprehensive and enviable experiences relative to your peers."

"All that sounds pretty attractive to me right now," I admitted.

"In my younger days, bedding attractive women validated I was desirable, wanted, and a stud. For some, it's being the victim; for others, it's being the fun guy. The belief that there are winners and losers in life compels us to scrounge for evidence we are winning, which requires constant comparisons to others for validation. Eventually, all of that is impermanent. That's when the midlife or late life crisis happens—if we are even fortunate enough to have the veneer on the illusion crack," he said, speaking very clearly and slowly. He wasn't saying anything new, but it was helping me to hear it again with a different spin.

"OK, for me, it's needing to validate to myself that I'm successful, which is validated by my title, annual income, and ability to own a home. I also need to be found attractive and worthy of love, which I look to a relationship for. I suppose it's important to me to have my physique look good for my age. This may be tied to being attractive, and I compare myself to other men my age. For some reason, it's important to me that people find me funny. I'm with you so far."

"Whatever our definitions of ourselves and our beliefs are, we eventually become no longer attractive, physically strong, or good athletes. We lose our intellectual edge. We haven't yet attained any significant spiritual accomplishment. We are no longer physically able to travel. So, we must live in our past with our memories to fortify our current identities to which we've become enslaved. Our material possessions become trinkets with which we surround ourselves to prove our value. What's left after it all disappears?" he asked.

"You just said it: our memories of who we once were or things we've done?"

"Sure, and that distance between who we were and who we are today becomes something we want to avoid thinking about. Find out what's left over without the memories, anticipated futures, and who you want to prove yourself to be for yourself and others. What's left if you set all that aside? Is it feasible that you are more than just a collection of experiences, possessions, or a certain net worth?"

I was pondering the series of rapid-fire questions he was throwing out and didn't answer, nor did he expect me to.

Eddie continued. "Even the spiritual seeker tries to collect experiences, theories, and knowledge through books and lectures. They meditate for a goal while trying to build up their spiritual identity and ego. How is that different from the CEO trying to prove they have attained success by creating a billion dollars of revenue? In reality, even the seeker is only a thought construct." Eddie paused to let that sink in.

"Are you saying, then, that no matter what the goal, whether it's to knock off a bank, feed the poor, buy a house for your kids, or run a marathon, it all ultimately and selfishly supports an identity we are either trying to create for ourselves or maintain?"

"Bingo! Introspectively, ask yourself what's compelling you to continuously chase and prove yourself to yourself. Follow it back to the beliefs you are attached to, hanging onto, and struggling to support. That will show you where you are stuck. Where are you when all that shit blows up and it's gone? What remains? If thinking about that scares you, you don't yet trust life or the process of life. Life, for many, is a threat to protect yourself from—which is ironic, as it's essentially what we are an integrated part of. But do we experience our connection with life or entertain it as merely a concept?"

"You mean, do we just *understand* concepts of the nature of the truth of it all, or do we *live* it on the experiential level?" I asked to make sure I was still following.

"Yep, but this sickness goes beyond just our personal beliefs. Do our collective societal beliefs truly reflect reality or obscure it? Look at the majority of humanity and how people suffer, not just physically but mentally, even when they are physically fine. What if our societal beliefs miss the point or are based on a flawed model of reality? After all, we look back every hundred years and wonder how the people generations ago did such horrible things to each other, destroyed the environment, believed in witches and slavery, etc. Remember when sugar wasn't bad for us, and a woman's worth was in how well she served her husband? Those were all accepted as reality at the time and then later rejected. Which parts of our way of life and societal beliefs today will be rejected in another hundred years? Just because we think something or have powerful feelings about something doesn't make it true. History is proof."

"So don't trust your thoughts but still use them to think about how they are wrong? It seems a tad contradictory, doesn't it?" I asked.

"It's like using a thorn to extract a thorn. The mind can get you to the edge but can never take you beyond it, since the fabric of reality is beyond the mind. It's like a boat that, if properly captained, can get you across the lake through a storm, but once you get to the other shore, you have to get off the boat to explore what's there," he said.

"So it's getting the mind honed as a tool to...what? Expose the limitations of the mind?"

"Expose the limitations of thoughts and break our identification with them. It's not easy, and you will be inconsistent, fail regularly at first, and get caught up in your mind and identity. It's kind of like golf. Sometimes, the ball flies straight; the next time, it's slicing or pulling. Does the golfer quit because it's hard? Or does he enjoy the game enough to keep playing? Can you keep playing without worrying about the score and enjoy the hole you're on at the time? Or, even better, what's the goal of dancing to your favorite song? It's not to get to the end; it's to flow with it in the now, connected to the beat. It's being versus striving."

"So, if I'm still with you, should I notice the mind and what it's doing to break my identification with what it thinks I am and eventually experience that I'm more than just my thoughts, beliefs, or identity construct?"

"Exactly! Who are you underneath those thoughts? Your attention needs to go there to experience the foundation of where you and this whole play originate from."

"Well, fuck. It seems like now I have even more to think about rather than less," I pointed out.

Eddie continued, "I've given you all this at once to hit you over the head with the proverbial two-by-four in hopes that we might shake a little something loose. Something that breaks your identification with thought and your physical form. There's only one place you can find your real self: this eternal instant that we are in this very second. This ever-changing present moment is all there has ever been or ever will be. It's the only thing that's real and always present. And you are it.

"Like Paul Coelho said, 'Maybe the journey isn't so much about becoming anything. Maybe it's about un-becoming everything that isn't you, so you can be who you were meant to be in the first place.'

The 'you' that starts the journey gets dismantled along the way. Sure, there will still be memories and preferences, and you'll talk and look the same, but that identity disappears in the exhale like wisps of smoke. But what's disappearing is the self-constructed jail you've spent a lifetime reinforcing that stands between who you think you are and what you really are. This journey is the only game worth playing. It is the search for the holy grail, but it's not out there like everything else we chase. It's deep inside, and you've always had it. This game takes you to the real, not further into the unreal. Life is kind of a game of hide and seek."

"Too bad I've never been a fan of hide-and-seek. How long does this process take?" This was an important question for a goal-oriented guy like myself.

"You are lucky, Toby. It's easier to question life when chunks of it are being ripped away. That's grace. If everything went according to your desires, it would take lifetimes to return to who and what you ultimately are. Life isn't sucking you further into the illusion. In its own loving way, it's spitting the real you out of the illusion."

"Eddie, in line with your golf analogy, you're like the golf instructor who ends a lesson by saying, 'Just focus on those fifteen things during your backswing, and you'll hit it straight every time.' It just confuses things even more," I confessed, as Eddie laughed at my analogy.

"Touché. In a way, I've just shown you where the sand traps are so you can avoid getting caught in them so frequently. My intention is to save you time if you are ready to listen. There is another part of the path a little further ahead, but you must get the bullshit out of the way first. Just be right here, right now, in this instant. Now get the fuck out of here and enjoy this beautiful day. It's all you have."

CHAPTER
THIRTY

Enjoying the day's beauty rapidly transitioned into thinking about what Eddie and I had been discussing. What he was saying was logical enough, raising the question of why I'd never considered any of these things, nor, for that matter, had anybody I'd ever met. Maybe society, as a whole, is averse to introspection.

I can't pinpoint exactly when I had decided to trust the yarn Eddie was spinning and take on the role of the student. Maybe in the East, this would be like following a guru. However, he didn't seem to be pushing any religion. It appeared to be more of a psychology of how the mind worked. He didn't seem to want me to depend on him, as he kept pushing me back into myself. It certainly didn't feel like I was being manipulated. It was I who kept asking him questions. I went to him when I felt like it, and he had no expectations. I guess that's why I trusted him. And then again, why not? My current approach to life obviously needed a tune-up or more of a complete body-off restoration.

And there I was thinking, off in my head, missing the beautiful day. At least I realized it and quickly returned to being aware of what was around me as I walked up the chipped and crumbling cement stairs to my apartment. Unfortunately, I became aware of Brian walking down the front steps.

"Hi, Brian. Beautiful day, huh?"

"Hey, Toby. Glad I caught you. I need to talk to you," he informed me. "We have a bit of a situation," he said with a sniff.

"Oh? What's up?"

"Well, I'm not going to beat around the bush here. You originally signed a six-month lease, which goes month to month after that. The owner of this building's daughter just got into the University of San Francisco and will be moving to the city, and he is giving you thirty days' notice to move out so she can move in. I know this sucks, and I wasn't anticipating this. I'm more than happy to be a reference for your next place. You've always paid the rent on time and are quiet. Other than pissing out the window at night, you've been a model tenant," he kindly pointed out, sniffing a few more times.

"If I promise to only urinate in the toilet, would that make a difference?" I countered, wondering exactly what he may have been doing in the driveway in the middle of the night.

"The owner doesn't know about that. But, as a best practice, you should investigate who's outside first," Brian said in a parental tone, running his tongue over his gums.

This news hit me like a steel-toed boot to the sack; so much for it being a nice day. As I counted all the ways I was being sequentially ass-reamed, it appeared I would be safer in a prison shower.

"Brian, this is a shitty time for this. I'm in transition on the employment front, and it could be rough finding another place without being able to demonstrate any income. I know you could care less, but in the spirit of full disclosure, I also just lost my girlfriend, my kids, and a good friend who died last night." At this point, I thought the most I could hope for was the small satisfaction of making Brian feel like a tool.

"Toby, we're buddies, and I wish I could do something, but I'm not the boss here. But let's keep a positive mental attitude, and I'm confident you'll land on your feet."

His little pep talk confirmed his passive dickishness. And what was up with the constant sniffing and tonguing of his upper gums? Could Brian be fueling his over-energized demeanor with a few bumps of the white dust?

"I'd like to thank you for something, but nothing comes to mind. Instead, being as 'we're buddies,' I'll take you up on your offer to give me a positive reference, even though the owner dislikes me."

"Sure. It's the least I could do, but the owner doesn't even know you."

"Well, could you pass a message his way for me?"

"No problem. What do you want me to tell him?"

"To go fuck himself. Just keep it simple," I said, knowing he wouldn't relay my message.

"Hey, hey. Remember PMA. Positive mental attitude."

"Sorry, I thought that stood for Pummel My Ass, which you've demonstrated you're proficient at." At this point, I just wanted to go inside, so I left sniffling Brian on the stairs, contemplating his PMA, and retreated to my soon-to-be ex-lair.

CHAPTER
THIRTY-ONE

I proceeded directly to my bed and began to masturbate to help recover from Brian's news. I didn't have to search for long in the BOMB (Beat-Off Memory Bank) to locate some prime fodder, since a recent deposit caught my eye. I was now reliving my last sexual encounter with Jax as she slapped my thrusting ass and yelled, "Fuck me like you mean it!" This highlight reel brought my brief, intense self-pleasuring session to its quick and rightful conclusion.

I missed Jax's sensual touch and silky, warm skin. I missed laying naked next to her with her head resting under my chin, making circles with her finger on my chest, while the jasmine scent of her dark hair gently carried me into a relaxed satisfaction that I was sharing this journey with someone I cared for and deeply respected. Someone willing to accept me exactly as I was, with complete abandon. Was it better to have loved and lost than to have not loved at all? That notion seemed like more of a shitty participation award designed to appease a brow-beaten ego.

And again, here was my mind, creating this narrative, convincing myself it was real. Well, if my idea of the me that's thinking this didn't really exist, there sure wasn't anything more real chomping at the bit to fill its place. Illusion or confusion? Not a bad t-shirt idea. Maybe I could hang that one next to my 'Bro got no dough, fired again!" t-shirt.

It seemed like at least a decade since I was living in our cute little two-bedroom condo with Gina and the kids, watering the brown spots in the lawn on Sunday morning in my robe and slippers, waiting for the likely hungover paperboy to eventually get around to doing his job. Upon further examination, it had been less than a year ago that I had managed to destroy my life, rebuild a new one, and successfully destroy that one. Was this due to dedication or dumb luck? This shirt would be green with white block letters.

"Dedication or dumb luck?" I suppose this is a belief choice most often subconsciously settled upon to support whatever made-up identity is trying to integrate either the unexpected fuckery just bestowed upon them or a remarkable accomplishment. If I had only been delivered some good fortune, I could chalk it up to dedication and take full credit without a second thought. Maybe I was just a dedicated fuck-up. That shoe fit.

And then that woeful bitch, Gina, getting me fired. And that's not just a made-up narrative. I knocked on the door, apologized for the wait, and greeted her by name. It was hardly a verbal assault by anyone's definition, yet enough to propel her into rash judging and name-calling. Both were well-honed skills she had cultivated. I even politely reminded her of the risk of keeping the cream on too long. But of course, Babs fired the evil man to cover her own ass should a lawsuit or lousy Yelp review materialize. Sure, I might have sprinkled in a few barbs for sport with a dash of name-calling, which didn't help my case much. She took my job and the illusion of being a father within moments of each other. She had been a heartless bitch all along, and I was a piss-poor judge of character when I married her.

What in God's name was I going to do now? The idea of scrambling for employment to sign a lease on another hovel before I was rendered address-free was overwhelming. Eddie had said, "When patterns break, doors open." I suspected he may have left "or not" off the end. Or maybe this was just the new pattern. At least now I was self-aware enough to enjoy being able to experience another mental breakdown and witness my own severely pathetic self flailing around like an unwanted carp on the shore, waiting for the fisherman's death blow. Maybe I needed to shift my focus to accepting my 'carpiness.'

A drunken night at The Plow was the logical place to start.

I HEADED out of my soon-to-be-vacated apartment, realizing how restricted my life had become. It had pretty much been limited to my apartment, The Plow, Eddie's cart, The Altered Ego Salon, and occasionally Jax's place. Of course, the latter two, recently eliminated, left just The Plow, Eddie's cart, and my apartment, which would also be removed shortly from this list if I didn't wake my slumbering ambition and respond to the latest developments.

Motivation comes and goes on its terms, as does much of life, which I was starting to take note of. However, questioning everything I believed in was obscuring the view of any North Star that might illuminate the road leading out of what was looking a lot more like one never-ending moonless night. Having nothing left to lose did provide the comfort of knowing I had nothing left to lose, for whatever that was worth.

Before rounding the corner, I could hear Irish music's tinny sound, which I didn't appreciate. By now, we could safely rule out that it was merely an exposure issue.

I had forgotten that Tuesday night was live music night at The Plow, but despite my bad luck and a ten-dollar cover charge, I entered undeterred. Crappy music brought with it crappy people who have remarkably stumbled upon the secret key unlocking the door to appreciating garbage music. Typically, The Plow would max out at fifteen to twenty people on a busy night, but tonight's entertainment had pushed that to about forty, plus the five band members. The small wooden parquet dance floor in the back quarantined about fifteen of those with the most questionable musical taste. The pool table was surrounded by three guys and one exceedingly verbose woman, the dim lighting working in her favor, contemplating their next shot in what appeared to be a close game. Connor was predictably behind the bar, exchanging superfluous chit-chat with five folks. I progressed through the chairs and tables holding a few small groups of unfamiliars. Big Sallie and RV Jeff's silhouettes solidified as I closed in on the bar. Their stools pressed together with her arm draped casually around his waist. The scent of sweat emanating from the dance floor mixed nicely with the ever-present stale beer smell like a fart in a sauna. Nobody else seemed to mind.

"Hey Connor, is this how bars in Ireland smell?"

"Hey, Toby! Where the hell've ya been, me boy?" Connor asked, smiling as he grabbed a Corona and the Patron bottle, meeting me at my usual spot at the end of the bar.

"Busy working on digesting a rather impressive shit sandwich," I said, not holding back. "On a scale of one to ten, how would you rate the quality of this Irish band?"

"Sober, a five or six. In about an hour, they'll be perceived at a solid seven-and-a-half. Extra fruit in yer beer tonight?"

"Touché. Why is there writing on Jeff's forehead?"

Connor poured my shot and a Jamieson's for himself. "He certainly has no problem talkin' about it. Why don't ya get it from the horse's mouth?"

"Ask Sallie?" I asked, unable to refrain from the faux pax of laughing at my own joke. Connor's face yielded a suppressed smile as we were interrupted by Jeff, who had noticed my attendance.

"Toby, where the fuck have you been?" It was now the question of the night. I guess a day off qualified a Plow patron as a missing person. "We figured you must have been in rehab."

Disregarding his inquiry: "What does it say on your forehead, Jeff?"

"Zen as Fuck," he answered with an exaggerated inhale and a confidently firm nod of his giant bald head.

Providing no reaction to the content, I needed to know: "Is that a tattoo?"

"Stick and poke, baby. Try before you buy. What do you think?"

"I've never heard of a stick and poke outside of dating strategy discussions. But it's nice that your shaved head ensures nobody will miss this masterpiece."

With what seemed unwarranted pride, Jeff explained, "Sallie did it with a pin and ink." Jeff looked at Sallie like a proud parent whose child had just aced their SATs. He gave her hand a gentle squeeze and left it on top of hers, returning his attention to Connor and me.

"That's not very nice. Were you asleep?" I inquired.

"No, dick fuck. I've been considering it for a while now, but it's a big commitment, so we decided to test it out and see if I was still as excited in a few months before going the permanent route."

"So it's basically like a drawing? Sallie drew on your forehead?" I still had no idea what a stick and poke was.

"It will wear off in a few months. What do you think?" he asked.

"Bad choices make great stories?" I answered after a dramatic silence, purposefully withholding the satisfaction of any honest answer to his question. "What does it mean?" If I were as determined to find another job as I was to push Jeff to the limit of his patience, I'd have secured two by now.

"It means I'm Zen as fuck. A spiritual badass. I'm present, baby, and you can't rock my holy chill." It was now game on. He was eager to demonstrate the embodiment of his definition of Zen by remaining outwardly unflustered.

"Is that what Zen means?"

"Yep. Calm in the face of chaos and, in your case, personal attack. I've grown a lot since our strip club adventure. Let's call it an awakening."

"Were you asleep before?" Brevity was my scalpel, extracting his latent and predictably burgeoning anger.

"A fuck-tard like you wouldn't understand," he said with a disgusted head shake and eye roll.

"Are you name-calling?" Checkmate.

"Fuck you, Toby!" Jeff was now visibly rattled. "I was going to buy your beer, but I've changed my mind."

Now laughing, which was a rarity, Connor interjected, "Toby's beer is on the house. Gotta give family an excuse to come back."

Offering an olive branch: "Jeff, it suits you well," I said, attempting a tone of fabricated sincerity. "And Sallie, despite the piss poor canvas you had to work with, your art is impressive."

"Thank you, Toby. See, Sallie, yet another fan!" Jeff was already rather attached to his new persona, which didn't seem all that Zen to me, but I clearly had no corner on truth these days. I was pretty sure my forehead tattoo would just say, "Lost."

Sallie was now engaged in conversation with the patron sitting to her left. She gave me a quick smile as she returned to her conversation. Underneath her calloused attitude was a warm, loyal, and loving human being. All bullshit aside, Jeff was a lucky man.

"Jax was in here last night," Connor said. "Didn't look so good. Said ya guys split up but no details." This caught me off guard. I didn't consider the possibility of running into her at our regular haunt.

"Yep, unfortunate. Different long-term visions of what we wanted. Would have been easier if we had a good fight or cheated on each other. Not so easy when you still care about the person with no anger or resentment to counteract the loss."

"We didn't talk much 'cause things were busy," Conner said, looking down at the glass he was washing. "She just kept to herself. Looked a bit strung out and didn't have her usual energy. But she could have just had a hard day or something. Anyway, sorry about the whole thing. You guys seemed to have a good thing goin'."

"Yeah, I thought so too. Most of what I've thought about most things seems to have been horseshit, it turns out. Thanks, though."

Much to my disappointed surprise, RV Jeff gently tugged Sallie's hand and led her to the center of the dance floor. The intro to the song had triggered an uncontrollable urge to move their bodies to the rhythm, which, to my untrained ears, was indistinguishable from the rest of their set. Connor didn't miss the opportunity to gloat.

Unfortunately for us, the place was filling up, and the table nearest the bar was populated with three young men who looked to be in their early twenties and were adept at talking loud enough to be easily heard over the hollow instruments and general ruckus. Equally as unfortunate, they were drunk and in a heated debate on muscle stimulation theories for optimum back and arm development. They looked more marbled than the average bloke, but none appeared ready to walk out on stage in a banana hammock and compete for the Mr. California title.

The tallest of the three, a blond-haired kid with the sleeves and sides cut out of his t-shirt, began to pontificate on the finer points. "Dude, you have to start with the compound exercises first while the secondary muscle groups are still strong enough to ensure your lats fail before your biceps. Classic chin-ups are the best. I knocked out seventeen in my first set this afternoon." I supposed this did qualify as a brag-worthy event. I was almost positive I couldn't get more than one in my current state of disrepair.

"Yeah, but if you pre-exhaust your biceps, your lats have to take up more of the load because your arms can't carry the set. Look at these Christmas hams," the dark-haired boy said. "They could do the entire set without even engaging my lats," he boasted, brandishing his less-than-impressive guns.

"The proof is in the pudding, wafer chest," the taller blond guy retorted as he rose to his feet, presenting his friends, along with anyone in the bar that cared to look, a full frontal lat spread. Luckily for him, he had proactively tailored his t-shirt to reveal his most prized muscle group. "If you ain't got the V, you most assuredly sit down to pee." The taunting was now underway. Given my choices of watching testosterone-infused meatheads have a posedown or watching RV Jeff and Big Sallie terrorize the dance floor, I decided to go to the restroom instead.

I approached the men's room, eager to piss on the ice they provided at the bottom of the floor-length urinal. This old-school amenity was always enjoyable and appreciated. Upon entry, I surprised a man with truly impressive arms and shoulders decorated with equally impressive tattooed ghostly faces and flaming hair protruding from under his black leather vest. His long blond mustache gave him a definite Viking aura. He immediately decided I was harmless enough to allow him to proceed to shove a car key, or in his case, most likely, a motorcycle key, into a small dark brown vial, producing a serving of fine white powder, which he immediately inhaled. He repeated this exercise a few times and politely raised the key to me, indicating he was willing to share in a gesture of goodwill or simply limiting his chances that I may choose to rat him out. Since he appeared not to be poisoned by it, I asked myself, 'What would Brian do?" and immediately took a quick bump just in case. Even after more than a decade since my coke phase, I still couldn't take the good fortune of free drugs for granted. "Thanks, bro."

"It's Brad. Just respecting my elders," he said, screwing the tiny white cap back on his vile and depositing it in the front pocket of his black leather vest. It was good to know I had reached the qualifying age of the elderly.

"Toby," I said as he turned towards the door, revealing the back of his vest, decorated with a skull with a yellow flowing feather headdress trailing it and the words "Hell's Angels" framing the graphic. I could now proudly add snorting coke with the Hells Angels to my list of recent accomplishments.

I returned to the bar to see that nothing had changed except Connor had refreshed my empty shot glass and beer. The music sucked, but the service made up for it. Brad was now standing at the bar, waiting for Connor to finish pouring him a Guinness. "Connor, Brad's beer is on me," I said, feeling noticeably tougher, being on a first-name basis with a man who looked like he'd kill you for a quarter.

With an expressionless nod, Brad said, "Thanks, Toby," in what I took for an appreciative tone, and he walked back to his table, where he sat solo, likely waiting for his friends to show up.

"Looks like ya run with a rough crowd these days," Connor said.

"We go back a ways. There is a big heart underneath all that leather and ink. Thanks for the refresh, by the way." The coke was now working its numbing path down the back of my throat but yielding minimal results beyond a slight improvement in my morale.

The aspiring bodybuilders had transitioned topics and were now intently discussing the advantages of eating chicken between sets of squats to maximize muscle growth and recovery, their volume increasing with each emphatic point made. I seriously doubted any of them would be getting laid that night.

"Pretty atypical crowd in here tonight, eh, Connor?"

"Always an adventure when this band plays. A common element that binds humanity is appreciating good music," Connor said with pride.

"Figures that I'm apparently outside the circle of humanity as a whole, then."

"Ya'll come around. It's just an exposure issue," Connor informed me. We were interrupted by some yelling, which unsurprisingly was being served up by humanity's bodybuilding contingent. This time, the bravado was directed towards another table with alcohol-inspired courage that, in my opinion, bordered on lunacy.

Then, a response from the other table. "Last chance to sit your paper ass down and shut the fuck up before I bury your punk asses." I thought it cordial that Brad was willing to offer a path to a ceasefire as he calmly remained in his chair with his half-finished Guinness in his hand; a knowing smile worked its way across his face, like good fortune had presented him with this opportunity. This was not his first time swimming in these waters; most assuredly, it wouldn't be his last.

Connor, no stranger to these flare-ups, offered a couple of options. "Ya' all have a choice. Take this outside or shut yer pie holes and enjoy the music," he said with the authoritative tone one would expect from an inn's proprietor. Unfortunately, it fell on deaf ears, which I'm sure also explained why those same deaf ears could tolerate the ridiculous music.

The blond kid, who will now be referred to as Latman, confidently strode around two other tables, stopping in front of Brad's. He calmly tossed his beer into Brad's face, who, remarkably, remained unfazed in his chair. His expressionless face signaled his comfortable familiarity with these types of developments. He then calmly set his beer safely beside his chair on the floor against the wall and rose to his feet.

Wasting no time, Latman lunged across the table headfirst into Brad, sending him reeling into the wall right behind him. However, this opening gambit had not taken the furniture into consideration, and it left Latman high-centered on the table, frantically grabbing at Brad's waist in a failed grappling attempt.

I was, admittedly, excited to see how this would unfold. Latman's friends were suddenly on their feet, realizing that backup may be needed. Brad had regained his balance and simultaneously leapt into the air and, on his way down, plunged his elbow into the center of Latman's spine, producing a cringeworthy CRACK before the table splintered and sent the two of them crashing down on top of the remnants. Latman remained motionless, most likely paralyzed with a broken spine. So much for the first mover's advantage.

"Jesus fuck," Connor uttered, which rang out across the now eerily silent bar. The band had stopped, seeing the commotion. The dancers looked around in confusion, trying to make sense of what was happening. Latman's friends were making a beeline towards their ailing friend. Connor was doing the same, his "persuader" firmly in hand as he navigated the tables and chairs on autopilot. Brad was already on his feet, ready to take on his next challenger, who happened to be the dark-haired kid with lackluster biceps. As he swung and missed Brad's face, Brad calmly grabbed a fist full of his hair and used it to accelerate the kid's face against Brad's raised knee, releasing a torrent of blood from the kid's shattered nose all over Brad's boots. Brad now looked unmistakably like Hulk Hogan with his flowing blond mustache and black skull cap bandana, administering classic all-star wrestling moves with the effortless fluidity of a ballet dancer on steroids. It was a beauty to behold.

With unexplainable quickness, Connor had already arrived on the scene, shoving Latman's remaining friend to the floor en route to the star of the show, who appeared more than ready to take things to the next level. I was concerned that Connor would be the next casualty or be arrested for assault with a deadly weapon. Over on the dance floor, RV Jeff, with a sixth sense for locating bar violence, was shoving people out of his way as women shrieked, men took cover, and the band frantically scrambled to pack up their instruments. Connor was moving at a full sprint when he brought the persuader down on Brad's hip, which had a minimal effect on Brad except for a brief, almost imperceptible grimace followed by an audible snarl. This guy was an uncaged beast, and I admired Connor and Jeff's courage as they engaged without hesitation— as if they could finally quench an aging, fiery thirst for mortal combat.

As Brad spun Connor into a headlock, Jeff smashed a beer glass he must have gathered en route into the back of Brad's head, which got Brad's attention as he spun around to face yet another contender, his arm still firmly around Connor's neck. RV Jeff and Brad were face to face with only inches separating them, providing Jeff the opportunity to slam his newly decorated forehead into Brad's left eye socket. He responded in kind, slamming his forehead into Jeff's, rendering Jeff unconscious and motionless on the floor. So far, Brad was three for three, with Connor's fate still undetermined.

Connor, clearly a veteran of pugilistic confrontation, used Jeff's distraction to swing the persuader like a batter hitting for the fences to land the game-winning home run, right into the outside of Brad's right knee, sending Brad staggering as he tried to maintain his balance, forcing him to inadvertently release his chokehold on Connor. Immediately, Connor drew back his weapon to unleash another blow. Brad, now moving with the jerky stagger of a compromised leg, caught Connor's wrist midair, saving the winning run from topping the fence, and spun it around Connor's back and up towards the ceiling, yielding a blood-curdling SNAP, as Connor's arm dropped lifelessly to his side. Brad's hand shot up and contracted around Connor's throat, slamming Connor's head against the wall. Brad's crushing grip pulled Connor's head away from the wall, and he proceeded to repeat the gesture, putting his entire body weight into this one and dropping Connor into a lifeless heap on the floor.

As this second blow accomplished its objective, I caught a blurry motion in my peripheral vision as something shot through the door with such blinding speed that identification wasn't possible. The trajectory was low and spinning, and what appeared to be its legs swept Brad's, dropping him immediately to the ground. Before Brad had fully landed, the Tasmanian devil, a blur of rags and scraggly hair, was on top of him, repeatedly slamming his elbow into Brad's temple and throat as Brad frantically kicked and squirmed to escape the machine gun volley of blows. Within mere seconds, Brad's twitching and kicking had stopped, and he was out cold. The whirling dervish had come to a stop over Connor's hunched body and was now holding the back of Connor's head.

The events were transpiring faster than I could begin to make sense of what was happening, leaving me stunned. About this time, the skateboard kid rode through the door, complete with long, greasy hair matching his torn black t-shirt and ill-fitting black baggy jeans. He came to a stop right in front of the whirling dervish that I only then realized was Eddie. The kid then executed that move where he casually kicks his board up into his hand.

Eddie looked up into the kid's narrow, angular face as the skateboarder began to speak. "It's his time, Eddie. Destiny wields a cruel sword, but, as you know, fate runs the game."

"Not this time, my friend. Fate can be changed, and tonight it will be," Eddie responded, returning his attention to Connor. I had no clue what was happening here, but they clearly knew each other, and the kid was less than sympathetic to both Eddie and Connor, in my opinion.

"You know the burden of those consequences, Eddie, and you alone will bear that burden. You alone," the kid ominously threatened.

Eddie briefly looked up at the kid, his ice-blue eyes shining so brightly that the intensity struck me from across the bar. I walked toward Eddie and Connor, navigating the other patrons leaving in mass.

"I am fully aware of the trade-offs and willingly accept them. Be gone with you," Eddie said, waving the kid to the door. In what appeared to be a frustrated pity, the kid shook his head and locked his coal-black eyes with Eddie's for a quick second—but he couldn't hold the gaze.

"I'll see you soon. I hope you regret your choice," was the last thing he said as he dropped his board to the floor and rode out into the cold blackness of the night.

Eddie's full attention was again focused on Connor as if he were a surgeon meticulously exploring the innards of his patient on the operating table. Suddenly, the lighting on that side of the bar intensified as if someone had turned the house lights on at the end of the night, and just as quickly, it returned to its previously dim bar lighting. Connor's feet began to twitch, followed by a slow opening and closing of his hands. "Welcome back, my friend," Eddie said to him as Connor's eyes opened with the hazy grogginess of someone waking up with a wicked hangover. "Nothing to worry about now. It's over. I took care of him," Eddie informed him.

Brad was starting to stir; however, he was quickly escorted back into his involuntary slumber with a swift kick to the side of the head, administered by a more than slightly pissed-off Big Sallie. It seemed punishing the biker had been prioritized above assessing Jeff's likely concussion.

"Eddie? Why...how...what are ya doing here, mate?" Connor asked, still shaking the cobwebs out of his head. "Fuck, my arm hurts. Almost as bad as my head."

Eddie let out a slight chuckle. "No soldier left behind, my friend."

Connor grabbed Eddie's hand, and I was now close enough to see tears in his eyes. "How often are ya going to keep saving me arse? It's got to be getting a bit exhausting after fifty-five years."

"How's every single fucking time?" Eddie replied. Connor smiled and carefully rested his head back on the floor.

Someone had called an ambulance, and the sirens grew louder and louder until the deafening pitch stopped right out front. The paramedics cautiously entered the bar, ascertaining the immediate risk of the situation. "Five wounded, none dead," Eddie said. "Probably need another ambulance to get them all to the hospital."

Eddie insisted on accompanying Connor to the ER, which the paramedics were OK with, as they loaded Connor and the blond kid, with what was without a doubt a broken back, into the first ambulance, deeming their injuries more severe.

Jeff had not only gained consciousness but was on his feet and already explaining how the events unfolded to the first police officer who arrived on the scene. It didn't take long for it to become apparent that Jeff had no details to volunteer as to how Latman and his friend arrived in their mangled states. The officer started trying to locate one of the remaining customers that could shed more light on the order of events. Apparently, I fit this bill since I had seen the whole thing without getting knocked unconscious in the process. I told the officer (Tony Gurfoille, garnered from his name tag) what I saw, while Brad and Latman's dark-haired friend were transported in semi-conscious states into the second ambulance and whisked away.

The officer suggested to the lone bar back, Jessie, that it would be best if The Plow closed for the remainder of the night, and Jessie was more than happy to oblige.

Jeff, having dramatically executed his right to refuse to get into an ambulance, was now behind the bar, scooping ice into a large zip lock to apply to his swollen eye and not missing the opportunity to pour himself a shot of Jamieson's for "purely medicinal purposes." Then he poured one for Sallie because he was a gentleman.

"I think I'm going to Uber over to the hospital to see how Connor is doing. Do you guys want to share a ride?" I offered.

"Thanks, Toby, but Sallie and I better stay here and help Jessie close up and make sure things stay calm." Although this appeared to be an obvious ploy to remain behind an unattended bar, it was possible that he intended to be helpful. Underneath all his twisted bravado, Jeff had a big heart, and Connor was the only father figure he had, for better or worse. If you can't trust family, who can you trust, right?

THIRTY-TWO

The cold fog provided a much-welcome reprieve from the dank and musty bar and a few moments of welcome solitude. By the time my Uber arrived, the adrenaline had finally started to dissipate.

It occurred to me that as my friends were being beaten and maimed, the thought never crossed my mind to help them. Instead, I watched the violence unfold like a boxing match, curious who would win. But I had always thought of myself as the kind of guy who would do anything for friends or family. I was yet again battering my self-image.

Knowing our destination was the hospital emergency room, the driver assumed the faster the better, bordering on reckless. "Hey buddy, no rush. We can take it easy," I said, and he reduced our speed to comply with the posted limit.

"Sorry, man. Just finished watching Fast and Furious 4, and a hospital run seemed like a good excuse to practice drifting on the city streets," he explained.

"Fair enough. My plan wasn't to check into the ER tonight. Just heading there to support a friend."

My mind was scurrying around, attempting to rationalize my lack of involvement in the altercation like a gerbil on an exercise wheel, getting nowhere despite an exhausting output. The funny thing was, I could see exactly what it was trying to accomplish and why. My behavior conflicted with my self-image, and to maintain the image of myself I identified with, my mind was exploring all possible angles to justify myself, trying to avoid the obvious alternative: adjusting my self-image to a less respectable version. I continued to observe this game of mental cat and mouse, somewhat amused, when the car suddenly stopped in front of the ER entrance.

"Here we are, my friend," the driver exclaimed.

"Gracias, amigo," I responded, unsure why I would default to Spanish while talking to a fluent English-speaking white male. I may have been developing a multiple personality disorder. As Eddie had said, I was becoming more aware of what I was not. My mind, emotions, and beliefs came and went, but something was constant. But despite my attempts, I couldn't quite grasp it, let alone define it.

When I entered, the ER had about fifteen people sitting around in various states of discomfort, waiting to have their emergencies addressed or, in some cases, even acknowledged. The room was starkly lit with fluorescent lights, intermittently spaced within the ceiling tiles, as was typical in most commercial spaces. The admittance desk was on the far left. Immediately on the right was an old lady in a wheelchair, sitting motionless, with her head buried in her hand, and a younger man holding her other hand, providing what little comfort he could.

A hefty man, who I guessed to be in his mid-forties, sat farther along the left wall wearing a softball uniform, holding a blue ice pack on his left shoulder, which I could only assume must be a dislocated or possibly a torn rotary cuff.

In another wheelchair sat a pale woman with stringy brown hair, wearing what appeared to be a handmade tan sweater, unevenly knit. She had either taken a blow to the head or was saddled with mental challenges, resulting in an ongoing monologue dedicated to the four hours of waiting she had already endured. She began loudly inquiring of nobody and everyone at the same time about why those who came in after her had already cut the line and been taken into the back.

Connor and Eddie were sitting quietly in the far back corner, Connor with an ice pack on his arm. I made my way through several other people with no discernible injuries to the vacant chair next to Eddie.

"How are things going?" I asked.

"They aren't goin'," Connor answered. "We've been here almost forty-five minutes. The paramedics determined my condition didn't warrant a spot in the express queue."

"His head appears fine, and a broken arm isn't an emergency, although, undoubtedly, less than pleasant," Eddie added.

Given no alternatives, we sat around in the awkward silence that tends to permeate emergency rooms, except for the ongoing monologue still being delivered by the pale, stringy-haired woman.

A dark-haired and olive-skinned Middle-Eastern-looking young man, probably in his twenties, and an older woman, who appeared to be his mother, entered the ER and stood in the queue to check in. At first glance, he seemed fine, except for his ridiculously trendy man-bun, which, in my opinion, was an emergency better suited for a barber shop. He was wearing a worn white t-shirt and a blue tarp around his waist, possibly another trending look I had yet to discover. Upon closer examination, his right hand was jammed as far up his ass-crack as one could while wearing a tarp. This wasn't your spontaneous public crack itch, as there was no itching, just constant pressure. My logical assumption was he had been sodomized, and validation was now critical. The TV above the check-in window, complete with no sound and a Giants baseball game underway, provided the opportunity I sought. I feigned interest to work my way to within earshot of the check-in station. They had now advanced to the front of the line and began conversing with the nurse. Unfortunately, the pasty brown-haired and marginally crazy monologue woman decided to elevate the volume of her complaints, making it challenging to catch every word. However, I heard the word "cyst" uttered, which satisfied my curiosity, so I returned to my seat next to Eddie.

"What's the score of the game?" Connor asked. "I think we're in extra innings, which is a minor miracle given our less-than-productive bullpen."

"No idea," I answered. "However, the guy in the blue tarp with his hand up his ass is combating what appears to be quite an anal cyst. Personally, given a choice, I'd prefer your broken arm." It was good to know that an ass crack cyst is also not an adequate ailment to qualify for immediate treatment. He was granted a wheelchair, which made little sense other than a consolation prize. Eddie went in search of the bathroom, which was forming a line to the left of the security desk.

"Jessie and RV Jeff are cleaning up and closing The Plow for you, so don't worry about that," I informed Connor.

"I'm sure Jeff is taking compensation in his favorite currency," he mumbled.

"He did take a nice bash to the head. Makes sense he needs some sort of medication. Pretty wild that Eddie happened to show up exactly when he did, huh?"

"That tends to be his style," Connor said, adjusting his ice pack with a wince.

"You thanked him for saving your ass again. Was the first time equally as dramatic?" I inquired, trying to make conversation to take his mind off his arm.

"I'd say quite a bit more dramatic. The first time he saved me arse was back in Nam. Don't talk to many people about that time in my life, mainly 'cause it's none of their business, but I understand you and Eddie have become close, so I guess I don't mind. Eddie and I and the rest o' our platoon were ordered to navigate a minefield one night. Let's say it wasn't goin' well. We were gettin' our arses blown to bits. In the middle of a minefield, retreatin' is just as dangerous as forgin' ahead, so we elected to follow orders and keep goin'. Eddie insisted I stay behind him and follow his path, figurin' if he got blown up, I would at least be able to avoid one more mine and have a chance. Eventually, we made it across to the other side. Everyone else wasn't as fortunate."

"Holy shit. Eddie told me that story and said only one person besides him made it. I had no idea it was you. That must have been...."

"Fifty-five years ago," Connor interrupted. "He didn't tell ye it was me because he wanted to respect me privacy. That's a pretty personal thing to fling around in casual conversation. Wouldn't ya say?"

"I suppose you're right. I didn't realize Eddie could move so fast. I mean, he shot in that door like a bullet."

"Used to be even faster, if ya can believe it. He was the Army's Taekwondo champion each o' the four years we were in the Rangers. The guy doesn't fuck around."

"You were Army Rangers?" I asked.

"Don't say it like it's a good thing. We got the worst of all the assignments. I call it a curse."

Eddie was now back from the bathroom and taking his seat.

"Hope you don't mind, Eddie; I told Toby about our little minefield exhibition. He inquired about the first time you saved my ass," Connor said, wincing as he tried again to reposition his arm in search of a reprieve that he was starting to realize wasn't going to be found.

"Already told him about that, no worries. Toby's family and I'm sure he won't go blabbing it around," he said, which I took as more of a directive.

"I can't begin to imagine. Great you guys have stayed close ever since," I added, trying to shift the conversation to something more positive.

"You go through an experience that intense with someone; it tends to create a trauma bond of sorts. When we got back, and

Connor opened The Plow, I decided to make the neighborhood my home. It was kind of an understanding that we'd look out for each other," Eddie explained.

"Eddie, what possessed you to come into The Plow when you did tonight? I don't recall ever seeing you in there, and it's five or six blocks from your cart."

"Don't know. Didn't think too much about it. Just realized I needed to see Connor and didn't need to dick around getting there. I tend not to question these things as the answers aren't always rational."

"Typical Eddie," Connor mumbled. The lad's got a sixth sense—always has."

"Connor O'Hara?" a nurse called from the doorway to the examination area.

Connor stood up, "That's me," he answered, making his way towards the door, Eddie and me in tow.

"Can't have the whole neighborhood in the back," the nurse said firmly. "Only one of you can come back with him."

"Neither of 'em needs to come back. They can keep each other company out here. I don't need any emotional support just to have my arm set and cast," Connor said with a 'don't argue' tone.

Eddie shrugged his shoulders, "You're the boss," he said and began walking back to our seats.

"You sure, Connor?" I asked, just in case.

"I'm not a fucking kid that just fell off a skateboard. I think I can handle it, but thanks for the concern."

"Alright then," I said, walking back over to sit down with Eddie as Connor followed the nurse into the back.

"How long do you suppose it's going to take?" I asked Eddie.

"An hour and a half, give or take. He'll have to wait back there for at least a half hour before the doc comes in. Then they'll have to take an X-ray, then set and cast it. Maybe two hours. Connor filled me in on the details of the shit show. Said the biker guy was a friend of yours."

"I had just met the guy in the bathroom. He was snorting some blow and offered me a bump. Then I bought him a beer. He seemed nice enough at the time. Plus, I thought it was kind of cool to be on a first-name basis with a Hell's Angel. It was the blond kid that started it. By the time Connor rushed in and started welding his 'Persuader,' the guy was just defending himself—but with some unnecessary roughness."

"Hey, switching topics, who was that skateboard kid? I've seen him around the neighborhood a few times lately."

Eddie huffed out a laugh, "That would be our friend Death."

"What do you mean death?" I asked.

"When did you see him around the hood?" Eddie asked.

"I reckon the first time was when I was kissing Jax, and he almost ran us over coming around the corner."

"If I recall, that was the night Mrs. Parker died. When else did you see him?"

"Second time he almost ran me over again...the night Cowboy died." I was starting to see the pattern.

"When else?" Eddie asked.

"Tonight."

"And Connor almost died," he added.

"Almost, but he didn't," I pointed out, challenging his theory.

"But he was supposed to," Eddie mumbled, turning his head to look out the window.

"But he didn't."

"Sometimes fate can be altered. There is a high price for that, but one I was willing to pay," he explained, doing little to help me understand what that meant.

"That's a little on the vague side. What the fuck are you talking about, Eddie?"

"I'm kind of opening Pandora's box here, but it's best not to worry too much about it," he said, rubbing his temples.

"The universe is a space-time construct that's pretty stubborn and was set in motion eons ago," Eddie continued. "Altering its trajectory by forcing a big change with downstream effects creates quite a karmic obligation—in this case, lifetimes."

"Eddie, I happen to think you are serving up a crap cupcake complete with sprinkles of determinism, fate, and supernatural jiz layered on top," I replied.

"Perhaps, but..."

We were interrupted startlingly. "You mess with the bull, you're going to get the horns!" a certifiably crazy-looking man with no shoes and filthy black feet belted out. He must have come in when we were talking, as he certainly wasn't there before. "Get off me, bitches!" he yelled, spinning around with his arms in the air as the security guards were doing their best to usher him out. After a threat that he wouldn't be admitted, he offered, in an abrupt about-face, to wait outside until he cooled off, which seemed to satisfy the guards as they accompanied him outside to monitor the cooling off.

"Anyway, what else has been going on lately?" Eddie asked, clearly trying to change the subject.

I decided to let his esoteric explanation of the universe go for the time being, as it sounded like a bunch of shit, and I was in no mood to reevaluate my understanding of all reality. I instead apprised him of the details of my recent eviction, and he kindly let me carry on about how fucked I was about to be, trying to find a new place with no job.

Eventually, he gently interrupted. "It is what it is. So, what's your plan?"

"It just happened this morning, and I haven't put one together yet," I answered, realizing it might be a good time to consider my next steps.

"How's Jax doing?" he asked.

"Don't know. Haven't spoken to her since the breakup."

"Not even just to check in and see how she's doing?"

"Well, it hasn't been very long, so I assume she may want some space," I said, not having thought about it.

"Hmmm..." he uttered in response, scratching his beard slowly with both hands.

"Hmmm...what?"

"Might be a good idea to check in on her," he casually tossed in.

"And what am I going to say? Hey Jax, I know I broke your heart, and I thought I'd check in to see how much you're suffering. Hardly seems compassionate."

Eddie rolled his eyes. "OK, Romeo, I'm on the outside looking in, but I would go with a slightly different approach. It's none of my business. Just thought I'd ask."

"OK, I'll bite. What would be your approach?"

"Maybe something along the lines of, 'Jax, I know this isn't easy for either of us or at least not for me. Regardless of the circumstances, I do miss and care a lot about you, and even though we may not be the best long-term fit, know that if or when you're ready, I'm always available to be a friend and someone who cares about you very much." That seemed smooth, truthful, and sincere, not to mention something I could never have come up with.

"Not bad. I'll consider that. Right now, I've got to figure out a plan, as my life is again spiraling into oblivion. 'No job' is a terrible thing to put on a rental application. I'm fairly certain I'm depressed, which makes it tough to get motivated. And, seeing and observing this, while feeling more aware, isn't changing a thing."

We sat in silence for a minute or two, then he spoke. "What are you willing to change to get off this wheel?" he asked.

"What wheel are you talking about?"

"Just a metaphor for the ups, downs, successes, failures, joy, depression, etc. That was the question I asked you to think about. Curious what you came up with?"

"Fuck, I don't know! It doesn't seem like much of it's in my control, and I'm giving up shit left and right with little choice," I responded, feeling perturbed.

"You're right. You don't have a choice in most of that. As long as there is an idea of a 'you' that needs certain external circumstances to materialize to feel OK, that same 'you' will have to feel not OK, discontented, sad, etcetera, when those external circumstances don't conform to your liking. 'You' can't know happy without the reference point of sad. 'You' can't know pleasure without a reference point of pain. Opposites depend on each other, and your concept of 'you' lives in a dualistic world."

"What are you suggesting? Give up 'me'? Wonderful. Now my only real friend is trying to talk me into committing suicide."

The barefooted, angry guy was now back in the room, considerably calmer and sitting in a chair waiting his turn. I couldn't help but wonder what was going on in his head, which of his beliefs about reality were different to the point of spurring his bizarre and unconventional behavior. He was in a state of internal turmoil based on his perspectives, identity, and beliefs, not much different than myself, except my orientation was probably more in line with our society's consensus reality. He was on his own wheel. I wondered what narrative he had spun up regarding his situation. Despite my curiosity, I decided it best not to engage him.

"I think you're missing the point, Toby, or I'm probably doing a crap job of explaining it. I'm not suggesting you whack yourself or anything foolish like that. I'm merely pointing out that your idea of 'you' is only a concept brought into existence by your thinking, fears, and desires for the future. When all that gets blown up, like right now, your identity searches to replace those beliefs and opinions, to propagate some sort of self-image and story to provide continuity to 'your' existence. So what if, as you witness the mind flailing for a new sense of stability, you short-circuit the program."

"I've been attempting that, and it's not going well. If I'm thinking about something that doesn't trigger any emotions, it's easier, but once I think about shit that makes me sad, angry, or mad, I lose myself, and things become too real not to take seriously," I said.

"Damn straight. The emotions are the trap. The fact you're seeing that this early on is pretty remarkable. It gets easier over time."

We were interrupted by a nurse who was impressively calm and friendly, given the insanity of what her shift must have been like dealing with all these crazies and distressed people. "Connor's going to be just fine. He has a mild concussion, a broken radius, and a fractured ulna. We'll be putting a cast on his arm soon, and I'd estimate he'll be ready to go in about a half hour."

"Great, thanks," I said, and she retreated into the back.

I was anxious to return to our conversation and pick up where we left off. Eddie had stood up and was stretching his hamstrings. "Starting to tighten up," he explained. Seeing an old homeless man stretching struck me as a bit humorous. I didn't see why they wouldn't stretch, but it was a refreshing combination of variables that made me giggle.

"Eddie, so again, you're saying there is nothing else to do but continue watching my ideas of what and who I am dissolve into nothingness and hope that somehow I'm better off afterward?"

"Yep. You pretty much got it," he said, retaking his seat.

"Seems high risk. Let yourself melt and hope it's not that bad. Is that the state of awareness you live from?"

"Yes and no. Of course, I have memories, preferences, thoughts, and emotions. I've just broken my identification with them. As a result, they've lost most of their fuel and intensity, which allows me to be right here and present with whatever is unfolding. It's all without effort anymore. That's how I'd describe it if I had to put it into words. I basically 'am,' and it's perfect however it unfolds."

"Well, it would be hard to get motivated to do anything if it's all just fine." I didn't say that it seems like an excellent recipe to fast-track your life into the shitter with an easy spiritual rationalization.

"You'd think so, huh? I still get up, make breakfast, figure out where to buy food, and visit with people and stuff, but it all just happens on its own, and I allow it to. The same shit gets done but not by thought-laden planning or a proactive effort to avoid imagined fearful futures. The mind isn't the initiator of all activity. Most people assume it is and never question it."

"Sounds like one needs to have a lot of faith for that 'let go and let God' kind of stuff, which I've never been a fan of."

"I don't like the dualistic aspect of the person being this thing, and a separate God is out there dictating what happens. As any particle physicist will tell you, it's all one continuous interconnected thing happening. But yes. At some point, the identity has to surrender to the source animating it all. At least it's faster that way. Or life can slowly chip away at the ego, and sooner or later, it just falls away. Either way is ultimately fine. People get overly worked up about it or attached to attaining something, creating more drag and cycles to play out."

"Still, there is a lot of trust required to throw your arms up and hope your mangled life pans out," I pointed out.

"Is the goal to have your life turn out a specific way? If so, grind for that goal and see what happens. If the goal is truth, let the bull-shit that got you here get off the bus. Admit that you know less than you think, pay attention without motive other than to be one with the present moment, and surrender to what each moment brings. You'd be surprised. But try it if you can set the fear down long enough. As long as we believe we are separate from life, life can spank us and is to be feared. So we resist life in every way possible, sure it will send us crashing onto the rocks. If you resist life, you resist the totality of what you are. You can't win that battle."

I was following Eddie, but all this raised my hackles. Again, he wasn't saying anything new, just repeating what he'd shared in earlier discussions. I'd be more open to it if it came from a Ph.D. in philosophy or a scientist. However, coming from a homeless man made me wonder if this was just a rationalized coping mechanism for an intelligent man left holding the short end of the stick. However, the fucker was perpetually content, thankful, and genuinely happy. He was also the most non-judgmental person I recall ever meeting. All traits I was sorely lacking. The reality was I wasn't yet willing to let go of my models of what I believed myself and the truth to be. And in arguing for them, I was indeed fighting for the right to keep them and all the limitations that came along with them. But the devil I knew was still better than the devil I didn't. The thought occurred to me that maybe I was probably just terrified of the unknown.

"Eddie, I appreciate your patience here. It's just hard for me to trust blindly. People who don't discriminate get taken advantage of all the time by others."

"My question for you is, at this point, what do you have to lose?" he asked.

"My sanity?" I said, almost joking.

Connor had already emerged from the back, walking in our direction, admiring his pristine, new, white cast. "Thanks for waiting, gents!"

"Let me sign that thing," Eddie said.

"No God damn way! Nothin' fucks up a great-lookin' new cast faster than a bunch o' graffiti. I don't want to look like some sixth grader with cartoons, pictures, and illegible signatures all over the damn thing. This is a man's cast, not everyone else's scratchpad. Let's get the hell out o' here," Connor said, angling towards the door. "I'm all checked out."

"He seems back to normal," I suggested to Eddie, who nodded in agreement.

"You want to crash at my place, Connor, in case you need anything in the night?" I offered.

"Well, there ain't a lot o' night left. It's already midnight, and it's just a broken arm. I've got your number and won't hesitate to ring you if anythin' alarming comes up. How about that?" he asked.

"Fair enough. Let's get an Uber to take us to your house, and once you're inside, Eddie and I can head home ourselves."

"Sounds like a sane plan," Connor said, as an incoming ambulance almost ran us down as we crossed the street to wait for our ride.

Connor lived in a flat up over on California and 3rd, only a few blocks from The Plow. If he had a concussion, which they said he did, it wasn't obvious. He was sharp and ornery as shit. We all got out of the car and stood outside Connor's building. San Francisco was a different beast in Richmond in the middle of the night. No traffic sounds, horns, sirens, or people. Just an unexplainable silent refuge in a remarkably dense urban jungle. The dichotomy left one with a smidgen of peaceful awe.

"Connor, was there any word on how the less fortunate victims are progressing?" I said, referring to the aspiring bodybuilders and Brad.

"Afraid not. Nor do I care. If they come around again, I'll call the cops. I'm glad nobody got seriously wounded or killed. And you said Jeff's OK?" Connor asked.

"He appeared no worse for the wear when I left. He may have a headache tomorrow, if not from the head butting, then from the tequila he was pouring himself," I answered, rolling my eyes.

"Well, top of the evenin' to ya boys, and a heartfelt thank-you for both bein' there for me. Proud to know ya, blokes," he said, surprisingly, giving us each an actual one-armed hug. Although I couldn't say I'd seen this side of him before, it was a relief to know it was there.

Connor headed in, and I walked with Eddie to his cart, claiming I had nothing better to do, but in actuality, wanting to ensure I knew his shit wasn't stolen and he was safely home. Everything appeared as he left it. I was anticipating other homeless types scouring his camp for anything of nominal value. Eddie seemed pleased as well.

"I'll probably see you tomorrow, Eddie," I said. "Thanks for the chat, and more importantly, thanks for getting things under control tonight." That was the understatement of the century.

"I'm glad I could help. You get a good night's sleep, Toby. Consider reaching out to Jax. No offense taken if you don't. Might not hurt, is all I'm saying."

"I'll consider it. Good night, pal."

As I took in the crisp night air, I noticed the fog had cleared, and I was looking at a starry sky, which in San Francisco meant you could barely see the stars with all the light pollution. Still, it was worthy of appreciation.

I'm sure it felt good for Eddie. Not every night you get to go to bed thinking, "I saved my best friend's life tonight." Eddie was one of the most bizarre characters I had ever met, both down to earth and not entirely of this world. A guy that had nothing but had everything at the same time and didn't give two shits one way or the other.

By the time I walked through my door, I had realized the excitement, adrenaline, and time spent in the ER had teamed up to leave me utterly ruined. I stepped over a pile of mail, plugged in my cell phone, ignored the two voicemails I had on my landline recorder, and fell into bed.

I was content to have a bed still to come home to. Who knew what tomorrow would bring, but I'd deal with that tomorrow.

THIRTY-THREE

The morning sunlight streaming through my window pulled me out of the deepest sleep I could recall having in quite some time. As my eyes began to gain focus, the clock alerted me that I had slept in until 10:15, an impressive feat.

As I went to the kitchen to put on a pot of coffee, my mind drifted back to my conversation with Eddie in the ER the night before. Already deep in thought, my mind was skipping from one topic to the next like a stone skipping across the top of the water, the skips getting more frequent and closer together as the stone's journey progressed. But I was aware of it as it was happening.

First, the skateboard kid, an incarnation of death itself, seemed far out but a bizarre possibility, given how everything had transpired.

Skip

Eddie's history with Connor back in Vietnam.

Skip

Trusting that things are unfolding as they're supposed to and not resisting.

Skip

Eddie suggested checking in with Jax.

Skip

I need to find a job ASAP.

Skip

I should get a run in first.

Skip

Oh yeah, I need to check my anus. I quickly ensured the bathroom lighting was the same as usual, and I was in the same spot on the floor. I assumed the position and snapped a selfie. It certainly seemed noticeably lighter, but that made no sense, and I wasn't able to focus long enough to figure out why it might have gone from a black hole where not even light could escape to a muddy brown yet still very unattractive poop chute. I had more pressing issues.

Thoughts kept interrupting each other, ensuring nothing was thoroughly considered. Yet, everything received at least a cursory acknowledgment, as if not forgetting to think about each of these would somehow ensure I was still in control. But in control of what?

To escape the spinning, I played my voicemails. The first was from Brian, reminding me that a walkthrough would be required before I could get my deposit back, and we needed to schedule that. It was a stark reminder that I had no plans for alternative housing, nor had I even started looking for another job.

The second message, again, was from a number I didn't recognize. "Toby, sorry to bother you this late. It's Jimmy. Please call me as soon as you get this. Thanks." This was certainly unexpected. What could Jimmy want to talk about other than my asshole-ness for breaking up with his sister? Then it dawned on me he must have caught wind of the drama at The Plow last night, and someone had probably informed him I was there. He was most likely calling to get the scoop from a first-hand witness. Maybe I could bounce the idea of checking in with Jax off him and see if it may be a good idea before actually calling her. I rang him back, and he answered on the second ring.

"Hi, Toby!" he said, obviously recognizing my number, "Thanks for getting back to me."

"Hey, Jimmy. Good to hear from you. What's up?"

"Toby, I've got bad news and may need help, but I don't know the best tactic. I'm freaked out, and so is Jax."

"OK, take a deep breath and let me know what's going on. And please don't tell me Jax is pregnant."

"No, fortunately, she's not, or if she is, she hasn't said anything about it. Toby, Jax is in the hospital. Stable but not in good shape and....."

I interrupted him mid-sentence. "Jesus Christ, what happened?" My heart rate immediately accelerated; its beats filled my ears. The thought of her maimed, hurt, maybe with cancer or something, was now sending me into a panic.

"She overdosed on heroin last night, Toby," he said and paused a couple of seconds before continuing. "Luckily, I stopped by unexpectedly and quite late as I was in the neighborhood and saw the light on. She didn't answer my knock, but the door was unlocked, and I figured she must be in the bathroom or something." Jimmy was talking so fast that he had to pause to remember to breathe. "And sure enough, she was but was on the bathroom floor motionless and then started to vomit. I initially figured she was sick with the flu or had been overserved at the bar, but she was out of it, and I knew something was wrong. That's when I saw the needle, rubber band thing, and a blackened spoon and realized what must have happened. I freaked out, called 911, and kept trying to wake her up."

"Holy fuck! Jimmy, I know for a fact she wasn't doing any drugs the whole time we were together, honestly, or I would have let you know, and we could have come up with a plan. She had told me about her previous addictions and her recovery and was so glad to be beyond that. You said she's in the hospital, so the paramedics must have arrived in time."

"God bless them. They were there in what felt like the longest five minutes of my life. Toby, I thought she was going to die in my arms," he said, his voice dissipating into a muffled sob. Eventually, regaining some composure, he continued. "I've never felt fear like that, Toby. The paramedics had some drug called Naltrexone or Naltrexine or something they immediately injected her with that shut down the process, but she stopped breathing, and they had to use those panel things to shock her like you see in the movies. It happened again in the ambulance on the way to the hospital. I felt so helpless. My sister was dying, and I could only watch and hope they could save her." He was now crying again.

"Jimmy, thanks so much for calling. What can I do? Anything you guys need, anything," I asked without hesitation, although feeling awkward about my role as an ex-boyfriend in a situation like this.

"Toby, you have to come to the hospital. I'm here now," he said as if somehow I could do something that the doctors and Jimmy couldn't.

"Sure...I will....But what if it makes it worse? She might be embarrassed, or it might just make her sad. I might be the last person she wants or needs to see right now," I said, concerned.

"Toby, when you guys broke up, and you left the Danube that night, she fell to pieces, wailing that her soul had just walked out the door and life had fucked her over yet again. She claimed she's never loved anybody like she loved you and would never find anyone close. She has been in tears daily, and that's not an exaggeration. I'm not saying you should get back together or anything. Knowing you at least care or could still be friends or anything could help. She's on suicide watch, Toby," he said as his voice cracked, and he paused to gather himself. "Maybe it doesn't make sense. I don't know; I'm grasping at anything that could save her from herself. She doesn't want to talk about it. She's likely embarrassed. I know she's been hurting and misses and cares about you, and it seems like having as many people she cares about as possible in her corner right now could help carry her through this. Am I crazy?"

"I get it, brother. On my way. Which hospital?"

"Thanks, Toby. Thank you so much. UCSF. Text me when you're in the lobby. We'll pretend you're family to get you in."

"Got it. I'll Uber. Be there in ten, tops." I hung up, threw on a pair of jeans and a t-shirt, grabbed my jacket, and halfway down the hall, realized I had forgotten about shoes and socks. Not willing to chance being turned away due to a no-barefoot rule, I quickly remedied the situation and was in an Uber within three minutes.

My mind was again skipping around from question to question without any organized progression.

How did this happen?

Skip

What would I even say to her?

Skip

Could she have been taking drugs and somehow kept it from me the whole time?

Skip

What was I going to say to her?

Skip

If I had been open to having a second family, would this have never happened?

And the stone kept skipping across the pond, and I was helpless to slow it down. A wiser part of me said, "Trust you'll know what to say. Just love her. She needs to feel that. Just love her." Immediately followed by the not so wise thought, "What if seeing me makes it worse and pushes her closer to doing it again?" Followed by the thought, "Don't flatter yourself." Then the wiser me voice, "Trust that things are happening for a reason you don't need to understand nor comprehend fully. Lead with your heart, not with your mind." I was all over the fucking map, flailing for something to grab onto like a drowning child, hoping there was a hand within reach to pull me to safety. But what was safety in this situation? Safety for my psychological well-being? Safety for Jax? *Skip...Skip...Skip.* Jesus, I literally couldn't think straight.

It donned on me that Jax was overdosing either at the same time

I was with Eddie waiting for Connor in the ER or possibly right afterward. If I had followed Eddie's advice and called her immediately, could that have helped prevent this whole thing? And what even possessed Eddie to encourage me to connect with her? Maybe it was a coincidence, but it was almost as if he knew something grim was in the wings, waiting for the perfect time to strike.

The Uber came to a stop, jolting me out of my circular thinking and back into the car. "Here we are. Hope everything's going to be OK," the Uber driver said.

"Thanks, man. I guess I'm just before finding out."

I got out of the Uber and waited at the crosswalk for the light to change. It was unseasonably warm. I estimated eighty degrees with a fierce blue sky and a mild breeze. On a sunny day, there are few more gorgeous places than San Francisco. People were sitting on the stairs of the hospital, eating sandwiches and drinking coffee, all appearing to be in good spirits, no doubt brought on by gratitude for the exceptional weather. The air smelled of the fresh asphalt being applied about half a block down the street. Much to my surprise, all this had a calming effect on me. The nervousness I was mired in gave way to genuine concern for someone I still cared for. Entering the lobby, I realized I had no idea where I was going and remembered I was supposed to text Jimmy. I let him know I was in the lobby. Although the lobby wasn't dark, it was relative to the bright sunlight. My eyes were still adjusting when Jimmy stepped off the elevator, scanning the lobby for me, and rushed over and gave me a firm hug, holding on for what would typically be an inappropriate length of time; however, in this case, it was more than warranted. As he eventually released me, I could see by his swollen eyes he'd been crying, and as the panic under the surface began leaking out, new tears started to form.

"I'm glad you called, Jimmy. We'll get through this with Jax," I said as a wave of calm confidence rolled over me. "Does she know I'm coming up?"

Jimmy was now dabbing at his eyes with his shirt sleeve and

appeared to be regaining his composure. "No, she doesn't. I didn't know how to tell her and wasn't sure if she'd refuse to see you. Something just told me she needs to see you, know you care, and not feel totally disconnected. It may be awkward, and who knows how she'll react."

"After a few minutes, if it's clear she doesn't want me there, I'll leave. Let's play it by ear. We don't want to overwhelm her trying to help," I said as Jimmy pushed the button to call the elevator.

"Sounds good. She won't eat, barely talks, and mostly just stares at the ceiling like she's awake but very far away, completely numb."

"Well, I imagine she's confused, disappointed in herself, scared, and feels like hell. She's probably half in shock," I said, realizing I didn't know shit about how she felt and was only projecting. I hoped that what Jimmy and I were about to do wasn't pure recklessness.

The elevator stopped on the fourth floor—the halls a sterile white, everyone quiet and walking briskly with purpose. Employees were wheeling carts of dirty laundry and carrying clipboards, and one woman was mopping the floor at the far end of the hall that we were heading down on our way to Jax's room. So far, nobody had inquired or questioned who I was. Security was a bit lax, especially if a patient was on suicide watch. Her door was closed, and we stopped outside before going in.

"Jimmy, if you sense it would be best for me to leave, and I seem oblivious, please say something immediately. If I can help, great, but if I'm doing more harm than good, we've got to shut it down, OK?"

"Absolutely. Why don't you go in first, and I'll hang back in the doorway. I think it's better if I'm not in the way or trying to tell her I called you and risk her losing her shit before she even sees you," he suggested.

"Sure." I remembered the wise voice in my head. 'Just love her.'

I walked into the small room with nothing but a bed, a single chair, and a nightstand. It reeked of loneliness and abandonment. I remembered that she was on suicide watch, which made more sense. They probably couldn't staff someone to sit there 24/7, but they could create a safe environment. Opposite the door, there was a decent-sized window that didn't open, and the room had its own bathroom to the immediate left of the door.

Jax was lying on the bed, looking like absolute hell. Her hair was greasy and uncombed. Her face was hollow, almost gaunt. Her normally olive skin was ashen, and she wore no make-up, not that she had ever needed any. She slowly turned towards the sound of the door opening, likely expecting Jimmy, with an expressionless face. It took her a moment to realize I was standing there. I don't know what I expected, but I hadn't considered the zero-reaction option. She returned to looking at the ceiling without a hint of emotion. I had no idea what to say and was just as curious as anyone else as to what would come out of my mouth that, remarkably, was starting to move of its own volition.

"Jax, I couldn't not be here. I know you are probably angry, numb, embarrassed, tired, and probably emotionally raw right now. At least, I would be. I don't care what happened or think any less of you. My life has become so royally fucked in the last week that I'm experiencing that exact list of emotions, and quite honestly, I feel like a pathetic excuse of a human being and wouldn't have wanted you to see my crumbling life." Still, there was no response, which prompted me to pack the awkward silence with as many words as possible.

"When Jimmy called me, suddenly, none of that mattered. You are going through a horribly hard and seemingly tragic experience, and everything in my head was immediately rendered irrelevant. I had to see you to let you know that I care, and that I love you very much and will move heaven and earth to give you anything you need and will always want to be a part of your life in some manner as long as it's not too hard for you. Friends share their journey and carry each other when they can't walk alone. I'm sorry I hadn't called you to keep communication open. I thought that may make it harder, but not talking to you has been much more difficult."

Jax stared expressionless at the ceiling as if nobody was inside. "I can leave if you want, and I'd understand that, but I would much prefer to stay. I can't tell you how good it is to be with and see you, even in these circumstances." Still, no reaction, as if she'd died right there with her eyes open. Maybe part of her already had. "Jax, please say anything, even if it's just telling me to shut the hell up."

"Shut the hell up." I had never been more relieved to hear those four words. She finally spoke, meaning she probably didn't have brain damage, and she wasn't furious or traumatized by my unannounced appearance.

I just stood in the doorway, doing what I thought was an excellent job of shutting the hell up, wondering what to do next. Jimmy stepped around me, pulled the chair over to the right side of her bed, motioned with his eyes for me to sit down, and returned to the doorway. Since I hadn't come up with any better ideas, I sat down in the chair. Her gaze remained fixed firmly on the ceiling. To avoid making her feel even more uncomfortable, I directed my attention to the nothingness on the wall in front of me, working really hard at continuing to shut up, attempting to give her a sense of control over something.

After about five minutes of silence so deep and cold that I was sure it would drown me, I put my hand, palm up, on her bed next to hers. After about two of the longest and most awkward minutes I can remember—and that's saying a lot with what the last few days had dealt me—she moved her hand on top of mine, wrapping her fingers around mine just hard enough to remind me of exactly how much I missed her touch. We sat like that, not saying anything, for what must have been another five minutes.

That's when I began sobbing uncontrollably, which quickly transitioned into what one may describe as wailing. No thought spurred this. Just a deep pent-up aching love that finally found its way to the surface, erupting like a volcano that couldn't be turned off. The intensity was, truth be told, frightening. We were two lost souls whose lives had unexpectedly been reduced to rubble. In a way, we were perhaps each other's only remaining foothold. Perhaps a bit melodramatic, but not entirely. Eventually, I looked over to see Jax was now looking right at me with tears running down her cheeks as she curled into a fetal position facing me. Her jade green eyes desperately probed my consciousness, perhaps in hopes of finding her lost self hidden in there somewhere.

I heard the door gently click and knew without looking that Jimmy had left us to ourselves. And there we remained for the next half hour, me holding her hand with both of mine now, as we both bawled our eyes out, not saying a thing as words would only dilute the pure emotional bond that we both needed at that moment more than anything else in the world.

We sat like that, streams flowing from our eyes, yet unwavering, until Jax crawled into my lap like a toddler ready for her bedtime story. We both held each other, crying for another twenty minutes or so in silence, knowing that the road out would be rough and hard to navigate, and neither one of us was fit to guide. I had so many questions for her about what so quickly contributed to her meteoric fall. She would share what she was comfortable with when she was ready.

"What happened to you that's so bad?" she asked, mercifully breaking the silence. I was relieved she was the first to speak, so I didn't have to risk taking the conversation in a direction that was uncomfortable for her.

"Lost my girlfriend, got fired from my job, evicted from my place, found out I'm not the biological father of my children, and the current mental breakdown. The typical stuff you'd expect from a guy like me."

"Well, now you can add 'drug overdosing ex-girlfriend' to your list," she said.

"That's a gift, Jax. Otherwise, I wouldn't be holding you right now. I appreciate you being willing to take it to such an extreme to get me to come around," I said, figuring humor may also imply no judgment. She punched me in the knee and buried her head in my chest. Her hair had lost its usual jasmine smell and now just smelled like dirty hair. She looked more skinny than athletic, or maybe that was just my projection. She couldn't have lost that much weight in what must have been less than a week. Had it been such a short time? So much had transpired. I then realized this would eventually end up right back where it started. Now more than ever, I was in no way, shape, or form able to be a father. Not so much because of being broke and jobless. More so because I didn't even know what was real, good or bad, imaginary, or who and what I was anymore—just a hollow, detached sense of nothing. What scared me the most was that I almost didn't seem to care.

We didn't say much else, both lost in our heads, trying to sort out our respective puzzles with too many missing pieces. I've since realized that 'sense' is relative, as things never make sense on their own. I was unsuccessful in trying to build an acceptable story—one I might be able to live with, because it would be only that—another story. The problem was that the stories weren't believable anymore, no matter how cleverly I manipulated and twisted the pieces and plots.

The door opened, and a nurse came in. He was a middle-aged, good-looking Asian guy, looking to be in his mid to late fifties. He was dealing with some follicular challenges up top but doing an excellent job of concealing the situation with the now trendy comb-forward hairstyle.

"Sorry to barge in on you. I need to take Jax's vitals and make sure she gets some sleep. I'm Rodney, by the way."

"No apology required. I'll sit here and stay out of the way," I said. "I'm Toby."

"Well, her brother has been here since she checked in, and we need to leave her alone for a while now so she can get some rest," Rodney informed me, prematurely closing our reunion, which seemed like the last thing she needed.

A vision of Jimmy going back to check in at The Blue Danube and Jax waking up alone, staring at the ceiling with that vacant, zombified look, trapped alone in the darkest corners of her soul, snuck through the back door of my mind. "When can I come back?"

"If you give me your number, I can call you once she wakes up?" he offered, which I thought was incredibly thoughtful. Spending each day working on the front lines of other people's nightmares takes a special person. This was a guy with a sense of purpose that went much deeper than a paycheck, and a part of me loved him just for that.

"That would be great, Rodney. Thank you. Jax, I'll be back later, provided that's what you want. I can understand if you prefer to be alone, and that won't hurt my feelings," I said, lying.

"I'd prefer not to be alone," she said in a voice devoid of emotion.

"I'll see you later then," I said, pressing my lips gently against her forehead. I stood up, still carrying her, gently laid her back down in her bed, then kissed her on the hand. Rodney put the little white plastic clamp on her finger to check her oxygen levels and began to put the blood pressure cuff on her arm. I patted Rodney on the shoulder and left, shooting Jax a smile over my shoulder on the way out.

I'm not going to lie. I was overwhelmed, and my capacity to organize a single coherent thought was even more compromised than before.

Walking back to my apartment, I observed my mind continuing to skip faster and faster.

What is my responsibility to Jax?

Skip

Fuck, where should I even start looking for another job?

Skip

I better grab something at the store for lunch.

Skip

What if I can't find a place before I have to move out?

Skip

Jax looked so pathetic. How did this happen that fast?

Skip

It felt so good to hold her. Could I start another family? No way in this unstable condition we had both fallen into. I haven't even begun to process the loss of my previous family.

Skip

How can I trust what's happening, like Eddie said?

Skip

Things are going to hell in a handbasket, and I'm not doing shit about it.

Skip

I can see if Connor needs a bar back.

Skip

It feels like my sense of self is a gallon of ice cream being emptied out one scoop at a time.

The same thoughts kept interrupting each other in random cycles. Maybe this is how crazy happens. Too much shit descends on your life simultaneously, exceeding your capacity to cope, and the mind just breaks beyond repair.

Mentally consumed and oblivious to what I was doing, I became aware that I had changed course and was now rounding the corner toward Eddie's cart. God, he must have been getting tired of my broken-down needy ass.

CHAPTER
THIRTY-FOUR

When I arrived, Eddie was kneeling over something alongside his cart. "Hi, Eddie," I said. He turned to face me, and it became clear he was fixing a flat bicycle tire. Then I noticed an old beat-up 1970s Schwinn ten-speed lying off to the right.

"Hey, Toby. Just in time. Can you slowly pump air into this inner tube so I can listen and see if the leak is coming from the valve or somewhere else? Normally, I'd just put it underwater, but my house doesn't have a working bathtub," he said.

"Sure." I walked around to where he had his bicycle pump. "Working on a new set of wheels?"

"Found this with a 'free' sign just around the corner. I figured it may be good for quick errands when I leave the cart, or I could sell it for a few bucks if I get it working again."

"Why not?" I said, kind of envious that he could tinker around feeling carefree while I had so many problems that I couldn't begin to sort my way out of.

"So what's up?" he asked, pressing his ear against the valve stem as I slowly pumped more air into the inner tube. "Wait a second before you answer. I think I hear exactly where the leak is coming from. Sure as shit, it's the valve stem. Looks like I'll need to find another inner tube. Anyway, sorry, what were you saying?"

"I wasn't saying anything. You had just asked what's up, and I was about to answer."

"Well, don't let me stop you."

"Eddie, I don't know what's going on. I'm fighting so many battles on so many fronts right now I can't focus on any of them long enough to figure out what to do.

"I didn't even have to check in with Jax, like you suggested, as her brother called me up in a panic and told me she had just overdosed and asked me to come to the hospital." I realized I had just unloaded like a cannon on the poor guy, but desperation prioritizes its interests over courtesy. "And don't you find it a little ironic that as we were sitting in the ER talking about Jax, she had a needle in her arm and practically died?"

"Not surprising," he muttered as he wrested the inner tube from the wheel.

"It sure seems a bizarre coincidence to me!"

"There's a synchronicity that seems to connect things at a level we aren't always aware of. Kind of like when you're thinking about someone and the phone rings, and it's that very person. Likely just coincidence, but maybe something more?"

"Well, now I'm dealing with Jax's overdose, the uncertainty of my role relative to her situation, and how my latent feelings I've been suppressing seem to be back with a vengeance. I'm now being woven back into the no-win situation that broke us up."

Eddie was now putting away a crescent wrench and stuffing the ruined inner tube into what appeared to be his garbage bag. "That sounds exciting."

"Well, maybe if you have an appetite for tragedy. And don't forget to combine Jax's overdose with me being fired and needing to show a new source of income to find another apartment in a few weeks. It feels like my head is stuck in a washing machine."

"That sounds dramatic, but I like it," he calmly replied, now on his feet, wiping his filthy black bike-tire hands on his pants.

"Well, I'm glad it works for you. Then, you'll also be pleased to know I truly think I'm now insane. Life just said, 'Checkmate, motherfucker.'" Eddie seemed unconcerned and almost a wee bit happy as I continued to lament my situation. "A little sympathy would be welcome here."

"It's an exciting time for you. When patterns break, doors open, and they are breaking all over the fucking place. Lucky, if you ask me. Aren't you eager to see what's next?"

"Not particularly. Whatever it is, it appears to be predestined to suck. I can't make sense of any of it anymore. Eddie, I'm losing my shit. I'm going crazy. Bat shit fucking CRAZY!"

"Let me ask you, 'who' is going crazy?"

"I know where you're going. The mind/ego trying to find a ledge to get a footing and reestablish itself or reinvent itself?" I was starting to get the drill.

"What is the mind scared of?" he followed up with.

"Fucking everything right now."

"Following the fear will lead you to the threatened belief. I have a feeling, in this case, it's fear of being nothing underneath all the bullshit, right?"

"Go ahead and add that to the list."

"If everything we thought we were is primarily our imagination, then what's truly real beyond just thought?" he asked.

"That's what I'm wrestling with, Eddie. I'm seeing this mental craziness happening, but observing it isn't causing it to dissipate. So, in addition to all this mental turmoil, there's the awareness of the turmoil as it happens, which is almost more distressing."

"Your ego is literally fighting for its life. The question is, are you brave and resolute enough to find out where your ego's death leads?" Eddie had a way of asking a series of rhetorical questions, prying open your mind just enough for the final question to punch right through your defenses and stab you right in the brain.

"Probably not. Whenever I think about it and where I want this journey to take me, it feels like I'm chasing another rainbow. And where will that leave me? Just more ass-crack crazy."

"Well, my brother, welcome to the edge," he said, giving me a friendly slap on the shoulder.

"I hate the edge," I said with all sincerity.

"Well, my new favorite nondual writer, Stephen Ladd, in his book *Spiritual Constipation*, sums it all up brilliantly—'Sooner or later, we all end up on the naked cross of our most cherished beliefs.'"

Eddie continued, "You know you're falling off into the abyss of the unknown. No stable foothold to anchor yourself." He paused as he pulled the bike carcass behind his cart, then resumed. "And at this point in the journey, deep down, you know you can't go back because your restless mind and the quagmire of tangled beliefs won't lead you anywhere but into more confusion. What got you here won't get you out because thought can't take you beyond itself. But you know you can't stay where you are."

"You've done a good job of describing it, I'd say. Life has generously served me up another fuckering."

"Or blessed you."

"A blessed fuckering. Fun to say, but no fun to be on the receiving end of," I pointed out.

"Ultimately, everyone on this journey ends up in this spot. Mostly, they are on their deathbed when they realize they have no idea what's on the other side and can only have faith that it's something to look forward to, or anything at all, for that matter. And in a way, 'you' are on your deathbed—not your body but your entire manufactured sense of self. Ah... the beauty of impermanence."

"Not to offend, but I'm aiming for a tad more permanence right now, Eddie."

"Nothing, absolutely nothing, stays the same. As our friend Ram Dass says, 'Suffering is the sandpaper of our incarnation. It does the work of shaping us,'" he quoted, extracting what appeared to be a small notebook from another bag he was now rummaging through. "Just let go and see where it goes, what happens next. I'm always here for you. So no fear of being lost and alone."

At this point, I wasn't in the mood for more insight into how broken I was. "Eddie, how can I trust anything when I've had my life blown to bits yet again, despite my efforts?"

"How can you not?" he said with a gentle grin. "Everything that happens to you is fuel for transforming yourself if you're open to it. Without the blessing of these experiences, you wouldn't have visibility into the thin veil of identity you're still grasping to hang onto.

"You, like most people, have the choice to spin up another narrative, but *you* are now aware that it's just more fiction you'd be hiding behind—a fiction that will eventually crumble, a fiction that you can no longer believe in," he said, casually looking for something else in his cart. His nonchalance was beginning to annoy.

"So you're recommending I sit here and hope things change? At this point, I can assume they will change for the worst, which seems to be the pattern."

"Toby, for most people, being a victim of circumstance provides a nice little reward. We absolve ourselves and our egos of responsibility for our situation. However, you have arrived at a place where your ego has become very thin and unconvincing. Don't try to bolster it by believing this is all happening to you for no reason."

"I'm just seeing the pattern of crap falling apart in every aspect of my life, and I feel helpless to stop it."

"This, too, eventually, like all patterns, will break. As a wise man once said, 'It is important to expect nothing, to take every experience, including the negative ones, as mere steps on the path, and to proceed.'"

"And who is this wise man you refer to that says these things?" I asked.

"Again, our friend Ram Dass. I figured a third party may have more credibility than just me saying the same shit over and over to you. Pick up his book more often." He opened the tiny notebook, thumbing through a few pages, obviously looking for something specific. "Ah... here we go."

"Ah...what?" I asked.

"Nothing. Just my little book of Alan Watts and Ram Dass quotes, in case I need to pepper you with more of them," he said with smiling eyes, which appeared aquamarine in the afternoon sunlight.

"Great. I'm now being flogged to death by spiritual quotes. Maybe I can meditate it all away," I said with as much sarcasm as I could muster.

"'All spiritual practices are illusions, created by illusionists, to escape illusion.' Another great quote from our man. You know he was a Harvard psychologist and professor?"

"Yes. I know, and thank you very much. So, no spiritual way out of my torturous existence, you're saying? Just trading one set of crappy illusions for another?"

"What if we were just pure loving awareness, here to have a human experience, kind of like a kid playing a video game? When the game's over, the character disappears. It wasn't real, but the kid still had an experience. Better than being bored, right?"

"Eddie, all I know is that this has to end soon, and I just don't know what to do," I said, trying to convey the sense of futility still smothering me.

"Here," he said, handing me his little notebook. "You know the drill. Open it to a random page and see what comes up."

"Fine, but I'm not finding any of this helpful." I took the book from his hand, opened it randomly, and did my best to decipher the barely legible handwriting. "'We are fascinated by the words, but where we meet is in the silence behind them,'" I read, looking at him for more commentary.

"That's the best one! Nice choice. He nailed it all right there, didn't he? So concise. I wish I could be that effective at communicating this stuff. That's why I love him so much," he said, unnecessarily pleased with himself. "You'll find yourself in the silence because you'll realize you are the silence. The only constant is the still essence of awareness that animates this whole fucking thing. Play in that space, and your orientation will shift into that state sooner or later when the time is right. Let go of your clinging and be patient. Remember that your current ideas of what you need to have, do, or be to find happiness have yielded very little of it. Why would you double down on such shitty odds?"

"Says the bookie. I'm shifting into survival mode here as food, shelter, and water are about to disappear for me. Once I get that shit under control, then maybe I can work out who or what my true nature is," I said, getting up to leave. At that point, I just wanted to go home, eat a frozen pizza pocket, and develop an employment plan while hopefully getting word from Rodney that Jax could have visitors again.

"Very well, you better go get a job then. Remember, I'm always around, even if I'm just a sounding board," he said as he made his way over to the bike and began to inspect the brakes.

"Thanks, Eddie. I do appreciate that," I said, understanding exactly why people would entertain suicide.

THIRTY-FIVE

I spent the better part of the stroll back to my apartment doing a masterful job of wallowing in self-pity, followed by pitying Jax, and culminating in taking a mental inventory of how much shit I was going to need to move. I was referring more to the upcoming physical move, but the amount of mental shit I had collected appeared far greater.

That was what pushed me over the edge, and I finally gave up. What else could I do? All my efforts on so many fronts had yielded precisely nothing. No matter what story I told myself, I no longer believed it. I, indeed, had nothing more to lose. And at that moment, I simply no longer cared.

If I'd learned anything, I'd learned whatever was going to happen would happen on its terms, and that's how it would have to be. I was exhausted trying to hold my self-esteem and identity together. I was determined not to build more bullshit stories and create more narratives. I would have to keep going, watch what happened next, and try to be aware of each moment the best I could. That's all I could do, and it summed up to doing nothing. And yes, the stakes were high. Insanity was a real risk, but now I had no choice but to deal with it—

what I had always thought of as sanity now seemed more insane than anything else. If sanity were purely finding an unexamined fictional narrative I could live with, I'd rather be insane than consciously decide to live life asleep—blind to reality.

I realized I was still holding Eddie's tiny notebook. I opened the first page and saw what appeared to be more of a note to Eddie than a quote.

Eddie, I put this together to keep you company on your journey. The journey home can be a lonely one. When you feel lost, open this randomly; what you may need the most will be right there for you. You may not think so, but you are the most promising student I've encountered in decades.
Pay it forward when the time is right. Safe Travels.
—The King

"The King": why did that strike me as oddly familiar?

Just then, the blinking red light from my answering machine caught my eye, causing a mild panic. Rodney may have called my house number instead of texting my cell. Maybe Jax had given him my landline. I couldn't figure out why I even bothered to have a landline. It was just a habit, I guessed. I pushed the play button and walked into the kitchen to grab some water.

"Hi, Toby. This is Babs at The Altered Ego. Can you please give me a call when you get this message? Thanks. Bye for now."

I was relieved I hadn't missed a call from Rodney but was apprehensive about calling Babs back. Maybe Gina had indeed posted a scathing Yelp review that had impacted business, and I would be sued. They were probably going to keep my final paycheck. I apprehensively dialed up the salon, bracing myself for another kick in the balls, which, luckily, I had now grown used to.

"Altered Ego Salon?" I could tell it was Jazmine.

"Hi, Jazmine. It's Toby, returning a call from Babs?"

"Oh, hi, Toby. She just walked down to her office. Let me put you on hold to see if she can take your call."

"No problem."

"Hi, Toby?" Babs asked.

"I'm afraid so," I replied.

"So Gina's attorney contacted me to notify me they would be suing us for neglect, not receiving services paid for, and a few other things."

"Not surprising. She tends to run hot. Not really one to settle down."

"Yes, I get that idea. Anyway, I explained to him we hadn't charged her, and she initiated leaving mid-treatment because she realized her ex-husband was employed here, and her embarrassment no doubt had fueled her anger. He wasn't aware of those details. Also, he seemed to understand that an argument with an employee at any establishment is not defensible in a court of law if no laws had been broken."

"I appreciate the update, but what does that all mean, Babs? I wish I could go back and change how things turned out, but I don't know what else I can do right now."

"I called to say…. Perhaps I overreacted a bit. Jazmine was replacing the towels in the hallway and heard almost everything. From what I understand, you weren't initially rude or disrespectful, and Gina exploded at you, throwing in some fairly aggressive name-calling and such. She said there was no way you would have known she was the customer, face down in the room when you entered. There was mention of potentially unnecessary sarcasm on your part, maybe even fanning the flames. Of course, given the situation, I very well may have responded similarly to such an attack." Babs stopped, creating an awkward pause that I realized was to allow me to say something.

"That pretty much sums it up. I probably shouldn't have needled her, but I was caught off guard, and my emotions got the best of me. Well, I appreciate the call, anyway," I said, somewhat comforted that I wasn't a complete scoundrel.

"One more thing, Toby. It has come to light that you weren't entirely honest about why you left your previous job. Gina mentioned, in her fury, you got terminated for pornography."

"I wish that weren't the case, but it was. I'm not a guy that whacks off to porn or spends hours wading through it because it turns me on. A coworker and I found it entertaining to try to surprise each other with increasingly more shocking and unbelievable examples. It's wrong, but it allowed us to find levity in a pressure cooker work environment. We never intended for anyone to see it, but a female coworker saw it on my buddy's screen when he was out of his office. I didn't tell you because I was sure it would kill the job opportunity. It's dishonest, but I guess I felt that I may be giving myself a chance by omitting it."

"Well, I'd like to offer you your job back if you haven't already found other employment," she said, catching me completely off guard. "I'm going out on a limb here to bring you back. Your Yelp reviews and customer referrals have improved business, and I recognize that. We will keep you focused on the male customers in the future to minimize potential client discomfort. Personally, I watch porn for pleasure and have no issue with others that do. What I do have an issue with is dishonesty. If you ever lie to me again, I'll cut your nuts off. "

This was good news. I wasn't looking at being a butthole bleaching receptionist as a career path, but weighing the choices, it was the only one I had, and my situation was certifiably desperate. For that matter, everything about me was desperate. Babs, a porn consumer? How much more bizarre could things get?

My lack of response created an audible silence. "Are you still there, Toby?" Babs asked.

"Sure. I mean... sure, I'm still here. And sure, I'll take my job back as long as we can change my title from 'Receptionist' to 'Specialist.' It just sounds more impressive, if you know what I mean. If we can do that, I swear I'll never lie to you again," I said with a laugh.

"Fair enough. You want to stage your glorious return for tomorrow at the usual time?"

"That would be great. Thanks, Babs. I appreciate you considering this."

"You do a great job, Toby, and keep morale pretty high around here, especially when it's busy and people are losing composure. I can't say you haven't been missed. OK, then tomorrow it is."

"Sounds good, Babs. Talk to you then," I said, hanging up the phone.

Well, shit. Maybe Eddie was right; the pattern of one crushing defeat after another had been temporarily broken. I didn't need the best job in the world right now. I just needed a job. Now, I could focus on my lack of permanent housing and my addict ex-girlfriend's challenges.

The idea of Babs as a sexual porn user still had me rattled, but good for her.

My mind shifted towards what had possessed Jax to get back on the black horse. Much like Babs, there had to be more going on in Jax's head than I understood. I guessed she would share when she felt she was ready. I just wanted her to feel unconditionally supported and valued by someone other than Jimmy and Summer. Often, family accepts you as you are, but that's not a clear indication the rest of the world doesn't think you're a complete piece of shit. Jax had given me that feeling of being valued despite my poor decisions and the shipwreck of my existence. I felt I owed her the same in return. However, seeing her again, even under the circumstances, reminded me how much I truly missed her. Being there for her was going to unravel any progress I may have started to make in moving on, but helping her get grounded again was much more critical.

Luckily, I was becoming quite experienced at creating future tragedies to endure. I would ultimately have the choice of disengaging with Jax again or starting a family as a lower-class bung bleacher with a recovering heroin addict for a partner. In a bad dream, at least, when you're trapped in a difficult situation, there's a chance you can wake up and have it all fade away.

I began to contemplate my housing options. Rents were skyrocketing in San Francisco. A year ago, "For Rent" signs dangled like Christmas tree ornaments decorating every block. The holiday had passed, and all the decorations appeared to be back in their boxes. Since I couldn't afford a similar hovel on my pay, I might have to find a roommate or two, an idea I hated. When you're down and out, something is appealing about having control over something somewhere in your life; for me, it was my apartment. Sharing an apartment would mean negotiating everything, being quiet late at night or early in the morning, coming home to a roommate watching what they wanted on TV, or finding the last hot pocket missing from the freezer. And then I realized that as I approached forty, I would be living the life of a college student.

Luckily, my ringing cell phone extracted me from my lackluster options. Rodney kindly informed me that Jax got a few hours of sleep and was now awake if I wanted to visit.

WHEN I ARRIVED, Jax was sitting up in bed, thumbing through what appeared to be a very old *People* magazine. It seemed to me that the last thing to leave a person on suicide watch should be a magazine that focuses on rich, famous, good-looking, happy people. The *National Enquirer* would have been more appropriate. People down on their luck seem to find stories of rich and famous people getting divorced, arrested, or generally miserable for any reason a healing tonic for their depression. Happiness, just like everything else, is relative.

Jax looked less catatonic and immediately glanced up when I walked in. Sunlight was streaming in the single large window, casting long shadows across the room.

"Thanks for coming back, Toby. I hope you didn't feel you had to, but all the same, I'm glad you did," she said, her voice still flat and monotone. I wondered how much of her physical condition versus mental space was contributing to her zombiesque persona.

"Well, I sure as hell wouldn't want to be alone if I were here. It's a pretty boring and demoralizing interior decorating theme they picked. It's completely fine if you aren't in the mood to talk. I'm happy to sit here and read my Ram Dass book that Eddie relentlessly quotes from."

"I'm happy to talk. May keep me out of my head as I can't seem to make much sense of everything yet," she said. "How is Eddie doing these days?"

"I could tell you he's fine or give you more details that could be somewhat depressing. It depends on what you're up for."

"Well, being that depression is my specialty right now, maybe the whole story. Misery loves company, especially if someone else's misery is distracting me from my own."

"I can't argue that logic. First of all, Cowboy was run over by a car and killed the other night, and I was gifted with the opportunity to witness the entire thing, including Cowboy dying in Eddie's lap on the way to the pet hospital. That's the bad news."

"Oh my God. That's horrible. Poor Eddie."

"Poor Cowboy," I said, figuring he got the worst of it.

"Obviously. I bet Eddie is crushed."

"He was, but the next day, we buried Cowboy in one of his favorite spots in Golden Gate Park, which I'm sure wasn't legal. And Eddie was back in good spirits. He seems to accept any hand he's dealt and is thankful Cowboy and him got to share part of their journey together. I almost think it hit me harder than it did him. I'm not a big fan of dogs, but I loved that little guy."

"Well, Cowboy also took a special liking to you, you have to admit," she pointed out.

"I suppose that's true," I replied, realizing that Cowboy and I did have a mutually fulfilling relationship.

"Then, a day or two later, Eddie showed up just in time to save Connor's life in a bar fight at The Plow. I'm sure it made him feel good that he could help out his best friend in a time of need."

"I didn't know they were even friends, let alone besties," she exclaimed. I didn't mention that 'bestie' was a trigger word for me, as it never failed to enrage me to hear such a stupid nickname. I decided to let it go.

"Yep. They served together in Vietnam, where Eddie had saved his life previously. That's why Eddie stays in the Inner Richmond near Connor so they can check in on each other. Sweet, huh?"

"Very sweet. Kind of like you being here for me right now. It feels good to have people care about you."

"Maybe it's a connection thing. People tend to be happier when connected to others on a myriad of levels. Life's unpredictable and serves up challenges like drinks at a happy hour. It's good to have someone that can drive you home if you get overserved, so to speak," I said.

"Some people don't know what that feels like. And others, when they realize their life is fucked, don't want to connect or burden others with their issues or admit they are falling apart, so they choose to be alone in their pain. Like me, I suppose," she said, taking the conversation to a deeper level that I was glad she was willing to let me access.

"Jax, I just want to say, don't feel obligated to discuss what you've been and are going through. Just because I'm here doesn't mean you owe me that. Of course, if you want to talk about it now or whenever, you know I'm always here for you."

"Thanks, Toby. I still need time to figure out where I'm at and where I want to end up. It's hard to be back at square one, in the hospital, our relationship over, unable to handle life without drugs, despite my intentions."

I could relate, with the exception of the drug addiction. "Jax, I suppose we are both victims of our patterns, but the sooner we see them, the less threatening they become, because we know we can get through the worst case and find a way to be whole again. We've each done it before."

"Sounds like Eddie's wisdom may be rubbing off on you. It's hard to be here with you and see you up close, knowing our longer-term journeys are taking separate paths. Quite honestly, it's a significant part of the pain I'm doing a wonderfully shitty job of dealing with. Even though being with you right now feels right, I'm only making this transition worse for both of us now." Her chin started quivering, and she turned her head away, trying to collect herself. I was at a loss as to what to say. I could be there with her only to hurt her later or let her go it alone in her darkest hour. It's like deciding to have that extra shot at the bar in the name of a good time, but yet knowing you'll be paying the fiddler the next day.

We were in pretty much the same place and had to decide whether or not to gamble for a short-term gain at the expense of the certainty of longer-term pain. It felt wrong, no matter how you looked at it, although I needed her then as much as she needed me.

Finally, I spoke, "I don't know what's best, but I know exactly how you feel. Ultimately, I'm willing to go through the pain of parting ways again if it helps you now, but not if it only makes it worse for you in the short term to wrestle with another grim challenge on the horizon. I probably need you right now as much as you need me. It would be easier for me if you were a little fatter and meaner. Then I could remain unattached to you," I said with a grin.

"Maybe I should get to work on that," she said and laughed her little laugh that, until that moment, I didn't realize how badly I missed hearing. "Maybe it's best if you check in sometime over the next few days, and we both think about what version of the relationship we could or couldn't live with before getting too comfortable falling back into our old patterns. It feels fucking wrong when I hear myself saying that out loud, but I know, inside, I have to take care of myself right now and find some hope going forward that is realistically attainable. Adult conversations like this suck."

"That they do. But if it gets dark for you, short-term help is a phone call away."

She took a deep breath and, after a loud exhale, said, "I'll call you before I reach for a needle and risk killing myself again if I figure that's the only way out."

"There's always another way out. It may be painful on many levels, but there is a path out, and if you don't think you can make the journey, I'll find the path and carry you out on my back if I have to," I said, meaning every word of it. "Nobody I care about is going to die alone under my watch. Or be tortured alive, for that matter. You are in the driver's seat here. Take whatever route makes sense. If you need me to take a turn at the wheel, wake my ass up and tell me it's my turn to drive, OK?"

"Deal." We simultaneously reached for each other's hands, as they do in the movies at just the right time, yet with forced smiles that create tiny dams to hold back the tears. "You should go now. I need to think. I feel much better and thank you for just being who you are, Toby. Knowing you're there when and if I need you…feels good."

It felt wrong to leave and right at the same time. I will check in with her tomorrow to keep the communication channel open so she won't feel awkward reaching out as more time passes. We exchanged a brief hug, and I left.

On the way through the hospital lobby, it hit me. The King! The King is what the homeless woman I saved from getting hit by the garbage truck outside the bar called that bizarre old guy in black who was standing on the suitcase. "The King! The King! He has a story just for you," she said. Then he told me that bizarre story about a guy on a mission to save himself from himself, but he didn't even know it yet. Then he said, "Safe travels," and patted my ass when I got into the Uber. That has to be the same guy who gave this book to Eddie. How many guys called "The King" are running around these days? I made a mental note to ask Eddie about him.

CHAPTER
THIRTY-SIX

The following day, after a fitful night's sleep filled with countless failed attempts to doze off, I remembered that it had been a few days since I had showered. The water cleansed my mind and filthy body, causing me to consider bathing more regularly.

I had a range of conflicting emotions concerning Jax's overdose. Regardless of which circuitous route I took to identify a possible situation that could work for us, the trail always led me to the same place. I had lost a family, and with how life was repeatedly shitting on me, I didn't trust that a new family wouldn't meet a similar demise. Ultimately, I was terrified of being a parent in another imploding family. When you're first married, the thought of your family falling apart doesn't cross your mind. You're buzzed on a cocktail of hype and hope for what's to come. After having experienced it all fall apart, fear of a repeated crushing defeat squeezes that hope and hype right out of you.

I briefly checked in with Jax, and she said she had slept well and was starting to feel a little more normal, but other than that, it was a reasonably uneventful conversation.

I then dicked around for a few hours before it was time to leave for work. On the walk over, I was slightly disappointed that I wasn't feeling more excited or at least somewhat nervous. It appeared I had developed a bit of an "I don't give a shit" attitude. Not negatively or obstinately, I just didn't care much about how things would go. At this point, I was starting to realize through my own experience that things would primarily go however the fuck they wanted, regardless of my preferences. My energy to try to control things had suddenly taken an unplanned vacation. Maybe they're talking about this when they say, "Life eventually just beat this guy down." Weirdly, it was nice not to be so invested. However, a part of me was sure that if caring couldn't stop the unfolding tragedy of my life, not caring probably wouldn't alter its course either.

Entering the salon, things appeared remarkably unchanged. I don't know why I would expect anything to be any different just because I hadn't been there for a couple of days, but a complete remodel in honor of my glorious return would have been exciting.

Jazmine and Babs were standing behind the front desk, eyes locked on the computer screen, reviewing the afternoon appointments. Feeling particularly carefree, I broke the ice with "I'm back in the crack and ready to pick up the slack," realizing that was a poor choice of words, considering the events that had led up to my involuntary departure a few days prior.

Fortunately, this greeting was met with laughter on their part and relief on mine that they hadn't connected the dots.

"Welcome back, Toby," Jazmine said, cracking her gum.

"Great to see you again, Toby," Babs said, walking out from behind the counter and giving me a somewhat formal handshake, signifying an unspoken new beginning.

"So, what's on the docket for today?" I asked.

"Jazmine and I are in back-to-backs, which is fantastic, given you are here, and we don't have to alternate watching the front. We need you to cover a lightening appointment for a MALE customer at seven o'clock. Nothing like jumping back on the horse, huh?" I figured Jax might disagree.

I wasn't expecting this and was relieved she still trusted me to effectively bleach people back to their younger years. Babs had clearly categorized the Gina incident as an outlier.

"No problem. Many employees aren't as passionate as I am about back door bleaching, so you've made a wise decision," I said with a deadpan look. After a quick chuckle, we reviewed the rest of the afternoon's appointments.

Babs excused herself to prep for her next visitor, leaving Jazmine and me alone at the counter. "Jazmine, I understand you saved my ass by sharing what you heard with Babs. I want you to know I appreciate it." Despite her quirks, Jazmine was a good soul who cared about people.

"Well, it's the least I could do. Babs was missing a few pieces of the puzzle, and I felt sorry for you. And, for the record, you have terrible taste in wives. That was one of the most uptight and...nasty women I've ever seen. She was like pure hatred marauding around in search of someone to unleash on. I suppose that's rude, but I hope you change directions in the future just because I care about you, Toby."

"I like how you worked 'marauding' in there, Jazmine. Any chance that's one of your vocabulary words?"

"Ha! YES! That was yesterday's word. But am I wrong? She seemed pretty damn hateful."

"Well, I won't disagree with you on any account there. I seem to have fantastically bad judgment in wives, but I'm working on it. Thanks for the concern, though. And if you know anyone attracted to guys with notoriously poor decision-making skills, I am available," I said with a laugh.

Jazmine committed to keeping a lookout for such a person and then dismissed herself for her three o'clock appointment, and I was again in sole command of the lobby of The Altered Ego Salon. I was 'the man' in charge upfront—the head honcho. Nothing happened without my blessing. Yes, I was a complete piece of shit, but I was no longer afraid to acknowledge that. I was also a courageous piece of shit that accepted his lot, which hopefully counted for something.

The next few hours passed without anything unusual transpiring, just greeting customers, answering the phone, and keeping the flow going.

As it started to get dark out, a large gentleman entered the lobby. When I say large, I mean about six-four or six-five, very muscular, and about thirty pounds overweight, creating a dominating presence. He wore a black motorcycle vest with no shirt underneath, perfect for displaying his thick black arm, shoulder, and chest hair. He was also wearing a little black leather biker-type captain's hat and a long pointed goatee that extended five or six inches below his chin.

If he were to fight Brad, the biker who beat up the whole bar the other night, Brad would surely receive the worst of it. That's when it occurred to me that I was the only person at The Plow that Brad knew by name, and he was aware that I was friends with Connor and RV Jeff since he saw me sitting and talking with them when I offered to pay for his drink. This was not good. He walked in, stopped, and stared directly at me, clearly indicating he was there to settle a debt. Less than two hours back into my job, we were about to have an assault in the lobby, and I would need to be hospitalized if I was lucky enough to live through it. Bikers were now becoming a daily nuisance for me.

I felt the need to say something, hoping to start a civilized conversation that wouldn't escalate, but this type of guy didn't seem like he talked a lot of things through. "Hi there. How can I help you today?" I said as if I didn't notice anything unusual about him.

"You Toby?" he asked, in a baritone so deep I wondered if there was a term for something lower than bass. Any back-pocket hope I had that I wasn't the intended recipient of a beatdown had since dissipated.

"Yes, as a matter of fact, I am," I said stupidly, forgetting to lie. I was now a confirmed target. I began considering my options: Try to hit him over the head with the computer keyboard to gain the first mover's advantage? Or make a run for the back door? Perhaps both. Keyboards weren't a frequently used weapon of choice for obvious reasons, so I opted for the back door and began to position my body for the sprint.

"That's what I thought. I'm here to see you."

This was very bad news, like when your Mom says, "Come into the kitchen. There's something I want to talk to you about." There's a chance it's nothing serious, but usually a very slim one.

"I'm Terry, your seven o'clock appointment. Was in here a while ago but didn't realize I had some pre-prep to do. Jazmine had to turn me away, but I'm high and tight and ready to roll now," he said with pride. "Figured it made sense to go with a guy this time. Don't want to make a woman feel uncomfortable again, if you know what I mean."

My mind was still in fight or flight mode, and it took me a few moments to process what he was telling me. Could it really be just a bizarre coincidence, and this guy had no affiliation with Brad or knowledge that I had witnessed a fellow biker fall in battle and that I should be killed out of principle?

"I get it. Smart choice. Why don't you head back to the second room on the left and, for lack of a better term, 'nude up.' I'll be there shortly." I couldn't help but chuckle at the humor of me just telling an intimidating biker to go nude up and wait for me. Babs and Jazmine had to be aware that this was the same customer that had elicited a cascade of vomit from Jazmine merely two weeks ago. Some welcome-back humor, at my expense. That I respected, but I was still admittedly rattled by it.

I took a few minutes to gather myself and bolster my courage, like a gymnast before starting the run to the vault. And, before I realized it, I was marching down the hall. I rapped my knuckles on the door a couple of times. "Let me know when you're ready," I said. Surprising him wouldn't be in either of our best interests.

"Ready for action!" rang out from behind the door. It crossed my mind that he might be waiting to administer a bully beat down but simply in a more private place than the front lobby. "Action" can mean a lot of different things.

I entered the room and made my way past a crumpled pile of leather boots, jeans, and what appeared to be a brand-new pair of white briefs. Either that or he took care to bleach his whites regularly. Perhaps a purchase to celebrate his newly shorn ass and soon-to-be revitalized sphincter?

He was on the bleaching table and had already assumed the position, on elbows and knees, ass pointed skyward, looking back over his shoulder, almost seductively. The thought crossed my mind that I had walked into a gay trap, my gaze shifting from his sultry look to the tattoo above his ass-crack that read, "Permission Granted."

"Funny tattoo," I admitted, doing my best to appear the confident professional.

"My old lady got it for me for Christmas just last year. She always gives such thoughtful presents."

"Very true," I admitted. "However, based on today's agenda, it would appear she isn't the only thoughtful one." Gay trap averted and beat down appearing less likely.

The circumstance I found myself in was so preposterous that I was stunned by the absurdity and unpredictability that permeated my life. Despite all my striving, struggling, and suffering over the last many months, it had deposited me here. I was in awe of the cosmic brilliance and humor of it all. And at that moment I couldn't care less. Caring hadn't served me well for quite a while now.

Moving closer, although the thick forest of ass-crack hair had indeed been clear-cut, I wasn't out of the woods just yet. The butt-hole targeted for bleaching had seen noticeable wear and tear beyond the run-of-the-mill hemorrhoid or two. I was face to face with a discolored cauliflower resembling a baby's fist.

It was a battlefield, and I wasn't fighting a mere battle here; I was fighting a war, knowing full well I was going in with inferior fire-power. I would make up for that by attacking with ferocity.

"Sorry about how beat up things are down there," he said sheep-ishly. "As an adolescent, I had a penchant for jamming things up my ass when I masturbated, ya' know?"

"Not at all uncommon," I responded to put him at ease.

"My sister's Barbie doll kind of did the trick for me," he wistfully volunteered. "She walked in on me once and lost her shit."

"Well, if you ask me, you're not much of a sister if you have a problem with your brother sticking your toys up his ass," I said, real-izing how comfortable I was in such a surreal conversation. I was enjoying the banter almost as if it was a foreplay of sorts. I figured this would at least be a good story for The Plow.

"My thoughts exactly!" he said with a firm nod. "Let the bleaching begin."

"I'm happy to warm up the bleaching cream," I offered.

After a few seconds of contemplation, he responded, "Not required. I've been training for this all my life."

"Really?"

"No, but it's funny to say," he answered with a slight giggle.

"That is super funny," I confirmed. This guy had a sense of humor.

"Terry, we'll start with a little exfoliation to ensure we get any dead skin cells out of the road, then the bleaching agent can do its best work."

"Smart idea," he said.

So I basically luffa'd his ass crack, setting the stage for the main event.

The artist was about to start another canvas. I was a master of my medium, and I applied the cream with a small soft applicator brush with laser-focused attention to detail. Skilled navigation around this jungle of flesh was not for those with fragile dispositions or weak knees.

"What happens now?" he asked.

"Terry, my friend, now we wait. It takes about twenty minutes for the secret formula to work its magic. It may tingle a little, which isn't necessarily bad and to be expected. I'm happy to leave you to yourself or hang out and chat. Whatever makes you feel more comfortable."

"Let's chew the shit. It'll make it go faster. What do you want to talk about?" he asked.

I was at a loss, and before I could come up with anything coherent, "Hey, I have a question for you. Maybe a long shot," came out of my mouth.

"Then shoot, brother."

"Do you know a biker named Brad? Big guy, like you with a Viking-like blond mustache?" I don't know what I was thinking, but it was too late. I realized by merely asking the question I was now a suspect. He would want to know how I knew Brad, and I couldn't think of any angle to position an honest answer to that. My palms were starting to sweat, and my throat already felt like it was being strangled. And even worse, he would surely tell Brad exactly where to find me.

"Yeah, I know Brad. Bad-ass motherfucker if there ever was one. However, he did get his ass profoundly kicked the other night at The Plow, down on Clement. He can't remember a thing about what happened—got his bell rung good. Funny you would ask about him, especially right after his little incident. And how exactly do you know Brad?"

"I was there. Met him before the fight broke out. Nice guy...before the fight, that is." I was stunned that my unsupervised mouth had just deposited me at the crime scene. God only knew what I'd say next.

"Well, then you know who beat his ass? If you know what I mean, I want to return the favor on Brad's behalf."

This wasn't going well, and I was starting to get dizzy, probably due to forgetting to breathe. I couldn't tell him the truth, or Eddie would get killed. I felt a stab of fear, but then something shifted. I suddenly became aware that "I" was something entirely other than this fear. The fear was just there like the chair in the room was just there, but my awareness had expanded so far beyond my thoughts and my fear that they seemed almost insignificant and fleeting. Something just opened up—and it wasn't Terry's ass-crack.

At that moment, sounds and thoughts began fading. They felt as random as anything else. I was observing them in the same manner as observing my surroundings, the smells of disinfectant, the biker's bleaching anus pointed at the ceiling, and the siren outside as the ambulance passed. Everything just came and went, but I was just the pure, unchanging awareness that housed all of it. It was as if I had just woken up from a long, bizarre dream.

There was no longer a sense of me as I knew myself before; however, everything was as much me as anything else, arising, silently present, and then disappearing. Words are symbols and can only approximate the experience, but there aren't words that describe ultimate reality. The concept of "me," as the individual I had always identified with, was replaced with perfect stillness. I was simultaneously everything all at once in perfect synchronization, like the gears of a fine Swiss watch, humming silently behind the scenes, while I was also complete nothingness.

Everything was perfect and was the only way it could ever be. I was the bleacher, the bleaching cream and the anus, and so much more. The clarity was blinding and more natural than anything I had ever known. Everything was exquisitely interconnected, one perfect whole dancing with and in itself, and I was the setting, the dancer, and the entire dance. There was no such thing as *other*.

I spontaneously uttered a gentle hum, like an extended Om, but not much of the "O" part, just a perfect "M" vibration, harmonizing with the sound of all of reality, the energy of this whole creation. It was like coming home after a long journey and remembering what and who I had always been behind the dream I thought was my life.

"Never seen the guy before," I noticed my mouth speaking of its own accord. "I understand he was some special forces guy who had just stepped in. Also, I've never seen a guy move that fast. The dude left immediately afterward. Wish I knew more." I was relieved that Eddie had remained anonymous in this unplanned outburst.

"Well, no matter how tough you are, there's always someone tougher. Maybe Brad'll think twice in the future," he said optimistically.

At this point, the fear was nowhere to be found. Just the awareness that all my drama and personal identity had all been only me playing an endless game of hide and seek with myself on so many levels. I could only laugh like a madman at the exquisite comedy of the whole game.

"What's so funny?" Terry asked.

"Sorry, but it amazes me how much effort people put into grooming, skin and nail care, and working out, and yet very few are detail-oriented enough to take care of their sphincters when it's such an easy thing to do."

"Agreed, my good brother!" Terry responded to my fictitious answer.

I continued to revel in the awareness that everything I had ever been seeking on this journey with Eddie had always been there, patiently waiting behind the scenes, but now the seeker no longer existed. What happened next didn't matter; the past and future were illusions of thought. The only reality, if anything was real, was the eternal, ever-changing present instant, which was the totality of who "I" really was. I laughed again. It was all me, and I was all of it and always had been.

My beliefs, aspirations, and my regrets were gone. I was only here, and I was only now, and there was no such thing as other. Terry, his bleach-filled cranny, my body, and all the sights and sounds in that room were one wonderfully playful dance of consciousness.

We then changed topics, talking about the gentrification of the Western Addition neighborhood that had recently been rebranded as North Panhandle. Then we talked about all the high-tech yuppies infiltrating South of Market and how San Francisco was going down the shitter. There was a brief discussion about the challenges of marriage (Terry was on his second wife) and the absurd gas prices. It was all perfectly normal, and it was all perfectly sublime.

We were interrupted by the ding of the timer as we debated the pros and cons of the space program's expense, given the pressing infrastructure needs in the US.

"OK, shall we see how we did? Just be forewarned: a second application is often necessary. If we tried to do it all in one treatment, we'd have to leave the lightener on longer, and it would burn your skin," I informed him. "I'm confident we'll see an impressive difference, however."

I proceeded to remove the bleach and get him good and cleaned up, taking extra caution to get all the nooks and crannies. It was indeed my finest work yet. "Terry, it looks like we've taken twenty years off your anus," I proudly informed him.

"Let me see," his voice as giddy as a schoolgirl's. I positioned the hand mirror so he could peer down between his legs and admire the excellence of my work. "Fucking A right! Damn, you're good at your craft, my friend. Damn good. I've been waffling on doing this for five years and wish I hadn't waited so long."

I appreciated his respect, basking in the thrill of his big win. "Alright, buddy, the back door has been restored to its former glory. I'd still recommend a final touch-up, as there's a good chance we could get it a shade lighter. I'll let you get dressed and meet you up front, OK?"

"Sounds good, my man," he said, climbing down from the table as I exited the arena, victorious.

A few minutes later, Terry arrived up front to settle his bill. Babs walked up just in time to watch Terry put an extra fifty-dollar tip in my hand. Noticing Babs, he said, "This guy's a master of his trade. You got a good man here who deserves a raise." At a loss for words, Babs raised her eyebrows in surprise, and a smile slowly worked its way across her face.

"Pleasure was mine, Terry. Thank you for your business. It was great to meet you. Do you want to make an appointment for your follow-up session now or call? It's best to wait at least a week as it could be sensitive." I asked.

"Why don't I monitor the sensitivity and then give you a call when it seems ready for round two?" he answered, giving me a solid fist bump.

"Fair enough. Wipe easy, my brother," I said, realizing Terry was a good man, not to mention a dedicated husband. It felt damn good to help relieve another's suffering. The unfamiliar feeling of gratitude swept over me in a loving embrace.

The door closed with the jingle of the bell, shortly followed by the low roar of what was surely Terry's Harley rumbling to life.

Babs informed me that she had to finish payroll and asked if I could close up front as Terry was our last appointment. Jazmine had finished her last session when I was tending to Terry's tush and had already left for the day. Retreating to her office, Babs left me alone in the lobby.

I turned off the "Open" sign and shut the blinds, and things continued to shift. My thoughts were barely noticeable and almost non-existent. The colors were vivid, like a sunrise on an early spring day when the greenery is surreal, contrasting a sapphire blue sky dotted with artificially white fluffy clouds. A quiet permeated everything, although there was no lack of noise emanating from the busy street outside.

The pure connection to everything blew my heart wide open, and I felt a love that exceeded even the strongest I had ever felt for my own children. Tears began to cascade down my face. I understood everything was perfect; all that had ever been and ever would be. And even that description severely fails to effectively communicate this new orientation.

My body was now packing up my stuff, putting my backpack on, and shutting out the lights, and it was all just happening, unprompted and thought-free.

Duality had dissolved, and although nothing had changed, nothing was remotely the same.

That's the best I can describe it: the final dissolution of Toby Tenderhill and the simultaneous birth of everything. The gratitude for being able not just to witness this new world but actually "be" it was and would be a gift that kept giving itself each moment.

At first, I questioned if it would fade, but it never did; only the questioning eventually dissolved.

Sure, my brain still worked to navigate life's logistics, but it no longer mattered what had happened or would happen next because those concepts were no longer real to me, just passing illusions of the mind. I would later talk and interact with people and go about my day, but that would unfold without premeditation. The action just flowed and was intuitively appropriate.

Eddie had been chipping away at the illusions that fettered me to a belief that I was a separate and broken individual. Eventually, my shell had become so thin it finally cracked open. Eddie lived in this space and, of course, couldn't describe it. It wasn't anything to be attained. Like he had said over and over, it wasn't additive. It was there all along. It was just masked by the baggage of all my concepts of who I believed I was and what I thought the world and myself to be.

I closed and locked the front door behind me and began the walk home, appreciating every car, tree, person, and store as if I were seeing them all for the first time.

I spent the remainder of the evening working through a week's worth of unopened mail, mostly junk, and paying a couple of utility bills. I began looking at apartments for rent on Craig's List and Facebook Marketplace. I talked to property managers and left messages. Later, I called Jax. Jimmy answered because she was asleep, which was not surprising as it was nine-thirty. He felt she was getting back to normal, at least physically, which was a good first step. I asked him to let her know I'd stop by midmorning tomorrow.

My mind worked as a tool to sort through things, plan a few

things, and converse with people; otherwise, it remained blissfully calm. A few routine thoughts would lightly surface and fade away, like steam, when removing the lid from a heated pot on the stove.

Before retiring, I grabbed my copy of Ram Dass's *Be Here Now* book and flipped it open one last time:

To him that has had the experience, no explanation is necessary, to him who has not, none is possible.

I gratefully laughed myself to sleep.

THIRTY-SEVEN

I awoke the following morning quite late, considering I had retired relatively early the night before. After entering the kitchen and unplugging my phone from the charger, I was pleased to see I already had four new voicemails. I quickly returned the calls, all from property management companies, and discussed the available apartments relevant to my needs. It was a tight rental market, but I had several options to consider.

Pouring water into the coffee pot, I changed course and decided to have coffee with Eddie instead. Things were different and still unfamiliar, although in many ways, more familiar than ever. I was eager to share with him and get his perspective on the shift that had transpired.

Brian was ascending the front stairs as I exited the building. As usual, he was dressed professionally in a blue pinstriped oxford shirt and khaki slacks, his hair neatly styled, and had a clean shave.

"Good morning, Brian," I said, walking down the stairs to meet him halfway.

"Hey, Toby. How's the apartment search going? Happy to be a

reference, you know?" Brian was actually a good guy, dealing with the challenges of his job like anyone else.

"I've been considering a few options, and I'm pretty sure I've got something figured out," I said contemplatively, with very little actual contemplation.

"Awesome. That was quick. Well, I don't want to keep you, but reach out if there is anything I can do."

"If it's any advantage to the owner, I would consider moving out early if he's willing to refund a prorated portion of the rent for this month, along with my deposit." This seemed fair.

"Let me check on that. He very well may, as I know he plans on doing some small renovations before his niece moves in and he doesn't have much of a window. I'll give him a call and let you know later today, one way or the other."

"Much appreciated. That will help in my planning—and one more thing. Thanks for being professional throughout all this. I'm sure it's not the most enjoyable part of your job." Fascinatingly, I had said something nice to Brian. Equally as fascinating, I did feel appreciative.

"No, it's not, but thanks. That feels good to hear. I'm trying my best," he said, continuing up the stairs into the building.

It was clear and crisp out, with an unusual offshore breeze. It was going to be a warm day. "Perfectly San Francisco," I said aloud as I contentedly strolled down Clement Street to The Blue Danube.

Jimmy was behind the counter, working on what appeared to be an order of avocado toast.

"Top of the morning to you, Jimmy!" I said, startling him.

"Oh hey, Toby. You snuck up on me. Give me just a second. I'm almost done here." He finished up, ran an order to one of the outside tables, and returned behind the counter. "What can I get you?"

"It's a good day to break my routine," I enthusiastically announced. "How about a triple oat milk latte with three squirts of that sugar-free vanilla syrup and a good amount of ground chocolate on top? Make that two. I've got to stop by a friend's."

"Coming right up. And by the way, thanks for checking in on Jax. I honestly think it's done more good for her than anything else. Contrary to popular belief, you're a good man, Toby," he said jokingly.

"Perhaps you're not giving enough credit to popular belief. Don't thank me like I'm doing anyone a favor. I couldn't not be there with her. Regardless of our relationship status, I can't help but love the woman. I'm going to head over there later this morning."

"I told her you'd be stopping by. Oh, I forgot to tell you. She said to wake her up if she's asleep."

"Sounds good. How are Jade and Summer doing?" I asked.

"Mama and baby are doing great. Man, I've never felt more exhausted. Sleep deprivation is a real ass-kicker, and Jade sleeps longer than most newborns."

"I've been there. It'll leave you pretty raw," I said, reflecting on those early days of parenthood, some of my life's most demanding and best days, wrapped up together like a bittersweet present: not exactly what you wanted, but much better than you expected. I supposed I'd repressed the joyful parts to protect me from missing the kids any more than I had to.

Jimmy came around from behind the counter, set the coffees down, and gave me what I considered an aggressive man-hug, complete with unnecessarily firm back slaps. "These are on the house. You have no idea how much I appreciate you," he said with what I swore were tears welling up in his eyes. I gave him another hug.

"Thanks, Jimmy. Very kind of you."

Eddie was sitting down reading the paper when I arrived, wearing what appeared to be new and remarkably clean navy blue Carhart work pants and new white Stan Smith sneakers. However, he stayed true to his no-sock policy and wore his familiar old red-hooded sweatshirt and stocking cap.

"Top of the morning, Toby," he said, setting down his paper.

"That's exactly what I just said to Jimmy, and top of the morning to you too, Eddie." I sat down next to him without waiting for an invitation and handed him his coffee. "Epic day, huh?"

"About as good as it gets. Thanks for the coffee; it smells good. I'm reading here about how bad the homeless problem is in San Francisco. Guess that makes me part of the problem. I consider myself upper class on the homeless spectrum after reading this, mainly because I'm able to refrain from panhandling, crapping on sidewalks, and leaving needles and garbage around."

"Well, as far as homelessness goes, you're definitely in the upper crust. Don't let it go to your head, though," I warned.

"I don't know what the hell is wrong with these people that do that crap. It's just disrespectful. It's mostly the addicts and the mentally ill, I suppose," he said, taking a sip of his coffee. "Damn, something different. This tastes fancy. Thank you."

"The pleasure is mine."

"You know, it's not that tough to manage out here. Easier than camping—more like backpacking when I think about it. Anyway, I'm sure you didn't come here to discuss the state of the destitute. How've you been since I last saw you? You look a lot less rattled today."

"It's been interesting, to say the least. And yes, I wouldn't consider myself rattled at all right now. Are you sure you want the details? I'm happy to continue talking about current events."

"The suspense is palpable. Sure, I want to hear what's on your mind," he said with full attention. "Your updates are the favorite part of my day."

"Let me run down the list. Jax is doing better. She's sleeping and talking, and she has her color back. We haven't delved into all the details of what brought her to the darkness that caused her to OD, but I didn't want to push her."

"I imagine she's sorting things out in her head first to get to a place where she can make sense of it. I'm sure she'll tell you more when she's ready, but what do I know?"

"Well, usually a lot more than most. Check this out: Babs from The Altered Ego Salon called me back, reconsidered my shit-canning, and gave me my job back. Even changed my title from Receptionist to Specialist," I proudly informed him.

"That's great. And what exactly do you specialize in?"

"Skin lightening, which, between us, is mostly anal bleaching. Kind of a butthole beautician," I said nonchalantly. "Of course, people do it for armpits, inner thighs, etc. Not glorious, but it does feel good to put people at ease and give them a warm, positive experience versus a potentially embarrassing one."

"I imagine you'd be good at that. Never underestimate the little interactions that can have a big impact on someone else's day," he responded, half joking.

"As always, right on the money. Maybe 'Eddie Money' would be a good nickname for you."

"I'd probably be mugged in the first ten minutes and every ten minutes after that," he said, laughing. Eddie had abandoned the paper entirely and was sitting cross-legged with his elbows on his knees, his chin resting on his hands. He seemed to have sensed or known something more significant was coming.

"Get this. So, yesterday was my first day back on the job, and I had to help with a bleaching appointment. I was happy to be back at work and in a good mood, but that's beside the point. Then this biker comes in, who looks a lot like Brad, that guy you fast-tracked to the hospital the other night. This other biker, Terry, knows Brad, it turns out. Anyway, I'm sure he's trying to find out who put the beatdown on his buddy because someone must have tipped him off where I worked and that I was at the bar that night. Oh, and he has no idea who administered Brad's beatdown, so don't be concerned for your wellbeing."

"I'm not," Eddie interrupted. "But go on."

"Ends up, he was my bleaching appointment. Anyway, I'm bleaching this beast of a guy's anus, as us Specialists do, and without thinking, I blurt out something about Brad, and Terry starts asking about who beat his ass and wanting to return the favor. I'm now scared shitless. And BOOM, everything shifts, and I'm not talking about an earthquake. I'm not me anymore. I mean, I'm much more than, for lack of a better term, 'the old me' and at the same time so much less. All the internal resistance to myself, life, others, my emotions, my identity, and the beliefs I was struggling to fortify just dissolved. They were never anything more than thought-constructed illusions.

"The 'I' that I had always thought myself to be was just this tangled mess of resistance I'd accumulated against reality on so many levels and had become completely identified with. When all that resistance dissolved, who I'd become to believe myself to be disappeared with it. Totally gone! What emerged was just a vast emptiness that is pure awareness, connected to everything in a seamless whole. Pure loving awareness of the perfection of absolutely everything with nothing painted on top of it anymore. It was as if the universe allowed itself to wake up and see itself clearly through these eyes. It feels so familiar, but in an almost ancient way, like it has never been anything other than this.

"Thoughts were happening as they are still right now, but within that all-encompassing clarity that ties everything together. That sense of me being separate from everything else just evaporated. Everything was perfect, and nothing needed to be done, although everything kept unfolding on its own." I struggled to explain it, and as the words came out, I realized I wasn't doing a very good job.

"Seems like a good first day back, all things considered," Eddie said.

"Not bad at all. As this massive transformation was happening, I ended up having a great chat with him, just enjoying my job and making jokes, and his back door turned out really good. More importantly, he was pleased. He even gave me a nice tip. I felt absolutely calm and just glad to be there versus lamenting my relegated profession.

"I can keep describing it, but at the same time, I can't. It seems like there aren't adequate words that fit the experience," I said.

"Of course you can't use words to describe it! Words always require a subject and an object. They force us to remain in a dualistic mindset and world. But let me give it a try if you think it may help?"

"Go for it. Please."

"'Unity' is the closest I've come, but that is still a symbol of a concept that requires the mind to think it." Eddie paused and, after a moment's consideration, continued. "For 'you' to experience 'unity,' it requires the subject of you and the object of unity being something else to be experienced by 'you,'" he said, licking his finger and rubbing a streak off his new sneakers. "'You are unity' is the best way to say it, but to anyone who hasn't experienced that, it sounds stupid, right?"

"Right! It does. No wonder it was so hard for you to try to beat it into my head: Thinking is not being."

"The irony is that you have always been 'it.' You had forgotten your true nature, a cosmic game of hide-and-seek, where the 'isness' that we all are loses itself within itself, only to eventually awaken to find itself again. That's the only point of it all—the experience of being. Everything else is simply beautiful distractions in ever-expanding layers. Welcome home!"

"Ha, that's what it feels like, doesn't it?" I said, appreciating his ability to articulate what I was struggling to describe. "It's just hard to take life so seriously anymore."

"It's fascinating. It's all so simple that we just simply forgot," he said.

"Does it ever go back? Is it permanent or a temporary thing?" I asked.

"Depends. Sometimes, people have a transitionary or integration period where they may fluctuate as their identity shifts in and out of being the individual. Now that you've had the experience, however, you would quickly recognize these fluctuations and, over time, permanently reside as, basically, loving awareness. But others may immediately remain aware of their true nature and don't lose themselves in the dream anymore. Either way is fine," he explained.

"What kind of surprises me is that I'm a lot more compassionate now," I said, shaking my head and realizing that when you connect with the totality of everything, you also gain a loving appreciation for everything. "It's funny how there is only one word for love in our language; however, the meaning I'd associated it with in the past isn't anything like what I'm experiencing now."

"That's most likely because you no longer experience yourself as a separate isolated thing loving some other separate isolated thing. It's no longer a subject, verb, object experience. It's no longer conditional. People love the best they can, but mostly it's dependent upon other people, pets, the weather, or whatever, conforming to their idea of how those other aspects of reality 'should' manifest. When you have a partner who doesn't tell you what you want to hear, has different ideas about what's important, or a pet that doesn't come when you call, suddenly you feel a lot less love because, in that reality, it all pertains to how it serves 'you' and what 'you' want from that moment. Despite what people say, it's most often conditional, and there is still an idea of 'the other' in relation to the individual."

"Excellent point. People love whatever gives them the feelings they want, but when that changes, love usually goes out the window."

"Precisely. Therefore, it can always be lost, isn't dependable, or needs to be different in some way. When it's all one connected whole, you feel yourself from many perspectives, and a sense of compassion for suffering surfaces," he said, pausing to take another sip of coffee. "It's all love, just different degrees of awareness that dictate our capacity to experience its potential. Love isn't something that comes and goes or can be given or taken away, is it?"

"Nope. It's the one thing holding it all together."

"Bingo. When we understand the illusion and how it works, it loses its pull, yet it's still fucking majestic, all the same."

"Right. Exactly!"

"It's a thing of beauty, Toby. I'm just grateful for the experience of being here as a witness and participant in this fantastic play. However it pans out, that's fine with me. I don't have ideas about what's good or bad, or right or wrong, because those thoughts seldom come up anymore, and when they do, they fade quickly," he shared.

I wished he'd shared his experience of this reality earlier, but at the same time, I knew it wouldn't have helped. It's like someone telling you about skydiving. You can understand it, but not having had the experience, all you can do is try to relate it to your own limited experiences, but that's just a thought game. You still don't know what that specific experience feels like. He had been helping me to clean the glass so I could see through it rather than telling me what it looked like from the other side, which would have left all the filth still in the way.

"Again, welcome home, my friend. So what's next for you now?" he asked.

"I guess we'll see how it unfolds, and I'll just be there to experience whatever I end up doing or not doing. For now, I'll keep working at the salon and move from my apartment since there's no choice."

"What about Jax?" he asked, standing up to stretch his legs.

"I don't know. I'll be anxious to see how that plays out. For now, I'll be there for her in whatever way seems helpful and appropriate. All I can do is love her. I'd prefer if she could find a content place to live from; however, I'll also accept her if she can't."

"I think that sounds about right." He was now brushing off the seat of his pants and examining his new shoes. "When are you going to visit her again?"

"Right now. I've got a couple of hours before work and nothing else time-sensitive," I answered, getting up to head out.

"Please say hello to her for me. Would you?"

"Of course. And Eddie?"

"Yeah?"

"In that little notebook you gave me, which I need to get back to you, the inscription on the front was signed by 'The King.' Who is 'The King?'"

Eddie laughed. "The King is an old friend of mine who was instrumental in helping me figure myself out after I returned from the war."

"A guy dressed in black from head to toe, black trench coat, and a black fedora with a red feather tucked in the side of the band?" I asked.

"You must have heard about him. Yep, that's The King, alright. I owe him a debt of gratitude."

"Why is that?" I asked.

"Like I said, our paths intersected shortly after I returned from Nam. I had PTSD, couldn't make sense out of life anymore, and was depressed and pretty much lost. Took me under his wing and helped me find my true self."

"I saw this guy, and someone referred to him as 'The King' right about when I got fired and things started to go to shit. He told me a bizarre story about a person on a journey he didn't realize he was on. I think the last thing he said to me was 'safe travels' after he gave me a pat on the ass. The thought never occurred to me that the story he was telling me was my own story."

"Hmm. Maybe that slap on the ass kickstarted your journey home. He was always a bit flamboyant. He is someone who has demonstrated the ability to affect physical reality. Rumors are he can make the wind stop and start, doesn't age, and other crap that's mostly rumors. Smart enough not to identify with that shit and let it suck him back into some bullshit spiritual ego-trip."

"Eddie, I owe you a debt of gratitude as well."

"Bullshit."

"You took my hand, walked me through hell, led me to freedom's gate, and waited with me until it opened. Call it grace or whatever you want, but I was lost or believed myself to be. You opened my mind just enough for me to find myself. I've got to say I love you, buddy."

"It's what I guess I was left on this earth to do," he replied, smiling. "Pay it forward someday if the opportunity presents itself."

"Have there been others?" I asked.

"Oh yes. A few. And there may be more. I hope so, but if not, that's cool. Now go see your lady," he said, waving me off.

THIRTY-EIGHT

I t was indeed a glorious day. People scurried around, completing their errands. I walked by a fish market that emanated the musty smell that only trays of dead fish on ice can produce. An employee of The Green Apple bookstore wheeled out the sale racks they positioned out front. One dollar each. I made a mental note to return to find a good novel to enjoy. I passed the fabric store where Jax worked or perhaps had worked, not knowing what fallout may or may not have occurred since she'd been missing in action. I was sure Jimmy had apprised them of her current situation by now. I turned the corner, and the smell of honeysuckle and rose caught my attention. I was standing outside a small flower shop and decided to pick up a nice bouquet for Jax.

After securing a bouquet of white lilies, peonies, and sunflowers for Jax, I saw a lovely bouquet of tulips, which reminded me of Gina. They were always her favorites. I decided *what the hell* and bought that one too and asked them to send it to my old home address with a note:

"There is too much to apologize for, but I can validate that you were right about me and my consuming melodrama when you said life is more

about who a person is than about what they achieve. Too bad the insight fell on deaf ears. I wish you the best and hope you find the happiness you deserve."

When I arrived at Jax's room, the door was open, and I found her sitting in bed watching the TV mounted high on the wall opposite her. Although she looked a little better, she still looked like she'd been through the wringer, but all I could see was a beautiful soul bravely engaged in the fight of her life, and I loved her for it.

She was consumed by a rerun of The Family Feud, hosted by the infamous Richard Dawson, who was not so briefly kissing each and every female contestant right on the mouth during the introductions.

Jax looked over, exhaled a relieved sigh, and produced a sincere grin. "Oh, Toby, those flowers are beautiful. That's very thoughtful."

Not seeing any other flowers in the room, I asked, "Are you even allowed to have flowers here?"

"They will likely put them in a plastic vase so I don't risk hurting myself." I handed them to her, and she inhaled a deep breath, taking in the aroma that must have been a refreshing contrast to the sterile hospital air.

"How's it going?" I asked.

"Much better. It seems eating and sleeping are good for the human body," she said with a tint of sarcasm.

"I think I read something about that once."

"They've been sending a shrink a couple of times a day to help me process this and identify the catalysts facilitating my demise," she informed me as she motioned me to sit down. I pulled the chair next to her bed as she positioned the flowers in the crook of her arm to continue enjoying their fragrance.

"So, is the therapy helping at all?" I asked.

"At first, it seemed invasive and annoying. After about the third session, it did seem to help. Until then, I was trying not to think about any of it, which I've learned is a typical defense mechanism that doesn't help."

"That's good, I guess. Right?"

"It is. I realized I had nothing to lose opening up about it all. The worst case isn't much worse than how I arrived. So, I decided not to resist and see how it goes. It's not all pretty, but at least I can now do a better job articulating it," she said with another hearty exhale.

She continued. "I realized you've been kind not to pry, but I feel I owe you much more of an explanation. My therapist says I have a tendency to not let people in, especially if I'm struggling within myself. I don't even let myself in most of the time."

"Well, you don't owe me anything. We can talk about it all day or not at all. If I'm honest, I have no idea what's helpful, and I don't want to inadvertently make things any harder for you than they already are." The circumstances aside, I relished the comfortable familiarity of simply being with her.

"That's sweet, and I appreciate your honesty, but I'm going to share the crux of it, and I want you to know before I start that this is all my issue to fix. I don't expect you to do or say anything, although, in a way, you are very much involved." I reached out and wrapped my hand around hers. Whatever she was about to share, quite honestly, I knew I would be OK with. Most of all, I was just glad she was willing to open up, and I could meet her in a space that I'm sure wasn't pleasant to endure alone.

Jax continued, "I'm not going to beat around the bush. I love you more than I was willing to admit even to myself. You opened the door to a deep level of intimacy, and I was scared to walk through. Up until you, I had never had a functional relationship. I'd never felt unconditionally accepted. Subconsciously, I had decided that you must not really know me, because if you did, you wouldn't be so smitten. As cliché as it sounds, I felt it had to be too good to be true. If I didn't love myself, how would it be possible for anyone else to love me? I didn't trust it would last, but a part of me desperately hoped it could."

How bizarre that we had both been going through the same

internal gyrations trying to protect ourselves from what we believed were our worst-case scenarios.

"You made life fun and meaningful. You made love safe, but I kept waiting for the other shoe to drop, and of course, it did—when you shared that you didn't see another family in your future. I guess I assumed that since you'd already had kids, a traditional family was something you valued. After we discussed it, I knew we had to go our separate ways, but internally, it set me off on a chain reaction." Jax stopped to gather herself, taking another deep breath and squeezing my hand tightly.

She continued, "My previous beliefs about me being not worthy of love, feeling destined to be alone, and feeling selfish for letting the idea of future children ruin the most hopeful relationship I've ever had all surfaced and pulled me right into my deepest insecurities and fears. I didn't see a way out and couldn't fathom dealing with the same cycle repeating itself again. The long and short of it was I found myself trapped in a life that, in my opinion, was no longer worth living. I was trying in vain to keep my head above water, but I could tell by the intensity of the struggle I was going to drown in the undertow of my fear and depression. I know that isn't rational and is fucked up, but the intensity of the feelings was much more convincing than any other logic." Jax paused and looked down, trying to resist breaking down so she could finish.

I started to speak, and she cut me off with a shake of her head. "I need to finish first. Just hear me out. So, the other night, I was wandering around with all of that ricocheting around in my head, and before I knew it, I was at the doorstep of my old dealer. I had numbed myself into a state of hopelessness and, subconsciously, needed an out. I needed to get high, even just for a little while, to escape. So I bought some smack, went home, and shot up like I was on autopilot. It was an old coping mechanism that I was familiar with, and I knew the decision would only make things worse, but, at the time, I was willing to trade that for a break from the pain. Once an addict, always an addict, I guess. Anyway, I stupidly didn't take the time to consider the dosage. I injected my usual amount, failing to consider I had been clean for eighteen months, and my tolerance had gone way down. As a result, I OD'd, and Jimmy, bless his soul, found me shortly before I would have died." Jax could no longer dam the tears and started crying. Not wailing or shaking, just tears of defeat. Tears of a reluctant acceptance of failure to control what was most important to her. I could feel her pain from the inside out. The intensity of an animal being trapped in a cage, eventually realizing, despite effort and hope, there was no way out.

I was in there with her, feeling her feelings and her shame, and it was OK. We were connected in this place where she didn't have the strength to stand alone, and I would buttress her until she could. I can only assume she felt the same as she leaned over and hugged me, long, hard, and blissfully silent. A loving hug that triggered a sense of unfettered gratitude. In that hug, the marrow of life. Connecting with her on multiple levels, the pain was as intense as the pleasure. We were alive, sharing this exquisite existence; for better or worse, it was a gift.

I could feel the wetness of her tears starting to soak through my shirt sleeve. This time, when I began to speak, she didn't stop me. With no clear idea of what to say, I watched and witnessed myself lovingly speaking my truth. "Jax, remember that movie *Brokeback Mountain?*"

"Please don't tell me you're gay. Turning lovers to the other gender would definitely put a candle on top of my layer cake of relationship failures."

I couldn't help but laugh. "Jax, every time I see you, I double down on my heterosexuality. Where I was going with the *Brokeback Mountain* thing is that cliché line, 'You complete me.' Not in a codependent way. It's more of a....it couldn't be any other way type of way. When you're ready, or if you find yourself ready, I'd love to love you in any way that works. And you know what?"

"What?"

"I've realized that being with you is much more important than

I ever thought. I'm starting to see things from a different perspective now. I guess what I'm getting at is if, at some point, we are together and having a family is an option, that's just all the more love to experience. Since I'm in a transition period, I don't think it's a prudent short-term decision. A certain amount of stability helps as a foundation for a relationship and certainly for having children. I guess what I'm getting at is—now I'm open to however it unfolds."

I certainly wasn't expecting any of that to shoot out of my mouth, but it did, and as I said it I knew it was true. Every word of it. Plus, it sounded Hollywood romantic, which was as cool as it was out of character for me.

"Toby, I don't know what to say. After all this, I have no idea if I want kids or not right now. If I can't figure my shit out, I have no business bringing a little human being into this world. Just thinking of anything beyond tomorrow is overwhelming. But I would like us to take it one day at a time without creating expectations for each other. Let's just see where it goes. I know I need to feel loved...to really believe I'm loved...and more importantly, I need to give love to somebody I trust."

"Well, ironically, I'm all about love as of late, so we're on the same path." I was in disbelief as to what had just transpired, but as Eddie says, when patterns break, doors open. You have to be paying attention to see them. And I was paying attention. Finally. "Thank you for overdosing. Impressive sacrifice you made to bring us here right now, ready to go wherever life takes us. The universe works in funny ways sometimes, huh?"

"Ha ha. But there may be some truth tucked in there somewhere. Still, I can't advocate an overdose as a best practice," she said with a smile.

By this time, Richard Dawson had moved well beyond molesting his contestants. Things had advanced to the bonus round, recapturing our attention. Our conversation shifted to lighter topics, and it was good to see her laughing again.

I DIDN'T TELL Jax about the dramatic shift in my awareness that had taken place. It just didn't seem appropriate yet, given her current challenges. After a couple of hours, we said our goodbyes, and I promised to check in on her the following day.

I ventured forth to an uneventful day at work, not requiring my specialist skills, relegating me to the joy of simply meeting and greeting people at the front desk.

That night, I treated myself to a McRib sandwich, which I vowed not to make a habit of again. Fuck, it still tasted delicious. Perhaps God's most outstanding achievement and gift for those open enough to receive it. There was a message on my machine from Brian when I got home, letting me know the owner was OK with an earlier move-out.

I effortlessly relaxed into a dreamless sleep. Tomorrow would be a big day.

CHAPTER
THIRTY-NINE

My alarm went off at 8 a.m., and I found myself exceedingly well-rested.

On the way into the bathroom, it occurred to me that I no longer cared one way or the other how beat-up, discolored, and generally threatening my anus may appear. Although I was suddenly content with the cards I'd been dealt, I had a hunch that I was curious to validate. Assuming the usual position and ensuring the lighting was consistent with previous photo shoots, I snapped a quick selfie. My suspicions were indeed correct. Pretty and pink and pristine. I chuckled to myself and the universe as I stood up, buttoning my jeans.

Today was the big move day. It was sunny and warm again without a stitch of wind, and the sky was a sapphire blue. It had rained last night, and everything smelled perfectly alive—the salty ocean air mixed perfectly with the scent of dog shit a woman was cleaning off the sidewalk. I was only wearing a t-shirt, and the sun on my arms was already warm, but not yet enough to draw a sweat.

I wouldn't be moving far, but it was exciting that something else significant was about to change at a foundational level in my life, mirroring all the other changes in the mental, emotional, and spiritual (for lack of a better term) realms of my existence. It was liberating.

I didn't have much to move. Jimmy had offered to let me put a couple of boxes of non-essentials like old yearbooks, photo albums, and a few sentimental belongings in his basement, which was generous. He told me he always felt that a fresh start was often better with less of your past weighing you down, so I took him up on his offer, and he stopped by to get the two boxes first thing.

I finished one last important errand to pick something else up. After which I turned in my keys to Brian and got my deposit back and the partial month's rent refund.

I walked around the corner, looking at everything with a sense of wonder and awe that this world could even exist, let alone with such diversity and beauty.

I rolled my shopping cart up next to Eddie's.

"Mind if we join you for a while?" I said as Eddie turned around.

"Stay as long as you'd like, Toby. I enjoy your company," Eddie answered.

"I will then."

"Who's that?" Eddie asked as a smile spread wide across his lips.

"That's our new dog, Eddie. A rescue I just picked up about an hour ago when I still had an address," I said with a wink. "It's a girl."

"It sure is. What's her name?" he eagerly asked.

"Cowgirl."

ACKNOWLEDGMENTS AND AUTHOR'S NOTES

Any author knows that writing a book is a lonely and solitary journey. Spending time alone leaves the mind with plenty of opportunities to question and doubt itself and provide overwhelming rationalizations for giving up. That's probably why fewer than two percent of new authors' books are published.

I had decided to give up multiple times. I was lost, discouraged, and overwhelmed by the amount of work and had no idea how to bring it together. In these darkest hours, my wife Linda and two daughters, Mia and Piper, and Linda's mother, Carolyn, believed in me more than I ever once believed in myself and showed no doubt that I would figure it out and get this thing published. Their unconditional support changed my mind every time I quit this project. They may have thought I was an incurable optimist during this project, but they had no idea how rattled I often was. Family carries you when you can't carry yourself, and their love carried me to the end. This book wouldn't have been without their unwavering confidence and support in me.

Lucky for me, others were also willing to pick me up off my knees and move this project forward. I'll start at the beginning.

The book started with only a title. A dear friend of over thirty years, Stephen Ladd, and I came up with a title and a tagline that struck us as so funny that we vowed to someday write a book for no other reason than to publish the title. If I'm being honest, I think Stephen came up with the title, and I laughed a lot, validating that it was the right one despite neither of us having the slightest idea what the book would be about and neither one of us having ever written a sentence of fiction.

Years passed, and not a word was written, nor was any content discussed. However, Stephen was then hard at work on his own book, *Spiritual Constipation: How to Get Shift Moving*, which inspired me to take a stab at writing *Zen and the Art of Anal Bleaching: A Back Door Journey From Darkness to Light*.

With no writing talent, it seemed my best shot would be to write something in the first person set in a city I knew well, touching on high-tech (an industry I worked in for the better part of two decades) and Eastern philosophy, which I'd studied for years.

I knew Toby's journey would require a mentor or someone to open his eyes and mind to new perspectives. That's when I remembered Eddie and his dog Cowboy. Yes, they were real. Eddie and Cowboy lived on the sidewalk down the block from the apartment my wife and I lived in when we were first married. Eddie's backstory about his childhood, experiences in Vietnam, and how he made money and survived on the streets are all true-to-life. And yes, I would buy 24-oz beers, and we would sit on the sidewalk and talk about life. Eddie may or may not have been enlightened. However, his perspectives and outlook seemed to indicate he was much more awake and aware than I was. And yes, these talks did force me to consider perspectives I possibly never would have. One day, Eddie was simply no longer there. He had mentioned moving to the South of Market district of San Francisco at one point, and I figured he must have moved on. Sadly, I never got to say goodbye or thank him and Cowboy for their friendship. So I decided to honor his memory by making him Toby's teacher.

Now that I had a couple of characters, I started writing without a plan, figuring the story would unfold on its own. I read Stephen King often takes this approach. However, it quickly became apparent that I lacked the creativity, experience, and talent to follow his approach.

Having never written a paragraph of fiction before attempting this project, I had no idea what I was getting into. My grammar was shit; I had no clue how it would end or what I hoped the reader would gain outside of a few laughs. After a year of flailing around, I puked out a horrific first draft, which I was quite proud of. I sent it to a few people who expressed interest in reading it and have yet to hear anything back. They were probably smart and put it down after a chapter or two, hoping I wouldn't follow up to get their feedback. Stephen Ladd, however, somehow slogged through the entire thing and provided excellent and detailed feedback, as well as some needed encouragement, as I was pretty discouraged after going back and reading the mess I had produced.

After a total rewrite, I felt comfortable sending it to a few more people who had expressed interest, as it now had a story to accompany Toby's inner journey. Stephen slogged through it again and provided more feedback and encouragement. Thank you, my busy friend, who logged scores of hours reading these two drafts and kept me going when I figured there wasn't much point in continuing.

Of the eight others I then gave it to, four made it through and got back to me with feedback, although the grammar, sentence structure, and flow were still, shall we say, less than reader-friendly.

James Christ, a dear friend, an English teacher, and an author, was immensely helpful with grammar, story-level feedback, and a few other suggestions and encouragement. Ann O'Hara also gave me much inspiration and feedback to keep me going.

My beta reader heroes are Geody Boetel and Kyle Wulff, who went above and beyond with pages and pages of notes at the story, scene, voice, and page levels, which spurred another major rewrite. It's possible it was empathy for a future reader's potential pain that motivated them, possibly pity for a floundering friend trying to salvage wasted time, or maybe they just really cared and knew more about good fiction writing than I did and were determined to help me get this book across the finish line. This book would be in a dumpster somewhere without their generous time and support.

Finally, I reached a point where it was as good as I could get it with my limited talent and skills. It was time to find someone with enough sack to actually publish such an outlandishly titled novel.

During the months of submitting the manuscript to countless literary agents and publishers and receiving rejection letter after rejection letter, Kendra Loo, Rodney Loo, Eric Wilcox, and Teke Kelly read the book, and their positive feedback inspired me to keep trying, even though the odds are minuscule for a first-time author to get published. They felt the book was funny and insightful enough to do whatever it took to get it out there for others to enjoy.

Eventually, another author and old friend from graduate school, John Mabry, who owns his own publishing company, The Apocryphile Press, read the book, loved it, and was willing to take the risk of publishing it. Thank you, John and the team at The Aprocryphile Press, for taking a risk and bringing this book to market. And thank you, Janeen Jones, for putting up with my grammatical handicaps, which surely made copy editing mind-numbingly tedious.

Old Hairy Jesus happens to be one of my nicknames. The other most common is Fuck Face. My wife may have thought that one up. At times, I grow my hair long, have a beard, and pontificate about philosophy. At some point, someone must have declared I looked like a caricature of an old hairy Jesus, and it stuck. I used it as a pen name simply because it's funnier than Dave Holmes, and my publisher, John Mabry, who has a hell of a sense of humor, didn't push back.

I'd also like to thank Jimmy, the owner of The Blue Danube coffee shop and the owners of The Green Apple Bookstore, for allowing me to use the actual names of their businesses, where some of the scenes from the book are set. I highly encourage you to check out these establishments when in San Francisco.

Jimmy is the owner of The Blue Danube and a wonderful soul

who made every visit my young daughters and I made to his coffee house a welcoming and fun visit. Although we've since moved an hour north of San Francisco, we stop by every time we pass through The City, hoping to catch Jimmy there.

The Green Apple Bookstore is a fantastic place to lose yourself for hours. New and used books fill a myriad of rooms, and I've spent countless hours discovering new authors and titles and just sitting around reading in this literary cathedral.

Finally, thank you, the reader, for being curious and funny enough to give it a whirl. I hope you laughed your ass off and possibly even pondered the nature of your mind and self along the way. If you enjoyed it, please take a moment to write a positive review on Amazon so others may pick it up and enjoy the journey as well. And please don't hesitate to snap a shot of the cover, or better yet, a picture of you reading the book, post it on Facebook or Instagram for a laugh, and let others know it's out there.

Old Hairy Jesus
Sebastopol, CA
May, 2024

ABOUT THE AUTHOR

Old Hairy Jesus (a.k.a. Dave Holmes) and his smokeshow wife, Linda, split their time between Johnsville, CA, a small gold mining town in The Lost Sierras and the Sonoma wine country town of Sebastopol, CA, an hour north of where the story unfolds in San Francisco. In these areas you will frequently hear mentions of the Sage of The Sierras or the Sebastopol Saint; both references to Old Hairy Jesus or OHJ as his friends affectionately call him.

OHJ majored in psychology, did his graduate studies in Eastern philosophy at the California Institute of Integral Studies, and accidentally spent sixteen years in Silicon Valley's high-tech circus, where he earned his PhD in Humility Studies from The School of Hard Knocks. The story pulls from these aspects of his life and his own transformational journey to reveal the foundations of Buddhist psychology through the lens of our contemporary Western culture.

Most importantly, while Old Hairy Jesus is not afraid to do tequila shots, he prefers to sip it over ice because he's very sophisticated.

Write him at oldhairyjesus@gmail.com

www.ingramcontent.com/pod-product-compliance
Lightning Source LLC
Chambersburg PA
CBHW030912050726
47498CB00003BA/704